RAVE REVIEWS FOR
TESS MALLORY!

CIRCLES IN TIME

"Ms. Mallory has not recreated the Robin Hood legend, but crafted her own magical tale of passion and betrayal that instantly grabs readers' attentions. What a pleasure to read!"
—*Romantic Times*

"Tess Mallory is a superb writer. She infuses her characters with true grit. Her heroine is gutsy and real, a role model. Passion and sensuality are Ms. Mallory's forte. . . . *Circles in Time* is an exhilarating novel: fast-paced, romantic, and satisfying. Highly recommended."
—*Under the Covers Book Reviews*

"There are lots of new twists to the Robin Hood legend in this delightful story of passionate quests."
—*Louisa's Magical Romance website*

MIDSUMMER NIGHT'S MAGIC

"Ms. Mallory writes a wonderful story blending the magic of Ireland and the chance of finding true love."
—*Under the Covers Book Reviews*

TO TOUCH THE STARS

"Fans of futuristic romance will enjoy the interesting premise and exciting resolution."
—*Romantic Times*

"IS THAT A SWORD UNDER YOUR SHIRT. . . ?"

"So how's about them Spurs?" she asked, stretching her legs out so close to his that he could feel the heat.

He opened his right eye and squinted at her, resolving to meet tease for tease. "Och, no ye don't. Tell yer tale."

Immediately Jix turned toward him, one hand snaking up to clutch at the front of his shirt, her calf curling over his.

"I'm really cold, MacGregor," she said, snuggling her head against his shoulder, sliding her knee up his thigh.

Jamie sat frozen, afraid to move as her nightgown slipped up toward her waist, exposing her bare skin, bringing it against his own. His own response was immediate and strong, and as her leg moved higher and higher up his thigh, he knew exactly when she became aware of his situation.

"Oh," she said, her lower body movement stilling with the one breathy word. Jix leaned closer to his ear and whispered, the touch of her breath almost sending him over the edge.

"Is that a sword under your shirt, MacGregor? Or are you just happy to see me?"

Jamie turned toward her, feeling like a man half-starved. He pretended to glare at her.

"Ye are an evil woman," he said.

Jix straightened, her laughter soft and seductive.

Two could play at this game. Jamie tilted her face to his and cupped her chin between his fingers. "Ye are evil, but I still want to hear yer story"—he looked at her mouth— "eventually. . . ." His thumb moved over her lower lip and her eyes registered surprise, as if she hadn't expected him to turn the tables on her. When her tongue darted out to moisten her lips he lowered his mouth to hers, capturing that wet, pink tongue with his.

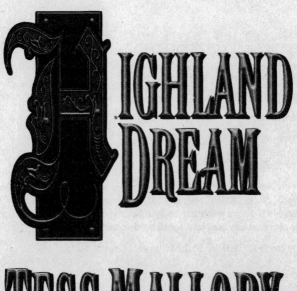

HIGHLAND DREAM

TESS MALLORY

LOVE SPELL   NEW YORK CITY

A LOVE SPELL BOOK®

March 2001

Published by

Dorchester Publishing Co., Inc.
276 Fifth Avenue
New York, NY 10001

Cover art by John Ennis
www.ennisart.com

ISBN 0-505-52444-9

The name "Love Spell" and its logo are trademarks of Dorchester Publishing Co., Inc.

Printed in the United States of America.

Visit us on the web at www.dorchesterpub.com.

To my sister, Jewell Dean,
who helped me find my faith again, through her own.
To my friend, Dawn Shepler,
who helped me find the magic again,
in my writing and my life.
To my husband, Sir Thomas,
who helped me find the moonbeams again, in the
beauty of our love.

HEY THANKS!

To: My agent, Roberta Brown—an incredible lady. You are the best.

Karrie Balwolchus—fantastic writer/line editor. Couldn't have done it without you, my friend.

My daughter, Erin—for being my personal editor.

Ty Treadwell (the PK), Ellen & Greg, Melissa, David & Ro, researcher Angie Els, and the Wild Ones—I love ya!

My family—Daddy, Blake, Heather, and Jordan; Cas and Meg; Jason, Julie, and Tommy. Also Cheryl, Tom, Linda, and the Cousins! Much love.

Nell Graham—you bring joy to my heart.

Shannon Story—my own special angel.

My editor, Kate Seaver—for your insights and your laughter.

And finally, as Jix would say—Thanks God—always there in a pinch!

Chapter One

"Permission to kidnap your daughter, sir!"

Retired Air Force Colonel Patrick Riley sat down heavily in his desk chair, a stunned expression on his face.

"Kidnap her! I'd like to lock her up in a convent and throw away the key! I·haven't had a good night's sleep since the two of you turned thirteen." He glanced up at Jix Ferguson. "Are you expecting a terrorist attack before dinner?"

"You never know. You're the one who taught me to be prepared." Jix adjusted the brim of the green camouflage cap she wore over her short auburn curls, and felt a pang of affection for the older man.

The colonel had been like a father to her, and what she'd just told him about his daughter's fiancé wouldn't make most dads' "Top Ten Things You Want to Hear Two Days Before Your Daughter Gets Married" list. She wondered what he'd say if she told him about her dream.

No, Jix, don't cloud the issue, she cautioned her more reckless side. *Besides, no one believes in your stupid prophetic dreams but you—and if you tell him that half the reason you want to stop this wedding is because you dreamed Samantha was marrying a man in a skirt, he may not believe either story!*

Fighting the urge to share her revelation, Jix shrugged, thrusting her hands down into the pockets of her green-splotched camo pants that perfectly matched her camo tank top, and wiggled her toes inside her blue Elmo slippers.

A smile touched his tough old lips. "Army green. Matches your eyes."

"I knew Mark was bad news from the moment I first met him but Samantha seemed so happy. . . ." her voice trailed away as the pain in the colonel's face stopped her.

Jix stood in the middle of the colonel's den, surrounded by model airplanes. They hung from the ceiling, the majority of them representations of Messerschmitt's, small German planes flown during World War II. The collection was the colonel's pride and joy—next to the computer company that had made him a millionaire when he retired from the Air Force to live in Austin, Texas—and of course, next to his only daughter, Samantha.

He raked one hand through his graying hair and released his breath explosively. "So you're telling me that not only is this jackass already married but he's talked Samantha into handing over all of her trust fund for him to 'manage'?"

Jix nodded. "As soon as they're married. Thomas has been investigating the jerk. It's a popular scam. A guy gets a job at a company, romances the daughter of the boss, and convinces her to marry him and to let him invest her money. Before you know it he's disappeared, along with her fortune."

"I wish Thomas were here right now," Riley said, clutching the arm of the chair tightly. "He could arrest that son of a—"

"He will!" Jix interrupted with a wry grin. "Having a brother in the FBI is a definite perk, but he doesn't want to embarrass you or Samantha. He wants her out of the picture before he makes the bust." She paused, then hurried on impatiently. "Colonel, Samantha's wedding is two days from now. What do you think of my plan?"

The colonel shook his head. "It seems extreme. I can still have that guy locked up in the next twenty minutes. I have connections in this town." He reached for the phone but Jix stopped him, her fingers closing over his wrist.

"Colonel, you don't really want that kind of a scandal, do you? Samantha would be humiliated in front of all her friends."

The older man frowned, his bushy brows knitting together thoughtfully as he released the receiver. "You're right. Then we'll tell Samantha," he said, "and she'll call the wedding off."

Jix bit her lower lip and squinted at him with one eye. "Uh, excuse me, sir, but are we talking about the same Samantha? Your daughter? My best friend? The one whose first complete sentence was 'Me don't want to?'" She shook her head. "You'll never force Samantha to dump Mark Winston Harrington the Third unless it's her idea first."

"If I remember correctly, someone else was pretty stubborn when Samantha tried to convince her that she was marrying the wrong man."

Jix's face reddened. "I was a lot younger then, and a lot stupider."

She turned away, pretending to examine one of the colonel's models. Her failed marriage before the age of twenty-four wasn't something she was proud of, but being reminded of Samantha's efforts to stop her from marrying Dirk the Jerk just intensified her own determination not to let the same thing happen to her best friend. If she had listened to Samantha, she'd have been spared some major heartache. Jix turned back to the older man in time to see him raise both gray brows, his eyes twinkling in gentle amusement. She laughed. "Well, I was lot younger anyway."

"You are not stupid, Jixie," he said sternly. "You just don't think things through sometimes. That's why I'm not sure about rushing into your plan."

"I never thought it would be Sam rushing into something like this." She reached up and touched one of the small airplanes hanging near her nose.

13

A wan smile reappeared on his face. "I just don't see how you can keep Sam from getting on that plane to New York. Damn the man for insisting the wedding be held there."

Jix sighed and sat down on the chair arm, draping her arm around the older man's shoulder.

"Sir—I have an idea about that."

The colonel groaned aloud, leaning his head against one hand. "Those words have struck terror into my heart since you were eight years old."

Quickly Jix outlined the rest of the plan she'd been working on since 2 A.M.

The colonel shook his head. "She'll never agree."

Jix raised one brow and smiled. "She won't get the chance. Just leave it to me, sir. I promise, this will work."

Riley shook his head. "Risky, extremely risky."

Jix put her hands on her hips. "Why, Colonel, have you forgotten? Risk is my middle name."

"No, it isn't. It's Isobel. Isobel Xavier."

She shrugged. "I'm open to alternatives, but time is running out."

Rising, the colonel took his wallet out of his back pocket and opened it, pulling a rectangle of gold-colored plastic from the leathery depths. He thrust the card toward her. "Here. I don't care what it costs. Save my daughter, Jix."

She reached for the card but he drew it back at the last moment and frowned. "Sure you can handle this?"

Jix tilted her head to one side and grinned, spreading her arms apart in an innocent gesture. "Colonel—this is me."

"Exactly. You have to promise me—no explosives, no rabid animals, and no international incidents."

"Why, Colonel, have I ever—"

"Yes."

Jix opened her mouth, then shut it abruptly. She glared at him for a moment before bursting into laughter. "That was a long time ago. Besides, the high school chem lab was old anyway."

"Sure it was."

"And I'd heard that the skunks in Montana were really friendly."

"Samantha said the shots were very painful."

"And it wasn't my fault that I lost my shoe at the top of the Eiffel Tower on our senior trip and it hit that cop on the head."

The colonel stood and brought his hands to rest on her shoulders, his blue eyes suddenly serious as he gazed down at her.

Jix looked up into those gentle eyes and swallowed hard, feeling guilty for her flippancy. She was just as frightened for Samantha as the colonel, but she couldn't allow herself to face the possibility that if she didn't do something, her best friend would be hurt emotionally—and perhaps physically. She hadn't told the colonel the rest of what Thomas had explained—how nine times out of ten the women involved in the scams were murdered, while the "husband" collected the insurance benefits on the policy he had conveniently taken out on his wife before her untimely death.

"Yes, sir?" she whispered, looking up at him.

"A lot is riding on this, Jixie-Pixie. Don't let me down."

The childhood nickname brought tears to her eyes and she quickly blinked them away, summoning a bright smile. "You can count on me, sir. We'll kidnap Sam tonight and be on our way to the British Isles by midnight!"

Riley shook his head and smiled. "Then God save the Queen."

Jix smiled back at him and stepped out of his embrace. She did have a plan. The fact that there were potential glitches here and there didn't worry her. She was used to flying by the seat of her pants, figuring things out as she went.

"You have my word, sir. Samantha is not getting married to that lowlife scum—not if I have to take her to the ends of the earth."

"The Highlands of Scotland," Riley said with a laugh. "That *is* the ends of the earth, isn't it?"

"Och, no, Colonel," she replied, slipping into a Scottish brogue and heading for the door. She stopped on the threshold and turned back, wiggling her eyebrows suggestively. "But 'tis the only place in the world where ye can find a man wearin' a skirt, minus his underwear." She paused and frowned. "Well . . . maybe not."

"Why, Jix Ferguson!" The colonel admonished her, his wink belying his tone of voice.

"Sorry, sir, no time for embarrassment now." She held three fingers to her forehead. "I'm on a mission."

"You're giving me the Boy Scout salute," he informed her.

Undaunted, Jix quickly slid another finger into place.

"Permission to kidnap your daughter, sir."

Patrick Riley returned the salute. "Permission granted." He smiled grimly. "Give 'em hell, Jix."

James MacGregor sat brooding in a cheap motel room just outside of London. He hated this assignment. Hated London. If the truth be known he wasn't all that fond of England. He missed Scotland every minute he was away, and had to remind himself daily that working for Scotland Yard meant making some sacrifices along the way. Shacking up in this horrible excuse for an inn was just one more.

The walls in the dismal room he'd rented by the week were so thin he'd become privy to the most intimate knowledge of the couple next door, knowledge that would take a good month to forget if he tried hard and drank a lot. At the moment it sounded as though their bed were about to come through his wall.

He sighed and turned his attention back to the cracked mirror in front of him, trying to ignore the bumps and thumps that shook the dingy paneling with synchronous frequency. Squeak, thump. Squeak, thump. Squeak, thump. He found himself humming along at times.

Jamie ran one hand over his head, spiking up the thick, wiry strands of hair that were in dire need of a cut. The

curls danced in flaming red abandonment around his face,
the brilliant color matching the bushy eyebrows that lay
over his piercing blue eyes like well-worn caterpillars.
Years of hard living had left deep lines in his face and
around a mouth almost hidden by a bushy mustache. Wrin-
kles creased the corners of his eyes and a sagging beneath
his chin denoted the advent of middle age. A threadbare
black T-shirt that rather dismally declared in green letters,
"I'm the Irishman Your Mother Warned You About,"
added to his overall scruffy appearance.

He gave one last calculating look at the picture he presented, then stood and pulled a worn gray tweed jacket
from the back of the chair. He shrugged into it and checked
the inside pocket. Everything was there: fake ID, fifty
thousand dollars in unmarked bills, and his Smith & Wes-
son. Now all he had to do was meet O'Shaunnesy. He
started toward the door when a sharp knock twice, pause,
then twice again, stopped him.

Tavish's knock. Tavish never came to this flat unless
something was wrong. He opened the door a few inches,
only to have the doorknob shoved into his stomach as a
burly figure hurried into the room.

Jamie shut the door and leaned against it. "And hello to
you too."

Tavish laughed and walked over to the bed. He sat down
and tested it once with a bounce. Almost in unison the
squeaking from next door increased. Tavish lifted both
bushy brown brows. A short, balding man, his stocky stat-
ure belied the strength Jamie had come to rely upon in his
partner. He had a right punch that could drop a bull, and
a mind as quick as a fox.

"Well, now, do they charge extra for the entertainment?"

"Tavish, what the hell are you doing here? This is
damned irregular."

The amusement left the man's face and he nodded.
"Aye, 'tis. O'Shaunnesy's not comin'."

"Why not?"

"He's evaporated, or been evaporated if you know what
I mean."

Jamie groaned, his Scottish brogue deepening with his growing frustration. While he usually tried to speak what the Yard referred to as "proper English," he and Tavish were both Scotsmen and he knew he didn't have to put on airs with his old friend and partner. "Och, I had a feelin' about this one. Why dinna ye just call me?"

"On that transmitter ye call a telephone?"

"It's a cell phone."

"Aye, and it's the most insecure piece of rattletrap that ever invaded the Yard."

"Well, this lovely paradise doesn't provide phone service," Jamie reminded him.

"Aye, and that's why I'm here."

Jamie sighed. "All right. Fine." He shook his head and crossed back over to the small mirrored dresser. He slammed himself into the unsteady chair and frowned at his reflection. "Do ye possibly know how long it took me to get ready for this gambit?"

"Aye. Sorry, lad."

"Damn, this is the part I hate," he said. He gritted his teeth, reached up, and ripped off one eyebrow.

The other followed. His ear-splitting howl of pain actually stopped the couple next door for at least thirty seconds before the thumping started again. Jamie grimaced as he pulled the auburn mustache from above his lips and tossed it aside. He reached up and jerked the thick mass of red hair from his head, placing it back on its Styrofoam wig head. He ran one hand through his own dark locks, glad to be out from under the hot wig. He needed a haircut, he noted, peering into the mirror. Living most of his life under one hairpiece or another made him forget at times to visit the barber.

His hair had grown to about two inches below his collar in the back and was getting pretty shaggy on the sides as well. His dark brows knit together as he glared at the reflection of his still timeworn face.

"Och, I hate it when people die ahead of schedule," he announced. "It fair screws things up."

"Aye," Tavish agreed.

Jamie sighed. "Ah, well." Hesitating for a long moment, he finally lifted both hands—and pulled off his face. He had almost gotten the pain under control and was contemplating what to do with the latex mask—Tavish being there gave him certain twisted ideas—when his partner spoke again.

"I dinna know how ye stand that mess on yer face," Tavish commented. He reached into the pocket of his houndstooth jacket and extracted a pipe. Another pocket produced a sack of tobacco and soon the sweet, smoky smell permeated the room. "I've got some good news for ye."

"I doubt that," Jamie said. "What is it?" The noise next door increased, and Tavish raised his voice, but his words were indistinguishable.

Jamie raised a hand to stop his partner's incomprehensible answer. He jabbed a thumb at the vibrating wall, and then held up one finger to indicate that the coupling would be through in a minute. The thumps and squeaks got louder, the bumps against the wall making him wonder if today really would be the day the bed came crashing into his room.

Tavish shook his head and relit his pipe, leaning back to wait. Jamie picked up a jar of cold cream and dipped his hand into it. He hated the greasy stuff, but it took off any lingering latex or makeup. He spread it over his face and frowned into the mirror. Damn, when had he gotten these dark vampirelike circles under his eyes? He looked like hell. Cathy would be horrified if she could see him. He smiled grimly.

His ex-fiancée had pumped his ego daily, telling him how square his jaw was, how handsome he was, blah, blah, blah. He'd eaten up the attention, but that had been six years ago, before Scotland Yard, before he'd broken his nose, before he'd caught the lying witch in bed with his best friend. He wiped the cream off. Like Indiana Jones once said, it wasn't the years, it was the mileage. He was almost thirty-six. Four years away from forty. And forty was just ten years away from fifty.

The couple reached their usual frenzied crescendo. Tavish stared at the wall, his dark eyes a little disconcerted, even for him. The heavyset man shook his head and turned away from the now silent paneling.

"Damn me, but that lad has stamina."

"Aye, try listenin' to his stamina half the night and ye'll no' admire him so much. Now, what were ye sayin'?" Jamie asked. The wall began to vibrate again and he groaned. "Don't they ever take a break?"

"Must be a Scot." Tavish commented, shifting his gaze back to the wall. "I said the orders for yer holiday came through."

Jamie blinked. "Ye said what?"

Tavish frowned. "Are ye deaf, lad? I said that the Yard approved yer request for a holiday. Two weeks."

Two weeks. Two blissful weeks away from Scotland Yard. Two wonderful weeks of not having to wear goop on his face or pretend he was a doorman or a cab driver or a cleaning woman. He hadn't had a holiday in over two years. His mouth curved up, and he knew he was grinning like an idiot, but he didn't care. "Holiday," he said softly. "Och, I thought they had forgotten me."

"Where are ye goin'?"

"Home. I'm goin' home to the Highlands." The mirror smiled back at him now, and the circles didn't look so dark.

"Your uncle lives up there, doesn't he? Lord Campbell?"

"My great-uncle. He hosts a medieval festival every year about this time. He's asked me to come, over and over again, but I was always workin'. He'll be overjoyed to see me." He pulled a suitcase out from under his bed.

"Then ye can get out yer bonny sword, eh? Good. Well, lad, I'll be in touch," he turned toward the door.

Jamie straightened, dropping the suitcase on the bed. "No, ye will not be in touch," he said, trying to make his voice stern. It was hard to do with Tavish grinning up at him like a cat caught in cream. "Ye will leave me the hell alone during my holiday." He moved to the wardrobe and began jerking out clothes and tossing them onto the bed.

"I'll give ye a call in a week or so," Tavish said, as though Jamie hadn't spoken. "Have a good time, laddie. I'll see ye when ye get back." Tavish moved to the scarred and battered door.

"Maybe I won't come back," Jamie said, the words coming out before he could stop them.

The man paused, his hand on the doorknob, his brows raised. "Dinna joke about that."

"I'm not jokin'. I'm tired of it, Tavish. I'm tired of it all." Saying it out loud made everything suddenly come into focus. All the things he'd been sorting through over the last few weeks, all the soul-searching, it all led to one conclusion: He hated his job. Jamie pointed to the shaking wall.

"I'm tired of eavesdroppin' on fornicatin' rabbits."

"I dinna blame ye for that, but I always thought ye liked yer bonny disguises," Tavish protested. "That ye had fun with it."

Jamie stared at him. "Fun?" He shook his head and took a deep breath, releasing it slowly before he spoke. "Tavish, have ye ever had yer eyebrows ripped off yer face?" he demanded, gesturing to his own. "Or had your neck break out from a latex reaction, or worn a woman's brassiere?"

A twinkle appeared in Tavish's eyes, but his voice was solemn. "Why, no, lad—why?"

Jamie turned away from that twinkle before he lost his temper. He stared at the quivering wall, feeling ancient and irritable.

"I've done them all, Tavish. I do some of them daily. Not the brassiere," he added hastily. There was a snort of what could have been laughter behind him, but when he glanced back over his shoulder, the man just nodded at him, not a smile on his face.

"Och, ye're just tired. All ye need is a wee holiday. Ye'll be right as rain in no time. Why haven't ye asked for a vacation sooner?"

"Right," Jamie said, shaking his head, "why didn't I think of it before now?"

"See ye when ye get back, lad." The door closed behind him.

Jamie turned with a sigh and began packing his clothes as the wall continued to shudder and shake. The last thing he folded was his kilt. He gave it a final pat into place, snapped the suitcase shut, then stepped over the wardrobe and took out his "bonny sword." He gazed down at the weapon and a feeling of pride swept over him as it always did when he held the MacGregor claymore. The sword had been handed down on his father's side of the family for over three hundred years.

Jamie pulled it from its scabbard and ran his hand over the ornate hilt, touching the heart of the claymore, the shimmering green stone at the center of the crosspiece. It seemed to almost glow with an inner light. He kept meaning to have a jeweler identify the stone. Some kind of emerald, most likely.

Sliding the sword back into the scabbard, he laid the weapon on top of his suitcase. Flipping open his cell phone, he checked the train schedule and found there was one headed for the Highlands in two hours. Enough time to catch a nap.

He crossed to the bed and stretched out, watching the dresser's mirror shimmy. Or maybe not.

Jamie put his hands behind his head and shifted his gaze to the ceiling. He'd be a liar—and probably not a man— if he said the noises behind the wall hadn't painted vivid images in his mind, images that made him think about his ex-fiancée and their long weekends in the country. Images that made him realize how lonely he was at times.

"Och, laddie," he said. "Don't pay it any mind. Think about two weeks in the Highlands without a care in the world."

Squeak, thump. Squeak, thump.

"Another cold shower tonight, Jamie, lad?" he asked the ceiling. "Don't mind if I do, thanks ever so much."

He crossed his feet at the ankles. After a moment he

began to whistle "Scotland the Brave," his feet moving
side to side, keeping perfect time with the music behind
the wall.

Jix watched as Samantha linked her arm through that of
the tall, handsome man beside her. She smiled up at him,
a glowing, radiant look on her face. The man had dark
brown hair almost reaching his shoulders and the bluest
eyes Jix had ever seen. His nose hooked at the bridge and
kept him from being too perfect, too pretty. His lips were
firm and chiseled, like his jaw, and as he looked down into
the blond woman's eyes Jix thought she'd never seen a
man look so handsome, or so happy.

Samantha was beautiful in a creamy white gown with
long white gloves. A garland of white and yellow daisies
encircled her head, and she held a small bouquet of the
same flowers in her hand. The man beside her wore a plaid
kilt of red, green, and white, a crisp white shirt, and a black
dress jacket. A white rose adorned his lapel. Jix's vision
blurred for a moment and she blinked, trying to see more
clearly. It was a wedding. She was at a wedding—Samantha's wedding. And the man standing next to her, gazing
down at her with such joy in his eyes, was definitely *not*
Mark Harrington the Third.

Jix sat bolt upright, her heart pounding. For a minute
she had no idea where she was. Then she remembered.
Releasing her breath explosively, she leaned back in the
comfortable first class airline seat and closed her eyes
again. It had been relatively easy to get a soused Sam onto
the connecting flight from New York to England. Once
aboard, Jix had fallen into a deep sleep.

She'd dreamed about Samantha's wedding every night
for the last two weeks. It was part of the reason she'd
asked her brother Thomas to investigate the man Samantha
planned to marry. Mark himself was the rest of the reason.
Jix couldn't stand the man. She smiled as she remembered
the day she had taken her concerns to Thomas.

Abandoned by her mother at the age of four, Jix had
lived with an eccentric aunt until the old woman died when

Jix was six years old. She'd spent two years in a Catholic orphanage until the Fergusons saw her at Sunday mass at St. Stephen's and asked about her. Kate and John Ferguson had four sons, but the two kind souls dearly wanted a little girl. The day Jix arrived at their home, her hand firmly gripped by Sister Margaret's, she had been terrified at the sight of four boys, all older and bigger than she was. But the four boys—Sebastian, Sean, Travis, and Thomas— treated her like a fairy princess, and the first night there she wept into her pillow with relief and a feeling of having finally found a home. The icing on the cake—a little girl her age, Samantha Riley, lived right next door. And next door to her, Chelsea Brown. Eight months later the Fergusons officially adopted Jix into their loving and rambunctious household, but the scars of those four years alone, unwanted, had left their mark.

Her smile faded at the thought of those empty years, and the fact that her adopted parents were now both gone, victims of an automobile accident. Jix resolutely turned her thoughts back to Samantha's problem.

"You just don't like him, Jixie," Thomas had accused when she first broached her fears about Mark. She had told him about her dream, something she didn't like to do. "Your subconscious mind is just taking your dislike of the guy and making up an alternate plan for Sam."

"But Thomas, you know my dreams always come true," Jix had insisted.

"Can't argue with that," he said.

"Could you just look him up? I mean, what would it hurt?"

He had ruffled her short auburn hair affectionately. "Okay, okay, I'll check him out. But only because I'm fond of Sam. Don't expect anything, though. Unless he has a rap sheet, I'm going to come up empty."

Well, surprise, surprise. Mark Harrington the Third had a rap sheet about a quarter of a mile long. Thomas had looked into the man's file a little deeper and come up with the information that Jix had spilled to Samantha's father. The question now was how to spill it to Samantha? She couldn't tell her about the dream. Sam had always laughed about Jix's clairvoyance. She was a no-nonsense kind of woman, a serious medical student at a prestigious school in Houston. Prophetic dreams didn't figure into Sam's way of thinking, even though she knew Jix often helped Thomas solve his cases, using images from her dreams.

Jix knew Sam loved her dearly, but their relationship resembled that of a mother cat who has taken in a stray chick. Mother cat Sam might love the chick and defend it from harm, but she'd never quite understand why it clucked instead of meowed.

Jix sighed. To make matters worse, from the very beginning she had been quite vocal about not liking Mark. How could she ever make Sam believe what she had to say was real and not just one of her harebrained schemes? Even if faced with hard evidence of her fiancé's wrong doings, Sam would probably claim Mark had changed and marry him despite Jix's misgivings. Sam might even accuse Jix of concocting the rap sheet to stop the ceremony.

"Jix? Are we in New York yet?"

Jix jumped at the sound of Sam's voice beside her. She felt a wave of panic rush over her as she turned toward her friend, and the window. Samantha Riley yawned and stretched, moaning as she lifted one hand to her forehead. "Remind me not to ever drink four margaritas in a row again. Especially when I'm flying to New York to get married." She giggled and glanced out the window beside her.

The window! *Mistake!* What had Jix been thinking— putting Samantha in a window seat? She'd been thinking that her friend—totally soused from too many drinks between Austin and Chicago—wouldn't wake up until they reached England. Before they left Texas, citing her status as maid of honor, Jix had taken charge of their travel plans, careful to tell Sam they would be changing planes in Chicago for New York. Since Sam expected the switch, it had been no problem at O'Hare for Jix to simply guide her woozy friend onto their connecting flight to London. Other than having to do a little fast-talking to a concerned flight attendant, making up a story about jet lag and antihistamine, everything had gone like clockwork. Her plan had worked beautifully.

But now Samantha was awake, asking questions, looking out that window that Jix had unfortunately forgotten about. Jix groaned silently. It was time to do what she did best—fabricate, exaggerate, invent! At least until they got safely on British soil. Then she'd tell Sam the truth and run for cover. She took a deep breath and turned with a smile to lie to her best friend.

Chapter Two

"My head feels as big as Dallas and I—" Sam stopped in the midst of a new complaint and lowered her hand from her forehead, leaning toward the window. "What is that?"

"What is what?" Jix asked.

"What is that?" Sam pointed toward the small window.

Jix leaned toward her, squinting. "It's a window, Sam. Gosh, you really should get out more."

Samantha rolled her eyes. "I mean what is that outside the window, down there?" She frowned, leaning her head against the glass. "It's all gray and—"

Rising halfway out of her seat, Jix leaned across the empty seat between them and pushed Samantha out of the way. "Let me see," she said, blocking the other woman's view, trying to remember that she was doing this for Samantha's own good. She stole a look at her friend and thought, not for the first time, how beautiful she was. Golden-haired, gray-eyed, intelligent, great personality— she deserved much better than that rat fink Mark etc. etc. the Third.

"Well?" Samantha asked. "What is it?"

Far below the plane stretched sparkling gray ocean. Jix sank back into her seat.

"Nothing to worry about."

"What is it?"

"It's—it's gray stuff. You know, clouds that sort of thing. You want to switch seats?"

"What for?"

"Sitting on the aisle makes me nauseous."

Samantha lifted one hand to her head. "Please, Jix, I'm not in the mood for your jokes." She turned to the window again. "Are you sure that's clouds? It looks like"—she leaned closer—"it looks like water. Like a whole lot of water." She swung around to Jix, her eyes widening.

Jix pushed her back in the seat with one hand and leaned across her once again, narrowing her gaze against the glare of the sun, thinking fast and coming up with nothing. "Well, what do you know? It is water. Lots and lots of water. You're right." She cleared her throat. *Get a grip, Jix,* she ordered herself. *You can bluff your way through this.*

"You're squishing me," Samantha squeaked. Jix sat back and immediately retrieved her purse from the unoccupied seat between them. She rummaged through it as Samantha watched, a puzzled look on her face.

"What are you doing?" Sam finally asked.

"Looking for my binoculars."

"Why?"

"So you can look at the water."

Samantha stared at her. "What are you talking about?"

"The water."

"What about the water?"

Jix stopped digging through her purse and sighed in a long-suffering way. "You want to see the water, remember? So I'm looking for my binoculars."

"I don't want to look at the water. And you don't have any binoculars in there."

Jix frowned at her friend, seizing at straws to keep Samantha distracted for as long as possible. "But you said you wanted to look at the water."

"No, I didn't."

"You did. I distinctly remember you saying—"

"Jix—what is wrong with you?" Samantha was glaring at her now and Jix swallowed hard.

"Well . . ." she hesitated, then rushed on. "You have to admit you're curious about the water."

Samantha sighed. "Yes, yes, I'm curious about the water. What is it doing there?"

Jix leaned across her friend again, this time poking one elbow down into Samantha's belly, making her groan.

"Would you please stop doing that?" Sam demanded.

"You asked me a question. How can I answer you if I don't examine what we're talking about?"

Jix peered down at the ocean for a full minute, her elbow digging deeper into Samantha's midriff, her mind racing. If she could just keep Samantha distracted until they landed in London, she felt sure she could make her understand what she'd done. Heck, Samantha had locked her in the linen closet just two hours before her wedding, trying to talk some sense into her thick head.

"Get off of me!" Samantha squealed, pushing Jix back into her seat.

"Really, Sam, you're making a big deal out of nothing. The water is doing what it's supposed to do—balance the ecosystem, keep sharks happy—your guess is as good as mine. I'm a writer, not a marine biologist." She slapped her hands together with a grin. "But, hey, how about a little drink?"

Samantha groaned. "Don't even mention liquor. I don't think I'll ever look so much as a beer in the eye again. And I thought that you were an actress—oh, sorry, that was last week."

"Beer doesn't have any eyes—I mean—beers don't have any—I mean—" Jix stopped, frowning, trying to sort out her verbs as Samantha turned again to stare out the window. "For your information I have entered Phase Three of my ten-part plan for my life, which means I am now a writer and—" Jix broke off as she saw understanding dawn in the depths of her friend's dark gray eyes.

"Uh-oh," Jix whispered, rolling her eyes toward the ceiling. "Uh, God, I could use a little help here. Sudden storm, engine failure, just be creative with the situation and—"

"Jix . . ." Samantha said slowly, her gaze still frozen out the window.

Jix straightened in her seat and turned to Samantha, smiling brightly. "Sure you won't have a Bloody Mary? They say there's nothing better for a hangover and—"

"Jix . . ." This time Sam's voice held a note of hysteria.

"Did I ever tell you about the time that I had too much to drink and ended up taking a shower in the fountain at the Botanic Gardens in the middle of—"

"Jessica Isobel Xavier Ferguson!"

The hushed use of Jix's entire name caused the words bubbling in her throat to die in a gurgling gulp. Samantha faced her, her bloodshot gray eyes round with shock.

"What—have—you—done?"

"Saved you from a fate worse than death?" Jix suggested hopefully. Guilt flooded over her as Sam's expression filled with horror. There was no reason to feel guilty. No reason at all. Samantha would thank her for this. Eventually.

"Saved me from—" Samantha began to shake her head in disbelief. "You didn't—you couldn't have—" she pointed one finger frantically at the window. "What is that?"

"Did you forget already? You told me, remember? It's water. A whole lot of water, and you were curious about it, but you didn't want to look at it with my binoculars and—"

"Jix!" Samantha practically shrieked her name.

Jix felt the proverbial walls closing in on her and took refuge in the defense mechanism she'd been cultivating since she was four years old—the fine art of wisecracking.

"You should really try to chill out a little, Sam. Remember your high blood pressure."

"I don't have high blood pressure."

"Well, you wouldn't want to get it."

"Jix Ferguson, you will explain this very minute how I

30

came to be on a plane hovering above some godforsaken ocean!"

Jix looked at the reading light and the air vent above her and sighed. "There she goes again. She doesn't mean it, God. So please don't crash the plane and take me down with her into the dark, pitiless, bottomless ocean just because she's tired and cranky."

"Tired? Cranky? I swear Jix, this time you've gone too far! You've—" She broke off, her eyes growing even wider. "So this is why you insisted on our flying to New York together, after Dad and the rest, and why you kept plying me with liquor the whole flight!" Her voice rose and her gray eyes were mere slits now. "You plotted this! You deliberately planned to keep me from marrying Mark!" She leaned toward her, her voice hardening. "Where are we?"

"Shhh—you're going to get us kicked off the plane!" Jix said, slumping down in her seat as the stewardess walked by and gave them an irritated look.

"I'm going to kick you off the damn plane personally— without a parachute—if you don't start explaining!" Sam threatened.

"Well, we did go to New York," Jix hedged. "And really, Samantha, I had your best interests at heart." She sighed. "I knew you were going to be difficult about this."

"My best interests? *My best interests?*" Samantha threw both hands up and suddenly caught sight of her wristwatch. She grabbed her wrist and brought the timepiece level with her bleary eyes. "It's twelve o'clock." She glanced out the window of the plane and blinked in the startling daylight. "It's noon. On Saturday?"

Jix nodded.

"On my wedding day?"

She nodded again.

"We aren't on our way to New York, are we?"

Jix shook her head.

"Where are we going?"

"Scotland?" Jix asked, her voice tentative.

With an oath, Samantha grabbed her startled friend by

the front of her tank top and jerked her forward, their noses almost touching. Her voice was dangerously calm, her words spaced carefully apart. "My wedding is in three hours. Turn the plane around."

"Uh, that's kind of impossible, Sam."

Her fingers tightened. "If you do not make them turn this plane around this minute, I will rip out your spleen and serve it to you for dinner. On a platter. With garnish."

Jix felt a swift stab of regret. "Samantha, we're going to have a great time and when I explain you'll understand. We're going to the Highlands," she said brightly, "and you're going to meet the man of your dreams there—I mean the man of my dreams. You see, I dreamed—" She snapped her mouth shut, her eyes widening. Oops.

Samantha's furious gaze burned into hers and Jix gasped at the anger she saw mirrored in her best friend's eyes. "Do you mean to tell me this has something to do with one of your ridiculous dreams?"

"No. Yes. Well, sort of."

"Sort of? You made me miss my wedding because of a sort-of prophetic dream?" Her voice had reached a fevered pitch and Jix carefully pried her fingers loose from her blouse and straightened her clothing, trying to put every ounce of sincerity she had left into her words.

"Sam, it's true. I dreamed that you were marrying someone else—not Mark! I dreamed you were marrying a guy in a kilt—this handsome, dreamy, hunk of a guy." Her voice softened. "It was beautiful. You had on a creamy white dress and a circlet of daisies in your hair and carried a sweet little daisy bouquet. He had on this Scottish outfit, you know, like in *Rob Roy*—kilt, tartan, brooch at the shoulder. I wonder if it's true they don't wear anything under—"

"Well, at least that explains your ridiculous outfit—for once!"

Jix glanced down at the red tank top that matched the red, green, and purple plaid, pleated skirt she wore. Then she readjusted the kicky little red beret she'd found in a secondhand store. Maybe the green knee-high socks and tassels and fringed loafers were pushing the envelope just a bit. The dark green jacket completed the look.

"What's wrong with my outfit?"

Sam didn't answer. Jix could see the panic growing in her friend's eyes; then Sam's hand closed tightly around Jix's wrist. Jix hurried to finish her story.

"Ow. Anyway, the point is, you looked so happy and he looked like he'd just been handed a million dollars and I thought—"

"You're serious aren't you?" Sam's words were hushed, disbelieving.

Jix blinked. "Of course."

"You mean it. You have made me miss my wedding because you dreamed that I'm supposed to marry another man!"

Jix sighed and lifted one shoulder in a half shrug. Sam had never believed in her dreams—why should she start now? "Well, I have to admit if that was all that had happened I might have hesitated."

"Oh, heaven forbid!"

"But, that wasn't all there was to it." She covered Sam's hand with her own and squeezed her friend's fingers sympathetically. "Sam, I found out information about Mark that changed everything, and I couldn't let you go through with the wedding."

"You couldn't—" Sam stopped as if trying to find the strength to speak. She jerked her hand away from Jix and shook her head, clenched her fists, then tried again. "You couldn't *let* me go through with the wedding? Miss 'I-Married-a-Drunk-Woman-Puncher' had doubts about the man *I* was going to marry so of course she had to *kidnap* me?"

She should've known Sam would take it this way. For someone who tended to be unemotional most of the time, her best friend certainly could overreact to a situation. After all, Jix hadn't thrown such a fit when Sam locked her in a closet on *her* wedding day. Of course, Sam had let her out before the wedding, but still, she could be a little bit calmer about the whole thing.

Sam sat there for a moment, shaking her head. "I can't believe it," she whispered. "I just can't believe it." Then her voice strengthened as she turned toward Jix, her eyes narrowed. "But why not? Why shouldn't I believe it? I'm forgetting, I'm dealing with Jix Ferguson the Jinx! Girl Catastrophe—Have Chaos, Will Travel!" She shook her fist at Jix, fury lacing her words. "How could you do this to me!?"

Jix didn't plan what happened next. She didn't know what made her say it—some little demon curled up in her brain she supposed. She folded her arms over her chest and lifted her chin.

"All right, Sam," she said. "I'll tell you the truth. I'm keeping you from marrying Mark because—well—because he's a transvestite!"

"I hate you, Jix Ferguson. I will hate you until the day I die. Or until the day you die—which may be sooner than you think! And as soon as I get dry—if that's possible in this squishy, moldy, freaking, godforsaken place—I'm going home!"

Jix sighed. Sam glared at her. Drenched to the skin, her silk suit plastered against her body, her blond hair hanging in wet clumps down her back, Sam was clearly not happy as they trudged side by side up the steep hill. The rain continued to drizzle down on them as it had for the last hour. Glumly Jix hefted her carry-on bag to a better position as she dragged her suitcase behind her. Those tiny little wheels didn't help much on a dirt road like this. She'd given up on trying to carry both bags, and Sam had refused to help. Petty, petty. Just because she'd missed her wedding and her luggage had been lost en route to London, Sam was in a bad mood.

Jix sighed and pushed back a lock of wet auburn hair that had tumbled into her face as they continued to trudge up the unpaved road.

"Look, Sam, I admit I made a mess of things. I'm sorry I said that about Mark but I thought if I told you something totally bizarre then you might believe me when I told you the truth," she explained.

"And the truth according to the gospel of Jix is that he's married. Why should I believe that anymore than your first ridiculous story?"

Jix let go of her suitcase and stopped. "Because I love you, dammit! I'd also like to remind you of something you seem to have forgotten—like the fact that you locked me in the closet just two hours before my wedding to Dirk!"

"I let you out, didn't I?"

"Yes, and don't you wish now that you hadn't?" The thought of the man who had destroyed her belief in marriage and love made Jix's stomach twist and she pushed the image of Dirk the Jerk out of her mind.

"Frankly, my dear, I don't give a damn!" Sam started walking again, and Jix picked up her luggage and hurried after her.

After their plane landed in England, Sam had become like a sleepwalker, not talking, her eyes glazed. Jix had gotten her on the train and soon they were headed for the authentic Scottish castle where Jix had arranged reservations and tickets to the authentic Scottish festival being held there. The train ride had been uneventful except for a minor incident at lunch involving a tripped waiter and a plate of haggis that ended up in Sam's lap, finally sparking her back to life and temper. She hadn't shut up since.

Once in Inverness, Jix rented a car and the two had headed for Meadbrooke. Even Sam seemed in slightly better spirits, or else she was busy plotting her revenge, but she appeared somewhat mollified as they drove across the beautiful Scottish countryside, blue-green meadows and purple mountains painting a fantastic backdrop to their day. Then everything had taken a turn for the worse.

First they got lost. Jix took the blame, but really, was it her fault that there were so many Scottish names on the map spelled alike? She should have turned left at Glensomething but instead turned at Glensomething else. It was an honest mistake! After wandering for hours—and getting a great first-hand view of Scotland, as she kept reminding her glum companion—they finally got on the right road to Meadbrooke. Then both back tires blew out. And it began to rain. Well, not really rain, not like in Texas where it rained hard and fast and they called them gullywashers, but more of a steady drizzle that permeated your clothes, your skin, your hair, lasted all the livelong day, and chilled you right down into the center of your bones.

Now, it was late afternoon and after walking for over an hour in the constant wetness they were both thoroughly drenched and exhausted. Even though it was only September, a brisk, cool breeze had effectively ended any hopes Jix might have had that Sam would look at the whole situation as an exciting adventure.

"Why would I lie about Mark?" Jix asked fervently, hurrying to keep up with her furious friend.

Sam stopped dead in her tracks. She turned toward Jix, raising one brow, her voice as cold as the rain. "Oh, puhleeze. You have been lying ever since the first grade when you pushed Johnny Bradshaw down in the mud and told the teacher that an alien had landed and stomped on him with its giant foot."

"I was a little kid. Good grief, you have the memory of an elephant."

"Okay, how about this? When the waitress at that Chinese restaurant last week asked if you were from out of town you told her that you were a refugee from Yugoslavia, and even taught her fake Yugoslavian words!"

Jix shrugged. "She enjoyed it. It didn't hurt anyone."

Sam shook her head. "Two days ago you told that encyclopedia salesman who came by your apartment that you couldn't buy his books because your mother was in a coma in San Salvador and you had to send her money every week from your salary as a Phone Sex girl! He ended up giving you money!"

"Well, I don't like pushy salesmen. It served him right."

Sam took a deep breath and closed her eyes for a moment, then opened them both and glared. "Jix, you lie for no reason whatsoever except that you're bored and want to wreak havoc in someone else's life!"

Jix sighed. "But that's not the case this time, Sam! Listen to me, will you? I only—"

"Is that it?" Sam's voice sliced through her explanation, dripping with sarcasm.

Jix glanced up to see her friend pointing straight ahead through the drizzle. A huge gray building loomed ahead of them. "Is that the 'castle' you've been ranting about?" Sam snorted and shook her head, water flying from her long blond hair. "It figures."

Jix raked her own wet curls out of her face and squinted through the rain at the structure ahead of them, hefting her carry-on bag to a more comfortable position. Disappointment sank into her soul. It wasn't a castle! It was a manor house. Beautiful, but no castle.

"Damn," she said, "can anything else go wrong?" Lightning crashed through the sky above them, and she squinted heavenward. "It was just a rhetorical question!" she yelled. She started walking again, trudging through dirt that was quickly becoming mud. Jix cast an accusing look upward. "And by the way, your aim needs work!"

An incredibly long driveway curved through an acre of beautiful rolling green meadow in front of them. Flanking it was a walkway of huge, flat stones leading to the house. Well, Jix shrugged, maybe it wasn't a castle, but it was the next best thing—a beautiful stone mansion that had to date back at least to the 1700s. In the distance, beyond the manor house, sat an incredibly huge boulder and even from where they stood, Jix could see ancient spirals and pictographs on it. Maybe that would appease Sam! She loved archaeology and old ruins and stuff.

"Okay, so it's not a castle, but you have to admit it's beautiful," Jix said, as they trudged up the walkway.

"I don't have to admit anything, except that I hate you."

"Are you going to keep acting this way all weekend?" Jix said crossly. "Can't you just make the best of things?"

Sam stopped and turned her face to the rain, standing motionless as if weighing her words before she spoke. When she finally did, it was with a solemnity that almost frightened Jix.

"I should make the best of things? You ruin my wedding and I should make the best of things? Everything is a joke to you, isn't it? But this is no joke. I will never forgive you for this, Jix Ferguson. Never."

As if to make the moment one of Jix's most memorable, the floodgates of heaven suddenly opened, and the drizzle turned into a downpour.

"Thanks, God," Jix muttered, "always there in a pinch."

Sam glared at her wordlessly, then spun on her heel and headed for the manor at a half-trot. Miserably, Jix followed. Did she mean it? Had Jix ruined their friendship forever? Her worry made the long walk to the house seem interminable. When they finally reached the entrance and climbed the few wide steps to the door, she groaned with relief, dropping her suitcase and flexing her fingers. She let the carry-on bag slip off her shoulder as well.

Sam silently stared at the huge, twenty-foot tall wooden structure in front of them. In the upper center of the beautiful oak door an incredibly large brass door knocker in the shape of a lion's head, polished to a dull sheen, silently welcomed them. There was no overhang and the rain continued to pour down on them. Jix longed to be inside, to enjoy the simple luxury of not being pelted by water. The possibility that she might ever be completely dry again seemed remote.

Sam picked up the knocker and let it fall three times, thud, thud, thud. The sound echoed through the wood and into the manor. They waited in wet dejection as a new sound of heavy footsteps echoed back to them. The massive door creaked open, and without looking up Jix took a step forward. Unfortunately the tip of her loafer caught in the dangling strap of her carry-on bag and she fell face forward onto the cold Scottish stone. Stunned, the wind knocked completely out of her lungs, she lay motionless trying to gather her wits when she felt herself being lifted by strong hands.

"Are ye all right, lass?" A deep, amazingly sexy voice asked.

Jix blinked, her vision clearing as the concerned face of

a man straight out of Scottish history looked down at her. She swallowed hard. No, not straight out of history—straight out of her dreams.

Jix stared up into the midnight blue eyes of the man Samantha Riley was destined to marry.

"It's great to see ye again, Uncle Angus," Jamie said, shaking the elderly man's hand.

Lord Angus Campbell shook Jamie's hand readily enough, but his sharp eyes narrowed as Jamie removed his mackintosh slicker, revealing Highland regalia. He took the raincoat from his grandnephew and gestured for Jamie to come further inside.

Jamie gratefully enjoyed the warmth of the house, brushing droplets of rain from his plaid. He'd barely made it to the manor from the train station before the Highland drizzle began.

"Well now, to what do I owe this singular pleasure?" the white-haired gentleman asked, hanging the coat on a rack near the door. He hooked it over the smooth wood, then turned and frowned at Jamie. "Not only do ye appear on my doorstep without warnin', but it would seem ye're ready for me wee festival as well—though I may have to hold it inside this year if the rain doesna let up." He paused. "Is that the MacGregor claymore ye have there?" he asked, his gaze flickering to the long, wrapped object Jamie held under his arm.

Jamie nodded and matched him brogue for brogue. "Aye. Would ye care to see it?"

The old man waved the offer away. "Perhaps later, laddie. Well, then, come in, won't ye?" He turned and led the way inside the house.

"I should have called," Jamie said, feeling awkward and ill at ease as he followed the man across the foyer and down a dimly lit hallway. "I've been meanin' to come and see ye for some time, but it's been a while since I had any time off from work. I hope I'm not puttin' ye out." Guilt laced through him. How long had it been since he'd visited? Two years? Three?

"Och, no, ye know ye have a standin' invitation here," Angus said, making a large sweeping gesture with his hand that encompassed more than just the sitting room they were walking through. "And how is everything down in Sassenach land?"

Jamie studied the house with renewed interest as they passed through room after room. An avid student of Scottish history, he had learned through his own research that a mighty castle had once sat in the same space, belonging to one of the Campbell clan. They had eventually been driven off their property by the British, and the castle destroyed. Later, the land had been granted to one of his uncle's ancestors and this smaller manor house erected on the site.

He hadn't seen the place in years. It had fallen into some disrepair since he last visited. The high stone walls still stretched up three stories high, but the roof sagged in places and the paint on the window casings had cracked and peeled. The side garden bristled with weeds and tall grass.

Did the manor have no servants? Jamie frowned. Just how hard a time was his great-uncle having?

"I'm glad ye've come, Jamie MacGregor," Angus said as he led the way through the grand hall and fancy dining room and into a smaller, more intimate dining room that was obviously used on a more daily basis. Jamie saw a plump, middle-aged woman in the kitchen beyond. He remembered sitting at the small eating table learning his alphabet from his great-aunt Katherine, Angus' wife. Great-aunt Katy was gone now and Jamie felt a swift stab of guilt for not coming to visit his elderly uncle more often since her death.

"Aye," he said, taking the chair Angus held out to him. "I'm glad that I've come as well." He leaned toward his uncle and this time his words were sincere, not stilted. "Uncle, I truly am sorry I haven't come to see ye in so long. Scotland Yard has overloaded me with work."

"And are ye happy in yer work, Jamie MacGregor?" his uncle asked, taking the chair across from him, his dark blue eyes, so much like Jamie's own, quite somber.

Jamie frowned, wishing he could sidestep the question, but knowing he couldn't. "At first I was happy," he said. "But after six years, well, I admit it grows wearisome."

"Have ye ever given any thought to my offer to ye some years past?"

Jamie blinked. He'd forgotten all about his uncle's request that he come and manage his property. In the excitement of being accepted by Scotland Yard, he'd turned Angus down and never given it a second thought. He flushed at the realization that he had treated his uncle's offer so callously.

"I'm afraid I was so swept away by the glamor of police work that it somewhat faded in my mind," Jamie admitted, looking down at his hands atop the wooden table. "I'm sorry, Uncle Angus. Ye deserved more consideration after all ye've done for me."

"I've done nothin'."

"But ye have." Jamie glanced up at him and took a deep breath. "Ye gave me and mother a home after Da died. Ye helped raise a rebellious thirteen-year-old." He looked away. "I haven't repaid ye very well for that, have I?"

Angus laughed and the sound startled Jamie into looking at him again. The silver-haired man was smiling broadly now. "Thirteen-year-old boys are practically grown. Ye were a good lad, Jamie, though a bit stubborn, and little trouble either to Katy or myself." He leaned back in his chair and took a package of tobacco and a pipe from the pocket of his worn tweed jacket. He nodded to himself. "Aye, ye brought us great joy."

Jamie watched as his uncle tamped down a goodly portion of sweet-smelling tobacco into the bowl and lit it. As the smoke drifted Jamie's way, he inhaled deeply, the familiar scent bringing back pleasant memories.

"But now that ye are here," Angus said, shaking the match out, "and since ye admit that ye are wearied of yer wee police force, why don't ye give my offer a second consideration?"

"That's kind of ye, Uncle but—"

41

"No. I need ye, lad." His eyes sparkled with something—hope, perhaps. Jamie shifted uncomfortably in his chair.

"I'm getting too old to run this place alone. Nothing would make me happier than to see ye established as laird of this place before I die."

Jamie smiled. Though the title was purely an honorary one in this day and age, he knew his uncle was completely serious. Scottish honor, Scottish history, was as vital to a Scotsman as his own life's blood.

"Ye know that yer great-aunt Katy and I were never blessed with children, and so ye are my only heir. British law decrees that I must either will my property to someone or gae it to the National Trust." He smiled at Jamie. "I'm getting old, lad, and I want to leave it to ye, but I willna do so if it will be a burden to ye. And I wish that ye would come now and begin managin' the place for me before it falls down completely!"

Jamie's head whirled with possibilities. If he took Angus up on his offer he could quit the force, perhaps learn blacksmithing and turn his hand at making swords, as he'd always wanted.

"I'll truly think about it, Uncle Angus," he said, then saw the doubt flicker into the old man's eyes. "I mean it. I have two weeks to give it some real thought."

Angus beamed at him. "Good, lad, that's all I ask."

A loud knocking at the front door sounded throughout the manor, reaching even the back dining room. The cook hurried through the doorway of the kitchen, her hands covered with flour.

"Och, Master Angus, I canna be answerin', if I dinna get my bread in the oven 't'will no' be fit ta eat."

Angus chuckled. "Dinna fash yerself, Edna. I'll answer it."

"Allow me, Uncle Angus," Jamie said, rising from the table. "Doesn't Henry work for you anymore?"

Angus sighed and shook his head. "Och, Henry's been gone two months. A better man's man will never be found."

Jamie patted his uncle on the shoulder as he passed, wondering suddenly about Angus's own well-being. Perhaps ill health lay at the bottom of his sudden urge to settle the matter of his heir. A great sadness settled over Jamie. Since the death of his mother, Angus was all the family he had left.

"I'll get the door." he said again, "and then tomorrow, what if you and I take a turn around the property and we'll talk."

Angus's face brightened and he smiled. "Aye," he agreed, "we'll talk. Greet them like a Campbell, lad, or at least like a MacGregor!"

It was an old joke between them, and Jamie grinned as he hurried toward the front door. Maybe he'd play up his heritage a bit if the people at the door were here for the festival. His uncle provided rooms for a certain number of faire-goers and many would be arriving that night, no doubt. He raked one hand through his hair, adjusted his plaid at his shoulder and waist, laid one hand on his sword, and opened the door.

A woman with short, disheveled auburn hair fell across the threshold before Jamie had time to react. It was as though the door had been supporting her weight and without it she tumbled to the ground, to lie sprawled practically in the doorway. Behind her stood another woman resembling a drowned platinum blond rat. Both women were soaking wet, and the blond had a look in her eye that made Jamie take a step back. The woman at his feet groaned, and Jamie quickly knelt beside her.

"Are ye all right, lass?" he asked.

She pushed up on her elbows and raised her head. Two remarkable green eyes gazed up at him with an expression close to wonder in their depths. In that instant, something quickened between them. Something he would call magical if he weren't a practical kind of man. She smiled and his heart turned upside down and inside out.

Chapter Three

"Are ye all right, lass?" the man asked again, supporting her with one arm around her waist. His touch was like a flame against Jix's skin. He wore a long-sleeved cream-colored shirt that dipped down in a "v" in the front, revealing dark, curly hair across his broad chest. Her fingers knotted in his wide sleeves as she dazedly drank in the sight of him. Her gaze raked over his dark brown hair that fell a little past his shoulders, to his black-lashed, midnight blue eyes. Dark brown brows arched above them, reminding her of Sean Connery in his younger days.

He had a straight, aristocratic nose, marred by a crook at the bridge, and Jix almost lifted her hand to her own, an old habit she'd almost overcome. Dirk's "love" had left her with a bump in the middle of her otherwise nondescript nose. The similarity made her feel suddenly as if they must be kindred spirits. Her attention drifted to his lips. Firm, sensual. She knew exactly what his kisses would taste like, how he would possess a woman's mouth. His chin was too stubborn, but she didn't care. She could be a mite stubborn herself. His jaw was strong, and his face had entirely too much character to be model-handsome, but she didn't care about that either. She liked men with character. He was a man who would not be easily led, she'd wager, but she didn't want to lead him, she only wanted to walk by his side.

Jix took a deep, ragged breath. What was she thinking? This was Sam's soul mate! He could be nothing less if God and the universe had given her such a vision of their wedding. But she couldn't help herself. The sight of him had robbed her of breath and coherent thought as she stared mesmerized into the deep blue eyes staring back at her. She knew him, as surely as she knew her own soul. Each time she had awakened from her prophetic dream, she'd felt a little closer to the dream-man. Even though she knew he was destined for Sam, she had felt a strange connection to him, the same connection she felt now.

She blinked. What was wrong with her? She'd kidnaped her best friend and risked ruining their friendship forever because she knew this was the man destined to be Sam's husband. Jix couldn't be attracted to him. She couldn't be feeling the heat of his hands on her waist, burning through her clothing. The rich, masculine scent of him couldn't be sending tingles across her now sensitive skin. She couldn't be feeling a sweet, hot fire pooling down deep inside of her. She couldn't want, more than anything in the world, to touch her lips to those firm, sensuous ones tilted up in concerned amusement.

No way.

She blinked again and tried to will herself to step out of his arms. For some strange reason, she couldn't do it. She stood paralyzed, their gazes locked.

His deep, amused voice chuckled down at her. "And do I pass inspection, lassie?"

Embarrassed, coming suddenly to her senses, Jix pulled away from his helping hands, regained her balance, and stepped back, her mouth still hanging open. It was startling, more than startling, to finally see the man who had haunted her nights for the last few months. That was what had caused her stupor. Of course, that was it.

"Uh, thank you. I tripped," she managed to choke out as he continued to stare down at her, bemused.

"Are ye all right now?" She nodded. He turned to Sam. "Are ye here for the festival?" he asked.

"No, we're here for the scuba diving!" Sam snapped, water running down her face. "Could we please come inside out of this lovely Scottish weather?"

"Och, of course, where are my manners? Come in, come in." He opened the door wider and gestured them into a huge vestibule. Jix and Sam gave a collective sigh of relief as they escaped the rain. The man strode out of the room, then quickly reappeared, carrying a stack of towels.

"Here, lassies, dry yerselves and then we'll get some hot tea into ye." His broad smile revealed even, white teeth. Jix's heart did a flip-flop.

Great. Now teeth are turning you on. Well, not just teeth, she thought as she watched him covertly. He stood at least eight inches taller than Jix's five foot four, and had the broadest shoulders she'd ever seen. He wore his shirt tucked into a brightly colored kilt of red, green, and thin bands of white. Another piece of the same tartan crossed his chest and adorned his shoulder, pinned in place by a round brooch—silver thistles around an incredibly large amethyst. Soft leather boots were laced to his knees. He wore a sword belted at his side, and an emerald stone shimmered at its hilt. He looked like an ancient warrior, and the image almost took her breath away.

Just then the man cocked one dark brow at her and grinned as if he knew what she was thinking. Jix looked away, turning her gaze toward the ceiling, the floor, anywhere but those laughing blue eyes. It wasn't that she was interested in him—no, not at all! But she was still human, still a woman, and she'd have to be dead not to be mesmerized by the hunk of a man standing in front of her.

"If ye'll tell me yer names I can show ye to yer room." His rich, Scottish accent combined with his deep voice sent a shiver through Jix, and she felt her knees going a little weak.

"I—" Her throat tightened as their eyes met once again.

"That is, I—" she swallowed hard, unable to take her gaze from the dimple appearing near the right side of his mouth. That mouth. Jix stopped trying to talk. She was incapable of speech.

"We have reservations," Samantha said shortly, "unless Jix has screwed that up too."

He glanced at Jix. Did she imagine the sympathetic look in his beautiful eyes?

"What names, lassies?"

"Samantha Riley," Sam said, her tone terse. "My"—she paused—"companion, can speak for herself."

Jix swallowed hard and finally regained a modicum of poise. She held out her right hand. "Hello. I'm Jix Ferguson."

He took her hand and immediately slow, soothing warmth began radiating up her arm, destroying her regained equilibrium. She felt mesmerized.

By the man from my dream. By Samantha's soul mate. Damn.

He released her fingers, giving her a curious look. Jix cast a glance upward. God had a very interesting sense of humor.

"Very funny," she muttered.

The man turned back to her with a puzzled frown. "I beg yer pardon?"

"Nothing," she muttered. "Just talking to myself."

"And that's the least of her problems," Sam said. "Believe me. Now that we've introduced ourselves would you mind telling us who you are?"

Jix winced at her friend's harsh tone, but couldn't seem to speak. Why was it the few men she ever felt attracted to always had something wrong with them? Her first love, Terry, had been an alcoholic. Her husband, Dirk, had been a violent S.O.B. Now this man—who obviously had nothing whatsoever wrong with him at all—already belonged to her best friend. Sometimes life was just unfair.

The man bowed over Sam's hand instead of shaking it. He straightened and inclined his head. "I am Jamie

MacGregor, at yer service, ladies. I'm Lord Campbell's grandnephew." He took Jix's hand again and bowed over it.

"Oh," Jix said breathlessly, "that's just grand."

He smiled again, a man totally secure in his power, his effect on women. Jix felt a swift stab of irritation and suddenly didn't quite feel so breathless. He was probably like all the rest. Arrogant. Conceited. Faithless.

He dropped Sam's hand. "If ye ladies will follow me, I'll take ye to the parlor for some tea while I find out which are your rooms." He turned to lead the way.

"No," Samantha said rudely. "I'm tired and I want to go to my room immediately. You can send the tea up."

The man blinked and Jix blushed, suddenly ashamed of her friend. "She'd be delighted," she said, grabbing Samantha by one arm and dragging her along with her. "Is it this way?"

Jamie MacGregor nodded, frowning slightly before a bemused smile touched his lips and he led the way.

Jix watched his kilt swing back and forth over well-muscled calves and a sigh escaped her. She clapped one hand to her mouth, hurrying after him, hoping neither he nor Sam had heard. No, Sam had his attention as she fired off one order after another. He kept nodding, a perplexed look on his face. Well, at least Jix had brought them together, but they wouldn't have much time to fall in love if Sam persisted in her demands to fly back to the States on Monday. Jix mentally rolled up her sleeves.

Before she got through with the two of them, Sam would be engaged to the man of her dreams and would have forgiven her best friend utterly and completely. Jix took a deep breath. And she and Jamie MacGregor would be nothing more than very good friends. Nothing more.

The parlor was a beautiful little sitting room with blue-sprigged curtains and lovely Victorian furniture. Jix sank down on the high-backed sofa and ran one hand across the dark navy blue tapestry, her fingers pausing over the tiny roses imprinted there. A fireplace graced one wall, its flames lending a cozy warmth to the small room.

"This is lovely," Jix said. "Isn't it, Sam? Isn't it just lovely?"

"It's wonderful," her friend agreed flatly. "Now can we please have our tea so I can go to bed?"

"Of course," Jamie gestured to the sofa. "Please, sit down."

With a long-suffering sigh, Samantha sat down beside Jix. The man made them both a small bow and tossed them a dazzling smile. "I'll be right back."

As soon as he was gone Jix turned on her friend, breathless, her heart pounding in her chest. "Sam—it's him! He's the guy—and you did everything but spit in his face!"

"What guy?" Samantha said crossly, folding her arms over her chest and slumping down until her backbone touched the seat of the couch.

"The guy from my dream—the *man* you're going to marry!" Jix sighed. "And he's gorgeous."

"The guy from—" Sam broke off and shook her head, giving Jix a hateful glance. "Look, squirrel-brain, drop this before I have to do you bodily harm."

Jix bit her lower lip. "But it's true, I—look, Sam, didn't you get a feeling or anything when you met him?"

Sam closed her eyes and rubbed her temples with both hands. "A feeling like what or anything?"

Jix bit down hard on her lower lip for a long minute until Samantha opened her eyes and gazed at her sullenly. Jix shrugged. "I dunno. Like maybe, ah, chemistry, a sense of destiny—lust?"

"Chemistry? Lust?" Sam snorted. "With that longhaired, wild-eyed—" Sam's own eyes widened and she sat bolt upright. "What have you done? Is this more of your underhanded insanity? Oh my gosh, did you arrange this? Did you *hire* that guy to seduce me so you could claim that your stupid kidnapping game was justified?"

"What a fascinatin' thought."

Both women froze at the sound of the deep, amused voice with the broad Scottish accent directly behind them. Slowly Jix and Sam turned around. Apparently the parlor had two entrances, the one through which they had come, and another, through the two French doors behind them. Jamie MacGregor stood grinning at them, holding a large tray on which a fat blue teapot and three cups sat, surrounded by bowls of sugar, cream, and a plate of scones.

His smile broadened as Jix and Sam sat in stunned silence. "Och, unfortunately, lass, I havena been hired either to seduce ye, or even ta flirt shamelessly, though I would no' be adverse to either suggestion."

"You must excuse my companion," Samantha said, rising to her feet with the grace of a queen, her voice like ice. She glared at Jix and lifted her chin haughtily. "She isn't quite in her right mind."

"Have a seat, lass," Jamie said calmly, "and have a wee drop of tea. Ye'll feel better if you do."

"No, thank you." Sam shot Jix a look of pure fury. If looks could kill, Jix thought, I'd already be six feet under. She stared down at the smooth wooden floor, wishing a wandering freight train would burst through the wall and run her down. "I find I am too tired for tea after all," Sam said.

"Verra well."

Jix glanced up and saw that Jamie's eyes still sparkled with humor, in spite of Samantha's rudeness. Maybe all wasn't lost yet. He crossed the room and placed the tray on the small marble-topped table in front of the sofa, giving Jix a wink that sent shivers right down to the bottoms of her feet.

"Let me show ye to yer room, then," he offered, bowing slightly toward Sam before glancing at Jix. "Would ye like to have some tea or are ye too wearied, like your friend?"

"Oh, I'm not tired," Jix said quickly, too quickly, and felt the heat flood her face again. "I mean, do you want me to come up with you, Sam?"

She peered anxiously at her friend. She should hope that Sam would insist she come up with her. Yes, that was exactly what she should hope. But she didn't. Never had she wanted something so badly as she wanted to stay right where she was, on the sofa, about to have tea with Jamie MacGregor.

"Oh, is she going to room with me?" Sam said in dismay. A sharp stab of grief pierced Jix's heart and she wondered suddenly if she had done irreparable harm to their friendship. Would Sam really never forgive her?

"Aye." Jamie lifted one hand to his head and rumpled his dark hair, his brows knitting together in perplexity. "I confess to being a bit confused, ladies. Are the two of ye friends or no'?"

"Yes," Jix said.

"No," Sam said.

Jix sighed and rolled her eyes, slumping back on the couch, feeling suddenly deflated as Sam continued to glare down at her.

"Ah." Jamie nodded, then took a deep breath. "Well, then, I'll just be takin' ye up to your room and perhaps another can be found for yer—for Miss Ferguson tomorrow. I'm afraid tonight the two of ye will have to put up with each other."

"I can find my way," Sam said, crossing to the parlor door. "Is the room upstairs?"

"Aye, second door on the left at the top of the stairs."

Jix watched her friend walk toward the door and knew she had to stop her. Jamie MacGregor was Samantha's soul mate, not hers. Jamie MacGregor was the man in her dream and nothing, no, not any force in the cosmos could keep him from taking his appointed place at her best friend's side. Whatever attraction Jix felt for the man was simply a combination of jet lag and the sexual frustration of being celibate for two years. She couldn't let Sam just walk away!

"Wait, Samantha!" she cried. She stumbled to her feet and circled the low table, unfortunately catching the edge of her skirt on the spout of the china teapot. Jix whirled to catch it a half second too late and the pretty pot crashed to the floor.

Jix sighed and shot Sam an irritated look. "Now see what you did."

"What I did?"

"We're sorry, Mr. MacGregor," Jix said, crossing to his side. "We'll pay to replace the teapot."

Sam whirled on her, furious. "I have had just about all I can—"

"But—but—" Jix glanced around for something, anything, to stall for time. Her gaze fell on the sword at Jamie's waist. "But you haven't seen his sword yet," Jix said, crossing the room and grabbing Sam by one arm. She pulled her toward Jamie MacGregor who had folded his arms over his chest and was frowning in perplexity again. Sam and Jix stopped just inches away from him as Jix gushed on.

"I noticed it right away and was immediately attracted to it." She felt the color rising to her face, and a slow smile spread across the man's face. What an idiotic thing to say! "I mean, it's so large, so long, that I—"she stopped, mortified.

A genuine grin split the handsome man's face and Jix wished the earth would open up and swallow her whole.

"Aye, it is large," he said, raising that elusive eyebrow again and gazing at her from beneath slightly lowered lashes. The expression in his eyes could only be described as sultry and Jix's heart beat a little faster. His hand lowered to rest on the hilt of the sword. "And 'tis fair long, I admit. You can handle it if you wish, but trust me, only I truly know how to wield it, how to gain the deepest thrust and slide it sweetly into the most reluctant scabbard." His eyes twinkled as Jix' blush deepened.

"Oh, brother," Sam muttered. "Puh-leeze." Before the man could move, she grasped the claymore by its hilt and with one swift pull, dragged it free from its sheath.

Jix almost gasped aloud at the beauty of the weapon. It was huge, almost four feet long, with a large, smooth, dark green stone embedded in the long hilt. The tip immediately dropped to the floor as the full weight of the weapon hit Samantha.

"There, look at the damn thing so I can go to bed and you two can get on with your innuendos."

"Sam, really—"

"Lass, you should be more careful—"

Both Jamie and Jix moved toward Samantha, almost colliding, but she raised the sword at the last minute, keeping the two of them apart.

"If I had any guts I'd just put this through her and rid the world of her particular brand of friendship," Sam muttered.

"Sam, please," Jix begged. "You're going to hurt yourself."

Jamie smoothly took the claymore from her grasp. "Here now, lassie. Let's not be makin' idle threats."

"They aren't idle," Sam retorted.

"Why are the two of ye so fashed with one another," he asked, his brogue thickening.

"She ruined my life!" Sam announced, jabbing one finger toward Jix. "She kidnapped me the night before my wedding, all because she didn't like my choice of a husband!"

Jamie's eyes widened as he turned to Jix. "Is that true, lass?"

Jix glanced up, still feeling dazed by the presence of Jamie MacGregor and the beauty of the sword he held. As he scrutinized her, she realized that even if he belonged to Sam, she didn't want him to think ill of her.

"I—I—well, she locked me in a closet on my wedding day!" Jix accused, and pointed back at her friend dramatically. She wasn't sure, but she thought the amused twinkle in Jamie's eyes faded a bit.

"I see. So ye're married then?"

Jix frowned. She was certainly making a mess of things. "No, no, I'm not. Not anymore. It was a mistake."

"A mistake yer friend tried to prevent?" he suggested, gently.

"Exactly!" Jix seized on his words. "And that's what I was trying to do for her! Believe me, if I had listened to what my best friend tried to tell me, I would've saved myself a lot of pain and heartache."

"Ah." Jamie nodded. "So you weren't just trying to get revenge for her locking you in the closet?"

"Of course not!" Jix stared at him, appalled that he would think such a thing. "I'd never do something like that!"

"No, you'd just get me drunk and put me on a flight to Scotland." Sam said bitterly. "And as soon as I get home again I'm filing charges."

"Why wait?" Jamie asked, one corner of his mouth quirking up. "I work for Scotland Yard. I'd be happy to take the two of ye down to the nearest police station right now. Or, if ye prefer, we can simply lock her in the dungeon and throw away the key."

Scotland Yard. Jix tucked away that little morsel of information. Sam had once dated a policeman, so maybe she was attracted to defenders of justice.

"A dungeon sounds perfect," Sam snarled. "Do you have a rack?"

Jamie grinned, and it lit up his whole face. Jix looked away and started counting the roses on the parlor wallpaper. "I'll have to check," he said.

"Great. Tomorrow we'll do one or the other." She shot Jix a quelling look. "But right now I just want to go to bed. Thanks for the look at your sword, Mr. MacGregor, and if you decide to run her through before the night's over, I'll give you an excellent alibi."

Jamie chuckled as Sam turned and started across the room.

"But wait!" Jix cried again. "I have to . . . um. . . ." she shot Jamie a look, then Sam. They would only be here for two days. Really just a day and a half because they'd have to take the train back to England on Sunday.

"What is it?" Sam said impatiently.

"Um, I—please, just look at the beautiful workmanship on this sword. Did you know there's Celtic knotwork all the way around the stone?"

Jix felt a brief surge of triumph as Sam hesitated. Her friend loved Celtic knotwork and collected it. If she could get her close to Jamie, she just knew that Sam would feel what she felt—that wonderful connection, that incredible chemistry.

"Well, all right," Sam agreed, begrudgingly. "Let me see it. May I?"

Jamie held it out toward her, his right hand on the hilt, the blade balanced across his left arm. Sam lightly traced the Celtic knotwork edging the brilliant stone. "It is magnificent," she said. "Is the stone valuable or simply ornamental?"

"Both. 'Tis symbolic of my family's valor in battle," he explained. "This sword has been in the MacGregor clan since time began." Sam gave him a skeptical look and he shrugged, smiling. "Well, that's the legend in any case. 'Tis said that the ancient gods gave it to the first MacGregor and it has been handed down from generation to generation to the bravest MacGregor."

"Are you brave?" Jix asked, before she could stop herself. The words came out husky and she bit her lower lip as he turned his burning gaze her way.

"All Scots are brave, lass," he admonished her. "For we're all descended from gods and kings."

Sam snorted. "Yeah. Right. You want to duck down a little, because your head is getting too big for the room."

Jamie grinned. "See for yerself." He turned the sword over and pointed to an inscription running down from the hilt about six inches. "Our family creed: *'S Rioghal Mo Dhream.*"

"What does that mean?" Jix asked, mesmerized by the soft cadence of his voice and the Gaelic he had spoken.

"Royal is my race," he said.

Sam's haughty demeanor gave way to honest admiration as she gingerly ran her hand over the crosspiece of the hilt. Jix found she couldn't keep from touching the sword either and for a moment, the allure of Jamie MacGregor was forgotten as she moved closer and smoothed the emerald stone with one finger.

"It's amazing, isn't it," she said, "that men really killed one another with such barbarous instruments?"

"Aye, and now we're much more civilized," Jamie said. "Now we use guns. At least back then it was a battle of skill and wits."

Jix frowned down at the sword. "Look at the stone—it seems brighter now, doesn't it, or am I crazy?"

"You *are* crazy," Samantha retorted, dropping her hand to her side, "but it does look brighter. Is"—she leaned closer—"is it glowing?"

"Yes! Oh darn, now it's stopped." Jix rubbed the stone again, and was disappointed when it didn't light up.

"That's odd," Jamie said, "it's never done that before. I wonder what caused it."

"Wait. Sam, put your hand back on the hilt again."

"I don't—"

Jix grabbed her friend's hand and placed it on the cross-piece, then quickly touched the stone. The glow returned.

"Look," she whispered.

The green of the emerald brightened until it was the color of a forest at twilight, permeated by an eerie glow. Jix began to tremble and tried to move her hand away, only to find that she couldn't.

"What the hell—" Jamie said in that same instant "—I can't let go of the sword."

"Me either," Sam said in disgust. "Is this one of your stupid pranks, Jix? Did you put super glue on the man's sword?"

"Of course not! What's happening?" Jix said, panic sweeping over her. She tried to take her hands from the weapon. She was stuck tight. "I thought we came into the library. Did we take a wrong turn and end up in the Twilight Zone instead? Where did you get this wacky pocket knife?"

"Like I told ye, it's been handed down in my family for generations," he said.

"Oh, that's right, the ancient gods gave it to you." She squinted at the ceiling. "Uh, excuse me, ancient gods—where is the off button for this thing?"

Jamie laughed and flexed his fingers around the hilt of the sword, then frowned. "Maybe there's an 'escape' key somewhere."

"Hey, Tweedle Dum and Tweedle Dee," Sam drawled, "could we focus on the problem here? We can't let go of the damn sword—what are we going to do?"

"Maybe we're supposed to ask it to let go of us," Jix suggested.

"It doesna have a brain, lass," Jamie said. "Nor ears to hear yer words."

"If it did, we'd probably have to do something a little more exciting," Jix said, "like repeat the family motto. How did that Gaelic ditty go again?"

" *'S Rioghal Mo Dhream,* " Jamie said.

As if on cue, the blade of the sword began to glow, and a soft humming sound filled the room.

"*JIX!* What have you done?" Samantha's voice was vibrating along with the rest of her, and the sword as well. Jix glanced at Jamie and saw his eyes widen, then he looked at her, accusation in his gaze.

"What did you do?" he cried. "What—"

"Me? Why does everybody always blame—"

It was as though the world had suddenly turned to glass. As though the reality of Jix and Jamie and Samantha had been flattened into a picture upon a sheet of glass, trapped inside and sent spinning through eternity. Jix spun through the blackness, voiceless, frozen, then the glass shattered! Free but blind, she cried out, the darkness swallowing her voice as the void wrapped around her. Falling, she reached out into the darkness and found . . . nothing.

The day her mother abandoned her, she had been filled with the same kind of nothingness as was found in this empty place. Her laughing facade had been stripped away and all that remained was her pain. She knew that pain and it rushed in on her, threatening to destroy her, to drive her insane. Jix screamed, or was that someone else screaming? She didn't know. All she knew was that she was falling, down, down, down, into a night that had no end.

Chapter Four

Out of the darkness strong arms wrapped around her and Jix clung to them. Some semblance of consciousness returned to Jix and she knew it was Jamie's arms holding her, Jamie alone keeping her from madness. The reality of his flesh beneath her hands, the warm, musky smell of him, the sound of his heartbeat as she pressed her face against his chest, all added together to bring her back from that sharp precipice of insanity. She became aware that Samantha was on the other side of Jamie, clinging too. Then all thought was suspended as the speed of their fall increased, and the sensation of a harsh, brutal wind whipped suddenly around them, twisting them in a dark vise.

Jix heard Samantha scream and she reached out for her friend, barely able to move her fingers from Jamie's waist. She groped in the darkness but Samantha was gone. With an inaudible sob she realized Jamie hadn't been able to hold Sam along with the sword. His right hand seemed almost paralyzed around its hilt. Sam had clung to him and now she was gone.

What have I done what have I done what have I done?
The words echoed in Jix's mind. Then she felt a sharp pain in her side, in her head, and knew no more.

Jamie awoke to the sound of men shouting and the clash of swords. He couldn't open his eyes, couldn't move. All he could do was lie prostrate and listen to a cacophony of destruction. He would wake up in a minute, he told himself. He would wake up in that fleabag hotel in London, or in his own flat or in the soft guest bed in his uncle's manor. In a moment, he would wake up. Another sound, this one closer, next to him, penetrated his blind consciousness. A soft, feminine sound, a sob caught in a woman's throat perhaps. The effort cost him every ounce of courage he possessed, but Jamie opened his eyes and found himself face to face with Jix Ferguson.

She lay on her side, facing him, eyes closed, lashes dark crescents on her cheeks. Her face was ashen, her lips blood red against her pallor, and a trickle of blood dripped down the side of her forehead. Her long auburn hair waved out beneath her like a flame upon the ground.

Jamie felt a chill run down his spine. Long hair? Jix had short, curly hair. Now it was long.

What the bloody hell is going on?
He tried to orient himself, feeling as though his brain had been coated with a thick goo, preventing him from rational thought. His fingers curled against the ground in frustration. The ground. They were lying on the ground, the air was filled with dust and the tortured cries of men, and Jix lay bleeding beside him. The thought propelled him out of the dirt, to his knees. He still held the sword; he leaned on the MacGregor claymore and tried to catch his breath, feeling as if every bone in his body had been shattered apart, then hammered back together again.

As he squinted through the murky air, Jamie saw that he and Jix lay in a shallow ravine, a large fallen tree balanced on the edge giving them protection from whatever lay beyond. Staggering to his feet, he stumbled up the slight incline and fell to his knees behind the gnarled log.

Cautiously he raised up and peered over the fallen oak. He stared for a moment, certain he had lost his mind. He took a step back and whirled, diving into the dirt to land flat on his stomach, his mind racing. Beyond the log, men wielding swords and battle-axes and pointed sticks and daggers and knives were slashing at one another. A battle. They were in the midst of a battle.

Impossible.

Jamie dragged himself up again and crawled to a better vantage point behind the toppled tree, his sword at his side. He peered over the barricade just in time to see a man wearing a plaid kilt of muted colors cut off another man's arm. Jamie's throat closed and nausea churned in his belly. Resting his head against the tree, he tried to pull in enough air to keep from passing out.

"Scottish dog!"

He looked up into two murderous black eyes Jamie knew he would never forget.

The man lifted a curved sword high over his head, and brought it down.

Instinctively Jamie lifted his own sword in time to block the attack, but the impact drove him back down the ravine. He lost his footing and sprawled beside Jix, his sword landing a foot away from him. His assailant jumped down with a fierce cry, and Jamie rolled just before steel slashed into the dirt where he had been.

There was no time to think, no time to wonder. Jamie grabbed his sword and turned, slicing the blade through the air even as he leapt to his feet. He caught the man in the arm and his attacker backed away, just as another man jumped down to continue the fight. Jamie lunged and caught the new man dead center; he heard the blade enter his assailant's body with a sickening crunch. The man sagged to his knees, his eyes rolling back in his head. Jamie pulled his sword from the man's chest and stared down at the scarlet blood dripping from the steel.

"What's happening?" he whispered.

Then they were on him—two from the front and one from behind—more men, clad in dark trousers and oddly cut coats, with two red sashes tied from shoulder to waist in an X. At first they overwhelmed him, then Jamie's training clicked in, the years of fencing and martial arts training he'd undergone using this very sword. Schooling himself not to waste energy trying to understand, he focused instead on fighting, trying desperately to pretend it was just another workout, just another exercise. *But* he thought grimly as he hacked and slashed at the men attacking him—*workouts don't leave another man's guts strewn on the ground.*

He defeated the three and turned to face another, and another, and just when he thought he couldn't raise the claymore one more time, three more men appeared. But these wore the muted kilts he'd seen earlier. Drawing on some reserve he didn't know he had, Jamie lifted the sword once again and prepared to fight.

The men didn't attack him. Instead one of them, the largest, grinned. "Och, laddie, put doon yer sword," he said, "I dinna ken what clan ye be from with your bonny plaid, but nae matter. This day the Sassenachs are the devils we all be after."

"Sassenachs?" Jamie asked, dazed.

"Aye, and thanks to yer help they've all turned tail and are halfway back to England."

Jamie let the sword drop slightly and stood with his legs apart, his knees bent. His breath was coming hard and fast as he looked up at the three, suspicious of their acceptance.

"Ye were fightin' them too?"

"Aye, laddie." They came nearer. The one who spoke was older than the others. He had a huge black beard that covered half of his face and large, bushy eyebrows slashed darkly over two piercingly intelligent blue eyes. "Ye just saved half a dozen of my men. Fer that, I am grateful. I am Fergus Campbell. What is yer name?"

"James MacGregor," Jamie answered, feeling a wave of dizziness pass over him. He swallowed hard. "What the hell is goin' on? I was at my uncle's castle and—"

But the man's bright eyes had grown hard and he took a step back from Jamie, raising his sword between them.

The other men around him lifted theirs as well and Jamie tried to find the strength to prepare for yet another fight. *Was it something I said?* he thought wryly.

"Ye've a braw nerve speakin' that name," Campbell said, his voice rough. "An' ye helped us? What skulduggery are ye about?"

Jamie wiped the sweat from his face and tried to think. Could it be some sort of reenactment staged by his uncle? No, of course not. He'd just seen men get their limbs chopped off. He'd just killed or wounded several men. The realization almost sent him to his knees, but he sucked in a breath of the cold Highland air and managed to stay on his feet.

"Look," he cleared his throat and broadened his brogue, "I dinna ken what's happenin' here, but I did help ye, did I no'?"

The big man nodded, grudgingly.

"I am James MacGregor and now I need your help." He gestured behind him where Jix still lay on the ground. "She's hurt and we must get her to a hospital."

The bearded man's gaze shifted to some point behind Jamie, and both bushy brows lifted as a slow smile slid across the man's filthy features. Jamie turned to find a crowd of men standing around Jix, peering down at her. Jamie crossed quickly to the woman's side and knelt beside her. The red and blue kilted skirt she wore was hiked up to her thighs, leaving little to the imagination, and he smoothed the material down, covering her legs. She wore no bra beneath her red tank top and as her chest rose and fell, it was little wonder the men were all staring. If the situation hadn't been so desperate he'd have stared too. But instead he ripped the plaid from his shoulders and draped it over the unconscious woman, then raised her shoulders from the ground.

"Lass?" Jamie said anxiously, smoothing her hair back from her face. "Lass, are ye all right?"

Jix's eyes fluttered open and two pools of green stared up at him in dazed confusion.

"Jamie?" she whispered. "What happened? What—?"

Her gaze shifted to a point above his shoulder and to his surprise she smiled. "Your uncle really pulls out all the stops, doesn't he?" she asked, her words slightly slurred. "But he'd better do some work on his safety features or he's going to find himself in a lawsuit." She moaned and lifted one hand to her head. "Ask that big ugly guy over there if he has some Tylenol."

"Ugly? Did the lass call me ugly?" Campbell puffed up like a blowfish.

Jamie tensed. He had a feeling these people were spoiling for a fight with him. "She hit her head," he explained, "pay no mind to her nonsense." He gathered Jix closer to him. "Don't talk," he said, his voice low. "Leave this to me."

" 'Tis a strange accent she has." The Highlander narrowed his eyes. "Is she Sassenach?"

Jamie's patience evaporated. "Look, will ye help us or no'? I need to get her to a hospital!"

"I'm fine, Jamie, really I am." Jix pulled herself out of his arms to a sitting position, then sat there blinking and swaying. "Where's Samantha?"

"Shhhh, be quiet, lass."

"Don't tell me what to do," she muttered. She sagged back against him, her eyes fluttering shut.

Campbell shook his head, his frown deepening at Jix's attempt to speak again. "I dinna ken what a hospital might be, but we have none of them." He watched the woman for a long moment before shifting his gaze to Jamie, understanding suddenly dawning in his eyes. "Och, now I ken who ye are and what ye be doin' on Campbell land. Yer uncle sent the two of ye to forge the alliance with Red Hugh, aye? We dinna expect ye before the winter snows."

He lifted the huge claymore he held and Jamie raised his own sword with his left hand, wondering if he could lower Jix to the ground and get to his feet before the man killed them both. Fergus Campbell laughed and hefted his four-foot-long sword up, then down in the scabbard at his waist.

Relieved, Jamie sheathed his own weapon and shook his

head. "Alliance? No, you don't understand. I'm James MacGregor—"

The man's smile widened even more. "Ye have courage, that is for certain. But if I were ye, lad, I wouldn't be shoutin' that name to the hills quite sae loudly. Especially since this field be littered with the King's men and some may still be alive." He nodded. "Red Hugh will be sore glad to see ye, lad, and yer sister, Maigrey as well."

Jamie looked at him. *Maigrey? Sister?*

"Now wait a minute, I—"

"Nae time ta wait, laddie, if ye want help for the lass. Worthington's men may be gathering and returning before long. Come along then and we'll take ye to Meadbrooke. Red Hugh's healer is likely there and she's the best in the Highlands."

Had these people lost their minds? What were grown men doing running around in the middle of the day in kilts fighting one another? Jamie didn't know, but Jix lay bleeding in his arms, perhaps suffering from a concussion or worse. She'd lost consciousness again and lay limply in his arms. Although he scarcely knew her, the thought of Jix being injured made him feel almost panicky. From the moment their eyes had met, he'd been connected with this woman—why, to what end, he didn't know. But he knew that he wouldn't let anything happen to her. He had to get help for her and if this nutcase wanted to call her Maigrey, that was just fine with him—as long as her injuries got treated, and soon. Jamie started to lift her in his arms when Fergus Campbell held up one hand.

"Your sword, laddie," he said, his voice firm. "Ye may be here to make peace and then again ye may not. But I'll have yer weapon in either case."

Jamie carefully lowered Jix back to the ground. He stood and unbuckled his belt, handing it over to the man. Campbell drew the claymore out of the sheath and whistled shrilly. Jamie knelt back down beside Jix, ignoring the man's exclamations. He lifted her, amazed at how little she weighed. A wee little thing, no more than five feet four inches tall, she was like a wee mouse next to his large frame. He gazed down into her pale, silent face, blood dried and caked down the side of her cheek, and his heart contracted.

"Don't you die on me," he whispered to her. "Damn it to hell, lass, don't you dare die." He tightened his hold and followed Campbell through the dust and dirt. Meadbrooke, the man had said. Was it possible he was being led to his own home? What would his uncle say when this band of wild men appeared on his steps? And yet, as they walked across the bright green meadow, Jamie's heart sank more with every step he took. Somehow he knew his uncle wouldn't be greeting them at Meadbrooke.

After walking for half an hour, Fergus called a halt, squinting into the sunlight. He lifted one arm and pointed toward the sun setting over the distant purple mountains. No, not toward the sun, toward the huge building silhouetted in front of the great orange ball.

"Meadbrooke," he announced.

Jamie stood transfixed. There before his eyes stood a great stone castle, its battlements stretching up into the twilight of the blue Scottish sky. This wasn't Meadbrooke. He was definitely not home. Then what—he sucked in a sharp breath of air.

Across the meadow leading to the castle lay a huge boulder, ancient, stark against the velvet green. On its side swirling spirals and other Neolithic pictures had been carved. Jamie swallowed hard. That boulder had stood there for countless generations. Just a few hours ago it had towered over the back of his uncle's property, marking one side of his land. Now Meadbrooke Manor was gone and in its place stood an ancient, towering castle of crumbling stone.

Jix twisted in the throes of a terrible dream. Wild Highlanders, like something out of *Braveheart,* had surrounded her and Jamie, threatening them with swords. Jamie waved a sword too, at her, or at the wild men, she couldn't tell for sure which. He looked quite wild himself with his hair long, streaming halfway down his back, his kilt bright amid the muted colors of the other men around him. Then the dream shifted and the Highlanders disappeared into darkness. She floated through the blackness, reaching for something, someone.

"Jamie?" she whispered.

"I'm here, lass, I'm here. Don't ye want to wake up now?"

She shook her head, frowning as a pain pierced her brow. A very small Highlander—or could he be a leprechaun? No, that would be Ireland, not Scotland—but in any case, some little jerk sat on her head with a tiny hammer, thudding away at her skull, pounding one rhythmic pain after another into her head. If she woke up, as Jamie had suggested, maybe the little demon would go away. It took tremendous effort, but at last she managed to open first one eye and then the other.

"Jamie?" she heard her voice croak out the word and blinked, trying to clear her vision. Jamie's face came into focus and relieved, she closed her eyes again.

"No, no, darlin', don't close yer eyes again. Stay with me, now, stay with me."

Jix smiled. Jamie wanted her to stay with him. He wanted her to stay with him forever. They would find a nice little cottage in the Highlands and together would have four beautiful children. She'd always wanted to have at least four children. She heard a soft chuckle.

"What are ye smiling about, lass?" Jamie whispered. She could feel his breath against her face. "Open yer eyes and look at me."

She did as he said and saw his sweet, concerned face, smiling down at her. She smiled back, when suddenly the little man on her head began swinging his hammer with alarming speed. Jix groaned aloud.

"Oh, my head."

"Aye, ye've taken quite a bump. I'm hoping ye don't have a concussion. Ye've got to try and stay awake now."

Jix blinked up at him as true consciousness cleared the fuzz from her mind. "Jamie?" She tried to sit up but he laid one large hand on her shoulder and pressed her back.

"Don't try to move. Ye're hurt and I don't know when I'll be able to get ye any real help."

She blinked again and let her gaze wander from his handsome face to the room in which she lay. Around her, gray walls rose up, hewn from massive stones fitted together in ancient solidity. Bright tapestries as large as her dining room back home adorned three of the four walls of the expansive square room that boasted ceilings over twenty feet high. A huge fireplace took up almost the entire fourth wall, and a bright, blazing fire danced there.

Dazed, she realized she rested on a huge bed whose four posters must have been carved from tree trunks a foot in diameter. They reached toward the ceiling and each ended in a carved rendition of a dragon's head. The bedclothes had a slightly musty smell, as did the entire room, but the dark green silken coverlet was warm and relatively clean.

"Where are we?" she said, appalled to find she could speak no louder than a whisper. She felt weak, as if she'd had the flu.

"In a hell of a lot of trouble," Jamie muttered.

The massive door to the room slammed open just then and Jix jumped and cried out as pain sliced through her head. A grim look settled over Jamie's features as two men entered wearing kilts and greatly resembling the rogues from her nightmare.

"It's time," one of them said.

"Can ye no' wait until tomorrow," Jamie said. Jix noted the unusual thickness of his brogue and frowned. "The lass is hurt."

"Red Hugh is waitin' and he'll no' wait fer long," the larger man said. "If ye want to plead yer case, ye'd best come with us." He glanced at Jix and his expression became a leer. "Ye can leave the lass here if ye want. I'll look after her." The man had the longest, yellowest teeth she'd ever seen, along with a face marred by pockmarks the size of olives.

Yeah, in your dreams, bub, Jix thought blearily. *My, the lord of Meadbrooke certainly likes authenticity in his festivals, doesn't he?*

67

"You can tell Lord Campbell that he's lucky I don't sue him," she said, still feeling more than a little put out.

The two men looked as if she had punched them in the stomach. Worried glances passed between them. The thought of a lawsuit must have them scared, she decided.

"Don't talk," Jamie said in a hushed tone.

She turned to face him. He looked a little green around the gills. What in the world was going on? "What?"

"Let me do the talking. I'll carry ye downstairs."

"But I don't want to go."

Jamie glanced at the two men, then back at her. "Ye're going with me." Broadening his brogue, he turned back to the men. "Dinna pay attention to her. She hit her head and doesna ken what she's sayin'. We'll go with ye." He narrowed his eyes. "Both of us."

The one who had volunteered to stay with Jix looked disappointed, but he nodded and gestured to the door. Jix felt even more confused. While she contemplated what in the hell was going on, Jamie moved to her side and slid his arms under her knees and around her waist. He picked her up and she blinked at him.

"Why can't I talk?" she whispered, relishing the warmth of his body next to hers. Her head even felt a little better when he was near.

"Because your accent will get us into trouble," he muttered.

"Oh." She lay back in his arms. It was all too confusing. Jix felt as though her body had been taken apart, molecule by molecule, and slammed back together again. Her brain seemed full of fuzz and she felt disoriented. But what did her Texas accent have to do with anything? She smoothed one hand against her thigh and frowned. Glancing down, she saw she wore a soft, crudely woven gown.

Curiouser and curiouser.

Jix fell asleep, and when she opened her eyes again they were in a vast hall, like nothing she had seen before except in old movies like *Ivanhoe*. Jamie still held her in his arms, a grim look on his face. The hall was huge, with a gigantic fireplace taking up most of one wall. These people really seemed to like their big fireplaces, Jix mused. Jamie could probably stand up inside of it without bumping his head. More tapestries hung around the hall, depicting great hunts and adventures. Her vision blurred and the pounding in her head kept her from paying further attention. Maybe tomorrow she'd take a closer look at this room, when she felt better.

"Jamie—" She curled her hand around the back of his neck and let her fingers explore the softness of his hair. "I really don't feel like doing the festival thing right now."

"Shhh, lass," he whispered.

"It's not that I'm not impressed," she insisted, staring around at the utter authenticity of the place. "I am, truly. And I promise I won't sue your uncle. But I really want—"

"Hush!" His dark brows knit together even as his blue eyes focused across the room. Jix sighed and stopped talking. He certainly took this reenactment stuff seriously, but then she'd heard Scotsmen were like that. To them the Battle of Whatever might as well have happened yesterday. Samantha would have liked this. She loved history. A nagging thought emerged from the fuzz around her brain.

"Samantha," she said softly. "Where is Samantha?"

"I don't know," he hissed, "now will ye be silent?"

Jix opened her mouth to retort when a man strode into the room and her mouth snapped shut. Shorter than the other men, he still had broad shoulders and a chest as wide as a professional wrestler. His thighs resembled small tree trunks and he had well-hewn biceps as big around as a melon. He wore a muted green and brown kilt but no shirt. Instead a piece of gray fur stretched across his chest, anchored over his shoulder and at his waist.

Brown leather boots, rough, weathered, and laced up to his knees, with fur adorning their rims, covered his calves. He carried a sword at his side, and more fur, this time in the guise of a cape, reached down to his ankles. It fastened at his right shoulder and then again on the left side of his waist. He had a thick shock of the brightest red hair Jix had ever seen and was the most exquisite example of barbarism that she could imagine. He strode across the hall and mounted a few short steps leading up to a dais on which a huge carved chair sat. The antlers of some great beast adorned the top, and, squinting in the dim light, Jix realized belatedly that the entire chair was made up of horns from some beast as big as a Texas longhorn. The man exuded confidence, arrogance, and control.

What an actor! Maybe Sam would appear any minute as a "captured princess" or something.

"Hi, Red, how's it hangin'?" she called, wondering why her words slurred. Jamie's arms stiffened beneath her and she pulled him closer, whispering in his ear. "Wow, your uncle really does it up good for the tourists, doesn't he?"

Jamie looked down at her, his dark brows colliding over concerned blue eyes. "It's not what ye think, lass," he whispered back. "Now please, for the love of God, let me handle things."

A wave of dizziness swept over Jix. "Sure, sure. I'll just be the spectator and enjoy the show." She waggled her index finger at the muscular man now taking his seat in the thronelike chair. "But I have to tell you that he is the best, the absolute best! The epitome of the wild, barbaric Highlander!"

Jamie groaned aloud. "These men are not from my uncle's festival," he told her, his voice low and trembling.

"Why are you so upset?" she asked, blinking up at him.

"Ye there!" The man's voice boomed across the room and Jamie turned back toward him. She sensed the tension in the room, especially in Jamie, and she frowned, wondering why he was so upset. Probably because she'd been hurt during the wild reenactment of the battle and he worried that she really would sue his uncle.

A little clarity returned to her thinking. How in the world had she and Samantha been taken from the parlor of the manor to the midst of the battle without their knowledge? No, Sam hadn't been at the battle. Her frown deepened. But she and Jamie had. How could that have been managed? Had they been drugged? Startled at the thought, she glanced up at Jamie's tense face and leaned her head against his chest, feeling safer than she'd felt in a long time. Jamie wouldn't let anything bad happen to her, or be a part of such a plot. For some reason there was no doubt of that in her mind. Besides, he seemed just as befuddled as she felt.

The man on the throne glared at the two of them, his eyes so dark they looked black in the dim light of the hall. She realized it must be night now; the only light inside came from the huge fireplace and from torches hanging from sconces on the wall. Golden shadows leapt across the stone floor and across the man's furious face as Jamie backed away from his scrutiny.

"What are you doing?" she asked, twisting around to see where they were going.

Jamie didn't answer but moved to where a rough-hewn bench sat against the wall. He set her down on it and turned back to face the redheaded man. Jix started to protest but decided she was too exhausted to take part in the farce. She lay down on the bench, propping herself up on one elbow, trying to get comfortable enough to watch the rest of the show.

"As I told yer man, Fergus, I am James MacGregor," Jamie said, taking a step forward. The two Highlanders who had led them downstairs took a step forward, too, and Jamie stopped, spreading his arms apart. "I am unarmed. Fergus has my sword. I come in peace."

"Aye, so ye say," the man on the throne rumbled. He glared at Jamie for a full minute, his hands clenched over the ends of the horned chair arms. "Ye have a raw bit of gall, speaking that name. I am Red Hugh Campbell. Are ye ready to put an end to the dispute between us and form an alliance?"

Jamie's broad shoulders stiffened. *Well, if this is a play,* Jix thought as she watched from her perch, *then Jamie is certainly good at his part.* A surge of admiration coursed through her as she studied him—tall, solid, handsome, his strong jaw locked fiercely. Clad in his Highland kilt and plaid, acting the part of a Scottish warrior, how could she not be attracted to the man?

A picture of Sam clad in a wedding gown, gazing up

71

into Jamie's deliriously happy face danced suddenly into Jix's weary thoughts and she shook herself. Jamie belonged to Samantha. It was Fate, Kismet, Providence. Why else would they have been led to the very man of her dreams? Her head ached more. Jamie's voice pulled her back to the performance in front of her.

"Aye," Jamie was saying, "I am here to forge the alliance in whatever way I can."

Red Hugh apparently didn't like Jamie's statement. He stood and took a menacing step forward, his fists clenched. "Whatever way ye can? And what does that mean, ye spalpeen?"

Jamie seemed taken aback and he hesitated, then cleared his throat and spoke again. "Why, whatever way ye deem expedient, of course. I wasna exactly informed about just how I should go about these deliberations."

Now Red Hugh seemed uncertain. "Ye weren't? Ye mean yer uncle dinna tell ye the agreement between us?"

Jamie shook his head.

"Weel, then, that makes this a wee bit more difficult." For the first time he looked directly at Jix, and she managed a small smile in spite of the demon still pounding on her head. She lifted her fingers and waggled them at the man, but his fierce expression didn't alter. This was getting a little creepy.

"I'm ready to go home, Jamie," she called to his back. "My head is killing me and this isn't fun anymore."

He shot her a look over his shoulder. "Whist, lass, keep still."

"Go home, is it?" Red Hugh took a thundering step down the steps toward her, and she shrank back against the wall. In a heartbeat Jamie moved to her side, his arms slipping around her as he gathered her against him. Jix could feel his heart pounding beneath her head as he cradled her to his chest. Never had she felt so protected. So safe. Well, fairly safe, she amended, as the redheaded man crossed the stone floor to them.

He thrust his face scant inches away from hers. From a distance the man had looked ruddy and blustery. Up close he had a nose the size of a pear, the same color as the bloodshot veins in his bleary black eyes. His red hair was liberally peppered with gray. Pockmarks slightly smaller than Fergus's olive-sized ones dotted Red Hugh's rough, grainy skin. She swallowed hard, for the first time in her life, utterly speechless.

"Ye'll no' be goin' home, lassie," Red Hugh said with a scowl. He glared at them both for a long moment. "Ye'll neither see home again."

Chapter Five

"What do ye mean?" Jamie demanded.

All at once the wild Scotsman's florid face broke into a wide grin. "Why, I mean that yer uncle has sent ye here with yer sister to forge an alliance of marriage." He reached out and took Jix's limp hand, lifting it to his lips. "Weelcome ta Meadbrooke, Maigrey. Yer new home. The marriage will take place in a fortnight. The alliance will be sealed."

Jix smiled back at him, relieved at his friendlier tone. She blinked as his words permeated the pounding in her head and reached her brain.

Jamie's sister?

New home?

Marriage?

"Jamie," she whispered, her fingers clutching the front of his shirt as she pressed herself against him, wishing she could crawl inside his warm, tough skin and hide herself. Her heart thudded inside her ears as she looked up into his face. "Jamie MacGregor, what the *hell* is going on?" As Red Hugh continued to beam at her, she frowned. "And what are *you* looking at?"

"She's feisty," Red Hugh said. "I like that in a woman, though too much is no'a good thing either."

"You don't know the half of it," Jamie said under his breath. Jix frowned at him. "Forgive my sister," he went on, "she's no' in her right mind, ye ken? She struck her head upon a rock today and has been speakin' nonsense ever since."

Too tired to fight anymore, Jix gave up. Let the men have their little game of let's pretend.

I hope Samantha isn't going through something like this! She'll never forgive me! Again.

"Verra weel," Red Hugh said. "I'll send my healer to have a look at her. I'll have food brought up to ye both and tomorrow a formal agreement shall be drawn up between us."

"Food? Did someone say food?" Jix asked. Her stomach rumbled, and she suddenly realized she couldn't remember the last time she'd eaten. "Food would be great. Oh, and could you send up some chips and dip? I feel a real attack of the munchies coming on."

Red Hugh frowned, but she didn't care. She was tired of being nice about this whole stupid festival thing. Her head ached and she still didn't know where Sam could be. She cocked one brow at Red Hugh. "Don't tell me you aren't getting tired of this whole charade? That outfit must weigh a ton."

"Charade?" Red Hugh had crossed back toward his throne and he turned, fury written on his features.

"No, no," Jamie said hastily. "She's talkin' nonsense again. Please, just ignore her. She needs to sleep. She'll be her auld self in the mornin', and I'll wager she willna remember any of this."

Red Hugh fixed a glare first at Jamie, then at Jix. She stared at him for a moment before remembering the first cardinal rule of defeating a bully—never let him know he's intimidating you. Lifting her chin slightly, Jix smiled at the man in the mangy fur, and to her astonishment, his bushy face broke into an answering smile. Jix laughed, though it cost her as the thudding in her head increased.

"I knew you were a sweetie," she said, giving him a wink. "We're going to get along famously, aren't we, Red Hugh?"

He nodded, one hand lifted thoughtfully to his lips. "Aye, lassie, I'll wager we will. Still, ye sound strangely, verra like an Englishwoman and that's nae good."

"Och, would ye rather I talked like this?" She deepened her voice, making it rich with a thick Scottish brogue. "Do ye no ken that I can sound like whomever I want, whenever I will? 'Tis a gift I have."

Jamie cleared his throat. "Please, Red Hugh, she really needs to sleep—" he stopped as the man began to chuckle.

"Aye, 'tis a gift ye have," he agreed, ignoring Jamie's words, his gaze raking over Jix, making her shiver a bit with the intimacy of the gesture. "But no' just fer soundin' like a Sassenach. I daresay ye've other gifts as well that should be explored. To bed with ye and to sleep. Tomorrow," he lifted his eyes to Jamie and his gaze hardened, "we'll talk again."

Red Hugh spun on his heel and stalked out of the room, his fur cloak flapping behind him.

The two men who had escorted them to the hall now appeared at their side again and marched them back to the chamber. Once there, Jamie laid Jix gently on the huge bed and she leaned back against the pillow with a sigh. A few more minutes of Red Hugh's scrutiny and she feared she might have disgraced herself and Jamie by passing out on the floor.

"Ye'll be comin' with us," one of the men said to Jamie.

A thin, lethal smile slid over Jamie's lips. "I dinna think so. I'll no' be leaving my sister to the mercies of this place. Tell Red Hugh that until the marriage takes place I'll sleep on the floor of the chamber, protectin' her maidenhood."

Jix snuggled down into the bed, once again feeling safe under Jamie's protection. Not that she had a maidenhead to protect, but they didn't need to know that. The two men shrugged and left the room. As soon as the door shut behind them, Jix turned to Jamie for an explanation. He was staring at her, hands on his hips, his dark blue eyes furious.

"Are you out of your mind?" he shouted.

Jix blinked. What was his problem? "You don't have to yell at me."

He shook his head. "Why would ye no' be silent when I asked ye to?"

She folded her arms across her chest, feeling suddenly stubborn. "Maybe because I don't take orders from men I hardly know?"

"From now on ye must do as I say."

"Look, I'm in no mood to get into a women's rights discussion with you, laddie," she said, leaning back against a hard pillow, "so let me just answer that by saying, 'forget it.' "

Jamie paced across the room and back, his hands clenched into fists at his side. He didn't say anything else and seemed to be lost in thought. Jix squirmed as she watched him, then glanced around the room.

"Hey, MacGregor . . ." she began, wishing she didn't have to ask him but knowing she had to or experience the consequences.

"What?" he snapped, coming to a halt.

"How authentic are your great-uncle's festivals?"

Jamie ran one hand across the top of his hair. His hair! Jix stared. When had Jamie put on that long wig? It looked great on him. Really sexy. She lifted a hand to her own hair. Long tresses had replaced her short curls. Was she, too, wearing a wig? Maybe that was why her head ached so badly. It had all this heavy hair on it now. But she had more pressing concerns than her latest hairstyle.

"His festivals are fairly authentic," he said, sounding weary.

"I hope not too authentic."

He shifted his gaze to hers and frowned. "What do ye mean?"

She squirmed slightly. "Is this a remodeled castle?" she asked, putting off his question. "It doesn't look remodeled."

"I dinna know anything about this castle, lass," he said, exasperation in his voice. "Why?"

"I just wondered, that is, I thought you might know—"

"What?" he demanded.

Injured, Jix lifted her chin. "I need to pee."

Jamie lay on the hard stone floor, hands laced behind his head as he stared up at the high ceiling. Even the two thick wolfskins he'd been given as a pallet didn't keep his back from aching, but he'd slept on worse. In the course of his police work he'd probably slept in the worst dives in London and on the most uncomfortable beds on the planet. His back was the least of his problems.

Red Hugh had agreed it was only right and proper that "Maigrey's" brother sleep on the floor of her room to guard her virginity until the wedding night. Jamie smiled grimly. He didn't know Jix Ferguson very well, but she'd mentioned being divorced, and besides that, she didn't seem like the kind of girl who would have guarded her virginity until she reached her mid-twenties. Not that she struck him as promiscuous, not at all. She just seemed like a girl with a zest for life that would naturally include love. If this marriage actually took place, he had a feeling Red Hugh would be very disappointed in his virgin bride.

Jamie frowned. *What am I thinking? This isn't going to happen. Jix is not going to marry this barbarian. It's ridiculous. No, we're going to escape from this moldering castle and somehow find our way back home.*

After finding a connecting door to the garderobe—what passed for a bathroom in the seventeenth century—and after eating the meager meal provided by Red Hugh, the two had settled down for the night. From the glazed look in Jix's eyes he doubted her coherency and prayed a little sleep would help her become more focused—and more cooperative—when she awoke. Red Hugh had sent word that the healer was busy delivering a baby but would be sent as soon as possible.

Jamie turned on his side and propped on one elbow, staring into the fireplace. He'd thrown his pallet as close to it as possible. The stone floor was damned cold, though it was only September. He stared at the red embers, musing. Maybe he shouldn't let Jix sleep too long without waking her. If she had a concussion it could be dangerous. She'd certainly been a ball of energy in the great hall, but he figured it would take more than a concussion to slow Jix Ferguson down.

Jamie sighed and tried to get his thoughts in order. He couldn't truly accept the bizarre events surrounding them, but as a practical man and a detective used to gathering evidence, weighing it, and drawing logical conclusions, he faced certain unalterable facts. His deductions so far pointed at one of three possibilities: a sensational, slick, expensive practical joke had been played on him; he had lost his mind and become completely delusional; or . . .

The thought of the last possible scenario made him sit up restlessly. Or somehow he and Jix, and perhaps her friend Sam, had been thrust backward in time. How, he didn't know. All he knew was that twenty-first century men didn't battle each other with swords and spears, or live in crumbling castles, or demand marriages to ally with another clan. So unless a terrible hoax had been perpetrated upon them, or unless he had gone nuts—both which he doubted—there was one answer: They had traveled through time to Scotland of the past.

He glanced over at Jix. She slept peacefully, the thick green coverlet pulled up to her chin. He had no sword, but was prepared to use every martial arts trick he knew to protect her. He stood, noiselessly, and walked the two feet to Jix's bed, gazing down at her motionless figure. She slept on her right side, curled up like a child, both hands under her cheek, her knees drawn halfway to her chest. The huge bed made her look even smaller than usual.

Jamie sat down on the edge of the bed. She was such a sweet woman, but so unpredictable. He couldn't imagine what it would be like to be in a relationship with such a woman. A man would never know what to expect from her. The thought was tantalizing. He reached out to smooth one long lock of red hair back from her face and she shifted beneath his touch, exposing the bruise where she'd hit her head. The blue-black color marred the otherwise creamy skin on her forehead. Jamie froze as she rolled to her back and stretched. The thick green coverlet fell away, the thin nightgown she'd been given to wear pulling tightly over her breasts. Jamie's heart beat quickened. She opened her mouth slightly and a small, pink tongue darted out to wet her full lower lip. He felt himself harden with sudden, hot desire and he turned away, stifling a groan as he rose from the bed and began to pace.

What kind of man was he, lusting after a sleeping woman, a woman who was hurt and confused? A woman who was so childlike, yet so incredibly sexy. And yet it wasn't just lust. He liked Jix, genuinely liked her. Clearly she was a person who felt passionately about things—friendship, loyalty—would she feel the same about love? A picture of Jix lying beneath him, naked, sated with the pleasure he had brought to her, flashed through his mind. She seemed the type of woman who would give herself wholeheartedly to the man she loved.

Unlike some women, he thought. His ex-fiancée Cathy had never truly given herself to him. She could never be spontaneous or free. He couldn't count the number of times he'd tried to kiss her only to be rebuffed because he would "spoil her makeup" or "destroy her hairstyle." She was so concerned with what other people thought that it had driven him crazy sometimes. He stopped pacing and glanced at Jix again.

Jix wouldn't be like that. Not Jix with her fresh face, scarcely touched by makeup except for a little mascara on her long lashes, and her natural, free-flowing auburn hair. He couldn't imagine her caring what anyone else thought about how she looked or acted. Was that good or bad? He hadn't quite decided yet. His eyes studied Jix's face closely, as though it would reveal an answer to his question. She no longer had her short pixie cut—she had long hair now, just as he did. How had that happened? Jamie ran one hand through his tangled dark brown waves. The same way it had happened to him, he supposed—whatever way that was. His head ached with trying to figure it out. Maybe his confusion and fatigue explained the reason his thoughts had strayed to his miserable experience with Cathy and why he stood practically panting over Jix.

Jamie turned away from temptation and crossed to the huge stone fireplace. A fire had been banked there, lending some warmth to the cold, cavernous quarters, the faint light from the glowing embers the room's only illumination. He moved toward the heat, trying to quiet his thoughts as flickering shadows touched the stillness of the chamber. He leaned one arm against the harsh stone and closed his eyes.

Crazy. I am crazy. I've been thrust into the past, for crying out loud, and shouldn't be worrying whether or not Jix Ferguson is my type. Besides which, I am not ready to get involved in a real relationship, and certainly not under these circumstances.

And Jix Ferguson had "real relationship" written all over her lovable face.

Never again. Or at least not for a long, long time. A sarcastic voice in his head reminded him that it had already been a pretty damn long time—five years to be exact. Oh, there had been other women, casual dating, but nothing long-term. No matter. He wasn't willing to risk himself again, and he sure wasn't willing to take that risk in the middle of a nutty drama like this. He knew from his studies in human psychology that people thrown together in crisis felt naturally drawn to one another. It would be easy to think you had serious feelings about someone when in reality you clung to one another for survival. It happened all the time in hostage situations.

Jamie opened his eyes and picked up a piece of wood stacked beside the fireplace, using it to poke the embers. Getting all his feelings straight in his mind made him feel better, more in control of himself. He would be polite, kind, and treat Jix Ferguson like a little sister. He frowned. Okay, like a younger friend—young being the definitive word here. She was probably about twenty-four, give or take a year, though she looked about nineteen at times. At his advanced age of thirty-five, that seemed pretty damned young.

Jamie heard her sigh and forced himself not to look over his shoulder. He drew in a ragged breath. Aye, too damn young. A mental image of Jix curled up on the bed danced in front of his eyes. He shook his head, trying to push the picture away as he turned to warm his back at the fireplace.

Jix sat in the middle of the bed staring at him, her green eyes luminous in the dimly lit room.

"Jamie?" she said, reaching one hand toward him. The sheer material of the gown dripped down from her arm, giving her the look of some celestial being. He moved quickly to her side. She touched his face, her eyes filled with confusion. "I thought I had dreamed it all. The battle, the castle, the man with the red hair."

"Shhh," Jamie said, trying to think of some way to comfort her. "It's all right. I'm here. I won't let anyone hurt ye."

Her eyes widened and she reached out with both hands, her fingers biting into his upper arms. "But is it true? Is it real, or have I lost my mind?"

"No, lass, it's real. Ye've no lost your mind."

"Then where are we?"

He shook his head, wondering how much he should tell her. Deciding the truth was best, he took a deep breath. "What I'm going to tell ye is going to sound crazy. I know I've tried to figure out any other scenario than the one that keeps staring me square in the face."

She frowned and dropped her hands from his arms. "What do you mean?"

Jamie took another deep breath. "How's yer head?"

"Better, I think. I have a headache but the pounding has stopped somewhat. Don't try to change the subject. Where are we?"

He took a deep breath. "Did ye ever hear of a story of H. G. Wells called *The Time Machine*?"

She tilted her head, frowning slightly. "Sure. Morlocks. The mannequin that kept changing clothes. Those white-haired people who lived on the surface—what were they called?" Her frown deepened, then she snapped her fingers.

"Kim Novak! She starred in the movie with—or was it Yvette Mimieux?"

"Aye, aye," Jamie said, shaking his head, "the point is, ye've heard of time travel?"

Jix raised both brows and gave him a tentative smile. "Okay, MacGregor, which one of us hit their head? Of course I've heard of time travel. I love Michael J. Fox."

He blinked. "Ye love who?"

"Michael J. Fox. You know, he was in *Back to the Future* and *Back to the Future, Part II*, and *Back*—"

"Aye." This time he let his frustration show. "Would ye just hit the pause button for a minute, lass?"

Jix stopped talking in mid-word and snapped her mouth shut. She folded her arms over her chest and looked at him patiently.

Jamie ran one hand through his long hair. How could he explain this without sounding crazy? Probably couldn't.

"All right, here goes." He took a deep breath and blurted it out in one breath. "I think somehow we've traveled back in time."

Jix nodded, her green eyes complacent.

He frowned. He'd expected a slightly larger reaction. "Did ye hear me, lass? I said that somehow we have traveled back to the past—to Scotland's past."

She nodded again.

He got it. "Ye can talk now," he said with a sigh.

"Thanks." She leaned toward him, her face animated. "Time travel! Do you really think so? I mean, I've always thought it would be so cool if—" she broke off, her eyes narrowing suspiciously. "Wait a minute. Is this some kind of joke? Did Samantha put you up to this to get back at me?"

"Of course not."

"Of course not. Sure." Her mouth turned up at the corners and Jamie had to steel himself not to kiss that infuriating smirk off her face. "We've traveled back in time. Of course, what could make more sense?" She touched the bruise on her head gingerly and winced. "Did you have to slug me to get me through the time vortex?"

83

Exasperated, Jamie slid off the bed and crossed the room to stand in front of the fire again, hands clasped behind his back.

"I'd like to think of something that did make more sense, believe me," he said, his voice harsh. He didn't blame Jix for not believing him. He turned back to her and caught the heated look in her eyes as her gaze darted guiltily up from his bare thighs. With a rush, Jamie realized he was half-naked. He'd removed his boots and kilt in order to be more comfortable while he slept, leaving on only the long saffron-colored shirt that reached to his upper thigh. Since he'd worn his kilt in the true regimental tradition, he had on no underwear. He felt his face growing warm.

"You're serious," she said, her voice husky, her eyes still hooded. Now concern lit her face and she held out her arms to him. "Come here, MacGregor."

Reluctantly he crossed back to her and sat down on the bed when she patted the spot next to her. He reluctantly perched on the edge, ready for flight.

Jix smiled at him and took one of his hands between hers. "Look, I love fantasy-land. It's one of my favorite places to live, but this is ridiculous. Although I still don't know how we got to that field, it's—" She paused, her glance flickering over his hair. "And when did you put on the wig?" Her smile broadened. "Come on, MacGregor, 'fess up." She raised her voice. "Okay, Sam, you can come out now. Joke's over!"

Jamie shook his head, relishing the feel of her hand still in his. "So ye still think this is all some trick, some elaborate hoax on the part of my uncle or your friend?"

Jix shrugged. "Sam was pretty mad at me. No telling what she might do."

He tightened his hold on her fingers. She tightened back. Jamie felt a rush at the touch of her skin against his and snatched his hand away, letting the minor irritation he felt surface. *Ye're protecting yerself, laddie,* a part of his mind told him. Another part answered vehemently—*Damn straight!*

"So you think that Lord Campbell would risk your life

and mine in a staged battle," Jamie demanded, "complete with real swords—a battle where men got their arms *actually chopped off*"—his voice kept rising and he tried to bring himself under control—"a battle where we could have both been killed. You actually think either my uncle or your best friend would have subjected us to such danger?"

Jix bit her lower lip and shrugged. "Well, maybe."

He shook his head with a sigh. "No, lass, they wouldn't have done that."

"I don't remember much about the battle. Or anything else. Was I downstairs in some kind of hall?"

Jamie opened his mouth and closed it. "Ye dinna remember? We went below and spoke to the laird of the castle, Red Hugh Campbell."

She shook her head. "No, I don't remember. Did I miss anything important?"

"Important?" Jamie looked away. Should he tell her that the laird of the castle expected to marry her in a fortnight and solidify the alliance between their clans? She'd had enough of a shock, he decided, without adding that to it. All in good time. He shook his head. "Nay, nothing important. He said we'd talk more in the morning."

Jix tilted her head in an endearing way. Did she know, he wondered, how absolutely cute she was?

"You know," she said, "maybe you just thought people were getting their arms cut off. You know there are tricks for that kind of thing. How do you think they do it in the movies?"

Jamie shook his head. "The movies. Do ye have any idea how much something like that costs? My uncle can't even hire a gardener! Why do ye think he opens his home to tourists twice a year? Because he needs the money."

"And just how are we supposed to have made this trip through time?" she demanded, a hint of sarcasm creeping into her voice. "Last time I checked, Scotty wasn't waiting to beam us up."

"I don't know," he admitted, wishing he had some answers to give her. "But if ye don't believe me, how do ye explain yer hair—and mine? I can only assume that the growth is some sort of affect of traveling through time."

Jix reached up and touched the long strands cascading over her shoulder. "Easy—it's a wig your uncle—" her eyes widened and her voice trailed off as she tugged on her hair. "Ow! Well, maybe not. Her brows scrunched together again, then she smiled. "Okay—hair extensions." She felt around her scalp, then dropped her hands back to her lap. "Not hair extensions."

"Do ye remember anything before the battle?" he asked. "The last thing I remember is being at my uncle's house. The next thing I know, we're here."

Jix frowned in concentration, closing her eyes and lifting one hand to her brow. "Oh, man, I hope whoever hit me is suffering as much as I am. Wait—" her eyes flew open and she turned to him, laying one hand against his chest in her excitement. And speaking of excitement . . . why was it that just the touch of this woman's hand made him want to throw her down on the bed and kiss her into oblivion?

"I do remember," she said. "We were standing in the parlor at Meadbrooke, looking at your sword. Sam and I were admiring it and then all at once it was like the whole world slammed together, like we were flattened out into pancakes, and then there was a black hole sucking us down." She grabbed him by the arm. "You were holding me, but you weren't holding Samantha and she—she—fell."

Jix's face turned ashen. Jamie put his arm around her and pulled her close. Together they leaned against the huge carved headboard behind them.

"Take a breath, lass," he ordered. "I remember a little of that, now. I couldn't let go of the sword. It was like my hand had been glued to the thing."

"So where is she?" Jix's voice dropped to a whisper as she looked up at him, her green eyes shining in the firelight. "If you're telling me the truth and we're lost in the past somewhere, where is Sam?"

He saw terror for her friend reflected in her eyes and

Jamie lifted one hand to her face, smoothing away a tear from her soft, soft cheek. The thought that Jix might be hurting made him hurt too.

"Och, lass, don't cry. I don't know where she is, but I promise I'll try to find her. Surely, she's here too, somewhere."

Jix's shoulders straightened. "I'm not crying," she said, though her voice quavered. "I never cry."

"Come here, lass." Jamie pulled her more tightly against him and to his surprise she relaxed and put her head on his shoulder. He wasn't sure at all that Sam had made the trip back with them. It had crossed his mind that when she'd slipped away during their trip through the blackness, perhaps she'd been killed, or lost in some other, more ancient time. But he couldn't tell Jix that. A sudden thought cheered him. "Perhaps she slipped back to our own time and is perfectly safe at home."

"Do you really think so?"

Jamie cupped her face with one hand and turned her toward him. He wanted to kiss her, to take away her fear. "Aye, I do. It's quite possible. But I'll still look for her, I promise."

"We'll both look for her," Jix said, moving firmly out of his embrace, her lower lip still trembling.

Puzzled, Jamie watched Jix bring her emotions back under control. She took a deep breath and lifted her gaze back to his, her mouth quirking up at the corners. "But if I do find out this is a trick—a payback for what I did to her—well, let's just say you'd better cover your nether regions and start running, Mr. MacGregor."

"I like it when ye call me Jamie," he said, fascinated by how smoothly she had shifted back into that teasing attitude of hers. A defense mechanism?

"I think I'll stick with MacGregor. You know," she went on, smoothing one hand down the long sleeve of her nightgown, her eyes locked with his, "I think you have the wrong idea about me. Just because I'm a little shaken up, don't think I'm some helpless damsel in distress."

"Did I say ye were?"

"No, but that's how you're treating me."

Jamie sighed. "Maybe that's how ye're acting. And maybe that's just fine with me, all right? This is a frightening situation and—"

"I'm not afraid," she announced, sliding even further away from him. She maneuvered onto her knees and grabbed a pillow, wrapping her arms around it and holding it in her lap like a shield. "Except for worrying about Samantha," she amended.

"You aren't?" Jamie frowned. Actually, she didn't look all that frightened. Most women he knew would have been in hysterics by now. Jix seemed to take the whole thing in stride.

She shook her head. "No, I'm not. Hey, I grew up with four brothers. Believe me, I've been through a lot worse than sleeping in some moldering old castle in the Highlands."

"Have ye now?" Jamie moved a little closer. "So time travel doesn't concern ye? And it doesn't bother ye that I have no idea how we got here? And of course ye don't care that we may be stuck here, forever."

She squeezed the pillow a little tighter, and her gaze slid away from his. "Something brought us here, so logically something has to take us home again."

"Logically?" He laughed, unable to contain his astonishment. "Excuse me, I didn't realize ye had traveled in time before so that ye ken the logic of such a situation. I'm so dumb, ye see, I thought there might be none at all."

"Now you're just being sarcastic and trying to scare me. Samantha! Ollie Ollie out's in free!"

"What are ye doing?"

Jix tossed the pillow aside and glared at him, hands on her hips. Jamie really wished she wouldn't do that. It made the gown pull so tightly in places he was trying like hell not to look.

She gestured around the room with one hand. "I'm calling Sam to come out of hiding. Really, this has gone far enough, don't you think?"

Obviously she wasn't afraid because she still thought it

was all a big joke. He linked his hands behind his head. Maybe keeping them pinned behind him would keep him from touching her.

"So tell me about these terrible things a lass like ye has lived through," he said, crossing his legs at the ankle atop the dark green cover on the bed. He wasn't sure but he thought it was an old-fashioned feather bed—a quilt-like comforter stuffed with down. He hadn't seen one in years. If it was, then their value to Red Hugh must be great if they rated such fine bedding. "Maybe it will encourage me that somehow ye'll get us out of this fine mess as well."

Her eyes widened. "I didn't get us into this mess," she retorted.

Jamie liked the spark of anger making her eyes suddenly blue-green instead of green. "Still, I'm sure ye've had plenty of practice." He saw her almost physically bristle. A crease darted down the middle of her smooth forehead.

"Practice at what?" she demanded.

Jamie sighed. "At getting out of messes. Really, lass, aren't ye listening to anything I say?"

She opened her mouth twice and closed it both times, as if unable to speak. "It's like listening to a baritone imitation of myself," she finally said. "Stop it. And what makes you think I've ever been in any messes?"

He laughed out loud. Jix bit her lower lip. As she sat there pouting, she looked about twelve years old. *Good!* If he could keep thinking of her as a kid, he could control these crazy feelings he had when he looked at her. No, he couldn't. As if to reinforce his decision Jix stuck her tongue out at him. It should have added to her childishness, but instead the sight of her pink tongue made him want to kiss her senseless.

"I don't know what you're talking about," she said. "But all right—if this isn't a joke, if this is really happening, then this is an adventure." Her face lit up and she grabbed the pillow again, clasping it tightly. "In fact, it's the chance of a lifetime! I'm a writer, you know and—"

"A writer? Ye're a writer?" Jamie saw the hurt spring

into her eyes and wished he could have hidden his surprise a little better.

"Well, I'm going to be," she said, lifting her chin. "And you don't have to sound so amazed. I'm not as stupid as you think."

"No, lass, I didn't mean it that way." He gave her what he hoped was an encouraging smile. "It's just that ye're so—so—"

"Ditsy?"

"I was going to say young," he finished.

"Oh." She paused, then shrugged. "I'm twenty-five."

Well, that's a little closer to my age, he thought. "What kind of books do ye plan to write?"

"Romances."

He raised his eyebrows. "Really?"

"Yes, really." She frowned at him. "Why does that surprise you?"

"Funny, I wouldn't peg ye for a girl who would write romance."

She bristled again. "And why not?"

Jamie folded his arms over his chest. He just couldn't help teasing her a little. She was so teasable. He pushed his eyebrows together as if in fervent concentration. "I picture ye more as an author of books based on catastrophe—ye know, twisters, earthquakes, Hurricane Jix—"

"Very funny," she interrupted. "For your information I'm a very good writer."

Jamie laughed. "I'm sure ye are, lass. So tell me about it. Is it going to be about a knight in shining armor who saves the damsel in distress from the evil villain?"

"Ha!" She tossed her hair back from her shoulder, her green eyes glowing with triumph. "I would never write such tripe," she told him. "My romances are going to be about brave, independent, courageous women who more often than not, save themselves and the hero!"

Sweet, sweet, sweet. Jamie smiled at her enthusiasm. "And what is the hero going to do? Twiddle his thumbs while she slays the dragon?"

Jix faltered and stared down at her hands, biting her

lower lip in thought. "Well," she amended, "I mean, he'll help too. But mostly he'll be there for the romantic part of the story."

"Ye mean the sex?" Jamie asked, feeling extremely hot for some reason.

Suddenly the air between them seemed very thick. Jix lifted her eyes to his. "Yes," she said softly, "the sex."

Chapter Six

Jix blinked. "Uh, I mean, no—it won't just be sex, MacGregor." She punched the pillow lightly, averting her eyes again. "It will be *love*."

"So ye believe in such things, eh?"

She raked her fingers through her tangled hair and winced. She stretched and yawned and shifted until Jamie almost groaned aloud.

"Um hmm, of course I do," she finally said, then yawned again. "Don't you?"

"I'm not sure," he said, fascinated as he watched her lick the end of her finger and rub it across her lips. Did she know what she was doing to him? He pulled his thoughts back to her question. "I used to. I think life has sort of knocked the romanticism out of me."

Jix dropped her hands back to her lap and leaned toward him. The soft white gown dipped lower and Jamie kept his gaze carefully averted. The room seemed very, very hot. He wished he could take off his shirt. He wished he could take off her shirt. He wished he could lick the edge of her finger and the corner of her mouth and the hollow of her throat and—

"What was her name?" she asked, her mouth quirking up in a knowing smile.

"What was who's name?" he asked. What were they talking about again?

"The woman who hurt you so badly."

Jamie sat up a little straighter against the headboard and cleared his throat, bringing his thoughts back under a semblance of control. "We're wasting time, lass. We should decide on what our next move should be."

"What was her name?" she asked again, sliding closer, her hands moving to rest on his knees.

He shifted uncomfortably but there was no where to go unless he jumped up off the bed. Gently he removed her hands and put them back in her lap with a brotherly pat. "Red Hugh is going to want to talk to ye in the morning. Are ye sure ye're all right? I was worried ye might have a concussion."

Jix rose to her knees and put her hands on his shoulders, her breasts almost brushing against his chest. She slowly lowered her mouth to just millimeters away from his ear. "What was her name?" she whispered.

"Cathy!" he shouted, grabbing her by both arms, startling her. "Her name was Cathy—are ye happy now?"

Jix sat back on her heels with a grin. "Yes. So how long were you together?"

Jamie blew a lock of hair back from his forehead in exasperation. "Ye are incorrigible, do ye know that?"

"Yes. Tell me about her."

"No."

"Fine." She stuck out her lower lip. "Then I won't tell you about my tainted love affairs."

"Suits me." Jamie crossed his arms over his chest.

"Me too," she said, imitating him, frowning sternly.

After a moment of watching her glower Jamie had to laugh. He held up both hands in surrender. "All right, lass. It seems I canna deny ye anything. Cathy was my fiancée. I found her in bed with my best friend. End of story."

Jix's smile faded. "Oh. I'm sorry, MacGregor. That must have hurt like hell."

He shrugged, absently picking up the edge of her gown and tugging it between his fingers. "Aye, it did at the time." He looked up at her. "Now it's yer turn."

Jix bit her lower lip and looked away, shivering slightly. "Is it me or is it getting colder in here?"

"Is it me or are ye the one trying to change the subject now?"

She grimaced. "All right, all right, you win. But let's at least get under the covers to talk. I'm freezing! Haven't they ever heard of central heat?"

"In a castle in Scotland? Not even in our own time."

"Well, I'm getting in bed." Jix pulled the covers back, wiggling under them in a way that made his heart race. She patted the space beside her. "Here, you're going to catch your death of cold in that shirt."

Jamie hesitated before slipping under the warm cover, stretching his long legs in front of him, leaning back against one of the large pillows. He closed his eyes and sighed as the tension in his back eased.

"So how's about them Spurs?" she asked, stretching her legs out so close to his that he could feel the heat.

He opened his right eye and squinted at her, resolving to meet tease for tease. "Och, no ye don't. Tell yer tale."

Immediately Jix turned toward him, one hand snaking up to clutch at the front of his shirt, her calf curling over his.

"I'm really cold, MacGregor," she said, snuggling her head against his shoulder, sliding her knee up his thigh.

Jamie sat frozen, afraid to move as her nightgown slipped up toward her waist, exposing her bare skin, bringing it against his own. His own response was immediate and strong, and as she slid her leg higher up his thigh, he knew exactly when she became aware of his situation.

"Oh," she said, her lower body movement stilling with the one breathy word. Jix leaned closer to his ear and whispered, the touch of her breath almost sending him over the edge.

"Is that a sword under your shirt, MacGregor? Or are you just happy to see me?"

He turned toward her, feeling like a man half-starved, then saw the glimmer of humor in her eyes. Disappointment coursed through him as well as a kind of relief. Jamie pretended to glare at her.

"Ye are an evil woman," he said.

Jix straightened, her laughter soft and seductive.

"Didn't you learn that already from what Samantha told you about me?" She asked smugly, rubbing his exposed chest with her fingertips.

Two could play at this game. Jamie turned her face to his and cupped her chin between his fingers. "Ye are evil, but I still want to hear yer story," he looked at her mouth, "eventually. . . ." His thumb moved over her lower lip and her eyes registered surprise, as if she hadn't expected him to turn the tables on her. When her tongue darted out to moisten her lips he lowered his mouth to hers, capturing that wet, pink tongue with his, never closing his eyes.

The kiss was hot, deep, intense, and she gazed right back at him, the heat in her eyes matching the heat building inside of him. Her arms slipped around his neck and his dropped to her waist as he deepened the kiss even more. He caught the soft moan she breathed and even though he knew he was moving way too fast, an urgency inside of him demanded he not stop. Maybe knowing they could be trapped here together forever, drove him. Maybe it was because she was just so damned irresistible.

His left hand moved smoothly from her waist up to her side, covering her breast, caressing her as his mouth moved against the side of her neck, his tongue painting smooth patterns down to the hollow of her throat. Jix melted against him, her body responding to his touch as he lowered his lips to her collarbone. Her hands moved to his hair where she laced her fingers into the long strands, clutching him to her more tightly as he lifted his mouth to take hers once again. Jamie slid one hand over the thin gown, over her soft breasts. She was beautiful. Perfect. Round. Sweet.

He was about to suggest they both lose their clothes, when all at once Jix jerked his head up, her hands flat against his ears. They stared nose to nose at one another, Jamie astonished, Jix's green eyes wide, not with passion, but realization.

"Your sword!" she cried. "Your sword is what brought us to the past! Just get it out and we'll be home again in no time!"

"What?" Jamie groaned as she slid away from him and the warmth of her body went with her. Standing beside the bed, she gestured with both hands, waving them in broad circles.

"Don't you understand—the sword! We were all touching your sword at the same time and then you said—what was it?—you said something in Gaelic."

"My clan's motto."

"Yes! And that's when everything happened!" She hugged herself against the cold and hurried toward the fireplace.

"You shouldn't be up," he cautioned. "Come back to bed."

"What year do you think this is?" she asked, standing on first one foot and then the other in front of the hearth.

Jamie released his breath explosively, irritation settling over him. "I don't know for certain. Castles like this in the Highlands existed anywhere from the 1300s till the present. But I did have one clue." Jix stopped pacing and waited expectantly. He frowned. He didn't want to talk about this. He wanted her back in bed beside him. When it became apparent that she didn't plan to move until he told her, he sighed. "Fergus said I was brave for speaking the name of MacGregor."

"That's a clue? Why?"

"In 1604 the English king declared the MacGregor clan to be nonexistent, and anyone claiming that name would be put to death. They lost their lands, their homes, everything." Jamie heard his own voice turn wistful. Funny, in spite of all the time that had passed since that calamity had befallen his ancestors, the Scots in him still felt the sorrow. *But the time hasn't passed, it's now.* He pushed the thought away, unwilling to examine it more closely.

"They soon came to be known as 'Children of the Mist,' for they were homeless, appearing and disappearing from one place to another like the Highland mist."

"That's terrible!" Jix said, outrage snapping in her green gaze. "Why did the king do that?"

"Political back-stabbing by another clan. Aren't ye getting cold?" He patted the spot beside him. "It's nice and warm over here."

She ignored him. "This is no time for fun and games, MacGregor, we've got to find Samantha and get back home again."

Jamie sighed and leaned his head back against the broad headboard. Apparently the romantic tone of the evening had evaporated, and it was just as well. Getting involved with someone like Jix would turn his world completely upside down. He'd known her one day and look what had already happened! He couldn't imagine what a long-term relationship might entail. Juggling piranhas would be easier.

"Even if the sword is what brought us here, lass, it isn't that easy."

Jix nodded and began to pace across the room and back, the nightgown trailing behind her. "Yes, because we don't know where Sam is. We've got to get out of this place and find her, but as soon as we do, we can use your sword to—"

"Lass," Jamie said, cutting her off. He hated to say it, but she might as well know the truth. "I dinna have my sword. It's gone."

Jix's outpouring of words stopped. She quit pacing, her green eyes looking remarkably anxious for a woman who claimed to be fearless. "What?"

"Fergus took my sword and I'll wager he gave it to Red Hugh."

She crossed to his side, looking so disheveled and beautiful, he almost pulled her down on top of him. But he didn't. He didn't know if their little repartee in the bed had been for real or just a game, and he didn't know if he had the guts to find out. Jix Ferguson wasn't a woman you could take to bed and easily forget. The thought of using her for the physical act of sex without something deeper between them repelled Jamie and suddenly he was the one who was afraid. What was this woman doing to him?

"We've got to get that sword." Jix said, moving to the bed and grabbing him by the front of his shirt. "You're a spy—surely you can do something about this!"

"I'm not a spy," he said, disentangling her rigid fingers. "I'm a detective. There's a difference. And right now we're locked in a room with two armed guards outside. We'll have to wait until Red Hugh starts to trust us."

"Do you think that will happen?" she asked. "Why should he trust us?"

Jamie hesitated. "There's something I haven't told ye."

"Something important?"

"Aye." He sighed. Might as well get it over with and deal with the hysterics now. "Red Hugh was expecting James MacGregor and his sister Maigrey to arrive to form an agreement between their clans—through marriage. He thinks we are those MacGregors. If we can keep him believing that we are who he thinks we are, then maybe we'll have enough freedom to find the sword and find Sam as well."

"Marry Red Hugh?"

Jamie braced himself.

Jix's face lit up. "What a great idea!" She jumped onto the bed like a schoolgirl, grinning at him.

Jamie stared at her. "What? Doesn't the thought of marrying that lout bother ye?"

She raised both hands to lift her long, heavy hair from her neck. He could tell she wasn't purposely trying to make him hot and hard, she was just thinking, but the effect remained the same. "I remember more now about last night. Red Hugh was the big one, older man, with hair about the color of mine?" Jamie nodded. She smiled and let her hair fall back to her shoulders. "Well, at least our kids would all be redheads. I've always enjoyed having red hair."

"Dinna joke about it," Jamie said, angry at the thought of Jix coupling with the likes of Campbell.

She jumped off the bed again and walked to the fireplace, standing with her back to it, her face thoughtful. Jamie's mouth went dry as the thin nightgown turned absolutely transparent against the firelight. He ran his tongue across his lips as she shifted her stance and her ripe silhouette beckoned him. For a moment he couldn't breathe.

"How soon does he want us to marry?" she asked.

"A fortnight."

"A fortwhich?"

"Two weeks time," Jamie translated. "But if we can get my sword back we can avoid the whole thing. Would ye like to tell me why this isn't upsetting ye?"

"Oh, come on, MacGregor," she chided, "this is exciting! How many women get the chance to marry a wild Highlander? Of course, I wouldn't want to actually go through with the wedding night, but the ceremony might be fun!" She lifted the sides of her gown like a dancer and moved from side to side. He could see the curve of her breasts, the faint shadows of her nipples, the darkness between her thighs.

Jamie groaned out loud. "Are ye trying to drive me mad?"

She frowned. "What are you talking about?"

"Get back in the bed," he ordered, scowling. To his surprise, she did, scampering across the floor and crawling in beside him, shoving her ice-cold feet against his.

"Warm me up, MacGregor. All right, so what if the real MacGregors show up?"

"Damn, yer feet are freezing!" She moved them higher, burrowed them under his thighs. Jamie closed his eyes and fought for control. "I guess we'll have to cross that bridge when we get there," he said between clenched teeth. He took a deep breath and let it out in a rush before continuing. "I've had a little practice at pretending to be something I'm not and for some reason, I'd wager ye have too."

"Pretty flimsy plan," she said, pointedly ignoring his

lightly spoken accusation. "What if he wants to marry me tomorrow?"

Jamie pretended to consider and decided to give her back a little of what she'd been serving up. "He said a fortnight. But if he does—" he waggled both eyebrows. "Have ye ever bedded a wild Scottish Highlander?"

To his surprise she didn't have a snappy comeback. Instead a shadow crossed her face. "Well, the American equivalent," she said. "My ex-husband—minus the charming accent."

"Och, from the sound of that I think ye're insulting Highlanders."

"Probably so. He was a real S.O.B."

Jamie leaned forward. "Did he hurt ye? I mean, physically?"

Their gazes locked and for a moment Jamie thought Jix was about to tell him something real, something important. But the moment passed and she smiled again, that damned protective smile he was learning to recognize.

"He was a bully more than anything. But you didn't answer my question. What if Red Hugh craves my bod and wants to marry me tomorrow?"

Jamie let the matter of her ex-husband drop. Time enough to dig deeper later. "He thinks I'm yer brother, that gives me some authority in this matter. I'll simply tell him that ye need more time to get used to the idea."

She nodded, sliding off the bed again and moving back to the fireplace.

"Now what? Can ye no stay put?"

"I get restless. I have a lot of energy and if I don't get it out, I can't go to sleep."

I'll help ye expend some of that energy, he longed to say. "Stay away from that fire," he cautioned instead.

But, Jix twirled right in front of it, sending her gown to billow out around her. She frowned at him. "Lighten up, MacGregor. You're spoiling the whole spirit of things."

"This really isn't good for yer head injury, do ye think? Come back to bed."

"No. I feel fine. Just a slight headache."

"Did anyone ever tell ye that ye're a spoiled brat?"

"Only my brothers."

"How many do ye have?"

"Four."

Four brothers. Another reason to avoid this woman like the plague. He had no desire to run the gauntlet of one brother's approval, let alone four.

Jamie grunted. "With that many of them, why did they no' knock some sense into ye?"

Jix stopped moving in front of the flames and for once, stood still. She bit her lower lip and gazed back at him. "My husband took care of that," she said mildly.

Silence stretched between them as Jamie wished himself into the nearest black hole. "I'm sorry, lass. My words were thoughtless."

She laughed. "No problem. When my brothers found out he was beating me up they made short work of him. Even though they aren't my blood brothers, they are sort of crazy about me."

"I dinna blame them," he said softly. She lifted her eyes to his and the genuine smile she gave him made Jamie feel like warm butter inside. "Ye're adopted?"

She nodded. "The Fergusons were great. It took a while to get used to so many brothers, but gradually I grew to love them." The shadow was still in her eyes. Jamie wondered why but decided to change the subject if talking about her family caused her pain. He never wanted to be the cause of Jix's pain.

"I always thought I must be missing out on a lot, being an only child," he said, steering the conversation in a safer direction.

Jix rolled her eyes and grinned. "Oh, you are. Getting your face rubbed in the mud, getting tickled till you're breathless, having all your boyfriends inspected—" she broke off and shrugged. "They're great. My adopted parents died three years ago and my brothers are all I have left. Well, except for Samantha, and another friend, Chelsea. They're like the sisters I never had." She sighed. "But I guess after this, Sam and I are kaput."

"I'm sorry, lass," he said gently. "My parents are both dead as well. My father when I was a child, my mother a few years ago."

Her eyes reflected the glow of firelight and he saw the glimmer of tears there. "It's hard, isn't it?"

"Aye," he said, wishing he could take her in his arms and comfort her. "Did ye ever know yer real parents?"

"No. Yes." She laughed and began pacing back and forth in front of the fireplace, twisting her hands in front of her. "I never knew my father. I remember my mother. She gave me to her aunt when I was four and disappeared. I always wondered why she didn't want me, but I had no complaints. Aunt Phronsie was great—" Jix stopped pacing and grinned. "She was a psychic at carnivals and I traveled with her."

"A psychic?" Jamie was entranced. No wonder Jix was such a fascinating person—she'd led a fascinating life. "A real one?"

Jix shook her head. "No, but—"

"But what?"

She hesitated then shook her head again. "Nothing. She was a con artist. She taught me the business and I loved her dearly, but she died when I was six years old. I lived in a Catholic orphanage for two more years before the Fergusons adopted me."

Amazing. By the age of six, Jix had been 'taught the business' of conning people. How could that be possible? She was one of the most open, unpretentious women he'd ever met. Jamie leaned back against the pillows on the bed and linked his hands behind his head again, trying to assimilate this new information with everything else he knew about Jix. He didn't miss her quick intake of breath, or the way she suddenly averted her gaze from his chest. So maybe her flirtation hadn't been just a joke, but it didn't matter. She'd had enough pain in her life. He certainly didn't want to add to it. Especially not under these bizarre circumstances. Jamie closed his eyes.

"You must work out."

He opened his eyes and met her cool gaze. "Every day."

"Why? In love with yourself, like every other man on the planet?" Her voice was teasing but her green eyes held a touch of cynicism he hadn't noticed before.

"No, I guess I just like to be in shape. Police work sort of demands it."

"I guess so," she said begrudgingly. She began to twist again in front of the fire. "Scotland Yard, eh? You do that accent well. Is it real or does that go with the job too?"

"Aye, it's real. I was born and raised in Scotland but I've lived and worked with Englishmen for years, attended English schools. I decided that in front of those wild Scots downstairs I should sound as Scottish as possible. I'd advise that ye do the same any time ye speak with them. Since ye can do a passable accent—"

"Passable!"

"—I'd say use it. Where did ye learn how to do that?"

She held her arms out gracefully from her sides. "I'm an actress."

"I thought ye were a writer," he said, feeling slightly befuddled. Trying to follow Jix's conversation was rather like trying to keep up with corn popping.

"I *am* a writer." She did a dancer's plié and lifted both arms over her head. "But I've been an actress for the last five years. It's part of my game plan."

"Game plan?"

"Sure." She lowered her arms, her brow puckered thoughtfully. "It's like this—I want to do a lot of different things in my life, so I decided when I turned fifteen that I would give each of my interests a try for five years. The first five years after that I was a dancer. Then I was an actress until I turned twenty-five—which was last month—and now I'm a writer. Next I'll be a sculptress." She gave him an appraising look. "I'd love to sculpt you sometime." Her gaze lingered on his arms; then she turned away abruptly toward the fire, holding her hands out to the slight warmth.

"An interesting way to live yer life," he said.

She whirled around back around and for a moment he saw anxiety on her face. "Doesn't it make more sense than

103

doing the same thing for twenty years and ending up hating it?"

"I didn't mean it as a criticism," he said. "You must be very talented." So maybe Jix Ferguson did care a little what other people thought. "Doesn't yer head hurt, lass?"

"Actually, I feel fine now. Maybe our 'trip through time' "—she grinned—"was the cause of my disorientation, not the bruise on my noggin."

"So ye still don't believe me."

"Oh, I don't know. Maybe." The next moment she had twirled like a ballerina in front of the fire, then danced over to the bed. She did another plié, this one deep, giving him a lovely view of the top of her breasts. "You have to admit it's pretty hard to—"

"Do you smell something?" Jamie said, suddenly alert. He wrenched his gaze from Jix's breasts and sat up, sniffing the air. It smelled like singed hair, or burnt material or—he looked back at her and with horror saw smoke curling up from the back of Jix's gown!

Jamie jumped up and grabbed Jix by both arms. She cried out, startled, as he picked her up and slammed her onto the bed.

"What the hell do you—"

A heavy woolen blanket lay on top of the more elaborate coverlet beneath and Jamie flipped it over her, cutting off her protests. He rolled her up in three neat, easy movements, quickly slid the roll off the bed onto the stone floor, and began pounding the base of the roll with both hands to put out any lingering fire as Jix's muffled cries for help faded and finally stopped.

"Damnation!" he cried, sitting down on the floor beside the rolled-up blanket, his breath coming hard as he realized how close Jix had come to real disaster. They were in the past. There were no burn centers to rush to, no friendly firemen, no 911, no paramedics. He gazed down at the motionless roll of wool. Why wasn't she struggling? Why wasn't she—?

"Jix!" He grabbed the end of the roll and pulled as hard as he could. The blanket unrolled, and Jix along with it.

She spun out of the blanket and sat crookedly in the middle of the floor, gasping for breath.

"Are you nuts?" she demanded. "What do you think I am, a burrito?!"

"More like Liz Taylor in *Cleopatra*," he said with relief. "Och, lass, I'm sorry." He staggered to his feet, almost shaking from reaction. "Ye were on fire. Are ye okay?"

"I was on what?"

"Yer nightgown." He leaned closer, hands on his knees, speaking slowly. "It—was—on—fire."

Jix finally looked down at the charred edges of the garment and blinked before lifting her eyes back to his. In that moment he saw a rush of emotions—gratefulness, hope, lust—all melted together in her big green eyes, in her hot and hesitant big green eyes. He reached down and offered her a hand up. Big mistake. The minute their hands touched, a different kind of fire danced from her fingers into his and straight into his veins. Heat surged in his chest, his loins, his head.

Jamie had to fight to keep from taking her into his arms. He shook himself back to some semblance of rational thought. This attraction was the last thing he needed. That either of them needed. They had to keep their heads, stay focused, sober. But as he helped her up from the floor and led her back to the bed, Jamie found it hard to think about anything except the way Jix's lashes brushed against her cheeks, and how soft her hands were, cradled in his. He cleared his throat.

"I fear I almost smothered ye. Ye sure ye're all right?"

She nodded, her gaze locked with his.

Jamie cleared his throat. "Ye'd better get back in bed. Do ye want to sleep in that gown?"

"Oh," she hesitated, then sat down and slid beneath the bedcovers. A few minutes later she handed her charred gown to him, her eyes huge in her face. Jamie took the gown and stood beside the bed for a long moment, watching her. She gazed steadily back at him. He retreated a step. If he planned to make it through this night without doing something he'd likely regret, he'd better keep his distance. He cleared his throat and leaned over to tuck the blanket in around her shoulders.

"I'll be right here beside ye on the floor," he said.

"The floor?" Jix pulled the covers down from her chin and frowned at him, the romantic haze he'd seen in her eyes replaced by practicality. "Don't be ridiculous. You'll catch your death of cold down there." She pressed her lips together thoughtfully, then glanced across the room. "Close your eyes, MacGregor," she ordered.

"Why—"

"Just do it or you'll be sorry." She threw back the blankets and Jamie hastily closed his eyes. He heard her padding barefoot across the room and could picture her, beautiful and naked, as vividly as if he had openly watched her. His face felt hot, then cold, then hot again. Damn.

"All right," she said, the bed moving as she slid in again. "Open your eyes."

He did, only to find her smiling at him, his MacGregor plaid wrapped snugly around her body. "Now, get in, and please keep your cold feet on your side of the bed."

Jamie stared at her in disbelief, coming to stand at full attention in a near state of panic. "I canna sleep with ye."

"Why not?"

Why not? Jamie drew in a ragged breath. Because he wanted to lick every part of her soft, sensuous body, from head to toe until she moaned his name. Because he wanted to kiss that luscious peach-colored mouth all night, mating his tongue to hers. Because he wanted to possess Jix Ferguson and be possessed by her. He managed to keep his thoughts to himself. Jamie cleared his throat. "We're supposed to be brother and sister, remember?"

"We'll get up early in the morning before anyone comes in."

"I canna do it!"

"I'm not asking you to make love to me," she said, leaning up on her elbows and glaring at him. Her anger faded. "Oh, you mean because of what I did before?" She blushed. "I was just playing with you, MacGregor. Don't worry, your virtue's safe with me. Just get in."

"Ye're practically naked."

She glanced down at herself. "The operative word here is 'practically.' I'm totally decent. If it bothers you that much you can sleep on top of the covers and put that fur you've been lying on, on top of you."

Yeah, he thought. Right. Like a few inches of cloth and fur would keep him away from her if he chose to pursue the fire building inside.

"Lass, I—" Jamie stopped. How could he explain that he didn't trust himself to sleep beside her, when he wanted more than anything for her to feel safe, protected? The last thing he wanted was for Jix to equate him with the scum she had been married to—someone who would hurt her. He continued to stare down at her, indecisive until she finally released her breath in exasperation and threw up both hands.

"Oh, for pity's sake! Get in, don't get in, sleep on the floor or in the freaking moat—"

"I'm not sure there is a moat," Jamie couldn't help saying.

"Fine. I don't care. Just let me go to sleep." Jix flung herself back and rolled over, her long hair curling down to her waist atop the covers. It caught under her arm and she had to wrestle with it for a minute. "I'm cutting this mess off tomorrow," he heard her mutter.

"I suppose I could sleep in the opposite direction," he ventured as she settled down into her pillow again, "head to foot, foot to head, ye ken?" There was a pause, then a pillow came sailing across the bed, hitting him squarely in the stomach.

"Be my guest, but if you tickle my feet you'll wish that Red Hugh had used that sword to put you out of your misery."

Misery is right, Jamie thought to himself as he lay down on the bed and positioned his pillow. Sleeping next to Jix Ferguson and not being able to touch her was going to be nothing short of absolute hell on earth. Jamie sighed. It was going to be a long night. He raised up and punched the pillow.

"MacGregor?" Jix said softly.

"Aye?" He settled down again. Her voice slipped over him like a silken sheet, soothing his soul. What was this woman doing to him? He had to get a grip.

"Thank you."

Jamie gazed at the ceiling, wondering what she'd do if he started nibbling on her toes through the covers. "For what, lass?"

"For playing fireman."

He smiled. "Aye, lass. And lass—"

"Yes?"

He hesitated, then raised up halfway on one elbow and looked at her. Jix rested against a huge pillow, her body half-lifted from the bed as well. Their eyes met so easily, so naturally, as if they had been used to looking at one another in bed forever. Her eyes were like green velvet in the dim light. His next words came unbidden, pulled from inside of him before he could stop them. "I wish I had been there when your husband was throwing ye around."

Something flickered in the depths of her gaze and he could barely hear her one-word reply.

"Why?"

"Because I would have broken his neck."

A tremulous smile spread across her lips. Giving a little sigh, she snuggled down into the bedclothes and turned away from him. After a moment she spoke, her voice shaking the slightest bit. "Thanks, MacGregor."

"Good night, lass."

"Good night."

She wiggled again, sliding down under the covers even more. Jamie wished for one instant that he was a sheet, or a pillowcase, or any inanimate object touching Jix Ferguson's wriggling body.

Ye have got it bad, laddie.

Jamie lay back, praying for the strength to somehow find a way out of this crazy situation, and to resist a woman who in all likelihood would turn his life upside down and inside out if he gave her half a chance.

Chapter Seven

Jix sat in the cramped wooden tub and sighed aloud. No matter that her knees were almost against her chest. Never mind that the soap looked like a lump of cloudy gelatin. Having hot water to soak and wash in was suddenly a rare and deeply appreciated luxury. Besides, even though the soap didn't lather much, it had a nice lavender smell.

She had awakened late in the morning to find Jamie gone. A serving woman arrived only moments later carrying a change of clothes and a tray with bread, cheese, and a cup of lukewarm milk. She bobbed into a curtsy and immediately left the room. Jix had made short work of the bread and cheese, and forced herself to sip the milk, which wasn't so bad after she got used to the rather strong taste.

To her surprise, two more serving women appeared minutes later, hauling a wooden tub between them and buckets of hot water. They'd readied the bath, then given her some privacy. Jix had spent the next hour learning the art of washing her hair and body in the small confines of the barrel-like bath.

Jix leaned her head over and dipped her long, newly

acquired hair into the water and scrubbed it a second time with the homemade soap. She wasn't used to having so much hair to wash, and it was amazing how many twigs and tiny leaves were now floating in the water. She supposed they were a result of her spill in the dirt during the battle that Jamie had described. The struggle she only vaguely remembered. Reaching up to touch the bruise on her head gingerly, Jix realized she'd been lucky to come away from the melee with only a bruise and a slight headache instead of a concussion or other major injury. No wonder Jamie had been so upset when she first awakened in his arms. A sigh escaped her and she dipped her head down to rinse, resolutely pushing away any thought of Jamie MacGregor's strong, muscular arms.

Where was he anyway? Why had he disappeared and left her alone? Not that she couldn't take care of herself— of course she could, but that didn't mean he should just take off without telling her. They had to stick together.

She fumed about his absence as she wrung the water out of her hair. The homemade soap had been difficult to use as shampoo but she resolved not to complain. At least she was less dirty than she had been.

Had Jamie gotten a bath? She hoped so. Just getting clean again would make a world of difference in her ability to face this new world. If it was a new world. She wouldn't put it past Samantha to have cooked up some kind of sweet revenge, but Jix doubted that even Sam was capable of this sort of extravagant payback. Jamie had been surprised that she wasn't afraid. She was a little surprised herself. Of course, it might be different if Jamie hadn't come back in time with her. How could she feel afraid when he was there with her, his strong arms ready to hold her, his ready wit prepared to defend her against such as Red Hugh Campbell?

Jix squeezed out the thin washcloth one of the women had given her and started trying to work some lather out of the soap. A picture of Jamie trying to fit in a small bathtub like hers darted through her mind and she giggled. Then Jix pictured him standing in the tub, naked, water pouring down over his muscular chest and taut stomach. She stopped giggling, a flush of warmth pooling in her middle and radiating in both directions. Her skin felt on fire suddenly and it wasn't from the now-lukewarm bath water.

She leaned her head back against the tub. What if she and Jamie had continued their little game the night before? Jix wrung out the washcloth. What had gotten into her anyway? What had she been doing tempting fate and her own passionate tendencies by coercing the man to play footsie under the covers?

A flush of shame flooded her cheeks. The truth was she had wanted Jamie. Badly. So badly that for a few minutes she'd totally forgotten he belonged to Samantha. He was Sam's destiny and she couldn't change that, and wouldn't want to—no, she corrected honestly, *shouldn't* want to— because Jamie was wonderful and Sam deserved a wonderful man instead of that jerk, Mark.

Still, she couldn't help the way Jamie made her feel, could she? But that was just chemistry. Of course, that was all. A sexual attraction and that could happen anytime, between any two random people. It didn't mean anything. Not a thing. She lifted one foot and started washing her toes. All she had to do was keep her distance and stop indulging in her natural tendency to flirt with someone who made her feel so comfortable, so at ease, so protected.

Jamie hadn't seemed to mind, but that wasn't the point. Just because his touch sent fire through her veins didn't mean it was all right to allow herself to feel that heat. She could resist him. If there was anything she had learned in her twenty-five years, it was how to control her emotions.

Jix closed her eyes, feeling a sudden depression sweep over her. Her mother's abandonment had been a terrible shock, especially since she had dreamed about it first. After that she thought for a time that her dreams came true because she dreamed them, and not because they were a premonition of the future. Aunt Phronsie had finally straightened her out and convinced her she'd been given a rare gift. But for many years Jix still believed it was her fault that her mother had gone away. After Aunt Phronsie's death, Jix had found her life plunging once again into that terrible darkness.

The Fergusons had saved her, opening new worlds of love, art, science, poetry, and so much more to attention-starved Jix. She'd been terrified of their four sons at first, but gradually grew to trust them. Still, there had always been a part of herself that she'd kept separate, hidden, even from them.

She'd always felt the need to distance herself from real intimacy—until Dirk the Jerk. And look what that had gotten her over the course of their brief marriage—a broken nose, dozens of bruises, two broken ribs, five black eyes, and a shattered heart.

Jix still didn't quite understand the power Dirk had wielded over her. She'd been afraid—not just of his fists, but of losing him. A high-profile newspaper columnist from Houston, Dirk had been orphaned at a young age also. At the time he seemed to be the first person who had ever really seemed to belong to Jix exclusively. Looking back now, she realized she'd viewed his circumstances as being the same as hers. She'd treated their relationship as if they had been two survivors who had found one another in the midst of a lonely ocean. As long as they had each other, they didn't need anyone else.

Her parents and her brothers had seen through Dirk's "nice guy" facade, and had been against the marriage, along with her best friend Sam. Even her shy, timid friend Chelsea had spoken up and begged her not to marry the man. But Jix had ignored them, sure that love could conquer any problems she and Dirk might have.

After the wedding she had moved with her new husband to Houston. Jix had thought it would be a grand adventure. But after only two weeks, Dirk had begun hitting her. At first her pride had gotten in the way of asking for help. Jix felt foolish, ungrateful, and stupid, for not listening to friends and family. She really didn't have any right, she reasoned, to go running to them for support, and couldn't bear to hear them say "I told you so." And so she had tried to reason with Dirk, suggesting counseling for their marriage. The suggestion almost put her in the hospital.

She reached up and smoothed the bump on the bridge of her nose, remembering. Not long after that, her brothers found out what was happening through a mutual friend. They'd arrived en masse on the doorstep of Jix's dingy, crummy apartment, like the cavalry charging over the hill. When Jix opened the door, her eye swollen shut, her nose bandaged, Travis, Sean, Thomas, and Sebastian had given Dirk more than a black eye and a broken nose. Jix had intervened before her brothers did permanent damage—though the bastard certainly deserved worse—and she had come up with a final, more benign, revenge.

They'd stripped Dirk and tied him to a chair. Jix had painted his entire body with honey and scattered a dozen of his *Playmate* magazines on the floor, open to the centerfolds. She'd next placed a call to a rival newspaper, giving them a "hot tip" about famous Houston columnist, Dirk Stafford. The next day, the front page featured an exposé—complete with photograph—of Dirk engaging in his secret sexual fantasy. According to the article not only was the man covered in honey, but ants had followed a trail of the sticky stuff to what they must have deemed a sweet bonanza. The look on Dirk's face was absolutely priceless. Jix and her brothers, along with Sam and Chelsea, had laughed themselves sick.

And no one had ever said "I told you so." Jix found a lawyer and filed for divorce. But the whole experience had taught Jix that she couldn't trust her own judgment when it came to men, and she resolved to never love any man that much again.

She dipped her hand into the now-cool water and let the drops trickle from her fingers, creating ripples in the bath as she stirred from her reverie, somber. Jamie MacGregor would have that kind of power over her and more, if she let herself love him. Not that she could imagine him ever raising a hand to her, but then she'd never suspected Dirk of being the violent bastard that he'd turned out to be. And what she'd felt for Dirk was a dim candle compared to the flame inside of her whenever she thought about Jamie.

"This is not good," she moaned, throwing her head back against the edge of the tub. "I am not going to make the same mistake twice. I am *not* going to fall in love with Jamie MacGregor!"

She would be his friend, she resolved, and she would help him find the woman he was destined to marry. Jix sat up in the water. Yes, that was the way to keep the demon of lust at bay—tell him about Samantha—all about her! What a great personality she had, how beautiful she was, how kind, what a good cook. In fact, Sam was everything Jix wasn't. She would help him get to know her friend and then by the time they found Sam, Jamie would be interested in learning more about her in person.

Relieved by her decision, Jix quickly finished her bath. The maids came back to dry her off and help her dress. The women patted her dry with clinical detachment. Jix was eager to begin her new plan, and she turned to the servants as they wrapped her in a huge piece of linen that she supposed passed for a towel in this century.

"Do either of ye know where my brother has gone?" she asked, remembering to use the brogue. One of the women bobbed her a curtsy. She looked tired and worn down and Jix felt suddenly guilty that this poor creature had carried heavy buckets of water up the stairs for her bath. She decided to get used to being dirty or find some other way to bathe.

"Aye, miss, yer brother be with the laird."

Red Hugh. Great. She didn't like it, not one bit. What if Red Hugh decided to kill Jamie or cut off his thumbs or something more important? Jix felt sure if she were present, she could coerce the big Scot into sparing the life of her beloved "brother," if it came down to that. But of course Jamie wouldn't think she would be any help at all in a negotiation. So far she didn't think she had scored any points for wit or intelligence in Jamie's eyes.

The servants bustled around, pushing her down onto a stool in front of a dressing table in a far corner of the room. Jix wondered if this chamber had once belonged to one of the laird's former wives? It didn't seem exactly feminine, in fact was rather Spartan, but the dressing table and the beautiful tortoiseshell comb and large hand mirror the women had placed on top of the mahogany table were old and costly.

She allowed the women to comb and arrange her hair, since she had no idea how to do it herself, then dismissed the two, assuring them she could dress herself. A few minutes later she almost called them back.

The clothes she'd been given were very flattering but something of a challenge to even the most dexterous. The dark green skirt worn over three soft petticoats brought out the green of her eyes, and the cream-colored blouse, made to wear off the shoulder, complimented her skin and hair. She slipped all those items on easily, fascinated by the fact that people in this century didn't wear panties. She picked up the last article of clothing from the bed. Some kind of corset? On closer examination Jix found it to be rather like a low-cut vest. She slipped on the light green garment and laced it up the front—or tried to. It was too small. Tugging on the leather laces, she realized her first appraisal had been correct. It wasn't too small, it was meant to act as a corset, or cincher. With effort she managed to squeeze herself into it and tie a bow at the top. Jix held the mirror up and frowned at the slightly wavy reflection. What she could see quickly turned her frown to a smile. Her waist looked two inches smaller and her bust two inches larger. She couldn't breathe but she looked great!

"Wow, maybe I should bring this style back once we get home again," she murmured. She smoothed a lock of hair back from her face.

"Stupid hair." She lifted the mirror higher to get a better look at the long, heavy mane. The maids had plaited a great deal of the thick auburn curls, looping the braids up to join together at the crown of her head in a bun. The rest of her hair hung down past her shoulders almost to the middle of her back, gleaming in long waves, finally untangled.

It was beautiful, but she hated it. It struck her as ex-

115

tremely silly that in the midst of this possible life-and-death situation, her mop of long hair had quickly become one of her main frustrations. She knew it shouldn't matter, but it did. Maybe being trapped in the past hadn't sent her into a hysterical frenzy like Jamie feared it would, but she still had to deal with it in her own way. And while she had to admit she looked good—even sexy—with long hair, waking up to such a phenomenon made everything so much stranger, so much more unreal. As though she wasn't really herself anymore.

And having long hair made Jix feel vulnerable. In her orphanage days she'd learned that the more hair you had, the easier a target you became. Hair could be grabbed and used to torment you. Silly, childish stuff, and yet the memories were still painful.

Jix refocused on her reflection in the mirror. She looked wan and discouraged, and from force of habit she brought a smile to her face, then licked her thumb and smoothed it over first one eyebrow and then the other.

Too bad she hadn't been carrying her purse when they went spinning back in time. She always carried a small makeup kit with her. She pinched her cheeks and brought a little color back to them.

"Guess I'm stuck with the real me," she quipped to her reflection. "If only I had a brush and some deodorant, I wouldn't complain. Much. I wonder if Sam had anything with her? She hates not having her makeup."

Jix sighed at the thought of her friend. Sam and her father had been so wonderful to her, and how had she repaid their love? By getting Sam lost in time. It was too ludicrous. At least Chelsea had been spared this insanity. She was glad she'd had the rare good sense not to drag their mutual friend into this "adventure."

Still holding the mirror, Jix moved impatiently to the bed, flouncing down on it. Jamie had better get back soon. They had to plan their next step in this crazy escapade. She smiled ruefully. If they got back home again—she stopped and corrected her thought—*when* they got back home again, she would have one hell of a story with which to begin her career as a writer!

With one hell of a hero, she thought wistfully. Heat flooded her cheeks and Jix lifted the mirror from her lap. Her eyes sparkled with desire, her lips parted as if for a lover's kiss, and her face was flushed, as if Jamie had just made passionate love to her.

"Okay, God," Jix said aloud, "I don't know what's going on but the joke is over. Time to bring Sam back into the picture." She closed her eyes tightly, clutching the mirror to her chest. "Before I screw up again."

Red Hugh Campbell slammed back another long draft of ale, letting the excess liquid trickle down from the corners of his mouth, into his rusty beard. He smacked his lips twice, never taking his eyes from Jamie even as he dragged his sleeve across his dripping face.

Jamie met his gaze, forcing his features into calm, refusing to outwardly reveal his concern over this meeting. He knew instinctively that his "host" had something up his dirty shirtsleeve—today at least the man had on a shirt—something sinister. Jamie had been a detective for too long to ignore the signals his gut was sending him. Besides, nothing else made sense. There were too many unanswered questions.

For instance, why would one of the Campbells—high enough in the clan to own land and a castle—choose to ally himself with a member of the outlawed MacGregor clan, essentially risking everything to do so? That morning he'd learned from the guards outside their door that Red Hugh had granted the MacGregors the run of the castle. They couldn't leave the castle, but were welcome to explore until the laird was ready to speak with them again. Jamie hadn't awakened Jix, wanting the time alone to find out more about where they were and when. By talking to some of the servants, and using his knowledge of Scottish history, he'd managed to glean enough information to approximate the month and year in which they were trapped—September 1605, the year after the MacGregor

117

clan had first been declared outlawed. He was pleased with the information he'd discovered, but realized that only Red Hugh could answer the rest of his questions.

Red Hugh claimed he wanted the alliance between the two in order to stop the MacGregor's theft of Campbell cattle. Jamie didn't buy it. Cattle theft—also known as reiving—between clans in Scotland was almost viewed as a competitive game of sorts. Besides, Campbell surely had enough men at his command to eliminate that problem or at least control it to some degree. No, there was something else afoot, something Red Hugh had to gain by this marriage of convenience.

"So, lad," Red Hugh said, thumping the goblet down heavily on the tabletop between them, "Ye wanted to speak with me, in private."

Jamie had asked to see him in the man's own chambers away from listening ears. He wasn't surprised when Red Hugh agreed. Whatever reasons he had for welcoming the MacGregors, Jamie had no doubt they were reasons he would not want widely known. They'd broken their fast there, and now it seemed Red Hugh was ready to get down to a real discussion.

"Aye," Jamie acknowledged. "I dinna think our business was anyone else's concern."

Red Hugh nodded, his red curls bobbing atop his head. "Spoken truly, for 'tisn't anyone's concern but ours."

The big man scratched his stomach, then belched. Jamie shifted in his chair, wishing he could open a window to air out the place. Red Hugh's unwashed body combined with the ancient fur he wore as a cloak kept a ripe smell permeating the room. But there were no windows in this chamber to open. A large four-poster bed, not as imposing as the one in his and Jix's chamber, but beautifully carved, sat in the center of the room on a slightly raised platform. There was a small ornately decorated chest and an unadorned wardrobe against one wall. The men sat in two simple wooden chairs facing the huge fireplace and the brisk fire dancing there. In all, it was a rather plain room for the laird of the castle.

"I want to know what this alliance is really all about," Jamie said bluntly. Relaxing his hands on the arms of the chair and resting his feet flat on the floor, Jamie purposely kept his body language open and receptive.

Red Hugh's rusty brows shot up. He reached across the table to grasp a large pewter jug and tilted it over to pour more ale into his cup.

"Do ye now?" He looked down into his goblet, then brought it to his lips as he nodded thoughtfully. He took a swig and lowered the cup, his sharp eyes shifting back to Jamie. "So, yer uncle dinna tell ye?"

"He dinna tell me anythin'," Jamie said, hoping he wasn't digging his own grave by possibly contradicting something the man already knew as fact. "Only that I was to come here, with Maigrey, to help forge an agreement between our clans."

"And ye dinna think that Maigrey's presence was curious?" Suspicion laced his voice and Jamie thought quickly.

"Nay," he said, trying to sound casual, "for my uncle often sends her with me to give her more chances to display her art."

Red Hugh's eyes brightened with interest, and more suspicion. "Her art? And what art would that be?"

Jamie grabbed onto the first idea that presented itself. Jix was a writer. She'd probably be able to tell a story or two, wouldn't she? She said she had been an actress too, so she ought to be able to improvise in any case. Afraid he would clench the arms of the chair and give away his tension, Jamie leaned forward slightly, linking his hands together in front of him. He smiled in a way he hoped was disarming.

"She has hopes of becomin' a bard," he said. "And I must tell ye, she is quite accomplished fer one so young."

"A bard, eh?" Red Hugh stroked his beard. "Well, 'tis an added bonus to the union then, isn't it?"

Jamie wasn't sure the man believed him and hastened to add more to the fabrication. "Her strength lies in her stories," he said, "though she has a fair singin' voice."

Red Hugh's blue eyes glistened with cunning and Jamie quickly shifted into full detective mode.

"So what is it ye want to know, Jamie me boy?" Red Hugh asked. "The terms of yer sister's betrothal?"

Jamie inclined his head. "Aye," he agreed, "but first I would like to know why ye want this marriage. Why align yerself with a MacGregor?"

Red Hugh glanced away, a deep chuckle rumbling through him. "Ye are a sharp lad, no doubt about that." He squinted back at him, fine lines fanning out from the corners of his eyes. "First of all, ye will cease referrin' to yerself as a MacGregor. That name is forbidden. From now on ye are my distant cousin, James Campbell. Ye have brought yer sister here to wed. Only those closest to me will know the truth of the matter."

Jamie nodded. "All right," he said. "But why the marriage? Why are ye willin' to take the chance?"

"Perhaps because yer sister is so bonny."

Although the man said it pleasantly, with no hint of a leer or lusty meaning, a quick surge of anger rushed through Jamie. He tamped it down, giving Red Hugh a knowing smile. "Aye, but ye dinna know my sister was bonny before we came. Besides, there must be plenty of young women in the Highlands lookin' for husbands, some whose clans would make better allies with less chance of angerin' the King."

"Aye, no doubt."

Red Hugh continued to gaze at him, an enigmatic smile curving his lips. So, the old fox was going to make him drag it out of him, was he? Jamie stood and folded his arms across his chest. He still wore his own kilt, tartan and plaid, though they were looking a bit worse for wear, not to mention his dirty and stained shirt. "I'll be takin' my sister and leavin' on the morrow," he announced, keeping his voice flat.

Red Hugh's face darkened and all humor left his features. He stood, and even though Jamie still bested him in height by several inches, he was well aware of the sheer confidence and power emanating from the man. It would not do to make an enemy of him, not if he wanted his sword back. Not if he wanted to live.

"What do ye mean?" Red Hugh demanded.

Jamie met his glower with one of his own. "I mean that I am no' a fool. If ye canna be frank and honest with me, then I canna in fair conscience allow my sister to marry into yer clan, nor to forge this alliance. There is something more to this than ye are admittin'."

Jamie saw the tension leave his face and the man chuckled again, nodding. "I like ye, MacGregor, truly I do, for ye are a braw laddie."

"Which will it be, Campbell? Do ye tell me what ye want of me and mine, or do I walk away with my sister?"

Red Hugh's thick lips twisted in a semblance of a smile. "Ye might find that a bit harder than ye think."

"Aye, I might," Jamie agreed. "But remember that although the MacGregors may be without land or home, they are no' without courage." He took a few steps toward the closed door and turned back, hoping he could bluff his way through this conversation without saying something that would give them away as the wrong MacGregors. "My uncle is waitin' for me to send word of the alliance. If it doesna come, he will be arrivin' on yer doorstep, with all of our clan, swords drawn."

"MacGregors canna possess swords any longer," Red Hugh said softly. "By order of King James."

"And MacGregors canna form alliances with other clans either," Jamie retorted. "By order of the King. So why are ye so eager to do so?"

Their gazes locked for a long, silent moment. When Jamie felt a bead of sweat beginning to form on his brow, Red Hugh threw his bushy head back and laughed, loud and long, clapping his hands against his broad chest as he sank back into his chair.

"I'm glad I amuse ye," Jamie said, making for the door.

"Come back, laddie."

Jamie looked back at him over one shoulder. Amusement still danced in the old sod's eyes, along with something more—respect? Perhaps the day could still be won. He turned and waited.

"Come back," Red Hugh said again, the laughter leaving his voice. "Sit doon, and I'll tell ye the lot of it."

Jamie did as he was bid and leaned forward, attentive, as Red Hugh began to speak. Soon Jamie felt his neck begin to tense as the man outlined his strategy. He finished and Jamie sat back, shaking his head.

"Ye want me to steal cattle on its way to the British stockade near the border," he repeated. "I dinna ken what yer purpose can be. Ye know of course that will bring the Sassenachs down on ye straight away."

Red Hugh's thick lips pressed together impatiently.

" 'Tis no' yer business why," he said, "just do it!"

"I can do better if I ken what is it yer tryin' to accomplish."

The man hesitated for a long moment, then shrugged. "Aye, why not? If ye betray me I have yer sister here with me." He shot him a narrow look. "And dinna think I willna kill her, even if I do admire her spunk. My plan comes before everything, and is in fact why I allow yer sister to marry into my clan in the first place."

"I would never underestimate ye," Jamie said.

"Aye. Well then, this is the way of it." He paused as if gathering his thoughts, then nodded. "My cousin Dougal Campbell is the chieftain of the Campbell clan, rich in monies and property and in the king's favor." He stood abruptly and began to pace back and forth in front of the fire, hands clasped behind his back.

"I take it there is no love lost between ye."

He shook his head. "Nay. I hate him and he hates me just as fiercely. He killed my younger brother and I in turn killed his."

Jamie frowned and shifted in his chair. He didn't think he'd ever get use to the barbarism of this age. He hoped like hell he wouldn't have to.

Red Hugh stopped pacing and faced him, his florid face red with anger, his right hand clenched. He lifted his fist and shook it. "I should have been chieftain! 'Twas my right! My father was the last chieftain but because I didna have the wealth my cousin had, and I wasna as well liked at court, the clan chose him and no' me."

"So what will my reivin' accomplish?"

"The MacGregors are well known for their abilities as thieves. And James MacGregor known for bein' the best thief in all of Scotland."

Jamie frowned. "I'm no' sure I like the sound of that."

Red Hugh laughed, one hand slicing down decisively. "Dinna fash yerself. 'Tis a compliment I'm giving ye. I want ye to lead a group of men—the fewer the better—and steal the British cattle. Harass them, do whatever damage ye can. Then I will make sure Dougal and the rest of the clan hear that it was *my* men who did the reivin'."

"And then?"

"And then?" Red Hugh smiled, his teeth yellow but even beneath his thick, unkempt mustache. "Then the clan will see that I am no' an old man, afraid of the Sassenachs."

"Ah." Jamie nodded, beginning to understand. This was an issue of personal pride for Red Hugh. "So that's what they've been sayin' about ye, I take it?"

"Aye. They say it because I made an agreement with the Sassenach commander at the stockade. Worthington is his name. A black-eyed, black-hearted bastard who takes pleasure in his violence against Scotland. At first I fought him openly, but after a time it became pointless. I was no longer willin' to sacrifice my men. So I made an agreement to save my people and the village from being attacked by the spalpeens."

Jamie considered his words, remembering the fierce black-eyed man who had almost killed him during the battle. "But the skirmish I fought in—"

"Aye, sometimes they'll attack if we wander too far from home and if there are enough of us that Worthington grows uneasy. Yesterday my men were travelin' to a meeting of the clan some miles away. But the clan doesna acknowledge the battles we have fought with Worthington—only what they call my cowardice."

"And what will keep this Worthington from attackin' ye now, if I do this?"

Red Hugh's beard spread wide and his crooked teeth gleamed in a yellow smile. "Why, I'll simply send word to Captain Worthington that 't'wasn't me at all. 'Twas those thieving MacGregors that have been roamin' the countryside. I'll tell him I've had trouble with ye meself."

"I see." Jamie's voice was tight with anger. He stood, facing Red Hugh. "So ye plan to use me and then turn me over to the Sassenachs for yer own gain."

The man shook his head. "Nay, laddie."

"Then what?"

"As soon as ye finish yer raid, I'll hide ye in a place where none can find ye."

Jamie turned toward the fire, considering. Could the old sod be trusted? What would prevent Red Hugh from betraying him after the deed was done? And what about before? "What if we get caught during the reivin'?" he asked.

The man's sharp gaze swept over him and once again Jamie saw the cunning ruthlessness mirrored there.

"Dinna get caught," he advised.

Jamie paced a few feet away, hands behind his back. He could agree now to do Red Hugh's dirty work in return for his sword. If Jix's hunch was right, they would be on their way back home before the laird could blink twice. It would be worth the risk.

"And if I do accomplish this action without gettin' my neck stretched, what then?"

"Then the clan sees what a strong leader I am, and I steal away some of my cousin's backin'. It will be a fine beginnin'."

"And what do the MacGregors get out of the bargain?"

"Yer sister gets a fine husband and a fine home."

Jamie fought back the smile threatening to form on his face. Red Hugh wasn't by any stretch of the imagination a young woman's heart's desire, nor was Meadbrooke Castle a 'fine' home. "I mean the clan," he went on, knowing it would be expected of him to ask, "what does Clan MacGregor get if we agree to this union?"

"My heartfelt thanks, and my protection."

Jamie's interest quickened. "What do ye mean?"

"I mean I will protect any member of yer clan that ventures across my lands. And," he paused dramatically, "I will no' turn them away if they are in need."

Jamie nodded, rubbing his chin and gazing thoughtfully into the fire. The people of Clan MacGregor might be living four hundred years in the past, but they were still his kin. If he could help them, and help himself and Jix at the same time—why not?

"And if I refuse?" he asked, just to see Red Hugh's reaction.

The older man's eyes narrowed. He crossed back to his chair and sat down in it, heavily, lifting his goblet to his mouth. He took a long drink and smacked his lips. "I dinna advise it," he said.

Jamie shrugged. "Seems a rather weak plan to me, but if 'tis what ye want. . . ." he paused. "There is a condition."

"Condition?" Red Hugh lowered his goblet and gave him a suspicious look. "I dinna like the sound of that."

"Ye're a fair man, Red Hugh. I'm taking a great risk and I dinna know if I can trust ye." Jamie leaned against the stone fireplace, his arms folded over his chest.

The laird leaned back in his chair and narrowed his beady eyes. "And what sum of money would make ye trust me?"

Jamie straightened. "I want no money. Only give me back my sword. 'Twas my father's and his father's before him."

Red Hugh hesitated, then nodded, clapping both big hands down on his thighs. "Aye. Once ye do as I ask, I will return it."

Jamie raised both brows. "I must have a sword when I go reivin'," he said.

Red Hugh's thick lips twisted in a semblance of a smile. "Aye, but not the MacGregor sword. I'll hold that until the job is done."

Damn. Outfoxed by the fox. But there was nothing for it but to agree. Jamie nodded. "When must I go?"

"In a week's time. That's when the Sassenachs receive their new lot of cattle."

It would be dangerous, but short of trying to take the castle apart by himself and find the sword, Jamie could see no viable alternative. He would search for it of course, but agreeing to Red Hugh's plan would buy him some time.

"Do I have yer word on it?" Jamie asked. "About the sword?"

Red Hugh rose and held out his hand. "Ye have my word as the next chieftain of Clan Campbell. Yer sword will be in yer hand as soon as ye steal the British cattle."

They clasped arms, their gazes locked. Jamie nodded and released his grip. "There is another matter I would discuss with ye."

"Aye?"

"I would ask that ye give my sister a bit more time to accustom herself to the idea of marriage. She wasna expecting this, ye ken."

Red Hugh frowned. "How long?"

"A month."

The other man considered for a moment, then nodded again. "Aye," he agreed, "a month."

Jamie took a deep breath and released it slowly. He ran one hand through his hair from crown to the back of his neck. Now all he had to do was stay alive.

What would Jix say about his being assigned to harass the English? One corner of his mouth lifted. He had a fair idea. She'd probably ask to ride along. His smile disappeared. On second thought, maybe he'd just keep this little glitch in their adventure to himself.

"Then it's agreed," he said.

"Aye, and tonight we will celebrate! Bring yer sister to the great hall at sunset. Mayhap she'll even grace us with one of her stories or songs."

"Aye," Jamie stood. "In that case I'd best go and tell her so that she may be preparin' herself."

Red Hugh waved him away. Jamie left the chamber, feeling as if a weight as heavy as the massive block of oak closing behind him had fallen squarely on his shoulders.

Chapter Eight

"Where did ye get that dress?"

Jamie's voice startled Jix and she jumped up from the bed, whirling toward the sound. She must have been totally lost in thought, she realized, not to have heard the huge door to their room opening and thudding shut again. The guards had followed him in and stood behind him, staring at her. She ignored them. Jamie looked tired and worried, but as he gazed at her, the weariness left his eyes, replaced by a heated intensity that almost melted her down to her toes. She held the skirt out like a fan and spun around in a circle, laughing as she came to a stop again and curtsied, anxious to see his reaction.

"Och, I just ran down to ye local Mart In Ye Wall and picked it up for just two chickens and a sack of corn," she said with a broad brogue. "Do ye like it?"

Jix felt the touch of Jamie's eyes as if he had physically caressed her. His perusal raked over her slowly, starting with the full green skirt, pausing at the corset-like vest, finally lingering on the swell of her breasts beneath the cream-colored drawstring blouse falling half-way off her shoulders. She'd never felt so sexy in her life.

"What's not to like?" he said. Something sparked between them and Jix suddenly found it hard to breathe. He held her gaze for a long moment, then as if realizing his evaluation might appear less than brotherly to the watching guards, Jamie cleared his throat and frowned.

"Aye," he said, his voice turning harsh, "what's not to like, if ye're a light-skirt and think to entice a man into yer bed. But 'tis a bit too revealin' for my sister to be wearin'."

Jix fell right in with his protest. "Och, ye always were too narrow-minded, Jamie," she scolded. "Besides, these were a gift from Red Hugh and ye can scarcely be against somethin' that my future husband gave me, now can ye?"

A quick, dark scowl darted across Jamie's face and Jix felt a sudden satisfaction in knowing that he wasn't acting, that the thought of her marrying that hairy old Scot sent a prickle of dread down his spine.

Stop it. She commanded her wayward thoughts. *He belongs to Samantha. Get over it!*

"Ye can leave us now," Jamie said to the guards. "An' stop starin' at my sister!"

The guards left reluctantly and Jix crossed to Jamie's side.

"So where have you been, MacGregor?" she demanded.

Jamie looked down at her, his blue eyes flickering over her, heat quickening into their depths. She blushed, feeling more deeply complimented than if he'd told her outright that she was beautiful. He lifted one hand toward her hair, pulling a long, soft curl toward him. His touch made her tremble and she had to put some distance between them before she grabbed the man and kissed him and died of embarrassment. She took a step back but Jamie still held her hair. Jix stopped and Jamie took a step closer.

"So, are ye used to yer long hair yet, lass?" he asked, ignoring her question, the long auburn strand stretched across the few inches between them.

Hair? Did she have hair? With Jamie so close she could be blind, bald, and naked and never realize it. Just the nearness of him sent tiny impulses pumping through her veins, hot, throbbing pulsations that made her dizzy with need.

"My hair?" Jix blinked. "Oh," she said with a laugh, "if I had my way I'd chop it all off but I figured that might be strange to these people."

"Good thinking." He dropped the curl and crossed to the fireplace, seating himself on the stool in front of it.

"What about you?" She cocked her head tò one side, drinking in the sight of him as he swung his plaid over his shoulders to fall like a cape across his back.

"Nay, I've not grown used to it yet, but 'tis the custom. Like ye said, it might draw undue attention if we do anything about it." Jamie stretched his hands toward the fire. "Och, it grows so cold at night in the Highlands, even in the autumn."

"Aye," Jix whispered, watching him. She hadn't realized it but the sun had set and their chamber had grown dark. He sat staring into the flickering flames, golden shadows transforming his features, carving harsh lines into his handsome face. His wavy dark brown hair fell from a center part to three or four inches past his shoulders, the locks shimmering with a red-gold hue in the firelight. His dark blue eyes had deepened until they were the color of midnight, a reflection of gold in the center giving him an otherworldly appearance. Jix felt suddenly as though she had ventured into one of the numerous Celtic deities' anterooms.

Unaware that he had turned into a Celtic god right in front of her, Jamie looked over at her and smiled, his face changing back to his own once again.

"I did get a bath, thank God, but 'twas hard to scrub this long mess. I admit I feel a bit like an English sheepdog," he said, trying to run one hand through his hair, but stopping at a snarl.

"Nay, laddie, never that," she said softly, then laughed self-consciously, moving to his side. "I think you look rather dashing."

Jamie cocked one brow at her. "Dashing? With this

mop?" He pulled at the knot and winced. "I'm almost afraid to see what might be living in it."

"Let me comb and braid it for you," she offered.

"Braid it?" He frowned up at her. "I'd look like a Native American."

"No, silly. You don't braid it in two tails like a schoolgirl." She picked up the comb from the dressing table and moved behind him, gathering his auburn locks between her hands.

Jix Ferguson, you are such a phony! A voice in her head taunted her as she stroked her fingers through his hair, caressing the silky strands. *You just want to touch the man, admit it!*

"Shut up," she muttered aloud.

"What's that, lass?"

She coughed. "Oh, nothing. You see, you just braid a few thin ones near the face." She combed the tangles out of several strands and began plaiting one. "It's a Celtic tradition begun by the gods, who used to braid the strength of the sun and the earth into their hair before a great battle." She gave the finished one a pat and began on another section, her heart thudding painfully in her chest. What she wanted to do was plunge her hands into his hair, lift the long strands from his neck and start kissing him there, at the nape, then trail kisses all the way down his back to his . . .

"I've never heard that story," he said, his voice pulling her back from doing something rash.

"Haven't you?" She tried not to notice how long his eyelashes were, and how warm his skin beneath her fingertips. She swallowed hard. "That's probably because I made it up. Okay, all done." She dropped the last braid and stepped away from him, feeling the need to fan herself.

"Thanks." He smiled up at her. "Draw a chair up to the fire and warm yerself," he said, then hastened to add, "but dinna get too near."

"Very funny," Jix said and stuck out her tongue. That spark of heat came again in the center of his eyes. Whew. She started to fan her face and stopped just in time.

"Ye made it up, eh?" he asked, pulling on one of his braids.

"Hmm? Oh, the Celtic gods—well, I've had little else to do today," she said in a reproving tone.

One dark brown eyebrow darted upward as he shook his head and smiled. "Have ye no' learned anything about yer lies?"

"They aren't lies," she said, aghast at his words. "They're stories. When you read a book are you reading lies or stories?"

"Maybe both? Verra well, lass, sit down, I have something to discuss with ye."

She moved one of the plain wooden chairs over beside him and sat, clasping her hands together on her lap so she wouldn't reach out and grab him. *Get a grip, Jix!* But it was difficult. Jamie MacGregor was unlike any man she'd ever known. Dirk the Jerk had been tall and wiry, although muscular enough to send her flying across the room several times a week. He'd been handsome in his own way, but looking back now she realized there'd always been something lacking in his cynical brown eyes. Integrity. Honor. Combine those two characteristics with someone who looked like Jamie and how could she help but fall for him?

Fall for him? Jix jumped up and walked away from the fireplace. She was not going to fall for Jamie MacGregor.

"Is there something wrong?"

"I'm just a little warm, that's all. Go ahead. I'll sit on the bed." She sank down on the edge, trying to look poised and attentive.

Jamie frowned but turned on the stool to face her. "I had a long talk with Red Hugh today and I think we're going to be welcomed here, for a time at least."

"What about your sword?"

His gaze shifted away from her and Jix frowned. She was pretty good at reading people and Jamie seemed to be worried about something. Or not telling her something.

"Aye, he agreed to give my sword back, in a few days."

Jix nodded, feeling vastly relieved. "That's great! But how did you—"

"Och, we're late," Jamie interrupted, standing and glancing out one of the narrow windows. "Red Hugh asked us to come down for supper with him at sunset." He shot her a grin. "I think he wants to see if ye've regained any of yer wits. I assured him that ye had. Don't let me down."

"Did ye tell him that I had little enough to start with?" she asked, jumping up from the bed and walking toward him. "But about the sword—"

"Nay, I did not say that," Jamie interrupted again. He shook his head and laughed. "Ye are an amazing woman."

His words caught her so off-guard that Jix almost stumbled to a stop in front of him. "I am?" she asked, suddenly breathless.

"Aye." He took her hand and gazed down into her eyes, his dark lashes half-lowered. "Any other woman in this situation would be howling like a banshee, complaining, whining, crying." He shook his head again. "Ye are incredible."

Jix drew in a deep breath as the touch of his hand against hers made her heart trip over its next beat. He held her gaze, his blue eyes liquid, gold pinpoints gleaming in their velvet depths. His mouth parted slightly as he lowered his lips to hers. Jix almost turned her head to avert his kiss. Almost. But at the last minute she gave in, letting his mouth melt into hers, giving his tongue access to hers, allowing the wave of need and hope and passion to sear into her soul as he kissed her.

He pulled away first and Jix found she couldn't look at him. "MacGregor," she began, focusing on his tartan. She stopped and took a deep breath.

"Aye, lass?"

Say it, Jix. "I don't think this is a good idea." She glanced up. His smile faded. She laughed and turned away from him. "Oh, you're a terrific kisser, don't get me wrong. It's just that, well, I'm sort of engaged to someone back home."

Silence. Then his voice, dry, disbelieving. "Really?" He folded his arms over his chest, cocked that dark brow in her direction again and smiled, knowingly. "Who?"

He didn't believe her? Why not? Did he think her such a loser that no man would want her? To make things worse her mind had gone completely blank. She couldn't even think of a fictitious man's name. She blurted the first name that came to mind, without thinking. "Uh, Dirk, my ex-husband."

The smile disappeared and Jix mentally kicked herself. Why had she said that? Now what could she do? Backtrack? Admit she lied? Act like it was a joke?

"What? Ye're joking! Even ye couldn't be that lacking in judgment."

Jix had started to tell him she was just kidding but at his caustic remark she snapped her mouth shut and glared at him. "For your information I am not lacking in judgment."

Jamie threw the plaid around his shoulders and glared back. "Aye, ye are if ye think to marry that bastard again. Are ye out of yer mind? Did he no' hit ye?" Jamie's accent thickened with anger until Jix could hardly understand him. "Dinna ye suffer at his hands enough? Are ye sae lonely an' sae lackin' in self-respect that ye'd gae with such a mon?"

"He's reformed," Jix said quickly. Jamie snorted. "It's true! He's been in counseling."

Jamie laughed and it was an unpleasant sound. "Has he now." It was a flat statement of disbelief.

"Yes, and you know, I really should apologize for acting so silly last night," she went on hurriedly. "I guess my head injury really affected me more than I realized and I—"

"Dinna fash yerself, lass," he said, his voice rough with anger. " 'Tis yer life and if ye want to tie yerself to a man who will fulfill some twisted idea ye have of love, then 'tis yer own business. We must focus on the task at hand. Let's go down to supper."

Jix flashed him a brilliant smile, determined not to let him see how his words had affected her. "All right then, laddie, let's no' be keeping the man waiting. I'm fair famished, I am." As if on cue her stomach growled. "Oops.

133

Sorry about that. I just hope they don't serve haggis. Did I ever tell you about the time that—"

"Perhaps ye'd best save yer stories for Red Hugh. He asked for ye to entertain him with one tonight." Jamie bowed stiffly toward the door.

Yep, he was furious. Should she feel complimented? He wouldn't be mad if he didn't care, would he? Lifting her chin, biting back a sigh, cursing herself for ever mentioning Dirk the Jerk, Jix gathered her skirt in her hands and raised the hem slightly from the floor. The soft leather slippers she'd been given to wear were a little too big. Still she managed to walk gracefully across the room, past Jamie and out the doorway. Jamie caught up and walked beside her.

"And please behave yerself," he hissed as the two guards fell in behind them. "Dinna do anything foolish."

Jix pressed her lips together, wishing she could turn and take a swing at the man. What had happened? Just because she said she didn't want to kiss him, he thought he could belittle her intelligence? Only last night he'd made her feel as though she was smart, witty, and creative. Now that she'd bruised his precious male ego, he had to be snide. She didn't know what made her more furious, his attitude or realizing that he was probably just like all the rest of the men on the planet.

"I know exactly what I'm doing," she whispered. He groaned aloud, further infuriating her. "I can play this part," she told him. "So you just worry about yourself and leave Maigrey MacGregor to me."

"Just let me do the talking," he ordered in a tone that raised the hackles on the back of Jix's neck. She stopped and spun around.

"You are not the boss of me," she said, narrowing her eyes. Maureen O'Hara in *The Quiet Man*, that was the image she needed to visualize for this performance. "And don't ye be forgettin' it, laddie." With a flounce she turned away and headed down the broad stairway leading to the Great Hall. Jix couldn't help smiling as Jamie started cursing under his breath.

She found it a little harder than she expected to negotiate the stairs in the long skirt and slippery shoes, and just before she reached the bottom her stomach growled, more loudly than before. Startled, she stopped short. Her sudden halt apparently caught Jamie off guard and he slammed into her back. She cried out, swaying precariously on the edge of the step, her arms flailing. Jamie moved as swiftly as a cat, wrapping one arm around her waist and one hand catching her directly over her breast. They teetered on the stairs as servants below and guards behind watched, their mouths hanging open.

The two regained their balance and Jamie snatched his hands away from her as if she had been on fire. Again. Jix pressed her lips together, furious that he'd had to rescue her.

"Thanks," she said tersely. He bowed to her, smoothing back his dark hair from his face, an amused smile lifting one corner of his mouth.

"Pardon me, Maigrey," he said, "but ye really should be more careful. 'T'would be unseemly to arrive in front of Lord Campbell in a sprawling heap, or burnt to a crisp."

Jix blushed to the roots of her auburn hair, from the intimate touch of his hand as well as his reference to her ignominious entrance at his uncle's home and the near disaster last night. She was a klutz. She knew it, accepted it. Hadn't she been thrown out of her first ballet class after pirouetting into Jodi Ann Kincaid, breaking the other girl's ankle? Just another in her long list of accomplishments. And just when she'd wanted Jamie to see her as feminine and elegant.

But she wasn't about to let him get away with his remarks. Regally she lifted her chin and stuck out her tongue. "You don't need an excuse to grope me, Mac-Gregor," she whispered. "Even if I'm engaged, I still enjoy a good time." Jix smiled at the stunned look on his face and raised the edge of her skirt to float gracefully down the last few steps to the entrance of the great hall. She glared triumphantly back at him over her shoulder. There! Let him chew on that for a while!

Unfortunately he wasn't looking at her. His eyes were fixed across the great hall. "Look, there he is."

Jix followed Jamie's gaze. Red Hugh stood with his hands on his hips, beaming. Thankfully, he didn't appear to have noticed their little mishap from where he stood, surveying his inner domain. The great hall had been arranged for supper and Jix sucked in her breath and blinked, overwhelmed once again by the size of the room. Ten long wooden tables flanked by wooden benches lined the cavernous chamber, all filled to overflowing with people in various shades of plaid and subdued colors.

On the platform where Red Hugh's "throne" had sat the night before, another long table had been placed, along with four chairs behind it. When the lord of the castle caught sight of Jix and Jamie, his face lit up. He gestured them over with both hands.

Jix took a step—only to sink down almost to the top of her ankle into a mushy mire. She looked down and discovered that a strawlike substance, in varying degrees of decay, covered the stone floor of the hall. A distinctly moldy odor drifted up to her nostrils and she grimaced. She'd read enough historical romances to know that this was the point in the story where the heroine realized the castle needed a woman's touch. She laughed.

"I don't think so," she said aloud.

"Are ye all right?" Jamie whispered, nudging her forward, one hand under her elbow.

Show time! "I'm just ducky. Did I tell you about the time I had a small part on *All My Passions*? So don't worry, MacGregor, I can handle this."

Jamie's grip on her elbow tightened. "Famous last words," he muttered.

"Bring my guests up here!" Red Hugh shouted across the hall, causing the people at the tables to turn and stare. Jix jerked her arm out of Jamie's grasp and started across the room. Chin held high, she swept across the rushes, mounted the few steps leading to the platform, stopped directly in front of the laird, and dropped into a deep curtsy.

"Please forgive me, Laird Campbell," she said, darkening her voice into the prerequisite brogue. "My brother tells me I was no' myself when we first met. 'Twas the blow to my head, ye ken. I am deeply grateful to ye for yer hospitality." She smiled at him and was amazed to see the real look of appreciation that flashed into his eyes.

"Dinna fash yerself, lassie," Red Hugh said, waving his hand absently. " 'Tis forgotten now." He put his arm around her and ushered her to the table. "I am honored to have ye at my table."

Jix lifted both brows in surprise. His attitude was certainly a turnaround from the night before! Immediately suspicious, she turned to Jamie as she sank down into the chair Red Hugh offered. What had happened to make the mad Scot so amenable?

"It seems our host is extraordinarily glad to see us," she said to Jamie under her breath as he took his place beside her. "Does this have anything to do with your early morning meeting?"

Jamie coughed, shifted his feet, and avoided her eyes. "I dinna know what ye mean."

Jix knotted her hands in her lap while keeping a complacent smile on her face. She had the terrible feeling that something had once again wrenched her life out of her own control. "Is there something ye would like to share with me, brother dear?"

Red Hugh's laughter kept Jamie from responding. Jix glanced up at the big Scotsman. His florid face was radiant with joy. Apparently he had overheard the last of their conversation.

"Aye, aye," he said, his deep voice booming, " 'tis a grand day, for yer brother has signed the agreement between us and as soon as the marriage takes place, our two clans will be officially united." He spread his beefy arms wide. "Now I welcome ye as kin."

Red Hugh pulled Jix out of the chair into his embrace. She yelped, certain she would be crushed in the big man's arms. His hug proved to be somewhat gentle, rather like being hugged by a large, awkward teddy bear. He released her and Jix stumbled back a step. Jamie had risen too and she slammed right into his broad chest. He reached a hand out to steady her and she jerked away from his touch. Red Hugh continued to beam.

Jix tried to form coherent words but couldn't. She clenched her fists at her side, almost shaking with anger. So Scotland Yard had signed the deal without even consulting her, without letting her be part of it! Never mind that they had discussed it the night before—she hadn't been part of the final agreement! By the time Jix took her seat again between Red Hugh and Jamie at the large trestle table, she was so angry she felt like punching both men.

As she sat steaming, servants began serving supper and Jix almost groaned out loud. The romances she loved to read had once again proved to be amazingly accurate. Castle food was usually described as, well, less than appetizing. In front of her sat a pewter plate filled with sausage that had a funny smell, onions, cheese, and bread. She stared down at it, Jamie's treachery pushed aside momentarily. This was her cue. In the historical romances the heroine would take over the kitchen and produce fabulous meals with her expert knowledge of the culinary arts. The thought appealed to her competitive spirit, but she knew her limitations. This heroine couldn't boil water. She picked up a hard crust of bread and examined it carefully. It looked all right but one could never be too careful when trapped in a time before refrigerators. She took a bite. Her stomach gurgled and she chewed rapidly before she lost her nerve.

Suddenly Jix became aware of Jamie's gaze. She turned toward him in mid-chew and saw not apology, not compassion, but a warning in his gaze.

"What is it, MacGregor?" she whispered. "Afraid I might embarrass you?" She wiggled her eyebrows and narrowed her eyes. "Be afraid, be very afraid."

Jamie cleared his throat and leaned across the table. "My laird," he said, addressing Red Hugh as the man shoveled food into his mouth, paying no mind to the bits falling into his beard. "Remember our agreement. My sister is to be

138

given a full month to prepare herself for the nuptials."

That announcement might have somewhat dulled Jix's sharp edge of anger, but it didn't. Not by a long shot! They'd talked half the night, couldn't he have told her his plan? But no, she was just a woman, not worthy of being taken into his confidence. She lifted the hard bread to her lips with both hands and tore off another bite, chewing it viciously, ignoring Jamie's nudge in her ribs.

"Aye, aye," Red Hugh said with a sigh. "I remember." His red brows collided. " 'Tis the only concession I gave ye. Come the first of October, Maigrey will be Griffin's bride."

Jix had just taken a drink of what turned out to be very good wine from a goblet placed in front of her. At the man's words, the wine went straight into her windpipe. She came to her feet, choking and sputtering. Jamie rose and pounded her on the back until she could regain her breath. When she finally did, she whirled on Red Hugh, uncaring of the startled glances of the people in the hall.

"Who—*Who* the *hell* is Griffin?" she demanded.

Red Hugh looked confused. "Why, my son, lass. The man to whom ye are now betrothed. A toast!" he cried, rising to his feet. Benches scraped backward as the people in the great hall came to their feet, holding their goblets and cups aloft. Red Hugh lifted his cup to Jix, his small black eyes shining with drink and pride. "To my son's new bride, Maigrey. Come the first Sabbath day in October, the two shall be wed."

"To Maigrey!" the people in the hall cried and tossed down their drinks. The hall immediately buzzed with excitement over the announcement and Jix whirled toward Jamie, hands on her hips. To her surprise, Jamie's dark blue eyes were wide with shock.

"So!" she cried and then remembered to speak in the Scottish brogue. "Not only have ye signed me away without even speakin' to me about it first, but ye give me away to some man I haven't even met!"

"But I thought—" Jamie began, his face stricken.

"Och, dinna fash yerself, lass," Red Hugh broke in with

a chuckle. "I dinna think ye'll be disappointed when ye see my Griffin. He's a braw, bonny lad."

Without warning, across the great hall, the huge double doors leading to the outside crashed open, the heavy wood slamming back against the stone wall. Jix jumped with a gulp and Jamie grabbed her, thrusting her behind him with one smooth motion. Too angry to even appreciate his protective gesture, she took the opportunity to punch him in the small of the back with her fist. It was like punching a brick wall. She did it again anyway.

"Later, we are going to talk, brother *dear!*"

"Aye, here's the lad now," Red Hugh said, "back from his hunt."

Jix heard Jamie's swift intake of breath and curious, she peeked around his broad back. The sight that greeted her took her breath away too, in more ways than one.

In the center of the hall stood a man at least six foot four inches tall, his shoulder-length hair as blond as a Viking's, his ice blue eyes fringed with dark lashes and topped by dark, expressive brows. He had a jaw of granite and sensuous lips beneath an aquiline nose. As he hefted the weight of a six-point buck slung across his wide shoulders, he paid no mind to the deer's blood dripping down a shirt that was open to the waist, revealing a bare, sweaty, muscled chest. He was barbaric, lusty, practically an animal, yet not a woman in the hall could take her eyes from him, including Jix.

He crossed in front of the tables to the platform and with a grin, bent over, letting the deer fall to the stone floor with a gruesome plop.

Jix was fascinated and repelled at the same time. This was Griffin? She was supposed to marry this marvelous masterpiece of male magnificence? She wet her lips as Red Hugh hurried down from the platform to clasp his son in his arms. The hall buzzed with excitement. Jix stole a glance at Jamie and saw with satisfaction that he looked as if someone had knocked the breath right out of him.

Good! She thought with childish triumph. *So it was all right for me to be betrothed to an old, hairy, smelly man, but now that I'm going to be matched with this wild young stud, maybe he won't think it's such a great idea!*

Her heart pounded suddenly against her chest. Would he care? Did he? Or was he just surprised? Her conscience prodded her and Jix slapped it away. Yes, she knew she had no business caring whether or not Jamie MacGregor was jealous. And even if he was, it could only be the result of a natural rivalry that would spring up between two macho males. He didn't want her. He just didn't want a young, handsome man to have her. Typical male. And after his high-handed way of doing things, he deserved to suffer just a little—even if he did ultimately belong to Samantha. Her lips curved up in a smile. It might be fun to tweak the serious laddie from Scotland Yard, just a bit.

Red Hugh turned now, his wide mouth splitting into a smile of pride as he gestured toward the platform. "Come, come," he called to her, "ye must meet my son—yer future husband!"

The buzz in the hall rose to a furor as Jix lifted her skirt and sailed across the dais and down the few steps. She paused at the bottom long enough to lift her chin and shoot Jamie a lofty smile of triumph. He stood, still looking shell-shocked, frozen in place as she swept over to the young giant. Griffin's ice blue eyes roamed over her with interest as she sank into a deep curtsy before him, quite aware that the position gave him visual access to her ample cleavage. She kept her voice soft, seductive.

"I am honored, Griffin of Meadbrooke," she said, "to be your betrothed."

Chapter Nine

From his vantage point Jamie watched the display, feeling gut-punched. This was the man Jix was supposed to marry? Of course, she wasn't going to marry anyone, but for the next month or however long it took him to figure out how to get his sword back, she would be expected to get to know her fiancé. After their meeting that morning Jamie hadn't worried about Red Hugh courting Jix. He'd seen the fatherly manner the man had taken toward the auburn-haired woman in their discussion and had known Jix could handle him. He had reasoned that Red Hugh only wanted an alliance, not a wife in fact nor—one could hope—in his bed.

But now he knew why Red Hugh had seemed so paternal—he'd planned to be Jix's father-in-law, not her husband!

"My," Jix said a little breathlessly as she rose from her curtsy, "ye certainly grow them large around here."

Red Hugh chuckled. "Aye, our bonny lads are of the largest size. No runts among them." He clapped the blond young man beside him on the back. "Griffin, lad, this is

Maigrey." She extended her hand and the giant of a man was about to take it when Jamie came to life.

"Pardon me," he said, moving across the platform and down the stairs, inserting himself smoothly between the two, elbowing Jix gently backwards. "I believe it is my place to present my sister."

Red Hugh shrugged, his hand dropping from Griffin's shoulder. "Aye, aye. But ye'll find we're no' much for proprieties."

Jamie's gaze met that of Griffin Campbell and did not like what he saw in the other man's eyes. Ruthless, determined, arrogant, selfish. He would take what he wanted without thought for anyone but himself. And Jix, foolish, angry Jix, had already set the tone of their relationship by playing the coquette. This man would probably beat her, too. Did she have some need to be hurt? Did she feel she somehow deserved such a fate? The thought of her returning to her ex-husband when they did make it back to their own time filled him with fury. In spite of saying it was her own business, Jamie already planned to find her brothers and alert them to her insane plan once they returned to their own time. He put the thought aside and lifted his chin, meeting arrogance with arrogance.

"I am James Mac—" he stopped, remembering Red Hugh's admonition about his name. "Campbell," he finished, "and this is my sister, Maigrey."

Griffin lifted his chin in haughty acknowledgment before turning to Jix. "Welcome to ye, Maigrey," he said, bowing slightly. "Yer brother is a wise man to give ye into my keepin'."

"I have no' given her into yer keepin'," Jamie said, louder than necessary. The hall fell into a hush and he fought to keep his temper under control. "Red Hugh has agreed to wait a month to give Maigrey time to acquaint herself with ye." He took a step forward and folded his arms over his chest. "And until that day, Griffin Campbell, I will be her shadow, her constant and vigilant shadow."

A thin smile stretched across Griffin's lips. "Ye wouldna be suggestin' I would try to bed the lass before our weddin' date, would ye now?" The hall began to buzz again.

Red Hugh chuckled. "Well, laddie, ye must admit ye have quite the reputation for such things." The two men laughed together.

Jamie arched one brow, controlling the fury ripping through him. If he were smart he would befriend Griffin, get to know him, get him on his side. The laird's son turned his gaze to Jix again and the heat of lust shone boldly in his eyes. Jamie clenched his teeth together so hard his jaw hurt.

So he wasn't a smart man.

"I'm suggestin' that ye would bed her this day and against her will," he said, biting off each word, "if ye thought ye could get away with it."

A murmur rose from the hall and Red Hugh laughed again even as his son's expression darkened.

"Perhaps it t'would bode ye well to remember just whose hospitality ye are partakin' of," Griffin said. He lowered his voice. "And to remember that ye are an outlaw with no land, no home, and scarcely a country."

Jamie dropped his arms to his sides, his hands curling into fists, lowering his voice also, until only Griffin could hear him. "And ye would do well to remember that ye are dealin' with a MacGregor, no' a mewlin' pup. And Scotland is, and will ever be, my country and my home."

Red Hugh cleared his throat. "All right, lads, 'tis enough. Come, let us finish our meal in peace. We can speak of this later." He led the way back to the table. "Here, Maigrey, sit ye beside me, and Jamie ye on my right side. Griffin, sit by yer betrothed." His eyes twinkled.

Jamie took his place, frowning at the two men, and Jix in particular. Things had slipped completely out of his control in a matter of moments and the knowledge made him very uneasy.

Once they were all seated, Red Hugh gestured to a man standing near the doorway. He disappeared and in a moment he and four more men entered the hall. They began setting stools on a stone platform about ten feet wide and a half foot off the ground, near the fireplace. The men left again and returned with musical instruments. Jamie recognized the bodhran, a type of Celtic drum played with a small mallet, as well as an oversized mandolin. One man carried a small harp, and another two sticks to which tiny bells were attached at intervals.

They sat down and began to play softly, some Celtic melody. The sound sent a chill down Jamie's spine, reminding him again that they were trapped in time, trapped in an ancient world. Trapped until Red Hugh relinquished his sword, or maybe even after. He took a deep breath and brought the rising panic under control. Casually he turned to the laird.

"I dinna think ye would be a music lover," he commented.

Red Hugh lifted one broad shoulder and let it fall. "Och, the ladies like it, and the lads are partial to the dance."

"I love to dance," Jix said.

Griffin took her hand and brought it to his lips. "Then ye must grant me one later, sweetlin'."

Jix smiled up at the man in a way that made Jamie's pulse pound. She turned slightly, giving Jamie a veiled look. So that was it—she was paying him back, in spades, for his decisions on her behalf.

Well, dammit, he'd only done what he'd thought best. They'd discussed it, hadn't they? So why was she angry? The only way they had a chance of getting home was if they could move about the castle freely. So he had agreed to Red Hugh's terms. But he hadn't known he was agreeing to Conan the Barbarian. He pulled himself back to the situation at hand.

Jix's voice trilled sweetly as she spoke to both Griffin and Red Hugh. Didn't the woman have any idea of how she affected men? Even her laughter sent a thrill of desire through his veins. What must it be doing to a man like Griffin, a man with no restraint and little civility? Stuck on the other side of Red Hugh, Jamie leaned forward, trying to hear what Jix was saying.

"I've been wonderin' about something," she said, tilting her head to one side and gazing up at Griffin appraisingly.

"Aye, lass?"

"A woman, a friend who traveled with us, became lost from us in a storm. I wonder if she may have come here for shelter?" Her long auburn hair fell across her shoulder and Griffin reached for one long lock. Jamie had to clench his hands together in his lap to keep from leaping to his feet and pounding the man.

"What did she look like, heart o' mine?" Griffin asked, his voice dark, liquid. Jamie watched as he took her hair and wrapped it around his fingers, pulling her closer to him. The man was so hot for her his hand was actually trembling. Jamie saw Jix stiffen, then relax and smile.

"Blond, taller than me, prettier than me," she said, her words coming out in a rush as she was pulled closer and closer to Griffin's lips.

"Och," Griffin said, his voice a whisper Jamie could barely hear, " 'tis impossible. No woman on earth could be prettier than you, bonny Maigrey." He bent his head to hers, and as his lips hovered scant inches above her mouth, Jamie thundered to his feet.

"If ye would give us yer leave," he said to Red Hugh, "I fear my sister is growin' fatigued. She is still recoverin' from her head injury and should rest."

Red Hugh's dark eyes twinkled with mirth, but he shook his head. "Nay, nay, Jamie. Ye said yer sister was a bard. Let her give us a song or a story then."

Jix turned slowly to stare at him and he shrugged. "Her head—" he began.

"I feel fine, brother dear," she said, rising from her chair, an odd smile on her face.

"But are ye no' wearied, Maigrey?" Jamie's throat tightened. What was she up to now?

"Nay, brother, I feel quite refreshed. After all, I did nothing all day but rest. And the least I can do is offer our host my meager efforts at entertainment. Ye would not have me refuse his request, would ye?"

Her voice was filled with innocence but Jamie knew better. She had that telltale gleam in her eye that meant trouble. Still, how much trouble could she get into, just singing a song?

"I suppose a wee song would do no harm," he agreed. With a sigh he took his seat again and watched as Jix made a curtsy to Red Hugh and Griffin before making her way toward the musicians.

She spoke to them for several minutes in a low voice, then had each one begin a tune under her instruction. One by one she added each player. The song sounded familiar but Jamie couldn't quite place it. She moved to the center of the hall and stood with her hands clasped together at her chest. The music swelled and she began to sing, her voice clear and true and gentle.

"At first I was afraid, I was petrified. . . ."

Jamie frowned. This song was familiar—what was it?

"I thought that I could never live without you by my side. . . ."

She began to move toward the table and all at once Jamie realized she was looking directly at Griffin Campbell!

Jamie felt dumbstruck, along with the rest of the hall, if the astonished faces of the people watching were any indication. Jix moved like one born to the stage. She lifted her arms toward the audience in a graceful plea, then lowered them to her side again. Suddenly she turned to the musicians and gave some sort of silent signal. The tempo changed, increased to a rock beat, and her hips began to keep the new rhythm as every man in the hall dropped his jaw.

"I will survive, I will survive!"

Jix swayed, she cajoled, her hips swiveled, her breasts wiggled as she told everyone in the hall why in spite of the odds, she would survive. She kicked, she danced, hiking her skirt up as she moved, and as she jiggled her way across the stone floor, Jamie couldn't stop the smile spreading across his face. She had guts, he had to give her that.

Unfortunately, guts combined with lack of judgment could get her into real trouble.

He surveyed the hall and his smile faded. The men sat literally drooling, lust lighting their faces, more than one shifting uncomfortably in his seat. He slid a glance sideways. Griffin Campbell had his hands clenched together so tightly on the tabletop Jamie thought they would crack. In another minute Jix might have the entire male population of the castle whipped into a sexual frenzy that would be uncontrollable. He shook his head and stood.

Jix had just wound up for her grand finish when Jamie began speaking, shouting out the words, causing her, along with the musicians' instruments, to stutter into silence.

"Enough!" he shouted. "I willna have my sister makin' such a spectacle of herself!" He turned to Red Hugh and glowered down at him. "She may be betrothed to yer son," he gave Griffin a contemptuous look, "but she's no' a common trollop."

Red Hugh managed to turn his glazed eyes toward Jamie. "Aye, aye, lad. Take her upstairs. Now."

He nodded at Red Hugh. "Until tomorrow then." He stalked across the hall until he reached Jix's side. When he got her alone, damned if he wasn't thinking of turning her over his knee and giving her a thrashing.

Didn't she know she was asking for trouble? Or didn't she care?

Jamie repeated the question out loud once the heavy chamber door closed behind them.

"Don't I care about what?" she asked, looking so genuinely perplexed, for a minute he thought he had misinterpreted the whole scenario. Then the corner of her lips curved up and he remembered he was dealing with a con artist. A sweet, sexy woman who probably never really meant anyone any real harm, but a latent con artist never the less. "What's wrong, MacGregor, didn't you like my performance?"

He ignored her question. "Don't ye care that ye're sending out signals like a sex-starved nymphomaniac to a man who could, with his father's blessing, break down this door, take ye forcibly from this room, rape ye, kill ye, do anything with ye that he pleased? Not to mention the rest of the blasted hall!"

148

His voice rose as he spoke and he began to pace, suddenly aware of how angry he really was, and how afraid. For no matter how hard he might try to protect Jix, if Red Hugh and his men decided to take her from him, there would be nothing he could do to stop them.

Her face paled and he caught a brief glimpse of fear flicker in her eyes. Jix glanced away from him and laughed. Acting completely unconcerned, she moved to the bed and sprawled across it, propping her chin on her elbows, facing him.

"You wouldn't let that happen, MacGregor," she said, kicking her bare feet back and forth playfully. "You wouldn't let anyone manhandle a woman." She paused. "Would you?"

"No," he said, "I wouldn't let anyone hurt ye." He took a step toward her, his fists clenched, wishing he could shake some sense into her beautiful head. "But after about five minutes what I might do would no longer be of any concern to them, or to ye."

She quit kicking her feet and raised both brows coolly. "Um, and why is that?"

He folded his arms over his chest. "Because, lass, I would be dead."

Jix shot him a startled look. She started to speak, but didn't. Instead she rolled over and slid off the bed, heading toward the door.

"Where do ye think ye're going?" he demanded. "We're not through talking."

She whirled around, her chin lifted defiantly. "I'm going back downstairs. I'm not going to let you scare me."

Jamie swore and crossed to her side. "Someone needs to scare you," he said, grabbing her by one arm and pulling her roughly toward him.

Jix gave a little cry, her left hand curling into his shirt to keep from falling against him. The tips of her fingers brushed against his skin, exposed by the open-necked shirt, and he felt branded by her touch. She looked up at him, her green eyes like dark forest shadows in the dim light, and Jamie felt mesmerized, intoxicated. But that only served to fuel the anger, the passion he felt for this woman so lacking in caution.

He seized her face between hard fingers and Jix cried out, her full lips parted, real fear now in her eyes. She pulled back as if she expected him to hit her, and suddenly all his anger dissolved. Her eyes fluttered shut as she continued to struggle against him.

"Open yer eyes, lass," he said, gentling his voice and his hands. She did as he said and this time there was once again defiance in the dark green flame. Good. She would need that banty-rooster arrogance to get through this alive. "I'm not going to hurt ye."

He felt her relax, but her expression was still wary and her hands still pushed between them, a barrier. He held her firmly but tenderly, looking into her eyes, trying to convince her, by sheer will, that she could trust him.

"This is no' a game, lass." He tightened his grip again. "Can ye fight me? Can ye?"

"I suppose not," she said, her gaze flickering up at him defiantly.

"Could ye fight yer damned husband?"

Jix looked away and shook her head.

He dropped her arm. "And ye canna fight these men either. The only thing keeping them from ye is whatever honor they may have, but mostly it is because they know they will have to go through me to get to ye, and that doing so could start another clan war. For some reason, Red Hugh needs the MacGregors," he paused. He planned to keep Campbell's plot to himself for as long as possible. "He wants to keep us happy, for now, but that could change."

Jix stood unmoving and he lifted one hand to her cheek, turned her face back to his. "I dinna want ye hurt, lass."

Her shoulders sagged and Jamie watched all the fight drain suddenly from her.

"I just thought it would sort of liven things up," she said with a shrug. "As usual, I was wrong. Just call me stupid."

"Ye are not stupid, and I grow weary of hearing ye say such a thing. Ye are a smart woman, but do ye not know that ye are also beautiful? These men are lucky if their women show them an ankle while walking in the court-yard. Can ye imagine what yer show downstairs did to them?"

She looked up at him, her eyes suddenly velvet. "You think I'm beautiful?"

Jamie had to smile. Did she really not know? "Och, lass, now ye're playing with me again."

Jix shook her head. "No." A wan smile touched her face. She crossed the room to stand near the bed, her arms clasped about her waist. "Dirk always said I was too big in the hips and that I should have my nose fixed."

"Too big in the hips?" Jamie laughed. "Ye have the most remarkable backside I've ever seen."

"Do you really think so?" She looked over her shoulder down at her rear and a genuine smile lit her face.

Jamie felt mutual pangs of anger and desire sear through him. He focused on the anger and tamped the desire down. "So this man who not only abused ye physically but it would appear mentally as well, this is the man ye've decided to marry again."

Her eyes widened, as if she'd forgotten she'd revealed her secret engagement. "Uh, he's changed, I told you."

"And ye trust him now, do ye?"

Jix closed her eyes against the harshness in his voice and before she could open them, before he could bring his thoughts or actions back under control, Jamie was beside her, taking her in his arms, blurting out the words before he could stop them. "I wish ye would trust *me*," he said.

She opened her eyes, startled, her hands pressing against his chest. "I do," she said. "More than you know."

"Enough to stop joking and pretending everything's all right when it isn't?"

One corner of her mouth lifted. "I don't trust anyone that much," she whispered.

"And I like yer nose," he said softly, leaning down to kiss the bump at the bridge. "It gives ye character."

"Oh, Jamie," she lifted her arms to his neck and her head fell back slightly. "What are you doing to me?"

151

Jamie slid his hands along her arms, over her shoulders, and skimmed up her neck to cup her face, his thumb moving gently over her lower lip. He tried to ignore the rise and fall of her breasts as her breath quickened, tried like hell to ignore the sudden, urgent need he felt to lay her down on the fur beneath their feet, to lift the long skirt from her silken legs and possess her, body and soul. Jix closed her eyes again as his fingertips skimmed the soft velvet of her jaw, trailed down her neck to her throat. Her lashes became dark crescents against her skin, and she parted her lips, this time giving a small, shuddering sigh.

He was lost. Jamie lowered his mouth to hers, barely touching her at first, letting the caress of her breath, the anticipation, drive him wilder. Her arms crept up his shirt front and around his neck. Was it his lust-filled imagination or did she press her hot, lithe body more firmly against his? No, she wanted him, as much as he wanted her. Her mouth opened and he cupped the back of her head, deepening the kiss, using his tongue to brand her with his touch, his heat. Her head fell back and she moaned, just a soft little moan, but it was enough. Jamie scooped her up in his arms and carried her to the bed, sliding them both on top of the coverlet without taking his lips from hers.

She burned him. That was the only way he could explain it. Her mouth, her skin, her eyes. They burned him, marking him, just as he wanted to mark her, to possess her and to let her possess him. He was crazy, he was delusional, he was suffering from the effects of time travel. He didn't care. At that moment all sense of reason fled from him. All that mattered was seeking her heat, her sweet, dark warmth.

He made short work of the soft white blouse she wore, pulling the drawstring that held it, then sliding the material below her two breasts. He cupped them in his hands.

"Beautiful," he said, loving the perfect way they fit in his hands, "ye are so beautiful."

"Jamie," she whispered.

"Shhh," he cautioned, cutting off her protest with his lips. He found her tongue with his, hot, demanding, and pulled her against him, his hands sliding up under the long skirt she wore. He smiled against her mouth as he realized there were no barriers between them and for the first time in his life he saw the wonderful practicality of kilts. Her hands slid over his shoulders and up into his hair as she opened her mouth to him. Her tongue met his again and her fingers ran down the back of his neck and knotted in his shirt from behind. She began tugging it and Jamie helped, letting her pull the confining garment out of his kilt. The tartan was pinned to the front of it and it was an easy matter to discard both, over his head.

Then they were skin against skin and her bare breasts burned against the firmness of his chest. He eased back to look at her and felt mesmerized. How could she ever doubt her own beauty?

Jamie wanted her now, without preliminaries, but refused to sacrifice what he knew could be a slow leisurely journey to paradise for a few moments of selfish ecstasy. His hands moved her skirt higher, taking his kilt with it and suddenly they were flesh against flesh, heat against heat. The catch in her breathing was so slight he might have missed it had he not been so intent upon pleasing her, on being alert to any movement on her part. He pulled away. She was trembling, her mouth quivering, tears shimmering on the eyelashes of the girl-who-never-cried.

"Oh Jamie," she said, lifting shaking fingers to cup his face as her green eyes filled with sorrow. "I can't do this, I just can't."

Jamie froze, terrified he had caused that pain in her eyes. "Lass, I'm sorry. I shouldn't have—"

"No, no, it isn't your fault, it's mine. I want you—you don't know how much I want you—but I can't."

He smoothed her hair back from her face and kissed one tear as it trickled down her cheek. She drew in a quick breath and he felt her shudder beneath him.

"I don't want to push ye into anything ye aren't ready for, lass," he said, pressing a kiss against her mouth, aching with longing for her.

"It's not that," she said, running her hands down his

side and driving what little control he had right out the window.

"Then what?" A sudden, terrible thought pierced him. Of course. What a fool he was. "It's because of him, isn't it?" She didn't answer. Jamie rolled to one side and sat staring down at her in disgust, feeling as though his heart had been twisted in two. "Answer me, Jix. Is it because of that damned bastard ye intend to marry once we get home?"

Jix sat up. Her red hair cascaded over her shoulders, golden glints from the fireplace highlighting the waves. The long curls sheltered her breasts from his gaze. She pulled her skirt down and drew her knees to her chest, wrapping her arms around her legs as she finally shifted her eyes to his.

"Yes," she whispered.

Chapter Ten

Trailing her fingers in the water, Jix sat on the edge of a stone fountain in the castle's rose garden. The last three days had seemed to drag on forever but this day might actually last for all eternity. Who knew? Time was screwed up, wasn't it? Maybe time as they knew it had simply ceased to be. She gazed down at her reflection in the pool of water.

"No, you stupid twit," she said, "it's just because you miss him. What a fool."

"Eh, miss? Was ye speakin' ta me?"

The castle gardener was down on his hands and knees digging at the base of one of the rose bushes. He had shuffled into the garden a few minutes after she arrived, clad in a long ragged tunic, greeting her with a bow and nonsensical muttering. He had long, gray hair straggling around his face, which was the dirtiest she'd ever seen— if the glimpse she'd gotten as he passed by was any indication.

"Nay, I was talkin' to myself," she told the man.

"Och, a daft one," he muttered and turned back to his digging.

Jix stuck her tongue out at his back. She was feeling particularly moody today. She'd risen at sunrise to catch Jamie before he left. As usual, she'd been too late. Ever since the night of what she inwardly called their "Almost Indiscretion," Jamie had gotten in the habit of coming to bed—or rather to the hard pallet on the floor—long after she'd finally fallen into an exhausted sleep, then rising before her and leaving the chamber.

She leaned her chin on her hand. She supposed Jamie spent his days looking for the sword, or at least she hoped so. That's what she'd been doing, fervently and painstakingly for the last three days. No dice. Jix sighed and took a deep, fragrant breath of the roses. For the last three days this tranquil spot had been her refuge, offering the only mental comfort she could find.

Maybe she should've told him the truth about her dream. She shook her head. No, she'd had too many experiences with doubters like Samantha to risk having Jamie think her a ditzy fool, too.

Even Griffin Campbell hadn't been around in the last three days to offer her some distraction. According to Red Hugh, his son was off collecting rent from a few of their outlying tenants. The laird had given her a tour of the castle and Jix had realized, with a sinking heart, just how big the place was and how easy it would be to hide a sword.

The castle had over fifty rooms inside the keep, upstairs and down, as well as the great hall that served as meeting/dining hall. There was a large kitchen, and the laird's study that, along with the hall, took up most of the lower level. Outside were an inner bailey and an outer bailey—courtyards of a sort. The inner bailey was reserved for the laird, his immediate family, and some of his most trusted men. The outer bailey was rather like a small village, with craftsmen and women hawking their wares. Many of the laird's renters lived within his gates, while others were scattered across the countryside.

The rose garden was actually to the side of the castle, enclosed by a fence and gated to keep out all but the laird's family. Red Hugh confided that it had been his wife's favorite spot.

Jix loved it, too. She wiggled her fingers to make a little splash across the surface of the water and smiled. Granite carved into big rounded squares enclosed a natural spring, forming a pool about eight feet across. The spring bubbled up from the bottom of the pool, and some ingenious medieval engineer had rigged a way to then take the water from the pool and recycle it by way of a lovely little rock waterfall positioned on the side of the stone enclosure. The rocks creating the pool were flat on top, making it possible to sit on the edge. Separate from the river used by the castle dwellers for their water supply, this fountain was reserved solely for the enjoyment of Red Hugh's family, and Jix had felt honored when he urged her to use it.

She wished she could share the lovely spot with Jamie. Where could he possibly be spending his time without her seeing him? Probably in the stable with some willing servant girl, she guessed. Someone who wouldn't play the tease. But she hadn't meant to tease. She wanted Jamie MacGregor more than any other man she'd ever known. But just as he had been about to take her to the stars, Samantha's face had appeared in her mind like a neon billboard. She had heard her friend shouting "Traitor! Betrayer! Slut!" and she couldn't go through with it.

Jix took a deep breath and released it, trying to push some of her inner tension away. She gazed up at the blue sky and watched as a butterfly drifted on a breeze into the garden and fluttered gently above the roses. It hovered for a moment, then dropped like a falling leaf to land on one of her hands. Iridescent blue wings opened and closed, their beauty bringing sudden tears to her eyes.

Irritated, Jix stood, sending the butterfly into the air. She was not going to become a helpless, crying, sentimental woman. This was exactly what she had feared! She almost let Jamie into her heart and look what happened—she was sitting here feeling sorry for herself because he was mad at her. Forget it. No sirreee bob. Not again. Not ever! She was lucky—*lucky*—that Jamie belonged to Samantha.

"Okay, God, I've learned my lesson," she muttered, lifting her eyes to the hazy Scottish sky. "I really have. Help me find the sword and Samantha and I promise, I'll really, really try to do better when we get back home. I won't pretend to be Yugoslavian or a phone sex girl or all those things that drove Sam crazy. Just please let me find her."

"Are ye talkin' to me, miss?" the scroungy gardener asked again, his voice as cranky as his scowl.

"No!" Jix reined in her temper. "I mean, nay, I wasna talkin' to ye. Please just attend to yer own business." She turned away, then gasped as she almost ran right into Griffin Campbell, all six foot four of him.

"Good morrow to ye," he said.

He wore an open-necked brown shirt with wide sleeves and collar. It laced up the front and had been tucked into what she had heard someone call "trews," which were loose trousers made from a kind of soft leather. The brown trousers in turn were thrust into knee-high brown boots. His long white-blond hair hung past his shoulders and his sensual smile made dimples appear in his lean, handsome cheeks. He held a silver goblet. He was beautiful, and yet Jix absolutely felt nothing when she looked at him. No desire, no lust, no oh-my-gosh-is-he-going-to-kiss-me, nothing.

Maybe because he's prettier than I am, she thought sourly. *Or maybe because he isn't Jamie,* a little demon in her mind suggested.

"Good morning, Griffin," she said brightly, arranging the folds of the dark blue skirt she wore. Red Hugh had generously provided several skirts and a variety of blouses.

"I was anxious to see ye," he said. "I'm sorry I had to rush away without telling ye goodbye." He held out the goblet. "Would ye care for some wine?"

Jix took the wine, noticing that his voice seemed softer, less arrogant. In fact, he seemed very different from the man who had practically seduced her at supper a few nights ago. He acted almost shy. Ridiculous. The man was a warrior, a lusty, sweaty warrior whose melting gaze in the great hall had been anything but timid. Still, she couldn't deny something was different.

She sipped the drink cautiously to give herself time to think. Griffin probably knew where Jamie's sword had been hidden. Maybe she could convince him to tell her. If he liked her at all, maybe she could distract him with, oh some mild flirting, and while he was distracted, she could ask him about the sword and maybe he'd answer. Yes, it might work. She lowered the goblet.

"Sit down, Griffin," she invited. He sat, but to Jix's surprise, made no move to touch her. She'd assumed that the first time he got her alone she'd be fighting for her honor. Interesting.

"I'm glad ye're back," she said, looking up at him through lowered lashes, hoping she looked sultry and not ridiculous.

He cleared his throat and coughed. "Aye, Maigrey, 'tis glad I am to be back. I've thought of ye every day."

Jix put the goblet down on the flat top of the fountain stone. She turned and laid her hand deliberately against Griffin's chest, leaning toward him. "And I've thought of ye every day too, Griffin, and every night."

"H-have ye?" he asked, pulling away from her slightly, his expression one of pain, not pleasure.

"Aye." She moved another inch closer. "After all, we are to be wed and that gives a lass pause for thought."

His Adam's apple bobbed up and down, and he leaned back a little further.

"In fact," Jix said softly, rising from the stone and sliding both hands up his shirt front, "I've been wondering what it would be like to—"

Griffin jerked away from her touch, practically doing a backbend in his haste to avoid her kiss. Startled, Jix grabbed him by the shirt and pulled back, keeping him from falling into the pool by mere inches.

They stumbled into one another, trying to regain their balance. Griffin pulled away as quickly as possible, his face red, flustered and apologetic.

"I'm sorry, Maigrey, I was—well, ye just surprised me."

"I'm so sorry, Griffin," Jix said. "I just don't seem to be able to do anything right."

"What's wrong with yer voice? Ye sound strange."

Jix's eyes widened. She'd slipped into her Texas drawl. Damn, she was already tired of keeping the Scottish brogue going. She cleared her throat. "Och, I just had something in my throat. Will ye walk with me?"

"I should—"

"Come along with ye," she said, forcing a lilt to her voice. "Ye've been away three whole days and I missed ye so much!" Jix linked her arm with his and led the way down the stone path that meandered through the dozens of rose bushes. She paused and bent her head to smell a dark red rose, drinking in the sweet fragrance. "Umm, it smells so heavenly."

"Aye," he said, giving her a wary glance.

Jix frowned. For all the world he looked like he was scared to death of her. But why?

Is it my breath? Maybe scrubbing my teeth with a twig just doesn't quite get the job done. And while it's true that I'm less than fragrant, what with having one bath since I've been here and no deodorant, but he's no rose garden himself.

"I'm sorry if I surprised ye," she said. "I just wanted to give ye a welcome-home kiss."

Griffin's face flushed and he wouldn't meet her eyes. "Aye, well, perhaps ye'd best wait on that until we're properly married, lass."

What in the world was going on? This same man had practically devoured her in front of the entire castle a few days ago. Had he changed his mind about marrying her or—? Jix had a sudden insight. "Have ye seen my brother today, Griffin?"

"Nay, lass, not today."

"Good. I mean, I'm glad he isn't around. He hovers over me like an auld man." She reached over and slid one finger down the middle of his chest. "I'm sure he wouldna approve of us being alone."

Griffin took a step back, then glanced behind him as if

to make sure he wasn't about to take another tumble.

Jix cocked one brow at him. "Griffin, are ye afraid of me?" He blushed and her jaw dropped. The mighty Griffin blushing?

"Of course not, Maigrey." He reached down and plucked a soft peach-colored rose from a nearby bush and held it out to her. Jix looked up into his eyes, expecting to see that panicky look again and instead there was a softness that hadn't been there before. She took the rose, feeling slightly confused. What was up with this guy? First he acted like he couldn't bear to have her kiss him, and now he looked at her like she was a banana split with a cherry on top. Yet he made no move to touch her or let her touch him. Fascinating.

"Thank ye, Griffin," she said, lowering her voice to a purr. "Ye are so sweet. I canna wait to marry ye."

The gardener was suddenly seized with a fit of coughing. He hacked and snorted and coughed until Jix thought the man must be dying. Finally he spit into the dirt.

"Hairball?" she asked, irritated at the interruption. The man ignored her. Jix turned back to Griffin with a smile.

"Yer brother doesna feel the same way," Griffin said.

Ah ha! Had Jamie been threatening him again? "What do ye mean?" She brought the rose to her lips, twisting it back and forth, never taking her eyes from his.

"I dinna think he approves of our marriage."

Jix smiled, stroking the rose petals down her throat slowly, languidly, gazing at him with sultry, bedroom eyes. She slid the flower down her chest to the crevice between her breasts, wetting her lips with her tongue, her eyelashes lowering, her head tipping back—

"Ow!"

"Are ye all right, lass?" Griffin asked, his voice filled with concern.

"It's just a thorn," Jix said, turning away and plucking the offending barb out of her breast. Too late she realized she had turned toward the gardener and he was watching her over one shoulder. He snorted again, a noise somewhere between a cough and a laugh. She glared at him, feeling like a complete idiot. Okay, forget the femme fatale routine. She casually dropped the rose and kicked it under a bush.

"I think ye are right about my brother," she said with a sigh, pulling Griffin on down the path, away from the obtrusive man on the ground. "He worries too much."

Griffin stopped and began plucking dead leaves from a rose bush, his brows knitting together as he avoided her eyes. "Aye, he acts fair strange about the betrothal." He paused, then rushed on. "Yesterday I told him I would like to move up the date of the weddin'. He looked at me with such murder in his eyes that I was startled." He glanced down at her. "If I dinna know better, I'd say he was jealous."

Jix opened her mouth then snapped it shut. Jealous? Jamie was jealous?

The gardener was seized with another coughing fit, but at least they were far enough from him now for it to be only mildly annoying.

"Jealous?" she laughed uneasily and laid one hand on his shirt. He took a step back, breaking their connection as he began shredding the leaves of another bush.

Jix felt totally confused. Every time she touched him, he freaked out. And yet, she could tell he was attracted to her.

"I know it sounds strange but he acts as though he is jealous of me. Do ye mean to say ye havena noticed?" he asked, breaking in on her thoughts.

Trick question? Jix considered. Was Griffin that devious? Did he hope to trick her into giving something away, or was she just being paranoid? She moved to another rose bush and bent to smell a fragrant red bloom. To her frustration the dirty old gardener had moved again and was just a couple of bushes away from them, digging happily in the dirt.

Jix straightened from the rose, careful not to touch the thorns. "Och, Griffin Campbell, brothers are no' jealous, they are protective! Do ye think there can be such a thing as a brother being too protective of his sister?"

"Perhaps," he said. "I would say 't'would depend on just how close a lass is to her brother."

Jix blinked. Griffin was a smart man. Of course, he was. He suspected they weren't brother and sister. Of course he did. The sexual tension between she and Jamie had been so thick at supper the night Griffin made his entrance that you could have sliced it with a knife. She had to fix this. Now.

"Jamie and I are close," she said, "but, I must confess, all is not as it seems."

Griffin looked up from the leaves in his hands and raised both brows. "What do ye mean?"

Jix sighed. "I canna deceive ye any longer, Griffin," she said, her voice hesitant, "not if we are to be wed. It's just that," she glanced at him, then quickly away, "well, Jamie hasna been entirely honest with ye and yer father."

The big Scot shifted his feet, looking vastly uncomfortable. "He hasna? What has he lied to us about?"

Jix let go of her skirt and clasped her hands together at her chest. "I dinna dare to tell ye. Ye wouldna want to marry me." She covered her face with her hands and moaned plaintively.

Griffin patted her shoulder, his touch awkward at best. "Now Maigrey, dinna say that. If we're to be married ye must learn to trust me."

She moved quickly into the crook of his arm, leaning her head against his chest as if she'd grown weak. She summoned a tear or two, allowing them to trickle down her cheeks.

Damn, I'm good. Maybe I should think twice about giving up my acting career. Not that there's much to give up.

"Oh, Griffin, if only I could trust ye." Jix looked up at him, raising her brows in fervent despair. "But ye must swear never to tell yer father, or to tell Jamie that I told ye."

He patted her again. Jix frowned. What had happened to the suave, worldly Griffin of supper a few nights ago? In private he was nervous, hesitant, and shy. A beautiful Barney Fife. What was up?

163

"I promise, Maigrey," he said, dropping his hand away from her shoulder. "What secret are ye hiding?"

The gardener started hacking again and this time Jix felt sure the man was going to expire in the dust. She pulled Griffin by the arm and led him a few feet away to a small wooden bench under a beautiful rose trellis. She sat and pulled him down beside her. He immediately moved a few inches away from her, his face a little pale.

Jix frowned and clasped her hands in her lap. "Och, Griffin, ye are so kind, I feel that I truly can trust ye. Ye see, Jamie is overprotective of me because, well, because," she bit her lip as if afraid to go on, then let the words rush out, "I do like the laddies, if ye ken what I mean."

Griffin's jaw dropped. "Ye mean ye are no' a maiden?" he asked, astonishment in his voice.

"No, no," she said hastily, realizing her blunder. "I am still a maiden." She wet her lower lip with her tongue and saw desire dart suddenly into his gaze. Why then did he act so standoffish? So hands-offish? "But that hasna stopped me from enjoying a laddie now and then and letting him enjoy me—do ye understand, Griffin?"

She looked up at him with what she hoped passed for adoration, then groaned as she saw the gardener walking toward them, head down, muttering to himself.

"Aye, lassie," Griffin said, a pained look on his face, "that I do. And yer brother doesna like ye, er, enjoying the laddies, is that it?"

Jix thrust out her lower lip into a childish pout and crossed her arms under her breasts. "My brother is a stuffy auld man who doesna ken that a young woman is filled with passion, and e'en though she might want to wait until her wedding night to totally give herself to her husband, well, there's something to be said for a little experience in the meantime."

The gardener shuffled closer to them, oblivious to the piercing look Jix shot him. He dropped to his knees again behind the trellis and started grubbing in the dirt. Jix rolled her eyes and tried to ignore him.

"Aye, experience," Griffin murmured. "Experience is nice."

Experience is nice? The statement brought Jix back to attention. *What is wrong with the man?*

"Dinna fash yerself about it," he said. "I will keep yer secret."

"Oh, thank ye, Griffin!" She threw her arms around his neck and kissed him on the cheek, then drew back slightly. His eyes were round, panic-stricken.

"Griffin? Griffin, are you all right?" she asked.

"Aye, aye," he whispered.

Time to strike. "Tell me," Jix said softly, keeping her arms about his neck. "Do ye know where yer father is keeping Jamie's sword? My brother is so fond of it, ye ken. If I could just tell him it's being well cared for it would make him so happy."

"S-sword?" Griffin stuttered. "I dinna know if my father would want me to—"

Jix pressed a kiss fully against his lips. If she didn't know better, she'd think Griffin Campbell had never been kissed before, but of course that couldn't be true. Red Hugh had boasted about his son's reputation.

"Och, please, Griffin—I'd be so grateful."

"No, I shouldna—"

She kissed him again, this time with more passion. Griffin started suddenly shrinking out her arms and Jix pulled away to find that he had slid completely out of her embrace and collapsed to the ground, a stunned expression on his face.

Griffin scrambled to his feet. Jix helped him stand and he grabbed her around the waist. She expected him to back away as soon as possible, but he didn't. Jix could feel him trembling. His eyes looked rather wild, and instinctively she stepped back, alarmed. From the corner of her eye she saw the gardener standing and shuffling toward them.

"Och, well, never ye mind, Griffin, I think I'll go in now myself," Jix said. "It was lovely speaking with ye, and—"

Griffin reached out and drew her back, his hand strong

165

around her upper arm. Jix's throat constricted as she saw the determined look on his face, his sensual lips pressed tightly together, his jaw firm with resolve. She realized all at once that maybe she wasn't as in control of the situation as she'd thought. After all, she wasn't dealing with a twenty-first century man, rather, one not far removed from the barbaric Celts who used to paint their faces blue and fight naked with clubs.

Another butterfly drifted by them and the scent of roses suddenly seemed almost cloying. They were alone except for the old man shuffling their way, who would probably cheer if the laird's son got a little. If Griffin attacked her now, would anyone respond if she screamed? And if she did scream, Griffin would know she had been lying about her "experience" and they would be ruined. Jix really couldn't imagine Griffin harming her. Of course, she had never dreamed Dirk would punch her in the nose for asking if he would mind drinking his coffee without cream.

"Excuse me, miss, but is ennythin' wrong?" a graveled voice asked.

Griffin scowled and Jix turned to face her rescuer. The gardener must have been a tall man once, but now was hunched over, a growth on his back, his limbs bowed with age.

"Get on with ye, man," Griffin cried, moving to stand between her and the man. "How dare ye interrupt a private conversation?"

The old man looked at the ground and tugged his forelock. "Yer pardon, yer pardon, sir, but I just wanted to be of assistance to the lady."

Griffin's hand came down on the hilt of his sword. "The lady is fine," he said, giving the old man a furious look.

"Young laird, be advised," the gardener said, his eyes narrow, " 'tis an ill wind that blows against those who would defile a maiden."

Griffin took a furious step toward the man. "Get out old man!" he shouted. "And dinna come back or I'll gut ye like a pig!"

The gardener didn't move, just stood there with a stubborn look on his horrible face. He had a huge lump of a nose, covered with a brown coating, and Jix realized he must have some sort of disease. His skin appeared to be crumbling away. She looked closer. No, his face was just covered with mud! Ugh. Strangely enough, his eyes gleamed with intelligence, and at the moment, anger. Interesting—for an ugly old man he certainly had lovely blue eyes.

"Griffin, darlin'," Jix said, "dinna grow so angry. I appreciate the man's concern, and there is a way he can help me."

"Help ye?" Griffin shot the old man another furious look. "Anythin' ye need, I can aid ye, Maigrey."

"Och, no, Griffin. I wouldna ask this of ye." She gestured toward the pool at the other side of the garden. "I dropped a bracelet in the pool yesterday and couldna reach it. Mayhap this kind man would fetch it for me."

"Of course he will," Griffin said arrogantly. "He works for me, does he no'? Fetch the bracelet, ye varlet!"

The servant ducked his head again as if remembering his place and shuffled back down the garden path toward the pool of water. Jix followed, her hands linked behind her, a smile on her face.

"Where be it, miss?" the gardener asked when he reached the stone enclosure.

"Back there." Jix pointed to the bottom of the pool on the other side of the rock waterfall. "I think it fell beneath one of the stones near the bottom."

Griffin stood to one side, his arms folded over his chest, an impatient look on his face. The old man leaned across the wide granite rocks, reaching down into the water, drenching his upper body as he did. When the gardener lifted one dirty foot to stretch a bit further, Jix planted both hands on his rump and pushed.

There was a tremendous splash as the man fell headfirst into the water, his legs flying upward. Water gushed out over the stones into the garden, soaking Jix's feet and the edge of her skirt. Griffin lifted one foot and shook the water from his boots.

"Maigrey, I dinna blame ye for no' liking the gardener's interference, but I planned to just have him flogged, no' drowned!"

"That's no gardener!" Jix said triumphantly as the man burst free from the surface of the pool gasping, the mud from his hair and face staining the clear water brown. "That is Jamie MacGregor!" She stood with her hands on her hips, gazing down into the furious blue eyes of her "brother." "How dare ye spy on us?"

Jamie stood, water coursing from his hair and body into the pool. He glared at Jix and stepped over the stones to shake like a dog, throwing water on Jix and Griffin.

Jix shrieked, holding up her hands to shield her face. Griffin wiped the dirty water from his face, a dangerous look in his eyes. He stepped over and grabbed Jamie by the shoulder.

"What is this game ye're about, MacGregor?" he demanded. "Ye think to spy upon me? When my father hears about it he'll lock ye in the dungeon and feed ye bread and water."

"It might be a nice improvement from the usual swill around this place," Jamie said darkly, jerking away from Griffin's grasp. He squeezed water from the edge of the ragged tunic he wore. "And I wasna spying on ye. I was just lookin' after my foolish sister."

"Foolish?" Jix was really furious now. Not only did Jamie not trust her, but he still thought her foolish—a mindless, silly woman. She clenched her fists at her side. "I am no' foolish just because I want a few minutes alone to get to know my betrothed!"

"Aye, but I said that ye canna 'get to know yer betrothed,' as ye put it, before yer weddin' night." He shot Griffin a baleful glance. "Have ye no honor, Campbell? Would ye defile her in a garden when ye have only to wait a few days to make it legal before God?"

"Dinna challenge my honor, MacGregor," Griffin said,

his face dark, his jaw tight. "Or ye'll find yer head on the ground beside ye."

"No!" Jix cried, moving between the two men. A tremor of premonition ran through her. She blinked and shook away the sense of foreboding. "Stop it, both of you—ye. Jamie, I want to talk to ye alone. Griffin, I'll see ye at supper, all right?"

Griffin stood like a stone for a moment, then turned to Jix and nodded. "All right, Maigrey, but talk to yer brother and advise him to rein in his temper, or he'll be rottin' in the dungeon of Meadbrooke on our weddin' day. All I wanted was to ask if ye would like to go for a ride on the morrow?"

"A ride?" she echoed. A ride. Out of the castle. Out of Meadbrooke. Finally, a way to look for Samantha! "Of course!"

"Not without me, ye won't!" Jamie said, his chin jutting out stubbornly.

"I am warnin' ye, MacGregor—"

"It will be all right, Griffin," Jix interrupted his tirade, her voice soothing. "Go on with ye now."

With one more furious glance in Jamie's direction, Griffin turned and strode out of the garden.

Jix turned back to Jamie, ready to read him the riot act, when he pulled her into his arms and kissed her—long and hard.

"Is that what ye were lookin' for, lass?" he asked, his voice smugly furious, his hands so tight on her waist that it hurt.

Jix gazed up at him, leaned back, and slapped him squarely across the face.

Chapter Eleven

Jamie stalked into their chamber, soaking wet, dirty streaks running down his cheeks, his face stinging. He could imagine what he looked like, wearing clothes fit for a beggar, coated in mud, muttering to himself. He had turned into a half-crazy lunatic because of an impetuous redhead. And now he had acted as loutish as her ex-husband and there was no excuse for it.

"Aye, lad, ye've sunk to a new low, in more ways than one." He pulled the wet tunic over his head and used it to wipe the dirty streaks from his face.

After Jix's abrupt rejection three nights ago and the reason given for it, Jamie had resolved to leave her alone. He didn't need her kind of insanity in his life, and if they ever did get back home again, he knew they didn't have a chance in hell of making it together. Even if he could convince her not to remarry her ex-husband, he had some serious reservations about entering into a relationship with a woman who would even consider returning to such an abusive situation. With that in mind, he refused to get further involved.

Jamie tossed the tunic to the floor and stripped off the clingy trousers he wore, then reached for his plaid and wrapped it around his middle. He liked Jix, actually adored her, in spite of how crazy she drove him. And without being too conceited, he felt pretty sure she still wanted him, regardless of her claim to still love her ex-husband. Jamie wasn't about to make love to her casually. He had no desire to have his heart broken again, and she was so damned tempting he didn't trust himself. So he had stayed away from her, coming into the chamber late at night, sleeping on the floor, rising before her. But he was still determined to protect Jix from Red Hugh's men, and especially from the laird's son, and so he had come up with a way to watch Jix without her ever knowing he was there.

Stage makeup in the seventeenth century was a little hard to come by in a remote area like this, so Jamie had improvised. Mud painted on his face to give him an aged look—if you didn't get too close—had helped to make a crude disguise. Ragged clothing had been easily obtained. Add to that the appropriate hunched-over walk, a wadded-up shirt for a hump on his back, flour in his hair to denote age, and a raspy voice, and Jamie had transformed himself into an old man.

In this costume, he had followed Jix for the last three days, hurrying in at night, eating after everyone else in the kitchen, waiting till she was asleep to wash up and go to bed. But today when he'd seen Griffin pawing her in the garden, he just couldn't stand by and watch any longer. So he'd blown his cover and his temper. And now Jix was justifiably angry. She probably wouldn't talk to him for a week. No matter. He had to leave the next day to reive the English cattle and there was a good chance he wouldn't make it back anyway.

Now there's some positive thinking.

Jamie stretched, reaching his hands over his head. His back was killing him after walking hunched over all day. This was the kind of stuff he did every day for Scotland Yard. He'd be damned if he'd do it on his holiday, too. On his holiday! That was truly funny. Who would ever believe he'd taken a vacation to the seventeenth century? He mused over the thought, then turned back to planning what he would say when Jix came through the door.

He would apologize of course. But what was wrong with the woman? Did she really think it safe to be in a secluded garden with a barbaric Celt who thought he was betrothed to her? The lass was absolutely without any common sense. No, that wasn't entirely fair. He figured she had met with Griffin to try to milk him for information about the sword. Jamie overheard her asking about the blade, but hadn't been able to make out the man's answer. He knew she'd already turned the castle upside down looking for the sword. Jamie had searched too, during times when he knew her to be safely occupied, but like Jix, had come up empty-handed.

And he knew that the reason she wanted to go riding with Griffin Campbell was to look for Samantha. He understood her desperation to find her friend, but if she thought she was going to ride out of this castle alone with that blond-haired bastard, she had another think coming.

What was keeping her? Surely she hadn't dared to go off with Griffin after his warning. Alarmed, Jamie clutched the plaid to his waist and rushed out into the corridor, coming to a halt at the top of the stairs.

Below him, Jix stood just inside the huge double doors of the vestibule, staring into the great hall. Jamie peered over the banister to see what had captured her attention. One of the cooks sat at a trestle table holding a little girl about four years old on her lap. The little girl was laughing, clapping her hands together as the woman bounced the child up and down on her knees.

Jamie's anger faded somewhat as he saw the wistful look on Jix's face. Was she thinking about her real mother? Or perhaps the aunt who had died. Or her adopted mother? There had been so many losses in Jix's life, and she had met them so bravely, just as she was meeting their challenge now. She had more courage than any woman he'd ever known, but he wasn't going to let her plunge recklessly into a dangerous situation.

"Lass," he said quietly.

Jix looked up at him, tears shimmering on her lashes. She blinked them back, and he watched as fury blazed back into her forest green eyes.

"I am not speaking to you!" she hissed, stamping one foot.

Jamie couldn't help but smile. The gesture was so petulant, so completely unlike Jix. She apparently took his smile for a taunt because she turned scarlet and ran up the stairs to their chamber, pushing past him. Jamie followed, reaching the entranceway just as she tried to slam the door shut. He stopped it with the flat of his hand and winced as his wrist jarred into his arm.

"Ye don't get off that easily. Let me in."

"No, you might attack me again." She was leaning her full weight on the door from the other side. Luckily for him, her full weight wasn't much. Jamie simply secured the plaid around his waist and then used both hands to shove the door open, knocking Jix to the floor. She lay sprawled on the stone, glaring up at him as he walked in and shut the door behind him.

"Hello, lass. Been a busy little bee today, haven't ye?"

Jix scrambled to her feet. "How dare you follow me around! Here I am working like a dog, trying to find the sword and arrange to leave the castle to look for Samantha, and you're busy playing secret agent man!"

Jamie frowned and leaned back against the wall, his arms folded over his chest. "I wasna playing at anything. I could tell Griffin and his father were growing suspicious of our relationship. I wanted to make sure ye were safe without them knowing I was keeping watch over ye."

"Ha!" Jix said, stabbing one finger toward him. "And you did a great job of that today, didn't you? Griffin is more suspicious than ever! The truth is, you don't trust me! You think I'm going to say something I shouldn't, or otherwise mess up, don't you?"

"No, of course not. I know ye have more sense than that."

That seemed to stop her for a minute. She looked at

him, hands on her hips, her head thrown back defiantly. Jamie wanted to kiss the defiance out of her. He wanted to rip off that sexy blouse and bodice thing she wore every day and toss it aside. He'd leave the skirt on though. Maybe put the bodice thing back on her, too. The thought of making love to her, half-clothed, made him grow hard. In the little he was wearing, it became quickly obvious.

Jix's gaze flickered over him, lighting first on his bare chest, then to the plaid around his waist, and his obvious desire. Her eyes widened as if she had just realized he was half-naked and ready for action.

He wanted to lose himself inside of her.

"MacGregor," she said breathlessly, "what are you thinking?"

"I'm thinking. . . ." he crossed to her side. She watched him with her lips parted, the look in her eyes almost fearful. Was she afraid of him? "I'm thinking that ye never look lovelier than when ye're angry and aren't tryin' to hide it. I'm sorry if I frightened ye before, lass. I would never hurt ye."

Color rushed into her face and he lifted his hand to smooth his thumb across the blush of her cheek. Her eyelashes lowered, then sprang back up as the plaid at his waist fell to the floor.

"MacGregor. . . ." Jix whispered.

His hand slid from her face to her collarbone and he traced the soft line to the center of her chest, then dragged one finger downward between her breasts, scrunching the blouse, stopping at the ties of her corset. He tugged her toward him and lowered his mouth to hers.

Oh yes. Jix Ferguson had the most exquisite mouth and she yielded it so sweetly. Her hands slipped around his waist and she moaned as he slid his hands down from her shoulders to her breasts. He opened his eyes and blinked when she stepped away. A second later his plaid hit him across the face.

"Stop it, MacGregor. There's no time for fun and games. We have work to do."

Jamie stared at her. "Ye are the most absolutely exasperating woman I have ever met. Do ye enjoy making my life miserable?"

"Speaking of miserable, I bet that's how Samantha is feeling right now!" Jix straightened her blouse. "We've got to find her! She is one of the nicest women I've ever known."

"Ye could have fooled me," Jamie said, wrapping his plaid back around himself.

Her eyes widened. "What do you mean? Sam is terrific. I did a terrible thing to her and of course she reacted. But she's my best friend. She's beautiful, she's talented, she's going to be a famous doctor someday. She cooks, decorates, loves kids"—she walked back and forth across the room, gesturing wildly with her hands—"I mean, she's everything I'm not! When we find her again, you two should get together and go out."

Jamie folded his arms over his chest. Now what was this all about? "Why?" he asked, bluntly.

Jix bit her lower lip and for a minute he thought she was going to cry. But instead she laughed again. How he was beginning to hate that false sound! "Because you'd like Sam, really you would. You two have a lot in common."

"What do we have in common?" he asked, moving toward the fire. "Where did these come from?" He picked up a pile of clothes from a chair—two pairs of trousers, or trews, and two clean shirts.

"Oh, I told Red Hugh you needed some clothes. Why don't you put them on before you get a cold or something."

Jamie smiled. "All right." He pulled the plaid from his waist and dropped it on the floor.

She glared at him. "Do you always have to think with your—your—"

"My what?"

"Your hormones?"

Jamie's face fell. "And here I thought I was finally going to get to hear some dirty language from ye." He picked up a pair of the trews. "I'm disappointed, lass."

"I bet," she said, turning her back to him. "Oh, but if

you like dirty talk, then Samantha's your girl! She's got a mouth like a sailor when she gets riled up and—"

"Enough, lass, enough."

Jamie pulled on the clothes and walked across the room. Gently he turned Jix to face him.

"Now what's this all about, really? We're in a rather precarious situation, don't ye think, to be playing matchmaker?"

Jix shrugged. "It was just a thought."

"Are we friends again, then?"

She smiled automatically and the gesture hurt him. He wanted her to smile when she was happy, frown when she was sad, and scream bloody murder when she was mad. In spite of his dip in the pool, he'd actually had a great day, because for the first time, Jix was really expressing the way she felt, and he loved it.

"Of course we are," she said.

"Would ye like to go down for supper?" he asked, extending his arm to her.

She hesitated. Her green eyes flashed up at him and for just a second, he saw the pain she was trying so desperately to hide.

"Let me change and I'll meet you downstairs. But later, we need to talk. We have to make a plan to find Samantha."

"Aye, lass, we will, on one condition."

She blinked. "What condition?"

Jamie reached up and rubbed his jaw. "Ye dinna slug me again."

The brightness returned to her gaze and she laughed as he opened the door to leave.

"I make no promises, MacGregor," she said lightly. "I make no promises."

"Ye're still pouting."

Jamie poured another drink. He and Jix sat at one of the trestle tables after supper, nursing their second bottle of wine. The rest of the hall was deserted. Red Hugh had gone to bed—supposedly. In actuality, he and Fergus were busy gathering the supplies needed for the raid against the English. In a few hours, just before dawn, Jamie and Fergus and four other men would ride to the border. It would take most of the day and night. Once there, they would attack the English soldiers as they herded their cattle toward the stockade, then return to Meadbrooke—in one piece he hoped.

"I am not pouting," she insisted, half-lying across the table, her long red hair trailing over her arms. She'd had four glasses of wine and just minutes ago Jamie had refused to give her anymore. She'd stuck her tongue out at him and begun to pout. Again.

"Of course ye are. Griffin practically ignored ye at supper."

"Shut up, MacGregor."

Jamie took a drink, savoring the wine. At least that was one area where Red Hugh never skimped. His food might not be fit for hogs, but his wine was the best.

"Are the two of ye plotting something?" he asked.

"Yes, your demise," she said, looking up at him, her green eyes unintentionally sultry, her words slightly slurred. He wanted to ravish her right there on the table, pour wine down her naked flesh and lick it off. Jamie blinked, realizing he'd missed the last thing she'd said.

"What did ye say?"

"I said, I asked Griffin where your sword is. Aren't you listening, MacGregor?"

He put his goblet down and leaned toward her, his hand closing involuntarily over her arm. He'd heard her ask the question of Griffin but hadn't been able to hear the answer. He'd assumed she'd had no success. "And what did he say?"

"He wouldn't tell me."

Jamie released his pent-up breath. Damn. "I'm not surprised."

She lifted half-closed eyes to his, a provocative smile on her lips. "Well, at least I tried. I thought I could kiss the information out of him. Aren't you proud of me? Giving all for the cause?"

Jamie released her arm and poured more wine into his pewter goblet. It had been difficult to keep from throwing Griffin into a rose bush when he saw him kissing Jix. Although, to give the man the benefit of the doubt, it looked like it had been mostly Jix kissing him.

"Aye," he said flatly, "I'm sore proud."

Jix smiled and shrugged. "Even if I'd found out I wasn't going to tell you."

"Why not?"

She lifted one hand and gestured to the great hall. "It's so obvious that you enjoy being here, playing Renaissance man, I didn't think you cared if we ever left." Her head fell forward again on her arms.

"Why do ye say that? Ye know I want to go home as much as ye do." Jamie took another drink. Did she really think that? Did she really think he was enjoying this?

Jix lifted her head from her arms, her eyes bleary but still alert enough to shoot sparks. "But you don't want to find Samantha as bad as I do. Why did you interfere with Griffin today? He wanted to take me for a ride. I could have ridden out and found Sam!"

"Why did I—" he shook his head. "Jix, ye just don't think before ye do these things. Ye're like a child—"

"A child!" She stood, her good humor gone. Jamie saw real, unadulterated fury in her eyes. "I am not a child and I'm sick of being treated like one. You sit around here with your injured male ego, skulking around the castle playing your little head games while I'm trying to actually do something to help us!"

"Head games? What are ye talking about?"

"I'm talking about this!" She bent over and hobbled in an erratic path across to the fireplace. "Look at me, I'm an auld man, I'm an auld dirty man," Jix croaked, then straightened. "How stupid do you think I am?"

"Ye paid me back for it. I still have water in my ears."

"Serves you right." Jix paused and gave him a long look. "You don't trust me, that's why you followed me."

Jamie looked down into his wine, struggling for words. How could he explain the nerve-shattering fear he felt every time she left his sight, not to mention the jealousy that seared him when Griffin Campbell cast his lusting eyes her way? He'd sound like a fool.

"I told ye, I just didn't want anyone to bother ye. But I suppose ye want that great piece of muscle slobbering over ye. Have ye slept with him yet?"

He immediately wished he could take the words back. Her jaw tightened and her eyes glimmered with either anger or hurt. Did she mean to cry or slug him? Jamie took another drink. Maybe she had the right idea. Get drunk and forget the whole damn situation. But he couldn't. He had to rise before dawn and ride across Scotland to steal cows from Englishmen.

"That," Jix said icily, "is none of your damned business!" She released her breath explosively. "And for your information I can take care of myself!"

"Och, here we go again." He slammed his goblet down and rose from the table. She had on a jade green dress tonight, different from the skirt and blouse ensembles she usually wore. The gown was cut from a beautiful brocade material, the sleeves tight to the elbow, then wide to the wrist. The low-cut, lace-trimmed bodice exposed more of her breasts than usual, while making her waist appear much smaller. The jade of the material deepened her eyes to the color of the Scottish meadows. The full skirt drifted romantically to the floor and as Jix stood there shooting fire at him from her meadow green eyes, he remembered suddenly, from her garb of three nights ago, that she probably wore no panties under her regal trappings.

Jamie jerked his gaze away from her and paced across the room, his mouth going dry, other parts of him growing hard. He could lay her down in front of the fireplace, right here in the great hall, and make love to her, driving the thought of any other man from her mind and her body. He could seduce her, make her feel things no other man could make her feel, and then afterward, exact a promise from her that she would never marry her ex-husband. He could tell Red Hugh the truth and Jix would never marry Griffin. He could hold Red Hugh hostage until he returned his sword. He could—Jamie took a deep breath. He could get his rampaging hormones under control.

Another breath and the red haze left his vision. He shook his head and glanced over at her. "Lass, what am I going to do with ye?"

Jix looked at him from across the room, lips parted, her eyes widening with surprise. The firelight sent soft shadows over her face, painting a golden glow across her skin.

"I can think of a few things," she whispered.

Jamie stared at her for a long moment, then practically sprang across the room, crossing the distance between them in three quick strides. He stopped abruptly a few inches from her. He longed to take her into his arms, but stood there fighting the desire, knowing he wouldn't be able to control his passion if he touched her again.

"Ah, lass," he said softly, "dinna tempt me."

A slow smile eased across her lips and he wanted to kiss her more than he wanted to breathe. But he didn't. Not even when she reached up and patted his face.

"Och, laddie," Jix said softly, using her brogue, "ye know I'm only teasin' ye. I'm a flirt and a tease and I dinna mean anythin' by it." She held his gaze as if she wanted to say more. Finally she turned and headed toward the stairs, a trifle unsteady from the wine.

"Jix, wait. What are yer plans for tomorrow?"

She slowly looked around at him and winked. "I don't think I'll tell you," she said. Jamie was suddenly aware of just how drunk she really was.

"Why not?"

"Because I can't remember." Her smile turned into a yawn. "That wine is getting to me. Let's go to bed." She started toward the stairs again, her skirt swishing rhythmically against the dirty rushes on the floor, her hips twitching back and forth.

"I can't think of anything I'd rather do," he said softly. Jix hesitated on the first step. She glanced back at him, a lopsided grin on her face.

"Och, laddie, and me almost a married lady."

Jamie raked one hand through his hair. He was tired.

Tired of wanting Jix Ferguson. Tired of dreaming of holding her in his arms, of kissing her hot mouth, of licking her from top to toe. He wanted her and it was like knowing you wanted to be a kamikaze pilot. Emotional suicide, that was what loving Jix Ferguson would mean. Loving her? Where had that thought come from? He looked up and found her green eyes gazing down at him, a softness and a yearning in their depths. He drew in a shuddering breath. She wanted him just as much. There it was, mirrored in her eyes. All he had to do was reach out and take her by the hand and lead her upstairs. He knew it as surely as he knew they were trapped in the past.

But he didn't take her hand. Instead he took another breath and spoke what had been on his mind half the day.

"Jokes aside, lass, I've been thinking."

"Dangerous habit, MacGregor," she shot back.

"Anything could happen while we're here, ye ken?" he said, wishing he could kiss that infuriating "I'm fine, everything's fine" smile off her lips. "And I just want ye to know that if anything should happen to me—"

The smile disappeared. "Don't say that!" She stepped down from the stairs and rushed across the space dividing them. She grabbed his arm, her fingers biting into his flesh. "It's bad luck. Say a prayer, quick!" Her face turned ashen and for a minute Jamie thought she would faint.

"Jix, what's wrong?"

She closed her eyes and began to tremble. Jamie moved quickly to take her in his arms and she clung to him, her arms sliding around his waist. He could feel her small fingers digging into his back.

"Lass, what is it?"

"Nothing's going to happen to you, do you hear me?" she said fiercely against his shirt. "And nothing's going to happen to Sam, either. We're going to find her and get the sword and we're all going to go back home." She opened her eyes and Jamie looked down into two pools of pain. "Do you hear me? That's the way it's going to be. I'm not going to lose either of you."

"All right," he said softly, "all right. Everything's going

to be fine." He brushed a strand of hair back from her face, his fingers lingering on her jaw. "Ye've had too much wine, lass. Let's get ye to bed."

To Jamie's surprise she let him lead her up to the chamber. There he helped her change into her nightgown and tucked her into bed. He kissed her on the forehead but before he could draw away she encircled his neck with her arms.

"What a nice big brother," she said, her voice slurred and slightly sarcastic. "I should have warned you about me and wine, though. It goes straight to my head."

"I'll remember that," he jokingly replied, "for a time when it might do me some good." Her breasts were soft and warm against his chest and it took all his resolve not to take advantage of the situation.

She giggled. "You don't need wine to get me in the mood, MacGregor."

"Hush," he said lightly. "Go to sleep, lass. Sweet dreams." He kissed her forehead again and moved out of her arms. She yawned and stretched like a kitten, then turned on her side with her hands folded under her cheek.

As soon as Jix's breathing became even, Jamie slid down beside her and closed his eyes. A few hours sleep was all he could hope for before rising and heading out on this foolish quest Red Hugh had insisted upon. He wanted to tell Jix. He hated to just leave and say nothing, but he knew if he told her, she would insist on going with him. No, it was better this way, even if it did make her worry. He'd tell Red Hugh to reassure her, to promise her that he would be all right, without giving away where he had gone, and why. Then he'd be back in two or three days and tell her where he'd been. Red Hugh would give him his sword. He'd find Samantha. They'd return to their own time. All of this would be like a strange and wondrous dream. Jix would go back to her crazy madcap world, and he would go back to Scotland Yard.

Jamie sighed, wishing there was some way to meld their worlds, to make them work together. But it was too risky. He wasn't willing to take a chance on hurting her. That was the last thing he wanted to do.

Chapter Twelve

Jix awoke in the night to find her mouth sour and Jamie lying beside her, his chest rising and falling with the rhythm of sleep. It was the first time he'd slept beside her in days and she enjoyed being able to lie there and look at him, drinking her fill of him, with no one the wiser.

He hadn't shaved recently and she wondered if he planned to let his beard grow and become as furry and barbaric as Red Hugh's. She hoped not. She loved his face, the strong line of his jaw, his stubborn chin. His lips. His eyes. His chest. Almost groaning aloud, Jix turned over, away from him. She had it bad. She really did. Jamie must have banked the fire in the fireplace, but a languid heat still clung to the air, making it hard to sleep. She closed her eyes and tried to picture something that would help keep Jamie MacGregor's chest from her thoughts.

A green meadow. Wasn't that what they always said to picture? A beautiful green meadow with butterflies dancing in the breeze and a trickling brook nearby. Maybe a little cottage in the distance. Jix drummed her fingers on top of her stomach. Bor—ing. Okay, start over. A green meadow and butterflies and a brook and across the meadow a knight on a shining black charger. She smiled. Yeah, that's the ticket. A knight—and oh, look—big surprise—it's Jamie.

Her heart began to pound a little faster as she imagined him swinging down from the huge beast and striding across the waving grass to her, pulling her against him, his mouth possessing hers. Her fingers wove into his long hair, tugging him closer as she molded her body into his, their mutual desire burning like a hot, molten—

Jix sat up, her breath coming hard, every muscle in her body on fire, taut with the need for release. She risked a glance at Jamie again, feeling the ache curl around her heart, then turned on her stomach and buried her face in her pillow.

Okay, so she would think about candy bars. Not James MacGregor. Candy Bars. Chocolate bars. Picture unwrapping the foil slowly. Taking a bite of the mouth-watering treat and letting it melt in her mouth. Mmmmm. Delicious. Jix felt some of the tension leave her. She broke off another piece and—what was she doing? She was handing it to someone—a man—a man with long, dark hair and burning blue eyes. She offered him the sweet. He took it but didn't eat it, instead he lifted her hand to his lips, and licked the melted chocolate from her fingers, drawing each one into his mouth, sucking them one at a time. Jix shivered with delight and when he took her lips again, he tasted of chocolate and salt and heat and—

"Well, hell." Jix flopped over on her back and released her breath explosively. "As Sam would say, I freaking give up."

Maybe it was the sound of Jamie's even breathing that finally soothed her into total relaxation, or maybe she was just more weary than she'd realized, but gradually Jix felt herself slipping into a deep sleep, her breathing soon matching the man's beside her.

She was in the meadow again, every blade of grass watercolor soft, as if it had been painted with a delicate brush. Butterflies danced around her and heather bloomed profusely across the beautiful dell. She could hear the trickling of a nearby brook and suddenly she wanted to break into song and dance, she felt so content. The smell of heather and roses permeated the air with their sweet perfume. In the distance she could see faint purple mountains soft with haze. She was completely alone.

Her contentment vanished. She was lost, confused. Why was she alone? Where were Jamie and Samantha? Jix gazed across the lonely field and in the far distance finally made out the turrets of Meadbrooke Castle. How had she wandered so far from the castle and why? She shaded her eyes from the unseasonably bright sunlight and turning, scanned the horizon in the other direction. The blue of the Scottish sky seemed unusually bright today, marred only by the haze of brown clouds near the ground. Brown clouds?

Jix blinked, one hand flying to her throat as she saw dozens of horses galloping toward her, dirt flying out from behind their hooves. She turned and ran, her long skirt tangling around her legs, trying to trip her. Jerking the material up to her knees, she didn't look back, but kept running.

Before long the horses caught up with Jix and rushed past her, as if she didn't exist. She stumbled to a stop, gasping for breath, and watched as men on horseback rode past. One of the men carried a flag atop a long pole. The British flag, red cross over white. Now Jix gathered her skirts again and tore across the countryside after them, afraid she would be too late to warn those in the castle. The sky grew darker as she ran, until she feared the darkness itself chased her, waiting for a chance to swallow her whole.

When she arrived at Meadbrooke Castle, Jix rushed inside. The hall seemed deserted. A tall man with black hair and piercing black eyes stood behind a table in the center of the room. The table was covered with a long black cloth, and lying across it was a bloody sword and a large covered serving platter. The man lifted the rounded lid from the platter. Horror welled up inside of Jix, but she could not give it utterance, all she could do was stare.

185

Jamie's disembodied head sat upon the platter, blood dripping from his neck and a gash on his head.

Then he opened his eyes.

The scream came ripping from her throat like a living entity trying to escape, then another, and another, until the agony of sound threatened to tear her apart.

"Lass, lass! Jix—wake up!"

Jix opened her eyes and found she sat bolt upright, trembling in Jamie MacGregor's arms. She threw her own around his neck and sobbed outright against his broad, comforting chest.

"Oh God, oh God, oh God!" she cried, the memory of the terrible dream assailing her even as she tried to push it away. She clung to Jamie, her heart pounding.

This had been the worst, the absolute worst dream she'd ever had. The only dream remotely close to it in terror was the one she'd had at four years old—the one in which she'd seen her mother abandoning her. The next day, it had come true. That had marked the beginning of her prophetic dreams. She'd had so many since she couldn't count them all. Some about minor things, some more important like her vision about Jamie and Samantha. But apart from the dream about her mother, she'd never had one filled with such fear until now.

"Easy, easy," Jamie whispered, holding her tightly. " 'Tis all right, lass, 'tis all right. I'm here with ye. I won't let anything harm ye. 'Twas just a nightmare."

"Oh Jamie," she whispered back, trying to control her panic, "hold me, please, just hold me."

"Aye. Dinna be afraid. I'm here."

Slowly, Jix's breathing shifted from frantically gulping for air to a more normal sound, but the panic inside of her had not abated. Jamie lay back, pulling her with him. She rested beside him, her arm around his waist, her head on his shoulder. He held her close, as if something infinitely precious. He was so strong, so very strong. How safe she felt, how wonderfully protected.

But nothing could protect them from her dreams. Nothing could protect them from a future already written, a future that must come true, no matter what. But how could it be possible? How could her vision of Jamie and Samantha marrying come true if he was destined to die in the past? Or had their trip through time somehow changed destiny and Jamie's fate?

She began to cry again. Jamie turned toward her, lifting her face to his with gentle fingers. *"Acushla,"* he said softly, "what is it? This is more than just a bad dream. Ye are the girl who never cries, remember?"

Jix nodded but couldn't speak, suddenly mesmerized by his dark blue eyes gazing into hers, by the touch of his hand on her skin. She saw the feeling quicken in him, saw the dark lashes dip down as if to hide the open desire, felt his fingers soften even more as they brushed away the tears from her cheeks.

"Jix," he whispered, and lowered his mouth to hers.

She melted against him, her hands lifting to his hair, that long, thick hair she had longed to touch. She laced her fingers into the dark waves as he ravaged her mouth. His hands slid down to cup her breasts and she leaned against them, wanting more of him, all of him.

Samantha. He belongs to Samantha.

She had to stop him. Jix knew she had to stop him. But she couldn't just reject him again. She owed him an explanation. Actually, she owed him far more, but she could at least start with the truth. She broke their embrace, breathless with need, determined to do the right thing.

"Jamie, I have to tell you something," she said, unable to keep from sliding her hands over his thick biceps.

But Jamie wasn't listening. He gently tugged the string holding her gown puckered at the neckline. It fell and he helped it along, pulling the soft material down below her breasts, exposing the sensitive, peach-colored tips.

Jix put her hands to his shoulders, to push him away, to tell him about her prophetic dreams. He lifted his face to hers, his dark blue eyes hazy with desire.

"Lass, let me love ye tonight," he said.

"Jamie . . ." Every time she said his name she lost more control.

"Shhh . . ." he pressed her to the bed and leaned back to pull his shirt over his head. He tossed it aside. He had taken off his kilt sometime in the night and now without his shirt, he sat beside her, completely naked.

A full moon lit the sky outside, the light dancing to them through the narrow window beside the bed. Jix stared up at him, breathless, watching the subtle play of shadows across his spectacular chest. She reached up and touched the dark, curling hair scattered there, lightly running her fingers over his muscles. His stomach was taut, hard, another part of his anatomy even harder, Jix realized. Her hand froze against his midriff as she gazed up at him. His long, dark hair spilled over his shoulders, silver-edged in the moonlight, his silhouette shimmering above her.

For a moment Jix felt as though she was about to be ravaged by some ancient Celt who had taken her captive. The thought made her heartbeat quicken. Then her heart began to thud in earnest as Jamie lowered his body to hers, brushing his chest against her sensitive breasts. Jix gasped and he caught her breath with his mouth, his tongue burning against hers. She lay limp, unable to lift her arms to hold him, everything inside of her crying out against this betrayal of Samantha.

Jamie moved his mouth to her neck, caressing her, speaking softly, nipping at her earlobe, kissing the line of her jaw. It was a moment before Jix realized he was speaking Gaelic, the sound like mythical music weaving around her mind, enchanting her with its beauty and passion.

She would make him stop, she told herself. She would let him touch her just for a minute or two, then she would make him stop. But the Gaelic spell continued, mesmerizing her, captivating her, as his hands moved over her body softly, first caressing each breast, then moving to gently slide across her gown, over her abdomen and down to her thighs. It was delicious, lying in his arms, eyes closed, not knowing where he would touch her next. Then his mouth closed warm and wet around her right nipple and she opened her eyes as hot ecstasy coursed through her body. She gasped, her hands moving of their own volition to his shoulders, passion surging through her as Jamie sent wave after wave of sweet fire flooding through her veins. He caressed her other breast, his thumb moving across the sensitive nub, sending more luscious sensations across her skin.

Jamie pushed her nightgown above her waist and pressed against her softness, seeking her, finding her. Desire exploded inside of Jix—deep, dark, uncontrollable desire—as Jamie's lips possessed her mouth and his body possessed her soul. All rational thought disintegrated and for a moment Jix thought she might, too.

Then Jamie lifted his face from hers and stilled his movement. He gazed down into her eyes and for a moment, just looked at her. For the first time in a long time, Jix felt truly beautiful, truly wanted, and not just for sex. Jamie's gaze told her that she meant much, much more to him than just a passionate fling. Panic filled her and too late, she knew she'd let everything go too far. Too late. There was no turning back now.

Gently he pulled her nightgown higher and Jix leaned forward, giving a delicious shiver as the cool material skimmed over her sensitive skin, over her breasts, over her head. Jamie dropped it to the floor.

"Jamie, Jamie," she whispered. He moved up to take her mouth, and slid between her legs again, hot and hard. She moved one bare foot up the back of his leg and gasped as he found her, sank into her, molded his hard, muscular body into hers. The length of him filled her and Jix slid her hands to the nape of his neck, stroking his hair, his shoulders, his back as she moved beneath him, mindless. Jix opened to him, not just her body but her heart, as she arched to meet him, over and over again.

Loneliness fled. Fear disappeared. The sorrows in her life vanished because Jamie MacGregor was filling her with his own surging life. His hands moved over her, under her, and she wrapped her legs around him, giving him deeper access to her molten core as something soft and wild and wonderful ignited deep inside of her. She moved with his rhythm, filled with a want, a need so deep it shook her to the very center of her being. She knew her actions were reprehensible. Jamie belonged to Sam. He was Sam's soul mate, her future husband. Jix knew that as well as she suddenly knew that she loved Jamie MacGregor. Just as she knew that she could no more have stopped him from loving her this night than she could stop the future from arriving, full fevered on their doorstep.

Jamie rocked her, shook her, sent her spinning into the heavens, then pulled her shakily back to earth before sending her flying again, all the time encasing her in the warmth and shelter of his strength, until at last she lay boneless, spent, her heart aching with fulfillment. Jamie found his own and the two lay trembling in one another's arms. He cradled her with a tenderness she had never felt from a man before. He kissed her forehead and whispered something to her in Gaelic, then murmured softly in English.

"Let me hold ye," he said, pulling her against him, his lips brushing the side of her neck. "Let me hold ye for the night."

Jix lay nestled in his arms, listening to his heartbeat. When she was sure he had fallen asleep, she let silent tears glide down her face. Jix had lived long enough not to equate sex with love. She'd been afraid and Jamie had offered solace. She had taken it. It was as simple as that. There had been no words of love on either side, in spite of what she thought she saw in his eyes. She'd been wrong before.

In the morning she would fix things. She would tell him it had been fun, a lark really, but nothing more. He'd be happy, glad even, to know that she didn't expect anything from him. Jix realized she should feel terrible guilt—after all, she'd betrayed her best friend—but even that had been pushed aside for the more frightening reality now facing her. Jix shivered beside the man she loved as the horror of her dream rushed in again and threatened to choke her.

Either Jamie and Sam were fated to wed—or James MacGregor was destined to die.

* * *

Jamie propped up on one elbow and watched Jix sleep. She lay curled in the curve of his arm and he memorized the soft outline of her cheek, the dark crescent of her lashes against her pale skin, the arch of her brow, the fullness of her beautiful lips. Never had he felt so complete, so content, so—dare he say—happy?

He had awakened in the night to find Jix reaching for him. No words passed between them, only passion, hot and liquid. She yielded herself so sweetly, yet so fervently, that it was all he could do not to murmur words of love into her ear. Yet he had not. It was all too new, too fresh, too tenuous to shatter with promises he might not be able to keep.

He would be leaving in a few minutes on this damned mission for Red Hugh and he had decided to tell Jix before he left. She deserved to know the truth, not to be sitting here worrying about him. She'd still be worried, he knew, but maybe that wasn't such a bad thing. Maybe she'd call in a few favors from God and keep him alive.

Jamie turned with a smile and found her awake, blinking up at him like a newborn kitten.

"Good morning, lass," he whispered, leaning over to kiss her.

Jix bolted upright, almost hitting him in the chin with the top of her head. She slid off the bed and began gathering up her clothes.

"What are ye doing?" he demanded. "Come back to bed. I want to talk to ye."

She laughed but the sound had no mirth. "Talk?" she asked, giving him a hard, knowing look.

Jamie reached out to pull her back, to keep her warmth in the bed beside him, but she shrugged out of his grasp.

"All right, come back to bed and let me make love to ye. Is that better?" he asked softly, leaning on one elbow and gazing up at her. Teasing him again, was she? But Jix turned away with another joyless laugh, her face flushing with color as she began to talk rapidly.

"Thanks for the invitation, MacGregor, but I think not." She turned and gave him a tremulous smile. "Don't get

191

me wrong. It was great fun and it'll make a wonderful chapter in the book I'm going to write, but . . ." Her voice trailed off.

Jamie frowned and sat up, pulling the covers around his waist. When they'd finally sank exhausted into sleep after their last round of lovemaking, he'd felt sure she'd been just as relieved as he that the fire burning between them had finally ignited and been wonderfully quenched—for the moment. As they'd lain together in the moonlight he'd even entertained the notion that he might be falling in love with Jix Ferguson.

Love! After his experience with Cathy he'd never thought love possible for him again, and even now he viewed it doubtfully. Love involved trust, and he wasn't sure he could ever trust a woman again, let alone someone like Jix. No matter how sweet and desirable she might be, she seemed to make a game out of everything. How could he possibly trust her? She was like quicksilver. Sometimes he had the oddest feeling if he looked away from her too long she might simply disappear, vanish before his eyes like some otherworldly creature. He had the sudden urge to touch her, to reassure himself she was real. Crazy, he knew, but he felt a little insane.

"Come over here and I'll give ye the next chapter as well," he said, stretching out on his stomach atop the covers, stark naked, reaching one long arm out for her. She looked down at him, her gaze raking over his body, her green eyes huge in her pale face. Her gown hung untied, half on, half off and she looked marvelously disheveled, her long hair tangled from their night of lovemaking. She ran her tongue across her lower lip and shook her head at his entreaty, but he smiled and watched the resistance in her eyes melt. Snagging her gown with one hand, Jamie gave a gentle jerk, bringing her tumbling into his arms.

Jix struggled, hands on his chest, but then he found her mouth, covered it with his and she moaned, sliding her arms around his neck and meeting his fire with a flame of her own. Within five minutes the power of her passion threatened to consume him. Her warmth, her spirit, surrounded him as she sweetly gave herself to him again, and he in turn sought to fill her with every part of his being. Her body was a solace, a welcome refuge and, as she moved against him in abandonment, her eyes closed, her mouth parted, he longed again to speak the words of love that had begun forming tenuously in his heart. But he didn't dare; he could only try to show her through his touch how much she meant to him.

"Ye are so beautiful," he whispered against her hair. Jix cushioned his face with her hands and turned him to face her. Green eyes searched his, reflecting back to him her molten desire—but there was something else there too, some unnamed fear. He nipped at her lower lip and she smiled. Jamie's heart turned over. What a darling she was. He deepened the kiss, his tongue painting promises above even as below he began to work a different kind of magic.

She was all the sweetness of life he had ever hoped to find and he wondered if she could taste and feel the power of what was happening between them. His mouth slid to caress her jaw, her throat, dipped lower to her breast and Jix arched against him. He could feel her heart pounding, then she spoke, her voice shuttered, a whisper.

"Love me, Jamie," she said. "Love me like it's real."

Jamie took her then, accepting the fire she willingly gave, offering his own in return, sending his life into her as if perhaps the very power of their lovemaking might take them home again. They made love frantically, almost desperately, each finding that pinnacle of bliss, then sinking blindly, sweetly into oblivion, melting into peace in one another's arms.

Jamie held her close as she shuddered beneath him, shuddering himself, the two of them awash with contentment. Warmth enveloped him, along with a wholeness he had never felt before. Was this love? It was unlike what he had felt for Cathy or any other woman—this knowledge that he never wanted to let her go, never wanted to wake up again without her beside him. He smiled at the thought and feeling suddenly joyous, flipped over to his back, carrying Jix with him. His smile faded as her long auburn hair tumbled over his chest like a cascade of silk and he looked up into her haunted gaze.

In the soft green depths of her eyes lay an agony he didn't understand, a regret that reached to the core of her soul. The sight of her obvious pain sent a swift stab of guilt through him. Something was wrong. He had sensed it immediately but instead of trying to find out what was the matter, he had acted like a randy bull and seduced her again.

"Jix, love, what is it?"

"Oh Jamie, I'm sorry," she said. "Please forgive me."

He blinked, taken aback by the hollow look in her eyes. "Forgive ye for what?"

She pushed away and knelt beside him, straightening her nightgown, shielding him from the sight of her bare, beautiful breasts.

"For making you think there could ever be anything between us. There can't be. Not in the past, not in the future."

"Lass, I dinna think ye understand," he began, thinking to assure her that she wasn't just a one-night stand, that he now fully intended to pursue whatever kind of relationship they could have in this crazy situation. She cut him off.

"No, I don't think you understand." Jix slid off the bed, and tugged the nightgown over her head, tossing it to the stone floor. He admired her body as she began pulling her clothes on with quick, hurried movements. She straightened her blouse around her shoulders, then picked up her discarded corset and slipped it on. She kept her gaze on the leather laces as she slowly tied the constricting garment around her. When she lifted her eyes to his again, it was like facing some cool stranger.

"I told you," she said, "this was fun, really it was, but that's all it was."

Jamie arched one brow. "Fun?" he echoed, disbelief washing over him. She had to have felt the same thing he'd experienced—the overwhelming rightness of their union.

Jix lifted her chin and her long lashes swept down and back up again. Emerald ice, he thought, as she continued to stare at him, nonplussed.

"Yes, didn't you think it was fun?"

She laughed then, a light little trill, and Jamie leaned back against the wooden headboard, staring at her, feeling like she'd punched him in the stomach.

"Like I said, when we get back home it will make a great chapter," she took a deep breath, "that is, if I go back with you."

Jamie felt his heart skip a beat. "What do ye mean, if ye go home with me? We'll all go home together once we find Samantha." In that instant he saw her bravado waver. Did she think that he didn't feel anything but lust for her and this was her way of protecting herself? After all, he hadn't awakened spouting words of undying love. Maybe she was just afraid of commitment. Or was this about her ex? Surely she wasn't planning to go back to him once they returned.

"There's been a slight glitch in our plan, Jamie," she said softly before he could pull his thoughts together.

"What kind of glitch?" He folded his arms across his chest, a sudden premonition sending a chill over his bare skin. "What is it, Jix?"

She stared at the floor, her long hair hiding her face. "I didn't realize it until now," she said, her voice so low he could barely hear her. "But after last night, well, it's just made everything clear to me."

Jamie thought he would go mad. Why couldn't she just say it? "What's been made clear to ye?"

Jix lifted her head and met his gaze evenly, her green eyes steady, decided. "I'm in love with Griffin Campbell," she said, "and I want to marry him, as soon as possible."

Jamie smiled. "Ye're joking."

She bit her lower lip and shook her head. "No, Jamie, for once I'm not joking."

"Ye canna mean it," he said, his brogue deepening unconsciously. He felt gut-punched. Again. Why was it only Jix had the power to make him feel this way? She couldn't be serious, of course. It was just one of her silly fabrications.

"I do mean it."

He threw the covers back on the bed and rose, naked. He crossed the room and tried to put his arms around her. She pulled away.

"I'm sorry, Jamie," she said, her voice shaking. "Making love to you only proved to me that I could never love you. That's why I did it. I was confused. We have so much chemistry between us that I thought maybe I loved you. I thought if we made love I'd be able to figure it out." She gave a little shrug. "Well, now I have. I don't love you. I love Griffin."

And as Jamie stood there, naked, shivering, she spun around on her heel and ran to the door, slamming it behind her before he could even call out her name.

Chapter Thirteen

"Griffin . . . are you trying to be a naughty boy?"

The blond Scot blushed scarlet. "I wanted a bit of privacy," he admitted. "Come in, please?"

Griffin had been eager to take her for a ride that morning, in spite of Jamie's warning in the rose garden. Jix had been surprised when they managed to leave without Jamie roaring out of the castle to stop them. After the first hour, Jix stopped looking behind them and decided, her heart sinking a little, that her last rejection of Jamie must have finally taken.

To Griffin's credit, he hadn't complained a bit when Jix insisted on stopping at every crofter's cottage to ask about Samantha. Now, hours later, she was exhausted and discouraged, and the sight of a beautiful little cottage made from white stone, nestled in a grove of oak trees, had made her first happy, then suspicious.

"We'll no' make it back to Meadbrooke this day," Griffin was saying as he helped her dismount. Suddenly Jix understood what was going on.

There was no denying the man was sexy. He wore a

black open-necked lace-up shirt tucked into black trews, his hunting tartan knotted over one shoulder, fastened with a silver brooch. A black stone in the center gleamed in the sunlight. Black leather boots were laced to his knees. Any woman would be crazy not to want him. He was straight out of one of Jix's favorite books. And it didn't matter to her one whit.

"Just what do you think you're doing, Griffin?" she asked nervously.

"What's happened to yer voice?" he asked, frowning as he tied the horses to the rough wooden fence surrounding the small house. "Ye sound queer."

"Yeah, well you don't sound so straight yourself," she muttered. But aloud she added her brogue, clearing her throat loudly before she did. "Och, forgive me, just a wee bit of dust in my throat." She settled her hands on her hips.

"Come in," he coaxed. "We can rest for awhile."

Jix sighed. She needed to rest. After dropping her bombshell on Jamie early that morning, she'd left their chamber and found an empty bedroom elsewhere in the castle. She had been too heartsick and weary to even cry. Instead she curled up on the narrow bed and tried to sleep. It had been impossible. When she finally returned to their chamber later that morning, there was no sign of Jamie. Avoiding her, again. He had probably disguised himself as a milkmaid—or hey, how about one of the cows Red Hugh kept tied near the kitchen?—to keep an eye on her. Maybe someone had tried to milk him and that's why he hadn't stopped her from leaving with Griffin.

Or maybe he just didn't care anymore.

"Will ye no' come in, Maigrey?"

Jix followed him up to a small gate. "It's a lovely place, but do ye no' think I will be compromised if I stay here with ye the night?"

Griffin's smile was hesitant as he ushered her through the gate and up the worn stone path to the front door. "I am the laird's son. No one would dare to talk about us." He took a key from the leather bag at his waist and unlocked the dark green door, then swung it open, gesturing for her to enter.

Jix walked inside, expecting dirty rushes on the floor like in the castle, and more interesting odors to add to her memoirs of this adventure. Instead she found a cozy little cottage, clean and neat. Wood was laid in the stone fireplace just awaiting the touch of a match—or in this time period, a tinderbox. A hand-knotted rug lay on the floor and atop it sat two rocking chairs. In the corner sat a wooden cupboard and near it, a round table with four chairs. It was all simple furniture, almost rough, but functional. Except for a beautiful brocade settee that was the centerpiece of the entire room.

Jix was surprised. She'd certainly never pictured Griffin living this kind of homey existence. There were four rooms in all—two bedrooms, the great room with the large fireplace, and another, smaller room, which housed a tremendous number of scrolls and books. Griffin a reader? It seemed unlikely, but why else would the books be there?

"This is nice, Griffin. But why did ye bring me here?" She turned and ran right into him. His hands closed around her upper arms to keep her from falling and her palms came against his broad chest. He stared down at her, his eyes wide and—was that fear she saw? No, of course not. Griffin was a warrior. And yet a fine sheen of perspiration beaded across his forehead and there was no mistaking the sheer panic in his gaze. He stood as one frozen, his fingers tightening around her arms. Then he crushed her to him, his mouth coming down on hers, hard. His kiss was tight-lipped, and about as exciting as when she'd been a teenager and she, Sam, and Chelsea practiced kissing the back of their hands in preparation for the real thing.

This was the Casanova of the Highlands? Maybe it was just because she loved Jamie, but this drop-dead gorgeous guy's approach seemed awkward at best. And she'd be damned if she'd let him manhandle her. Jix pushed away from him and broke the embrace, frowning. Griffin's eyes flew open and he searched her face. Apparently not finding what he'd hoped for, Griffin dropped his hands from her arms and sank down into a nearby chair, cradling his head in both hands with a groan.

With a sigh Jix patted him on the shoulder. "It's all right, Griffin. You just caught me by surprise."

He rose and shook her hand from him, storming across the room and back again. He was so tall that if he lifted one arm he could touch the ceiling. Jix felt very small beside him, but for some reason, she wasn't afraid. Griffin's anger was obviously toward himself, not her.

"Nay, it isn't all right!" he shouted. He stopped, his blond hair standing wildly about his head, his blue eyes wide with—terror? What was this big Celt afraid of?

"Griffin," Jix said in a coaxing voice, holding out her hand to him, "come here. Sit down and we'll talk." She led him to the brocade settee and sat down.

He stared at her for a long minute, then with a groan sat beside her. "Ye might as well ken it before we are married," he said, his words soft, broken. "I am only half a man, Maigrey, and if ye dinna want to marry me, I wouldna blame ye."

Jix felt a sudden knot of compassion twist inside of her. Was Griffin gay or just impotent? Poor man! How he must have to hide his condition from his father and from the other men! Or had he been able to? But what about his reputation with the ladies? Was it all a facade to keep the truth from the clan?

"Talk to me, Griffin," she said softly. "I willna be critical of ye."

"Ye canna help me, Maigrey." He shook his head, lacing his hands together between his knees. He looked up. "I'm hopeless."

"Let's start at the beginnin', shall we?" Jix said, laying one hand over his. "Do ye like women?"

"Do I—" Griffin looked startled, then dumbfounded. "What do ye mean?"

"Do ye like women?" Jix asked again, keeping her voice level. If he was gay, she didn't want him to think that she was being critical. "Or do ye like men the better?"

"Do I like men the—" He stood up, his face red, his

hands flexing and unflexing. He paced across the room and back four times until apparently he was able to compose himself. Jix had no idea why he was suddenly so upset. He finally returned to her side, breathing hard, shaking his head. "Maigrey, I dinna like men. 'Tis not my problem."

"Ah. Well then, do ye have erectile dysfunction?"

He frowned at her. "Do I have what?"

"You know, do ye, er, have trouble getting the starch into yer sheets?"

He shook his head. "I dinna like starch in my sheets."

Jix bit her lower lip and tried again. "No, I mean, when ye're with a woman, do ye feel somewhat deflated or are ye able to point the way to paradise?"

He stared at her again, then suddenly his sensual lips turned up into a broad smile and he laughed. "Oh, I ken yer meanin'." The smile disappeared. "Ye think that I have no blood in my cock?"

Jix blushed and looked away. "Well, do ye?"

"Och, lass, ye misunderstand. When I say that I am half a man 'tis no' because I am no' *capable* of pleasing a lady, and is certainly no' because I dinna like them!" He laughed again, but the sound was tense. "If anythin' I like them too much, which makes my problem all the more fashin'."

Jix shook her head. "I don't get it. If you aren't gay and you can, uh, perform, then what's the problem?"

"What's wrong with yer voice? And I *am* gay—that is, I'm as happy as the next man, except for this one thing!"

She cleared her throat and hid a smile. "Just tell me then, straight out, Griffin. What's the problem?"

He looked at her, then at the floor, then at his hands, then finally back at her again.

"I canna—I dinna—I havena—" He stood and began to pace again.

"Oh for pity's sake, sit down, you're driving me nuts," Jix said, tapping the space next to her. He sat, his face pale. "I willna criticize ye, Griffin," she said, remembering to use the brogue. "I want to help. I—" she broke off as understanding swept through her. "Oh." She smiled at him. "Griffin, are ye a virgin?"

He didn't look at her but kept his eyes on the ground. "Aye," he said miserably, "and if anyone finds out, 'tis ruined I am, and my father will probably disown me!"

Jix nodded, biting her lower lip to keep from laughing. "Ah—ah, I see." She swallowed a giggle and tried to look as serious as possible. "Yer father doesna know, then?"

Griffin jerked his head up. "Nay! No one knows!" He stood and began to pace. Jix blinked. The man was making her dizzy.

"Everyone thinks I'm this great ladies' man, that I've had more lasses than any man in the clan." He stopped, his face stricken as he glanced at her, shaking his head. "When the truth is, I'm naught but a fraud." He covered his face with his hands. "Dinna look at me, Maigrey, I am too ashamed."

"Griffin, Griffin, Griffin," she said softly, clucking her tongue. "Ye know nothing about women, do ye?"

He dropped his hands from his face and spread them wide. "Isna that what I've been saying?" he cried. "In humiliating detail?"

"Tell me something—do ye expect yer wife to be a virgin?"

He frowned. "Aye, of course."

"Then why do ye suppose that yer wife would be disappointed when she finds ye are as well?"

He shook his head. "A woman wants a man that can please her. It's the man's place to lead her through the weddin' night, ye ken?"

She sighed and leaned back against the settee. "Yes, sure." Seventeenth century male logic. "But Griffin, how on earth have ye managed to remain a virgin?"

He looked away, one tiny muscle in his jaw tightening. When he looked back at her again, she saw pleading in his eyes.

"Ye willna laugh at me, Maigrey?" She shook her head and reached over to squeeze his hand. He took a deep breath and released it, then sat down again beside her. "When I was a wee bairn I saw my father sneak into the barn one night. I followed him. There I saw him with a woman who wasna my mother. What they did—well, it looked like fun." He grinned at her, then looked away. "But she wasna my mother, ye ken?"

Jix nodded, feeling sorry for the little boy who had witnessed such a thing.

"I kept wonderin' if my mother knew." He shrugged. "When I got older and the other lads prodded me to gae with them to the whores, I couldna. I kept thinking about the lady I would marry. Would she ask me if there had been others? Would I tell her a lie if there had been? And all the while I kept rememberin' my father in the barn."

Jix laid one hand on his shoulder. "Oh, Griffin, what a sensitive soul you have."

He laughed, this time the sound caustic. "Och, dinna say that, Maigrey. If my father knew these soft mewlings he would no' just disown me, he'd probably lock me in the tower and throw away the key. I am no' sensitive, but mayhap I am a romantic. In any case, ever since that time, whenever I am around a woman, I am seized with a terrible fear, a terrible tightenin' of my limbs. I begin to tremble and I canna even think straight! Once I even lost my dinner while trying to seduce a chambermaid. I told her I was ill and she believed me, thank God!"

"I would never have guessed. You put on a good show," Jix amended, "in public, at least."

"Och, aye, I had to learn how to keep the other men from findin' out. The truth is I'm a weaklin'."

Jix reached out and turned his face to hers. "Griffin, ye are not a weaklin'. Ye are a fine man and I am fair impressed with the way ye view a couplin'. Do ye not ken that a woman wants to make love, not just have sex? I truly don't think ye'll let her down on her weddin' night."

Griffin frowned, looking confused. "Och, Maigrey, 'tis ye I fear disappointin' on our weddin' night."

Oh. Of course! She was his betrothed! She summoned a smile.

"I'm not worried about it, Griffin."

His eyes bored into hers hopefully. He took her hand and she could feel him trembling. "Then Maigrey, will ye—could ye—" he broke off and ducked his head. "Ye said ye had been with other lads."

"Aye," she said, "does that make ye respect me less?"

"Nay, nay," he said quickly. "Ye see, I've wanted to have such sport, thinking it might help me gain the courage some day when the right lass did come along. But—" he broke off, then lifted his head. "Maigrey, will ye help me? I feel I must find out somehow with ye, or else release ye from our betrothal."

Well, I thought I'd heard every line in existence, Jix thought cynically. But as she gazed at him, the defeated look on Griffin's face convinced her otherwise. He really was in dire need of a little sex education. Did she dare? The thought of touching any man but Jamie filled her with nothing but emptiness. Could she teach Griffin how to please a woman without actually engaging in the process herself?

Mentally Jix rolled up her sleeves. She stood and turned to face him. "All right, Griffin, I'm goin' to help ye. But ye have to agree to do whatever I say, all right?"

He nodded, eagerness shining in his eyes.

"Tonight we'll get a good night's sleep—in separate beds"—his face fell a little—"then the first thing in the morning, I want ye to go to market."

Griffin raised both brows. "Market?"

"Aye." Jix smiled. "I want ye to buy some squash."

Jamie lay flat on the top of a hill beside Fergus Campbell, silently watching six Englishmen below move a shaggy herd of cattle in a straggling line. The red-hued animals walked at a quick trot, bawling as their herdsmen kept them moving forward. The English stockade—a foreboding castle taken from its previous owners—was only four miles away. Red Hugh had scrawled a map in the dirt that morning before the five men left Castle Meadbrooke. Now Jamie glanced up at the sky appraisingly, wishing the sun would hurry up and set and give them a chance to strike under the cover of darkness.

It had taken longer to get here than he'd figured it

would, though they had been pushing themselves since before sunrise. Sunrise. The thought reminded him of his night of passion with Jix, of her leaving his bed before the break of dawn, of her declaration of love for Griffin Campbell. He clenched his fists. He couldn't think about their tumultuous relationship now. He had to focus, to concentrate. Six years with Scotland Yard had honed his skills until he could turn off distracting thoughts like Jix Ferguson. Well . . . he could try.

The men were exhausted, their horses equally so. If he could, he'd wait until the next day to attack, but the Englishmen below seemed to have no intention of making camp. They were moving in a hurry, probably planning to make the stockade before they lost daylight. If Jamie's ragtag band hoped to get the cattle without trying to fight a war against the entire regiment, he mused, they had better strike now.

He nudged Fergus. The big man nodded and whistled, the sound identical to a bird Jamie had heard just that morning. Five yards away, another "bird" answered, then another, and yet another. Five men, including Fergus, six including himself. Jamie had decided to keep his band of thieves to a minimum. All six wore green and brown hunting plaids and kilts. Red Hugh wanted the English to know that Scotsmen were responsible for the reiving and in this early time period, tartans had not yet been assigned to the clans. Jamie had debated about wearing his bright MacGregor tartan, thinking it would at least stand out and give Captain Worthington something to look for. In the end he had discarded the idea, deciding he would be target enough without the bright hues of his plaid.

Fergus began backing away. Jamie followed suit until they were far enough back from the edge of the hill to not be seen by those below. Their horses stood patiently in a grove of trees and the five men ran almost noiselessly across the short distance, jumping into their heavy, tall-horned saddles with practiced ease.

Jamie tossed them a grudging look of admiration and mounted his own more slowly. He'd been given Hunter, a beautiful bay gelding with an obedient disposition and the ability to run like the wind. Jamie couldn't remember the last time he'd even been on a horse and had been surprised to find he'd not forgotten much since his days at his uncle's estate. As he slid his right foot into the stirrup and settled into the dark leather, Jamie squinted up at the sun, now finally dipping below the distant purple hills.

"Are ye ready, Fergus?" he said softly.

"Aye," the big man answered. "I'll take Duncan and young William with me."

"And Ian and Donnal with me." Jamie tightened his jaw. "Remember, it's no' important to take the cattle with us. 'Tis the same to Red Hugh if we simply drive them into the woods to be lost."

"Och, such a waste," Fergus observed, stroking his dark beard. "Mayhap we can manage to take one?"

He had such a plaintive tone in his voice that Jamie couldn't help but grin. "Mayhap," he agreed. "But only if it doesna endanger us. I have no desire to be captured by the English and rot in their prisons." All the men nodded soberly. "All right then," Jamie said, "let's do it."

As agreed upon, the six walked their mounts to the edge of the hill; then split up—Fergus and two men heading across the crest of the hill, Jamie and his men picking their way down the slope. The Englishmen and the cattle had passed them by now and Jamie and his men rode easily behind them, the lowing and hoofbeats of the herd covering the sound of their pursuit.

Shadows slid across the ground, turning the Scottish green to black. Jamie peered through the fast encroaching darkness and saw with satisfaction that Fergus and his men were now making their way down their own slope, some fifteen feet ahead of the English and the cattle.

"Well met!" Fergus cried. "We've a man injured. Can ye help us?"

"Out of the way, Scotsman," one of the English called. "Or ye'll have two men hurt."

Jamie gestured to his two men and they split from him, one on either side of the shifting cattle. Fergus's men did the same on the opposite side, drawing their swords. Dusk was a grand time for their attack. The dimness of the day made it hard to discern shapes, and caused a general confusion among the English. Horses reared, cattle bawled loudly as men shouted and the sound of steel against steel rang out. Jamie and his men plunged into the fray, surprising the enemy from behind as they whooped their way through the milling cattle.

It didn't take long to dispatch the man closest to him, though Jamie tried hard to give him only a disabling wound and not a fatal one. In the shadow of the twilight he doubted the herdsmen would be able to identify any of their attackers.

"Ard Choille!" he cried, giving the MacGregor warcry, wondering if he would bring more wrath down upon his kinsmen with his actions. But he had agreed with Red Hugh that 'twas the only way to make sure the English knew who was responsible.

With one more shout, Jamie began driving the cattle nearest him away from the herd. He slapped the flat of the sword Red Hugh had provided against the rumps of the bony Highland steers, driving them into the woods. The other Scots did the same and before long all that was left of the entourage were the Englishmen still battling two of Fergus's men, four herdsmen unconscious or dead on the ground, and one cow contentedly munching grass in the midst of the meleé.

Fergus's men finished their battles, leaving the last two Englishmen on the ground, then the six Scots split up again, plunging into the woods in different directions, sending the confused cattle even deeper into the Highlands. As they had planned, all the men would meet up later at Meadbrooke, after leaving elaborate trails that crisscrossed one another, creating a muddled mess that led nowhere.

Jamie ducked under a low-hanging branch as he followed yet another steer through the underbrush. The shaggy red of the beast gave him something to watch for as darkness slid over the land. What would Jix say if he told her that she and Scottish cattle had the same hair

207

color? He grinned in spite of himself. He didn't think she'd appreciate it one bit. His smile vanished as the steer dodged right and he followed. There wasn't going to be another reiving, not if he had anything to say about it. Once he returned to the castle, he would demand his sword back from Red Hugh, and he and Jix would return to their own time—with or without Samantha Riley. Right. Sure. Like Jix would agree to that.

A cold breeze kicked up around him as he finally lost sight altogether of the steer. He slowed his horse to a walk and halted, listening for any sign that he was being followed. Nothing. The only sound was that of an owl hoot-hooting in the inky shadows of the woods around him. Jamie glanced up at the darkening sky and saw the moon rising. With a sigh he prodded his mount forward with his heels. He had to keep moving. The Englishmen would recover soon and no doubt would try to find the men who had robbed them of their next month's beef.

He pulled his plaid more securely around him as his horse picked his way blindly across the rocky terrain. He ducked his head against the rising wind, wondering absently if Jix lay curled on her side asleep in the grand bed at Meadbrooke, or if she was awake, missing him as much as he missed her. Or did she dream of Griffin Campbell and her wedding day?

His jaw tightened. Most likely the latter, though he didn't believe her admission of love for Red Hugh's son. He might have been out of commission with women for a time but he still knew when a lass had feelings for him. He frowned and burrowed deeper into his plaid. No, Jix had lied about loving Griffin, of that he was sure. Did that mean she had lied about going back to her ex-husband, too? Or had both lies just been her way of letting Jamie know she didn't want him?

One corner of his mouth lifted. Well, she could've fooled him. Because by damn, he could swear she had wanted him at least twice last night and once this morning.

Ahead of him in the still inky black woods came a sudden shout and the sound of horses or cattle trampling

GET UP TO
5 FREE BOOKS!

Sign up for one of our book clubs today, and we'll send you
FREE* BOOKS
just for trying it out...**with no obligation to buy, ever!**

HISTORICAL ROMANCE BOOK CLUB

Travel from the Scottish Highlands to the American West, the decadent ballrooms of Regency England to Viking ships. Your shipments will include authors such as CONNIE MASON, CASSIE EDWARDS, LYNSAY SANDS, LEIGH GREENWOOD, and many, many more.

LOVE SPELL BOOK CLUB

Bring a little magic into your life with the romances of Love Spell—fun contemporaries, paranormals, time-travels, futuristics, and more. Your shipments will include authors such as KATIE MACALISTER, SUSAN GRANT, NINA BANGS, SANDRA HILL, and more.

As a book club member you also receive the following special benefits:

- **30% OFF** all orders through our website & telecenter!
  (Plus, you still get 1 book FREE for every 5 books you buy!)
- **Exclusive access to special discounts!**
- **Convenient home delivery and 10 days to return any books you don't want to keep.**

There is no minimum number of books to buy, and you may cancel membership at any time. See back to sign up!

*Please include $2.00 for shipping and handling.

YES! ☐

Sign me up for the **Historical Romance Book Club** and send my THREE FREE BOOKS! If I choose to stay in the club, I will pay only $13.50* each month, a savings of $6.47!

YES! ☐

Sign me up for the **Love Spell Book Club** and send my TWO FREE BOOKS! If I choose to stay in the club, I will pay only $8.50* each month, a savings of $5.48!

NAME: _____

ADDRESS: _____

_____

TELEPHONE: _____

E-MAIL: _____

☐ **I WANT TO PAY BY CREDIT CARD.**

☐ VISA   ☐ MasterCard   ☐ DISCOVER

ACCOUNT #: _____

EXPIRATION DATE: _____

SIGNATURE: _____

Send this card along with $2.00 shipping & handling for each club you wish to join, to:

Romance Book Clubs
20 Academy Street
Norwalk, CT 06850-4032

Or fax (must include credit card information!) to: 610.995.9274. You can also sign up online at www.dorchesterpub.com.

*Plus $2.00 for shipping. Offer open to residents of the U.S. and Canada only. Canadian residents please call 1.800.481.9191 for pricing information.

If under 18, a parent or guardian must sign. Terms, prices and conditions subject to change. Subscription subject to acceptance. Dorchester Publishing reserves the right to reject any order or cancel any subscription.

through the underbrush. Jamie turned Hunter in the other direction and kicked him hard in the side. He bent over in the saddle, trying to avoid low-hanging tree branches to no avail. They whipped him across the face, sending stinging strokes of pain into his flesh. Another shout. The British. Jamie spurred the gelding, giving him his head, unable to see very far ahead, hoping like hell the horse knew more than he did about running for your life across the Scottish Highlands.

They left their pursuers behind. The miles passed and Jamie grew more weary as Hunter made his way through the wooded area and across rocky crags, down into meadows and across Scotland. Finally he knew he must give his mount a break. He slowed the gelding to a walk, then guided him into a small copse of oak trees. They both sat there breathing hard, a slight vapor appearing in front of their mouths from the cold night air.

"A chilly night, eh?"

Jamie spun around, drawing with one fluid movement the sword Red Hugh had provided him. A man sat on a dark horse. A red ember burned near him, seeming to float in the air, giving the appearance of some sinister magic. He moved forward out of the shadows, into the full moonlight. Black eyes gleamed like hard, silver coins. He held a slim cheroot in one hand, a sword in the other, his reins looped over the tall saddle horn. Every muscle in Jamie's body tightened. The man from the battle during which he and Jix had first appeared in the past—the man who had almost killed him. Captain Worthington? Jamie took a chance.

"Aye, Captain," he said softly, " 'tis always so when evil is abroad in the dark."

A broad smile split the man's face and the ember arched into the air. "Take him," he ordered.

Jamie jerked his horse around in time to parry a vicious blade from behind, then kicked Hunter in the side and plunged between two trees into the darkness. Behind him the captain shouted orders and Jamie heard the thunder of men on horseback rushing after him. He rode across the rough countryside, dodging trees, holding his sword in one hand and reins in the other, cursing movie actors who made it look so damn easy to be a hero. He swerved down one incline and up another, through trees and across rolling rocky glades where he was exposed to his pursuers. Then Hunter mounted a hillock and at the top there was Captain Worthington. He must have circled around. Jamie slashed out at the man before he could gain the upper hand, but Worthington parried the blow and lunged forward.

Jamie gasped as the point of his foe's blade bit into his left shoulder. He kicked at the man's horse, driving him back long enough to turn Hunter and head down the hill. Blood flowed from his wound and Jamie ignored the pain lacing through his shoulder as he bent low over the saddle and rode for his life.

Moonlight sent shivery silver shadows across the ground and rocks, and ahead, clear as day, Jamie could see he was coming to a ravine, a deep, craggy drop-off in the Highland terrain. He gauged the gap to be about twenty feet across. He glanced back over one shoulder. Worthington was less than a hundred yards behind him. Scotland Yard had taught Jamie to make lightning-quick decisions. Sometimes they were the right ones. Sometimes they weren't. Glancing back once more, he made up his mind. He tossed the sword aside and gathered the reins in both hands, lying as flat as possible in the saddle, heading straight for the gorge at full speed. When they reached the edge he kicked Hunter in the ribs and the gelding lifted his legs and soared into the air, landing on the other side. Almost.

Hunter's front hooves hit the rocky earth squarely but his back legs found no purchase. He tried to scramble his way to more stable ground, but Jamie's weight pulled him back. Jamie urged the gelding forward. He wasn't going to make it. They would both plunge down into the blackness at any moment. They were so close.

Thinking quickly, Jamie threw his body sideways out of the saddle, hitting the edge of the rocky precipice hard. The breath left his lungs and he gasped for air as his hands closed around sharp rocks to anchor himself. But as Hunter gave a mighty, frantic shove with his back legs, pushing to higher ground, one hoof lashed out at the last minute and caught Jamie in his injured shoulder. His hand slipped. He started sliding and desperately grabbed at the crumbling rocks as he fell. He couldn't stop his descent. He thought of Jix; then he was falling—down, down, down, into the black bowels of the Highland earth.

Chapter Fourteen

"No, no, no, not like that!"

Jix had tried to be patient but, honestly, Griffin Campbell was one of the most inept men she'd ever met when it came to learning how to touch a woman! He reached out again and squeezed, too hard. Jix jumped to her feet.

"Griffin!"

He looked up at her from the settee, startled, his fingers jerking together, crushing the overripe squash that represented a woman's breast.

"Ye just sent that woman screaming for the first aid kit," she said, shaking her head.

Griffin stood and flung the pieces of squash from his hand, wiping the moisture on the back of his trews. He stalked across the room and back, stabbing his index finger toward the settee.

"I dinna ken first aid, but 'tis no use. I canna do it, Maigrey. 'Tis not a real woman and I canna make love to—to—" he crossed back and sank onto the cushions, gesturing beside him, his voice pleading—"to squash and watercress!"

Jix sighed. She had decided to create a sort of doll for Griffin to use as a practice dummy for his romantic attempts. She'd taken old linens and stuffed them with hay to create a scarecrow-type figure. Using charcoal, she had drawn a face on a small pumpkin that served as the head, then had taken two large overripe summer squash, connected them with a ribbon, and hung them around the dummy's neck, creating breasts.. The watercress was placed strategically lower—not that she thought they'd ever get to that part of the lesson the way things were going!

"Griffin, ye must be gentle!" She said from her chair opposite where the doll still sat on the pale green settee. "How many times must I tell you—ye—less is more?"

"I canna do it," he said again, shaking his head. "I must resign myself to livin' alone for surely ye will never marry me now. I should never have told ye."

Jix took a deep breath and scolded herself silently for not being more patient. The poor man was desperate and she was his only hope. She rose and crossed to his side. "It's all right, Griffin," she said with a smile. "We've only just begun and it takes time and experience to learn these kind of things. Let's just take a little break."

A pitcher of icy cold water from a nearby brook, along with two tumblers, sat on the table in the corner. Jix poured them each a glassful. She held one out to him and he took it, his eyes mournful.

"Can I no practice on ye, Maigrey?" he asked. " 'T'would have to be easier than this way."

Jix hesitated, then grinned and set her glass down on the marble-topped table in front of the settee. She put her hands on her hips and thrust her chest out provocatively. "Sure. Go ahead, give it yer best shot."

Griffin's brows furrowed together as he lifted his hand and cupped it, slowly bringing it toward her right breast. When he was about four inches away, he started shaking, sweating and turning red all at the same time. He dropped his hand back to his side.

"I canna."

213

"That's why I made Minnie Pearl here for ye," she said, patting him lightly on the jaw, her voice sympathetic. "I thought if ye could practice on a woman that couldn't slap yer face, ye might be able to overcome yer nervousness."

" 'Tis no use." His expression was resigned as he sat back down on the settee, beside the dummy. "Maigrey, I release ye from our betrothal. I canna marry ye."

Jix opened her mouth and closed it. Here it was, her way out. She should grab it. Maybe Red Hugh would still give her Jamie's sword. Doubtful. She had to go through with this.

"Griffin, what are ye sayin'?" She leaned down and lifted his face to hers. "Don't ye know that I love ye? Don't ye know that—"

"Maigrey, dinna say more." Griffin put his own goblet down and stood. He moved away from her, stopping in front of the fireplace. The laird's son had built fires in all four of the fireplaces in the cottage as soon as they arrived. He stared into the firelight, his hands on his hips, letting the flames paint a soft glow across his sad face. Jix felt a tug at her heart as she watched him. Poor Griffin.

"Griffin?" she ventured.

"Ye dinna love me," he said. "I wish that ye did, but I know that ye do not. I know ye are marryin' me to seal the agreement between our clans, nothin' more." He glanced back at her. "Or is there more to it than that? Is there some reason that I dinna ken?"

Jix opened her mouth to tell him that he was wrong, that she did love him. But for once her ready wit failed her. She was tired of the game, tired of pretending to be something she wasn't. "Griffin, you're right. I don't love you. But I need your help. Can I trust you?"

He raised one brow. "What's wrong with yer voice?"

"Can I trust you?" she said again.

"I've trusted ye with the worst secret a man can have. I think ye can trust me in return."

Jix drew a quivering breath. If she told him the truth about who they were and how they came here, would he think her crazy? Take her to Meadbrooke and have her thrown into the castle dungeon? If only she could tell him, then maybe he would help her find Samantha and help Jamie regain his sword. She crossed the room to his side. Looking up into his eyes she saw what appeared to be true compassion, real warmth, but she was still afraid. Jix drew a ragged breath.

"I can't love you, Griffin," she said, not bothering with the brogue. "Because I love someone else."

"Ah."

That was all he said for a long time. Poor Griffin. For the first time she wished Chelsea had come with them on their trip back through time. Shy Chelsea Brown would be a perfect match for timid Griffin Campbell.

"I thought perhaps ye were," he said. "So I canna say I'm surprised."

Jix froze. She'd been afraid that Griffin suspected she and Jamie weren't really brother and sister. She supposed she might as well admit it and tell him the whole, crazy story.

"It's true, Griffin. I don't know how you figured it out, but it's true. Though I don't know what difference it makes. Jamie isn't in love with me."

His mouth dropped open. "Yer brother?" he asked, horrified. "Ye're in love with yer brother?"

Jix's eyes widened with equal horror. "You said you knew!"

"I thought ye meant my father!" He took a step back. "Lass—I'm fair shocked."

"No, no, you don't understand!" Jix cried. Now this was a fine mess she'd made of things. "Jamie isn't my brother! We just told your father that so that he would help us. Jamie is no relation to me at all. He's the man I love, but I can't be with him because he's destined to marry my best friend, Samantha."

Griffin's dark brows collided in confusion. "The lass ye've been looking for?"

"Yes."

Griffin nodded, then his frown deepened. "Let me see if I understand this." He pulled her down on the hearthstone, looking rather fierce. "First, who are ye really?"

Jix cleared her throat. "Jamie really is James Mac-Gregor."

"And ye are?"

"Jix Ferguson."

"Jix? What kind of name is that? And a Ferguson? I was about to marry a Ferguson?" He looked outraged. "Why did the two of ye lie to my father?"

"It's really a long story, Griffin." She hesitated, but had to know. "Have I hurt you too badly?"

He shook his head. "Nay, lass. Dinna misunderstand—I want ye like any man in his right mind would want ye, but I knew there was somethin' missing between us. I had always hoped that when I married it would be for love, so in a way I suppose I'm relieved. But dinna change the subject"—he gave her a stern look—"let us talk about ye and MacGregor. Ye are in love with him, but ye say he is destined to marry yer friend, who is lost? Were they betrothed?"

With a sigh Jix explained her own peculiar power to see the future and her dream of Samantha and Jamie being married. Griffin nodded along with her story. "Ye have the Sight," he said, not batting an eye at the strangeness of her tale. " 'Tis common in Scotland."

"But there's more."

She told him the other dream of the English attack on Meadbrooke, and of Jamie's head on a platter. His face darkened with worry.

"An' ye say yer dreams always come true?"

"Yes. And there's more."

It was time to 'fess up. Thirty minutes later, she felt a little less sure of her decision. It sounded so insane.

Griffin stared at her, blinking. "Ye are from the future."

Jix nodded, watching his face closely. So far during the telling of her grand adventure he'd sat perfectly still and silent. Now he made the flat statement in a voice filled with wonder and awe. He smiled, amazingly white teeth gleaming in the dimly lit cottage as he looked down at her.

"Och, well, that explains yer odd speech at times." He

stood and walked toward the settee, then smiled back at her. "But truly God has favored ye, lass. And favored us by bringing ye here."

Jix blinked. "You mean, you aren't afraid of me? You don't think I'm an evil sorceress or something?"

Griffin gave her a puzzled look. "Why would I think that? Ye've been nothin' but good and kind to everyone."

She laughed self-consciously and rubbed one hand up her arm. "Haven't you ever heard about the angel of light?"

"Och, ye mean the evil one? Ye're no' his servant."

"How do you know?"

He left the room, heading into the far bedroom. In a moment he came back carrying a black book. "Put yer hand on it."

Jix had the presence of mind not to hesitate. She immediately placed her hand on the Bible.

"Now, swear to me that ye dinna serve the divil or his minions."

"I dinna serve the divil or his minions," she said obediently. He nodded and set the book aside.

"Ye see?" he asked. "Ye have proven yerself."

"I might be crazy. Don't people in this century throw nutcases into Bedlam?"

"Not . . . ? Aye, ye might be crazy," he agreed, smiling. "I've had some thoughts in that direction, but I dinna think so."

She shook her head, still smiling. "I don't understand. How can you accept this so easily? How can you believe that a sword could send three people back in time?"

"Och, 'tis easy to explain. Come with me." He turned and walked toward the small study. She followed him, curious at his easy acceptance of her story. He stood in the center of the room and proudly stretched his arms as if to encompass all of the books and manuscripts and scrolls on the shelves.

Jix tried to understand what he was telling her. "You have a lovely library?" she said, half statement, half question.

" 'Tis no' compliments I'm searchin' for, but a way to help ye understand why I believe ye. I am a student, ye ken. I have studied Brahe, Kepler, William Gilbert, oh and of course Copernicus—" he broke off with a laugh. "I could go on and on, but suffice it to say that I believe there are more wondrous things in heaven and earth than we can e'er imagine." He winked at her. "And then there is always the magic of the little people to fill in the rest."

Jix had to sit down. There was a chaise lounge near a polished desk at the back of the study and she crossed to it, her knees suddenly weak. "I feel so relieved to be able to tell someone!" She looked up at him. "Griffin—will you help us? I can't let my dream of Jamie's death come true."

Griffin held her gaze. "Tell me, did ye know that the captain of the English at the nearest stronghold has black hair and eyes? And that he is known as the Executioner for his habit o' cutting off his enemy's heads? 'Tis said he does it because he is fair superstitious and thinks if he beheads his foes they canna return to haunt him."

Jix shivered, in spite of the warmth of the room. "No," she said, "I didn't know."

"Did ye tell Jamie of yer dream?"

"No, I couldn't bear it."

"What about my father?"

"No. I was afraid he'd think I was crazy." She shook her head. "There's no way to stop it from happening, Griffin—Jamie is going to die!"

Jix covered her face with her hands and Griffin hurried over to sit beside her. He patted her on the shoulder, still keeping his distance. She hugged her arms around her middle, rocking back and forth as she struggled to bring her emotions back under control.

"Och, Maigrey—no—Jix, is it?" He said. "I'll have to get used to that name. Have ye considered, Jix, that yer dream is only one possible outcome of the future?"

She stopped rocking and glanced up at him. "What do you mean?"

"My mother had the Sight, so the truth of such a thing isna strange to me." His gaze searched hers and he patted

her again. Jix could feel him trembling every time he
touched her and was overwhelmed by his kindness. If only
there was someway she could help him. "But have ye ever
tried to change the outcome of yer dreams, before they
came about?"

A brief, searing surge of hope made Jix look up.
"Change it?"

He dropped his hand from her shoulder, his gaze intense. "For instance, if ye dreamed someone was about to
come to harm, did ye no try to warn them, to prevent the
harm?"

Jix considered his words. She shook her head. "My
dreams have never before been about harm coming to anyone."

"When did ye first know ye had the Sight?"

She got up and crossed to the small fireplace in the
study, wishing the heat could drive out the cold suddenly
encasing her heart. "When I was four years old, I dreamed
that my mother abandoned me. The next night, she left me
on my great-aunt's doorstep. I never saw her again."

Griffin's voice softened. "That was tragic, lass. So ye
have never dreamed before of death?"

"No. My adopted parents were killed in a—an accident,
and I've often wondered if I had dreamed about it, could
I have changed what happened?" She shrugged. "Usually
my dreams are of happier tidings. Oh, sometimes of finan-
cial troubles or perhaps an illness, and occasionally I help
my brother with his work catching criminals but I haven't
dreamed of death." Her throat tightened again and she
lifted her hands to cup her face. "How can I live without
Jamie?" she whispered. "This is all my fault."

"Listen, lass, here is my thinkin'," Griffin said thoughtfully, his blue eyes serious. "The great God has ordained
what happens, that much is certain to me. And mayhap He
gives ye knowledge of events before they happen. However, how do we not know that the reason He's givin' ye
the knowledge of a tragedy is so ye can help prevent it?"

Jix frowned. Her own religion was composed of a
hodge-podge of beliefs, but at this point she was willing

to bow to Griffin's confidence in his theology.

"But if everything is preordained," she mused, "how could I possibly keep God's plan for someone else's life—or death—from happening?"

"Well, lass, what if yer intervention in the matter is, in fact, part of His preordination?" Griffin smiled.

Her heart quickened again with hope. "Are you trying to say you think we can keep my dream from coming true?" she asked.

"I can tell ye that once my father learns of yer dream, the English won't catch us napping when they come." He nodded thoughtfully. "If ye hadna told me of yer dream, that wouldna be true, so it must make a difference in the outcome. But what I truly believe is that yer dream is a vision of one of the paths of life that might come true, dependent upon what decisions we all make."

"You're amazing." Shame crashed down on her, then guilt pressed in and threatened to beat her senseless. She turned and stared into the fire. "And I am such a horrible person."

"What is it, lass?"

Jix shook her head, unable to meet his eyes. "I dreamed Samantha and Jamie would be married—and she's my best friend—but I—I—" she broke off. She didn't want Griffin to think worse of her than he already must.

"But ye love him anyway." She nodded. "Och, lass, my theory might also be true concernin' yer friend's marriage to Jamie. Mayhap the outcome is changin', even as we speak."

Jix drew in a deep breath and turned back to him. "I know what you're trying to say, Griffin, but the fact of the matter is that I knew Jamie was meant for Samantha and I still went after him. God's gonna get me for that."

He frowned. "Went after him? I dinna ken—"

"I still pursued him. You know, chased after him?"

Griffin leaned back against the chaise lounge and smiled. "Och, ye mean ye played the flirt with him. Well, 'tis no law against that."

"Except the law of friendship."

"Nay, I think ye beat herself overmuch, lass. Ye dinna plan to fall in love with him, did ye?"

She shook her head.

"Ye fought against it, did ye no'?"

She nodded.

"Does yer friend love him?"

"She barely knows him."

"Och, then dinna fash yerself." He stood, slapping his hands down on his thighs. "And I dinna think the good God will 'get' ye—whatever that means."

Jix twisted her hands together. "I need to go back to the castle, Griffin. I have to talk to Jamie."

"Aye, lass, I think ye do. And we have a few things to be tellin' my father as well."

"Griffin," she lifted her gaze to his. "Will you help us now? We have to get the sword back from your father."

He smiled and patted her shoulder. "Ye can count on me, lass. After all, ye have information that could destroy me."

Jix shook her head, her mouth curving up in response. "I'd never do that to you, Griffin." She held out her hand. "Friends?"

He took her hand in his large one and squeezed it so tightly that Jix had to blink back tears. Realizing what he'd done he pressed a quick kiss to her knuckles.

"Och, what a blunderin' bull I am. Of course we're friends, lass. Now, let's be off before—what did ye call her?—Minnie Pearl demands my lusty presence again."

Jix smiled and went into the other room to throw out Minnie Pearl's breasts.

As they headed back to Meadbrooke an hour later, Jix grew more and more anxious. She pleaded with Griffin not to stop for anything and when they arrived, their horses were spent and she suspected the bones in her rear end had been driven into her spine. A near panic had formed like a lump in her throat the last few miles. Jix felt almost frantic to talk to Jamie, to discuss Griffin's theory, and she could only hope he didn't think the worst of her for going off alone with the handsome Scot.

They arrived at the castle long after supper. Red Hugh greeted them with a worried look on his face and quickly had food and drink brought to them in the great hall. He sat across from the two of them at one of the trestle tables, his rusty brows knit together, his dark eyes anxious. Jix watched him covertly between bites of stew. What was wrong with Red Hugh? As soon as the edge had been taken off of her hunger, she took a long drink of wine and asked the question plaguing her since their arrival.

"Where is Jamie? Does he know we're back? Did he know we were gone? I hope he isn't too angry."

Red Hugh sat like a stone statue, staring at her with a bleak look in his eyes. "Nay, lass, he doesna know ye left or that ye have returned."

A small prick of apprehension darted through her. "Why not? Surely by now he's looked for me."

"Yer brother is no' here." Red Hugh said flatly, his hands knotted into fists upon the tabletop.

Jix glanced at Griffin, who suddenly became very busy buttering a piece of bread. "Griffin? Do you know what's going on?"

"What's wrong with yer voice, lass?" Red Hugh asked.

"I lost my brogue," she retorted, "and I don't know where to find it. Where is Jamie?"

Red Hugh cleared his throat. "Maigrey, I want ye to know that I've come to think of ye as my daughter. When ye and Griffin are married, ye will be part of our family. Ye ken that, do ye no'? And now, now ye can marry Griffin as soon as ye please."

A cold chill crept down Jix's spine and she stood up slowly, her heart constricted within her chest. She pressed her fingertips against the table, fighting for balance. "Red Hugh," she said, "where . . . is . . . Jamie?"

Griffin stopped eating and stared at his father, too. "Da? Has he no' returned?"

Jix turned. "Returned from where? You mean you know something about this?"

He looked up at her hesitantly, then nodded. "He was to do somethin' for my father." He frowned and he glanced back at Red Hugh. "What happened, Da? Why has he no' returned?"

Red Hugh stared down at the table for a long minute, then lifted his bleary eyes to hers. "Lass, 'tis fair sorry I am to have to tell ye this. Yer brother is dead."

Chapter Fifteen

"No," Jix whispered.

The room began to spin and she fell backward. Griffin jumped up and caught her as she went over the bench. When she opened her eyes again she lay in the dirty rushes, looking up at Griffin's stricken face. Red Hugh hovered behind him.

"It's not true," she said. "I won't believe it."

"Och, lass, are ye all right?"

"It isn't true," she said, holding onto Griffin's arm, feeling dazed as he helped her to her feet.

"Ji—Maigrey, ye need to lie down. Ye've had a terrible shock." Griffin said. "Let me see ye to yer room."

"No." She snapped her head up to face Red Hugh. "Jamie isn't dead."

The laird shook his large red head. "Och, lass, I know ye dinna want to believe it, but 'tis true. Yer brother went out on a dangerous task fer me."

"For you? What task?"

"He agreed to reive cattle from the English—"

"Reive cattle?" Jix interrupted. "What does that mean?

Is it like shearing sheep?" That didn't sound good. Had Jamie gotten kicked while trying to shave a cow?

"No, lass, it means stealin'," Griffin said.

"Borrowin'," Red Hugh corrected. "Or takin' back the cattle that they have 'borrowed' from us."

Jix shook her head and the room began to spin again. "Wait a minute. What are you talking about?"

"The lad agreed as part of the marriage contract that he would lead a reivin' party against the English. Unfortunately, the English captain and his men gave chase to them and accordin' to Fergus, Jamie tried to jump a ravine, and dinna make it." Red Hugh looked honestly apologetic. Jix wanted to punch him in his ruddy, pockmarked nose.

She clenched her fists at her side. "Fergus came back but Jamie didn't?"

"Aye. All the men made it back except Jamie." Red Hugh patted her on the back. "I'm sorry, lass." He walked out of the great hall, shaking his bushy head. Jix let him go, waiting until the laird had gone out the door, before turning to Griffin.

"He isn't dead," she said between gritted teeth.

Griffin's blue eyes were filled with compassion. "Jix, I know this is hard for ye, but—"

"He isn't dead." Jix crossed her arms over her chest and lifted her chin. "You knew he was going to do this awful thing for your father, didn't you?"

"Aye."

"You knew and you didn't tell me!"

Griffin looked away and shrugged. "I dinna see that it was any of yer concern. 'Twas yer brother's decision."

"I see, and I'm just a woman. I shouldn't have a say in any of this? Is that what you mean?"

He raised both hands and shook his head. "I can tell I'd best no' answer that." Griffin sighed. "Look, lass, yer bro—that is, Jamie knew he was takin' a risk. I never did understand why he was willin' to do it."

"Your father said it was part of the marriage contract." She narrowed her eyes. "Did you refuse to marry me unless Jamie did this?"

"Och, no, lass, why would I hesitate to marry a girl as bonny as ye?"

"I don't know, but there's one thing I do know." She leaned forward, rising up on her toes until she was almost in Griffin's face. She poked his broad chest with one finger.

"Jamie isn't dead and you're going to help me find him!"

Jamie came back to consciousness slowly, his head pounding, every inch of his body feeling battered and torn. It took tremendous energy but he finally managed to open his eyes, and immediately wished he had kept them shut.

Blackness surrounded him. He started to sit up, but thought better of it. Even though he felt dazed, he remembered exactly what had happened and where he must be. He was somewhere in the belly of the ravine he had tried to jump. But how? The gorge had seemed bottomless. Jamie reached his hands out on either side of his body and felt the crumbling edge of a ledge with his right hand, the ragged side of the cliff with his other.

"Always there in a pinch, God," he said hoarsely, echoing one of Jix' favorite sayings. Except for minor bruises and scrapes, and an aching shoulder from being clipped by his horse and stabbed by Worthington's sword, he seemed to be all in one piece. It was a miracle that he hadn't broken something or bled to death. Apparently the wound in his shoulder had clotted on its own and wasn't too deep. He tried to push to a sitting position and pain laced up his leg from his ankle. Okay, maybe one break, or a sprain. Still, considering the fall he had taken, he was extremely thankful.

But as he slowly managed to sit up and began evaluating the situation, Jamie saw that he had probably received only a short reprieve from death. The walls of the ravine rose straight up from where he sat, the sides steep, jagged. He couldn't tell how far from the top he was, but as his eyes grew more accustomed to the darkness, he could see that, short of sprouting wings and flying away, there was no way in hell he could get out of this dark prison.

Jamie leaned back against the rock, his injured leg stretched out, his other leg bent, his arm resting on his knee. Jix would be worried. She'd be angry at first when she learned he'd left and hadn't taken her into his confidence. She'd badger Red Hugh until the old man would probably tell her everything. Then she'd be frantic. In a day or two, she might even demand that Red Hugh or Griffin come and look for him. He moved his foot and a chunk of dirt and rock fell into the black abyss below him. Belatedly he realized that the ledge on which he sat was very unstable. The wrong move might send it and him plummeting into the dark chasm.

Jamie closed his eyes. If he was going to die, then he would die thinking of Jix and what might have been. What if they hadn't gone back in time, he wondered? What if she and Sam had simply come to his great-uncle's festival and they had met and he and Jix had discovered this hot attraction they had for one another and acted upon it? They would have seen each other exclusively for awhile, then gotten engaged and set a wedding date. They would have married in the spring and gone to live at Meadbrooke Manor, where Jamie would have managed Uncle Angus's estate and learned the fine art of swordmaking, and Jix would have written her books for the next five years.

When the time was right, he and Jix would have had babies. First, a little girl that looked like her, then maybe a boy with her green eyes and his dark hair. He smiled in the darkness. She'd make an incredible mother. Offbeat and determined to do things her own way, but still incredible.

He blinked. When had he decided Jix Ferguson could be responsible enough for motherhood or marriage? When had his doubts about the two of them changed? Jamie smiled grimly. He guessed knowing you were about to die put a different spin on things. He'd always worried that when he reached the end of his life he would have terrible regrets. Now he had arrived at that doorway, and he did. If he had it to do over, he would have confessed his love to Jix as soon as he'd felt it. He would have broken down her walls of defense until she couldn't deny her love for him either. For somehow, sitting there, waiting for the ledge to fall, Jamie knew in his heart that Jix Ferguson loved him just as much as he loved her. Something was keeping her from admitting it, but it was there just the same.

"Jix," he said softly, "wherever ye are. I love ye, lass."

"Faster! We have go faster!"

Griffin's horse plunged in front of hers and Jix had to pull her big gelding, Thunder, up short to keep from running into Firestorm. Griffin reached over and grabbed the reins out of her hands and she turned on him, furious, to find he was just as angry.

"Ye canna race like this at night across ground ye dinna know!" he shouted, jerking on the reins, twisting her poor horse's head over one shoulder in order to turn her around. "Ye will break yer neck and then what will I tell Jamie if he *is* still alive? That I allowed ye to kill yerself? I dinna think so!"

"But Griffin—"

"Dinna 'but Griffin' me!" His handsome face was livid in the moonlight. "Ye will do as I say or I'll take ye back to the castle where ye belong!"

Jix glared at him. She had coerced the man into leaving that night to hunt for Jamie, but he was turning into a real pain in the neck. She shifted in the saddle, readjusting her trousers. Griffin had given her some of his discarded clothing, knowing she could ride faster without a bulky skirt. The trews almost swallowed her whole, but she had looped a belt around the top and drawn it tight. One of Griffin's large black shirts reached to her knees, and a black cloak engulfed her. Wearing her new ensemble, Jix felt more her old self than she had since arriving in the past. And Griffin Campbell wasn't going to keep her from finding Jamie.

"I've been riding Samantha's horses since I was ten years old!" she yelled. "I've won ribbons! I have to find Jamie. He may be hurt, Griffin, now get out of my way!"

"Ye will let me lead and travel safely, or so help me God I'll knock ye out of that saddle and carry ye back face down over my stallion!"

That sobered Jix pretty fast. From the look on Griffin's stern face she had no doubt that he meant what he said. She swallowed the lump in her throat and tried to think rationally. He was right. She didn't know this countryside and could just as easily go plunging headfirst off some cliff as across an open meadow. She shivered, thinking of Jamie plunging over the side of the ravine. Had he realized what was happening? Had he seen the ravine and been trying to jump it, as Fergus had suggested, or had he fallen into it unawares? She took a deep, ragged breath.

"All right," she said. "I'll follow you. Can I have my reins back?"

"Do ye promise?"

Jix gave him a reproachful look. "Would I lie to you?"

Griffin laughed shortly. "Only if ye're breathin'. I think I'll lead ye for a bit."

"I promise, Griffin. Please, give me the reins."

After a long moment, he did. "But if ye do this again—"

"I won't. We're wastin' time."

"Let yer horse walk to breathe a bit before he keels over."

Jix listened impatiently to her horse's labored breathing. She felt a pang of guilt. She didn't want to hurt the animal, she just wanted to find Jamie. Had to find him. He wasn't dead. As if he had read her mind, Griffin turned to her.

"What makes ye so sure that Jamie isna dead?"

"I've had two dreams about Jamie's future."

"Aye, and in one of them, he lost his head."

Jix closed her eyes, feeling the despair of his words settle over her. "I know," she said, opening her eyes and darting him an angry glance. "But he was at Meadbrooke Castle when that happened. That's why I know he isn't dead."

Griffin shook his head. "Ye have that much faith in yer dreams? What if they are wrong this time? Ye dreamed Jamie married yer friend, too, and it doesna look as though that is possible. What if yer dream of his losin' his head was just a premonition of his death?"

Griffin made perfect sense, but something deep inside of Jix said he was wrong. Her dreams were very specific and she knew, without a doubt, that Jamie wasn't dead.

He couldn't be.

"No, he's alive. Can we move along now?"

Griffin nodded and the two set off at a fast trot. As they rode, Jix glanced up at the moon. It was beginning to set, but the night was still almost as bright as day. Their first stop would be the ravine where Fergus had seen Jamie disappear. Jix felt sure if he had, indeed, fallen into some sort of gully or hole, a strong man like Jamie could easily have climbed out of it. She fully expected not to find him there, and that was going to be the hard part. If Jamie had escaped, he might be wandering, dazed, alone, and blunder right into an English patrol. They rode for another hour, and just when Jix felt her derriere might never have feeling in it again, Griffin pulled up.

"It's just ahead," he said, pointing in front of him.

Jix kicked Thunder in the sides and dashed ahead of him. Griffin hurried to catch up with her, grabbing her horse by the bridle and bringing it to a stop.

"Sorry," she said, sliding out of the saddle.

Griffin glared at her but swung down and together they ran toward a long, dark shadow in the ground. He reached it first and Jix skidded to a stop at his side, grabbing his arm to keep from going over the edge. Her heart pounded painfully in her chest and she covered her mouth with both hands as she stared down into the great gaping maw of a bottomless black chasm.

"Oh, my God," Jix whispered against her hands, then lowered them slowly into fists at her side. The ravine was a jagged tear in the earth, a pitiless void. It was like a black hole, absorbing all the light that came near and obliterating it. And Jamie? Her heart thudded against her chest.

"Now will ye believe it, Jix?" Griffin asked, leaning over the edge, one hand on his thigh. "There is no way a man could survive such a fall."

Jix shook her head. "I don't care. He isn't dead. Jamie!" She called down into the gorge. "Jamie MacGregor, are you there?"

For what seemed like hours Jix called, screamed, cried, and cajoled, until she lost her voice and could no longer say his name. She sank to the ground and leaned her face into her hands, weary and heartsick. The faint pink fingers of dawn laced across the sky and Jix struggled back to her feet. She stumbled to the edge of the gorge and looked down. Griffin hurried to her side. The sides of the precipice angled sharply outward, then back in at places. She couldn't see anything remotely indicating that Jamie was alive and somehow clinging to the sides of the steep rocks. The bottom of the great gulch was still hidden to them, the blackness still so deep that the dawn's light couldn't penetrate it.

"Och, Jix," Griffin said softly, "there's a wee village just down the way, and an inn. We can ride there and break our fast, then decide what to do next."

Jix nodded and let him lead her away. She felt weak from hunger and thirst and worry. She started to mount her horse, then lowered her foot to the ground and leaned her head against the saddle.

What if Jamie lay at the bottom of the ravine, alive, weak and hungry and thirsty, unable to speak, his throat too dry from lack of water? What if his leg were broken, or his back, and he lay in agonizing pain—

The fear and sorrow Jix had held at bay all day flooded into her soul. She fell to her knees and wept, sobs racking her body, her fingers clutching the ground to keep from falling off the world, a world without Jamie. How stupid she had been! Denying her love for him because of a dream. Feeling disloyal to Samantha when her friend barely knew the man. Lying to the one man who had been able to erase the painful memories of Dirk the Jerk. Telling him she didn't love him. If only she could see Jamie now, she would confess to him that in all the world, in all the universe, in all of time, Jamie MacGregor was the only man she would ever love.

231

Griffin knelt beside Jix and put his arm around her. She leaned her head against his shoulder, squeezing her eyes shut, fighting against the power of her pain. He hugged her tightly as the tears ran down her face.

"Thank you, Griffin," she said hoarsely. She looked up at him and her fingers tightened around his waist. "Griffin—you aren't shaking!"

He shrugged and smiled. "Och, well, maybe I'm gettin' used to ye. Shall we go on to the village? There may be news of a man brought in, injured, or mayhap yer friend is there."

"Aye." Jix dashed her tears from her face and let go of Griffin's strong arms reluctantly. She walked over to her horse and gathered up the reins, then put her foot in the stirrup and hauled her body wearily up and over the heavy saddle. "Let's go."

They hadn't gone three feet before Jix pulled Thunder to a halt. Her throat tightened and a feeling swept over her so intense, so horrifying that she couldn't move. She began to tremble. Jamie *was* in that black abyss. She knew it. She felt it. She would stake her life upon it. He was hurt and needed her help.

"Jix—what's wrong?" Griffin called, stopping ahead, Firestorm twisting impatiently beneath him.

Jix couldn't answer. She threw her right leg over the saddle horn and slid off her mount, then crumpled to the ground, her knees too weak to hold her. She staggered to her feet as a cold chill seared down her spine. Griffin dismounted and hurried to help her.

"He's here," she whispered.

"Och, lassie, I know ye want to think so, but there's no way—"

Jix grabbed Griffin's arms and shook him, and even though her strength had about as much impact on the big man as a mosquito shaking a bear, she got his attention. Her voice wasn't much more than a rasp, but she had to make him understand.

"Griffin! Listen to me! You said that I have the Sight. All right, then—something is telling me that Jamie is here.

232

He's in that black hole and he's alive and we have to get him out! Will you help me?"

Griffin gave her a long, searching look, turned and glanced at the ravine, then turned back to her. At last he nodded. "Aye. What do ye want me to do?"

Jix almost wept again with relief. She threw her arms around his neck and hugged him tightly.

"Och, lass, let's no' tempt fate."

She blinked the moisture from her eyes. "All right. First, help me call for him. He may be injured or unconscious. We have to locate him if at all possible before we do anything else. And second—" Jix looked him up and down. Griffin wore his plaid, his tartan, his trews, and a shirt. It might be enough. It would have to be. She gave him a rueful smile.

"And second, take off your clothes."

Jamie's throat felt raw, dry, scratchy, as though someone had stuffed cotton down his gullet when he wasn't looking. He opened his eyes, gratified to see that the sun had finally risen. He felt the back of his head gingerly. His hand came away bloodied. Well, that explained why he had lost consciousness again. He only hoped he didn't have a concussion. Not that it would matter anyway if the shelf beneath him gave way. Carefully he sat up and looked around, able at last to truly ascertain his chances of survival.

The ledge on which he sat protruded about four feet out from the side of the ravine. A slight overhang shielded him above and he slid out just a bit so he could gauge how far down he had fallen. He sat back again, appalled. Twenty feet. Only twenty feet from the top of the ravine. But it might as well be twenty miles. The sides of the gorge were formed from sharp, slatelike rocks that crumbled easily. There were no handholds that he could see. If he had rappelling gear he might make it, or even a good rope. But bare-handed?

Jamie slid back under the overhang, moving slowly lest more of his precarious perch slide into the darkness below. It was hopeless. He linked his hands over one knee, trying to ignore the various aches and pains as well as the rumbling in his stomach and the dryness of his throat. He would think about Jix instead. Jix and her green eyes sparkling with mischief, Jix with her auburn hair, now streaked with gold from being in the Scottish sun so much. Jix with her soft, soft lips and her sweet, sweet breasts, and her fine, unconquerable spirit.

The first time they made love, Jamie knew immediately that he was not taking anything from Jix Ferguson. What he received was given freely, without reserve. He hadn't realized at the time how precious the gift she had given him really was. Now he did. He wished he could tell her, along with the fact that he loved her more than he'd ever thought possible.

"Jamie!"

The whispered word came to him on the breeze wafting its way down the side of the ravine. Jamie sat up. Had he imagined it?

"Jamie!"

There it was again. Hardly audible.

"MacGregor!"

Jamie leaned forward. Now that he hadn't imagined. It was Griffin Campbell's deep baritone voice. And—Jix? Was Jix with him?

"Here!" he called, his own voice hoarse, weak. He cleared his throat and tried again. "I am here!" he cried, pushing his strength into the words.

At the top of the chasm, directly above him, barely visible to him beneath the overhang, a familiar red head appeared and two anguished green eyes gazed down at him.

"Jamie!" Jix cried, sounding hoarse and distraught. Tears flooded down her face and Jamie felt a quick surge of hope. She had come looking for him. Even if he died, he at least could say good-bye. But no, this was terrible—he didn't want Jix to see him die.

She stretched one hand toward him. "Oh, Jamie, thank God we found you!"

"Are ye all right, MacGregor?" Griffin called, his blond head appearing beside hers.

"Aye," Jamie called back as best he could. "I'm no' much hurt, except for my ankle. I may have broken it, but I suspect it's just a sprain."

"Oh, thank God, thank God." Jix was crying again and Jamie felt suddenly impatient to be out of this hole so that he could take her in his arms.

"I'm all right, lass," he called. "Now use that brilliant mind of yers to help me out of this mess."

"Where were you last night?" she demanded. "I called and called and you didn't answer. Oh Jamie—" she broke off again, her tortured voice trembling.

He couldn't help but smile. "I must have stepped out for a minute. Ye mean the two of ye were here last night?" The overhang must have shielded him from their search.

"Early this morn, actually," Griffin corrected. "We have an idea on how to get ye out—or rather, Jix has an idea. But with yer ankle hurt—" he broke off.

"Jix always has ideas," Jamie chuckled, then his eyes widened. "Did ye say, 'Jix'?" He cleared his throat. "Who is Jix?"

"I told him the truth," Jix called down.

"Ye did *what?*"

"I told him the truth about us. Now shut up, MacGregor, and let us figure out how to get you out of there."

Jamie sat back against the stone wall. She had told Griffin the truth! Knowing Jix, that could mean any number of things. When he got out of this mess, he supposed she would explain. All at once he didn't feel like his survival was such a long shot. He pushed back with his good heel to straighten his back, then gasped as almost half the ledge sliced off and fell into the dark ravine.

He scrambled back just in time to keep from tumbling to the bottom. About two feet of the ledge's width remained, just barely enough room to sit beneath the overhang and dangle his legs over the side. Jamie swallowed hard. He could hear Griffin and Jix arguing at the top, her rasping voice punctuating Griffin's deep rumble.

"Uh, lass," he called, his heart pounding as he looked straight down into the mouth of the earth. "Griffin?" The voices above were growing louder, drowning out his words, and finally Jamie put two fingers in his mouth and let loose a piercing whistle. The quarreling stopped, and Jix's face appeared again.

"What is it Jamie, we're trying to—"

"Uh, lass, my situation has just gotten a wee bit worse."

Jix's eyes widened in horror. "Griffin!"

Griffin looked over the edge and his eyes widened. "Och, damn it to hell."

"Aye, my sentiments exactly," Jamie agreed.

"Now I'll have to let her do it."

Jamie's heart almost stopped beating. "Now ye'll have to let her do what?"

There was more argument above him, and Jamie's heart started beating double time. "What's goin' on up there?"

"Hang on!" Jix cried, her voice sounding a little improved, but much too excited. He knew that tone. She was about to do something crazy. "We're figuring something out!"

After another minute, something came flying over the edge of the gorge. Rocks crumbled past him. Jamie had a hard time making out what the object was at first but as it slowly descended he realized it was a hodgepodge of clothing tied together—a green and brown tartan tied to a green and brown plaid, tied to a shirt, and, lastly, what looked to be a pair of leather trews tied to something he couldn't make out. A rock had been attached to the end and it inched by his perch.

"What the hell are the two of ye doin'?" he shouted, then his breath caught in his throat as he saw Jix swing over the edge of the cliff, hanging onto the makeshift rope for dear life. "No," he whispered. "No. NO!"

Jix's hand slipped and she grabbed for another hold, finding it in the knot between the shirt and the trews. She wore only a shirt that came to her thighs and a pair of boots. He could only assume that she had given up some part of her wardrobe for this insane plan.

"You almost made me fall!" she yelled. "Now shut up, MacGregor, and let me rescue you!"

"Campbell!" Jamie roared.

"He's busy!" Jix retorted, sliding down another foot. "Don't distract him, he's monitoring the knots for slippage and he's got the end tied around the saddle horn of his horse. Do you want him to come talk to you or do you want him to keep me from ending up at the bottom?"

"When I get out of here I'm goin' to kill him for lettin' ye do something so dangerous! An' then I'm goin' to raise welts on *yer* bottom for talkin' him into it!" Jamie trembled with the force of his fear. He would rather dive head-first by his own volition into the black abyss than sit helplessly as Jix tumbled to the bottom of the horrible pit.

"There's no other way, you stubborn Scot! Griffin's too heavy for this stupid rope we made!"

"An' how do ye plan to bring me up? On yer back?"

"Stop talking to me! You're breaking my concentration. This isn't as easy as it looks!" Her foot slipped against the crumbling shale and a large chunk went flying to the bottom of the ravine.

He stopped talking. Jix inched her way down and Jamie held his breath as she slowly descended into the chasm. By the time she reached him, his entire body was drenched with sweat and he was shaking.

"Now what?" he asked, fighting to keep the tremor from his voice. "I dinna think this ledge will hold the two of us."

Jix braced her feet against the side of the cliff. She had reached a position next to Jamie and their faces were so close that if he leaned out, he could have touched his lips to hers. He didn't dare. Just in the last few minutes more of the shelf had crumbled. Not a lot, but enough to tell him that every movement was dangerous. Jix cast an anxious glance at the narrow perch on which he sat.

"Okay, this is the tricky part."

Jamie took a deep, calming breath. "Jix, listen to me, love." She blinked at the endearment and he hurried on. "This willna work. Go back up and just throw the rope back to me, ye ken?"

"I had planned to switch places with you and have you

go up first, then you and Griffin could pull me up."

He shook his head. "Why am I surprised? Why did ye no' just throw the rope down to me in the first place? No—don't answer that—just go back up!"

But she didn't. And as she hung between earth and sky, biting her lower lip, indecision in her gaze, Jamie felt his heart might burst with love for this selfless, beautiful, totally insane woman.

"Your ankle—I was afraid you couldn't make it," she said, her voice raspy.

"Jix—"

"I was afraid you might not be able to climb up by yourself."

"Jix—go—"

"I was going to tie the rope around your waist and have Griffin pull you up."

"Jix Ferguson, climb back up that rope this instant or so help me—"

Her face suddenly contorted in horror. "Jamie—I'm slipping!"

It all happened in a matter of seconds. Jamie grabbed Jix around the waist with his left hand, diving for the makeshift rope with his right even as the ledge beneath his feet crumbled into oblivion. Above he heard Griffin cry out as the strand of clothing stretched further and the two of them swung out over the bottomless ravine.

"Oh poop," Jix said, clinging to his neck. "I guess this wasn't such a great idea after all."

Above them, the shirt between the plaid and the trews began to tear.

Chapter Sixteen

"Drop me!" Jix cried.

"What?" Jamie tightened his hold on her. "Dinna be crazier than ye are!"

"Just drop me and you'll make it!" Her voice was getting higher and Jamie recognized the signs of hysteria. "I deserve it! It's all my fault! Drop me! If I hadn't—"

The only resource Jamie had was his mouth and he pressed his lips against hers, effectively silencing her for a moment. He pulled away. "Now listen to me," he said, his tone carefully calm. "Put yer feet against the rock, ye ken?" He put his own booted feet in place and after a second, Jix put hers beside his. His arm muscles cried out for relief and his ankle felt as though it might snap in two, but he ignored the pain, sweat pouring down his back. "Campbell!" he shouted. "Have ye flown to Argentina? Where the hell are ye?"

Griffin's head appeared over the edge. "Sorry!" he cried, frantic. "The knot almost slipped. I had to repair it!"

"Well, ye've got a tear in the shirt—tie something around it!"

Griffin disappeared, then quickly returned and tied a kerchief in the middle of the shirt. "I dinna know if it will hold but that's all I have."

"It'll hold! Make the horse walk forward, do ye ken? Slowly—and Jix and I will walk up the wall to ye!"

"Aye, aye!" Griffin called, and disappeared again.

"Now hold onto me, lass," Jamie said softly.

"Jamie, I'm scared," she whispered.

"Dinna be afraid, I willna let ye fall." Their eyes met for a brief second and Jix pressed a quick kiss against his lips, then tightened her hold around his neck.

Together, inch by inch, they crawled up the side of the ravine as Griffin's horse moved forward, keeping the line taut, keeping enough momentum going to pull them up the side. Just as they reached the top, Jamie heard a loud rip and he threw Jix forward. The rope snapped but because of his thrust, Jix landed on the flat of the earth. Jamie dived at the same time and hit the edge of the ravine, gasping as his breath left his body. Strong hands grabbed his arms and dragged him over the edge. Jamie lay on his back, groaning, then the breath was knocked from him again as Jix fell against him, sobbing. He blinked back his own tears of relief, shaking with the knowledge that he had almost lost her forever.

He sat up and held Jix until she stopped crying, then smoothed her hair back from her forehead and gazed down into her eyes.

"Och, lass, thank ye for rescuing me."

She burst into tears again and buried her face against his neck. Griffin knelt down beside them, shivering. He wrapped a black cloak around Jix's shoulders.

"It was too thick to tie into the rope," he said. Jamie glanced up and saw the Scot was stark naked. He sat up and pulled Jix with him. This was certainly no time for proprieties, but Jamie held out his hand anyway.

"Thank ye," he said.

Griffin shook his hand, then helped Jamie and Jix stagger to their feet.

"Thanks again," Jamie said.

"Aye, but—"

His words were cut short by the impact of Jamie's fist slamming into his eye. The blow sent the Scot tumbling to his bare backside. Jamie towered over him, rubbing his fist.

"That's for lettin' her take such a dangerous, foolish, idiotic risk!"

"Jamie!" Jix shrieked. "It wasn't his fault!"

Griffin groaned, one hand covering his eye. "Aye, I deserve it. I dinna wish to interrupt yer thrashin' of me, but there are horses comin', and they are no' Scots." He nodded toward the east, one hand over his eye.

Jamie turned. Dirt billowed into the air. Not just a few horses, but a lot of horses. A detachment from the stockade, looking for the reivers? Jamie bent down and picked Jix up in his arms, kicking the rope toward Griffin.

"Do ye know a place we can hide?" he asked as the man gathered his clothing and threw it across his saddle. Jamie watched him climb up and wince as he sat down naked against the hard leather.

"Leave me here!" Jix cried suddenly, struggling in his arms. "I can send them the wrong way! I'll tell them that the reivers ravaged me and headed the opposite direction!"

Griffin shot a worried look at Jamie. "I dinna think—"

"Lass, shut the hell up!" Jamie cried, shaking her. "Do ye think I would risk losing the woman I love more than life itself to save my own skin? Now, get on the horse!" The cloak covered her somewhat, but he ripped his plaid from his shoulders and wrapped it around her waist, then slapped her on the behind.

Jix gave him one astonished look, but mounted her horse without another word. Jamie quickly got on behind her.

"Follow me," Griffin called, bunching the clothing rope in front of him in the saddle. "I know a place."

He kicked his horse into action and Jamie turned the gelding after him, smiling grimly as he saw Griffin's bare bottom jiggle against the saddle. A true Scot, he thought and glanced down at Jix. She sat leaning against his chest, her eyes closed, her fingers twisted in the hem of his shirt.

Good. He didn't want her gazing at Campbell's tigh
buttocks. A dark thought crossed his mind. Or had she see
them already?

"Where are we?" Jix asked, her voice croaking again.

The combination of playing Super Jix to the rescue
screaming her lungs out, dangling above a bottomless pi
and fearing Jamie was about to die because of her lame
brained idea had about done her in. She needed water des
perately, but said nothing. If she ached for a drink, hov
much more did Jamie need something to quench his thirs
after being trapped on that ledge all night long?

'The woman I love more than life itself.' Had he reall
said those words? How she longed to talk to him, but no
in front of Griffin. That would be unkind. She still wasn'
sure that Griffin hadn't been a little hurt by her admissio
of love for Jamie. Not to mention Jamie's fist. Luckily, th
Scot hadn't seemed to take offense to Jamie's attack.

Men—go figure.

"It's no' much farther. This is a place I dinna think th
English will come," Griffin said, pulling his plaid aroun
him.

He'd handed Jix the 'rope' a few miles back and she'
managed to pick out the knots to release her own trew
and belt and the large piece of green and brown materia
that made up Griffin's plaid. It covered him well and a
least helped keep off the chill night air. After Jix donne
her trousers, Jamie had donated his plaid to cover th
man's lower half.

They had been riding for what seemed like hours ove
rocky terrain, down craggy hills, across stark stone, skirt
ing dark crevices more frightening than the one that ha
swallowed Jamie. Jix felt weary beyond belief but she kep
working on unknotting Griffin's clothes. It was the leas
she could do. As she worked, Jix pictured what a col
night in September would mean back home. Not that ther
ever were any cold nights in Texas before December. Bu
in the few cold winter months awarded Texans, on a nigh
like this she would snuggle down in bed with a warm quil

and a good romance novel. She'd fix a tray complete with a cup of hot chocolate or maybe a café au lait and a pile of her expensive favorite cookies. Except now that bed would be empty without Jamie beside her.

"There's a place up ahead," Griffin was saying, his voice pulling her back from her reverie. "It's in a hollow, and if we keep the fire small, I dinna think the—" his voice trailed off. "Damn."

Jix looked up from the task in her lap, her fingers gripping the clothing. Ahead of them the ground dipped down, sloping steadily to the bottom of the hill. A soft glow permeated the base of the hollow.

"What is it?" she asked softly.

"Someone's already there. We'll have to go on."

Jix groaned aloud, then felt the heat flood to her face. "I'm sorry," she said, embarrassed at her outburst. "I'm fine. Really. Let's push on."

"Nay," Jamie pulled back on the reins. "I can go no further. Mayhap these wanderers will share their fire?"

Griffin shot him a quick glance and raised his brows. Jix knew the Scot didn't believe Jamie's claim of weakness anymore than she did. He was stopping for her. Taking a chance for her.

"No, let's go on," Jix insisted, turning in the saddle to face him. "Jamie, I—"

"Lass." He lifted one hand and stroked his fingers down the side of her face. "Do ye think I can wait much longer to get off this horse and hold ye in my arms properly?"

His mouth touched hers and Jix cupped his face between her hands, opening her lips to him. His tongue met hers and warmth coursed through her as he made a heated promise without using any words at all.

"All right," she said, drawing away, "but be careful."

Griffin dismounted and Jamie slid off too, winced, then turned and held up his arms to Jix. She started to refuse but he grasped her by the waist and she had to put her hands on his shoulders to keep from falling. He lowered her slowly, letting her body slide against his, the evidence of his desire obvious beneath the tight trousers he wore.

"Is that yer sword, MacGregor," she whispered, putting on her brogue for a moment, "or are ye just glad to see me?"

"Och, lass, so very glad to see ye."

They stood together, Jix's arms around his waist, his holding her tightly. Griffin cleared his throat and Jix jumped back, embarrassed.

"Yer pardon," the Scot said dryly, "but I fear we have company and I am in sore need of my clothes."

Jamie and Jix turned. Behind them stood a group of men, swords in hand. They wore the brightest colors Jix had seen in all her time in the past—reds, blues, greens, yellows, vibrant and bold. Their shirts had wide, wide sleeves, and their pants were wide-legged as well, stuffed down into black boots, billowing over the edges. Kerchiefs were tied around their necks or heads, and sashes at their waists. The leader of the group had black hair and eyes and for a moment Jix felt faint. The man in her worst dream had this sort of coloring—but no, this man had sallow skin, and his eyes were not filled with murder or malice. His eyes were wary, to be sure, but nothing more. And he wasn't tall enough to be the man in her dream. She blinked. These were gypsies.

"Gypsies," she said.

"Aye." Griffin tightened the plaid around his waist, adjusted the one at his shoulder, then walked forward to greet them as if he were the King of England clad in regal trappings—black eye and all. "I am Griffin Campbell and we mean ye no harm."

Jamie drew Jix back from the men and protectively moved in front of her. She gazed at his muscled back, his broad shoulders, longing to lift his shirt away and smooth her hands over his bare skin, assuring herself that he was real. She closed her eyes, feeling more confused than she ever had in her life. Finding Samantha seemed more elusive than ever, marrying Griffin was out of the question, and staying alive was proving to be extremely difficult. So many decisions to make, when all she wanted to do was love Jamie MacGregor and be loved by him. She sighed.

"Are ye all right, lass?" Jamie asked, his voice low.

She started to answer, started to tell him she would never be all right without him, when he turned toward her and frowned slightly.

"Ye told Griffin of our relationship—did ye tell him about our little trip through time as well?"

"Yes, I did." He shook his head and closed his eyes as if bemoaning the fact that he hadn't dropped her down the ravine after all. "Jamie, I'm sorry," she said hastily, "but we need his help! He's willing to get the sword for us!"

Jamie's dark brows rose. "Is he now? And why would he be willin' to do that?" There was no mistaking the accusation in his voice.

Jix felt her heart sink. Here it was again—his lack of trust. So his words of loving her had just been to quiet her, calm her after their near misadventure. For without trust, there could be no love.

"Gee, I dunno. Maybe that last lap dance did the trick!" she snapped, turning away. She clasped her arms around her waist, digging her fingers into her own flesh as she blinked back tears. She could feel him watching her, thinking, as he stood motionless behind her, then his hand was on her shoulder. She wouldn't turn around.

"Lass," Jamie said softly, "I'm sorry."

Jix glanced over her shoulder and saw real apology in his eyes. She let him turn her to face him but reached up and stopped his hand as it moved to cup her face. "You said something strange back there at the ravine." She put his hand firmly away from her. "You said something about not wanting to lose the woman you loved more than anything else on earth."

Jamie smiled down at her. "Did I?"

So, he was going to deny it. Jix took a deep breath and tried to sound casual. "Well, maybe not. I was sort of hysterical for a few minutes. Maybe I imagined it. Never mind."

"Lass, I—"

Griffin came bounding over to them, interrupting what-

245

ever Jamie was about to say. The big blond Scot was wearing a grin from ear to ear.

"They'll be happy to share their fire with us," he said, "an' their meal, an' they have no love for the English." He nodded, a satisfied look on his face. "I think we can safely rest this night."

"Wonderful," Jix said flatly. "Let's go."

They followed the gypsies back to their camp, Jamie limping beside her. He and Griffin found a place for the three of them to sleep, not too far from the central fire. The gypsy leader, called Malkov, even provided them with some extra blankets. Jix snuggled into one beside the fire and dived into a bowl of succulent stew one of the gypsy women handed her. Jamie and Griffin sat one on either side of her devouring their own food, passing a bottle of wine first to her, then to each other until it was all gone.

One of the gypsies got up and began to play a beautiful haunting melody on a violin as Jix ate the last bite of her stew and leaned back, feeling utterly replete.

"Do ye need to find a place to relieve yerself?" Jamie asked quietly in her ear.

Jix frowned at him, then laughed, feeling the effects of the wine. Leave it to Jamie to think of the essentials and spoil the moment. She was still angry with him, but presently felt too content to do much about it. Besides, she did need to pee.

"Yes, thank you." She nudged Griffin. "We'll be back in a minute."

Griffin nodded, his glazed eyes on a beautiful, dark-haired gypsy woman who had risen to the tune of the violin and now swayed to the music, her body writhing with the rhythm. So he wasn't exactly pining away for the lack of her love, Jix thought wryly, as she and Jamie left the camp.

Jamie led Jix up the hill from the camp to a grove of trees and bracken. She was almost afraid to go inside the dense thicket, and for the first time since their arrival wondered about snakes.

"You first," she said brightly, peering into the darkness.

"I have no need." He gestured to the trees. "Hurry up. I dinna want to miss the dancing."

"I thought you were a gentleman."

"Och, surely a lass who can scale a cliff with naught but her lover's clothes can handle any wee beastie in the forest." His mouth lifted in a dark smile.

"He is not my lover!" His words made her so angry that she stormed into the woods, kicking her feet out in front of her. In Texas she'd been taught that the first person stirs up a snake from his nest and then it bites the second. Angrily she wished Jamie was walking behind her. "And don't you dare watch me either!"

She came out of the woods a few minutes later determined to ignore him, expecting to immediately return to the camp. But Jamie stood leaning against one of the larger trees, his arms crossed over his chest as he gazed at the moon. He had pulled his hair back into what Griffin had referred to as a 'queue,' and his face gleamed with shadowed silver in the moonlight.

Jix felt drawn to him, and as if some ancient magic had decreed it, she walked slowly to him, placing her hands on his crossed arms. Jamie lowered his gaze to hers, his midnight blue eyes soft with longing. It was the most natural thing in the world to lift her mouth for his kiss. It was the most natural thing in the world to let him take her in his arms and twine hers behind his neck.

They stood in moonlight, two silver statues soft against one another; then Jamie stepped back and Jix shivered as his hands moved over the ties of her cloak. It slid from her shoulders to the ground. He lifted the hem of her shirt, pulling it over her head. Her belt came off next, tossed aside. The too-large trousers fell to her feet and she stepped out of them, now totally naked but for her boots, feeling pagan and magical under the cold Scottish moon.

Jamie loosed his plaid and swung it around her shoulders, then slowly disrobed until he, too, stood like a figure in some ancient tale of yore. He led her past the grove of trees, into the meadow beyond that lay shimmering beneath the starlight. He took the plaid from her shoulders and spread it across the ground, then sat down and lifted his hand to her. Jix sank to her knees beside him and he fell back, drawing her down with him. She slid on top of him and for a moment they simply looked at one another, their bodies pressed together, nothing between them, no clothes, no pretenses, and suddenly Jix wanted no lies between them either.

"Jamie," she said, hardly daring to speak above a whisper, so mystical did this place seem with the meadow at their backs and the brilliant stars and moon above.

"Ye want to know why I said what I said." He cradled her face between his hands. His hair had come undone from its leather tie and she couldn't resist raking her fingers through it, spreading the long waves across the plaid. She couldn't speak. Couldn't tell him her need. If he refused, or made a joke, she couldn't stand it. Jix Ferguson serious. Well, that was one for the books.

"Yes," she said at last. "I want to know."

Jamie gently smoothed his thumb across her cheekbones. "Because I meant it," he whispered. "Because I love ye, Jix Ferguson, more than life itself. I love yer laugh and the crazy things ye do. I love how ye try to hide yer feelings, and laugh away yer pain, and I promise, I will spend the rest of my life making ye feel safe enough to be honest with me, always, in every matter, in every way."

Jix felt stunned. "You don't have to say this," she said. "I want to make love to you. You don't have to—"

"Och, lass," he said, his hands sliding down the side of her neck to her shoulders. His dark brows pressed together fervently. "Do ye think I say this to get ye in my bed? Nay, lass, I say this to keep ye in my bed. Forever."

"But Samantha—"

He touched her nose with one finger. "We'll find Samantha. Now that Griffin knows the truth and is willin' to help, we'll find her in no time."

"I didn't sleep with him," she said, as he pulled her mouth down to his. The kiss was sweet, warm, delicious. When he pulled away, his smile was gentle.

"I know ye didn't. 'Twas just my male ego getting in the way of my brain."

She moved slightly and was rewarded by his quick intake of breath. "Which brain are we talking about, laddie?"

His hands slid down her back and Jix arched against them as Jamie grew hard and hot beneath her. "I think ye are about to find out, lass."

They made love quickly, both of them feeling an urgency to reclaim life, both heady with wine and the intoxication of their feelings. Afterward, Jix lay on top of him, totally limp with satisfaction, feeling wild and uninhibited, exulting in the power Jamie had given her.

How had she not realized this? Being loved by a man like Jamie wouldn't rob her of anything. Being loved by a man like Jamie would only increase her own innate worth. She would tell him, confess her love for him. In a minute. Her eyes closed as exhaustion from their perilous day claimed her. She would tell him as soon as she awoke, she amended, feeling Jamie's rhythmic breathing beneath her. As soon as they both awoke. She smiled. Yes, as soon as he opened his eyes again, she would take that final step and admit, to his face, that she couldn't live without Jamie MacGregor.

Chapter Seventeen

Jix walked aimlessly across verdant green meadows, the smell of heather and roses heavy in the air. She felt lost, confused. Why was she alone? Where were Jamie and Samantha? She gazed across the lonely field and in the far distance finally made out the turrets of Meadbrooke Castle. How had she wandered so far from the castle and why? She shaded her eyes from the unseasonably bright sunlight and turning, scanned the horizon in the other direction. The blue of the Scottish sky seemed unusually bright today, marred only by a haze of brown clouds near the ground. Brown clouds?

Jix blinked, one hand flying to her throat as she saw dozens of horses galloping toward her, dirt flying out from behind their hooves. She turned and ran, her long skirt tangling around her legs, trying to trip her. Jerking the material up to her knees, she didn't look back, but kept running.

Before long the horses caught up with Jix and rushed past her, as if she didn't exist. She stumbled to a stop, gasping for breath, and watched as men on horseback rode past. One of the men carried a flag atop a long pole. The British flag, red cross over white. Now Jix gathered her skirts again and tore across the countryside after them, afraid she would be too late to warn those in the castle. The sky grew darker as she ran, until she feared the darkness itself chased her, waiting for a chance to swallow her whole.

When she arrived at Meadbrooke Castle she rushed inside. A tall man with black hair and piercing black eyes stood behind a table covered with a long black cloth. On top of the table was a bloody sword and a silver serving platter, with a large cover atop it. He lifted the cover. Horror welled up inside of her, but she could not give it utterance, all she could do was stare.

Jamie's disembodied head sat upon the platter, blood dripping from his neck and a gash on his head.

Then he opened his eyes.

Jix sat up gasping for air.

The dream. The dream had returned.

"Jix, lass, what is it, what's wrong?" Jamie sat up beside her on the plaid. The moon had gone behind a cloud and she could barely see him in the darkness. Suddenly he seemed very far away.

Jix gulped down the terror and tried to stay calm, for on the heels of her panic had come a clear understanding.

The reason the death dream had replaced that of Jamie and Sam's wedding was because of her love for him. Her love, combined with their trip through time, had somehow altered the future, and now it was her fault Jamie was destined to die. Her love for him had eradicated the dream of Jamie and Sam getting married, and replaced it with Jamie's death.

"Nothing. Just a nightmare," she said, pulling her knees to her chest and hiding her face against them, despair flooding over her.

"What was it about?"

She shook her head. "Jamie, I almost got you killed today at the ravine with my stupid idea." Jix lifted her panicky gaze to his sleepy one. He snapped to instant attention, and a cloud blew past the moon in time to light his face and let Jix see the concern in his dark blue eyes. He was so beautiful. She reached out and touched his jaw with her fingertips. "I'm not going to let my love destroy you like it's destroyed everyone else in my life."

"It willna," he said softly, capturing her fingers and pressing his lips to them. "Love doesna destroy, lass."

"Mine does." She pulled away from him and stood uncertainly. "Mine always does."

"Lass." He shook his head, rising to his feet. He picked up the plaid. "Dinna do this. I love ye and nothing is going to keep us apart now."

Jix stared at him, longing to expose her fears, but she couldn't. He wouldn't understand. He would laugh away her concern. And then he would die. Panic welled up inside of her as she found her trews and pulled them on.

"Jix." Jamie moved beside her, picking up his own clothes. He draped her cloak around her shoulders. "Ye havena caused any of this."

Her throat tightened as she clutched the edges of the warm covering around her. "Yes, I have. If I hadn't interfered in Sam's life, none of this would be happening! Your life wouldn't be in danger. The worst thing that would have happened to you would have been marrying Samantha! Why do I do these crazy things?"

"Marrying Samantha?"

Jix shrugged out of the cloak and pulled her shirt on over her head, then picked up the thick cape.

"When will I ever learn?" she asked, her heart aching. "Does it make me feel like I have some kind of control over my life or something? Do I really think I can keep bad things from happening to the people I love? Maybe these are my motives, but the truth is, I'm a walking disaster! I've caused nothing but destruction!"

"Lass, calm down, ye aren't makin' any sense." Jamie reached out to her but she slapped his hands away. He stepped back, the shock registering in his eyes.

"Leave me alone, Jamie," she said softly. "I shouldn't

have made love to you again. This is not going to work."

"What isn't going to work?" he demanded.

"You, me—us! It's like I told you, it was fun but—"

He started pulling his own clothes on. "Och, dinna start that again!" He jerked his shirt on and pulled the borrowed trousers up and over his naked skin. Jix turned away, her heart aching, unable to look at him any longer and still remain strong.

"It isn't going to work!" she shouted. "Now, please go back to camp. I need to be alone." She wrapped her arms around her waist and glared back at him defiantly. "Do you *ken*, alone?"

His midnight eyes held her angry ones, and he pressed his lips tightly together as if trying to hold back his anger, or his frustration. Finally he released his breath in a long sigh. "I canna leave ye out here alone," he said.

"Then just—go sit there—on the side of the hill. I need time to think."

He took a step forward and turned her around, smoothing a lock of hair behind her ear as he leaned down and kissed her mouth gently. Jix felt as though her heart might burst with longing as his lips touched hers. How could she give up Jamie? How?

How can I not give him up if I know it will save his life?

"Go away, Jamie," she whispered against his lips.

"No," he said. "I'm no' leavin' ye alone. Talk to me, Jix. Talk to me now." His hands cupped her face and he searched her eyes. "Ye're going to tell the truth, Jix Ferguson. For once in yer blessed life."

"I'm telling the truth! I don't want you! Go away and leave me alone!"

"Aye, that is the song and dance ye keep feedin' me—ye dinna want to be with me, or ye canna be with me for some mysterious reason known only to ye."

Oh, don't look at me, Jamie, not with that angry passion in your eyes. She closed her own eyes but his image still burned in her mind. His hair streamed back from his face, the wind picking up the long dark strands and sending them gently into the air. She wasn't afraid of his furious expression because she knew now how easily it could change to gentle love or amusement. But he wasn't amused right now and she would never allow his love to claim her again. She opened her eyes.

"Jamie, you don't understand," she said.

"No, I dinna understand." He dropped his hands to her waist and pulled her into his arms. Her hands involuntarily moved to his chest as he gazed down at her, his dark eyes searching hers. "I dinna understand that when ye're in my arms and ye look into my eyes I can see the love ye have for me, but ye willna admit it. I dinna understand that when I make love to ye, ye burn so hot that I feel at times my soul is goin' to catch afire, and yet afterward, ye cry or run away."

He pulled her more firmly against him and Jix began to struggle, trying to push away. "And when ye struggle against me," he said, his voice softening as he lifted her face to his and all the fight left her body, "I dinna understand why just a touch from my hand will calm ye and why ye kiss me as if ye think to never see me again. Why all this"—he brought his mouth scant inches from hers—"if ye dinna love me?"

"Jamie . . ." His mouth was so near. Jix closed her eyes and her head fell back and she felt his lips on her neck, her ears, her face, her mouth. She kissed him back with all the love in her heart, her throat tight with unexpressed tears.

Then Jamie ended their kiss gently and with one last stroke of his hand over her hair, set her away from him, his face somber.

"When ye decide to be honest and tell me what's really goin' on, I'll listen," he said. "Until then, I'll no' touch ye again." Without another word, he turned and walked away.

Jix stood indecisively, watching him go, feeling bereft and as sickly abandoned as when her mother had left her on that long-ago day. But wasn't this the best thing, after all? If she stopped trying to fix things with Jamie, maybe he would turn to Sam when they found her, and maybe he wouldn't die. Because if one dream came true, the other one couldn't. If Jamie and Sam fell in love and planned to be married, then that would take away the death dream.

Right, God? *Right?*

Silence was her only answer. She let Jamie walk away.

Jamie was wide awake and fighting to keep from waking Jix up and having it out with her again. She had walked into camp a few seconds after him. She had ignored him and crawled between her blankets where she promptly fell asleep without a word to him. He sat beside her, leaning against a tree, unable to stop thinking. Unable to stop hurting.

He loved her. There was no doubt about that. And he truly believed that she loved him. He didn't really think she had a few screws loose, although at times he was tempted to wonder, but he knew something was terribly wrong. Why did she fight so hard against him? Why did she make love to him and then turn around and tell him it wasn't going to work?

Jamie ran one hand through his hair, dragging his fingers to the nape of his neck. And what was all that about his marrying Samantha? He frowned. Now that he thought about it, Jix often ended up talking about Samantha after one of these outbursts. He glanced down at the sleeping woman. Was there some connection? Maybe she thought she didn't deserve happiness since she had ruined Sam's marriage. Knowing Jix's loyalty to her friend, that might just be the problem.

But another time she had tried to convince him that he should go out with Samantha, and come to think of it, that night at his uncle's manor, Sam had accused Jix of hiring Jamie to seduce her. He frowned. Did Jix think he was interested in Samantha? Why would she think that? He'd disliked the woman from the moment she first opened her mouth, although later, after finding out they had hiked so far in the rain, he had been more compassionate. But why, after all he and Jix had been through, would she think he would want to hook up with Samantha? It made no sense at all.

Jamie leaned back against the tree and linked his hands over his knee, watching the gypsies dance, weary of trying to figure out Jix Ferguson, and yet wishing desperately that he could. He turned his attention to the bright colors and laughing eyes of the Romany people. This was a tribe with no small children and the leader had told him they often "celebrated" into the wee morning hours. They didn't fear the English because Captain Worthington sometimes called upon their fortune-teller to come and read his palm, and his men always enjoyed the gypsy women and paid well. Malkov had said that Worthington was very superstitious. It was practically his only weakness. There should be some way to use that against the man.

Across from him, Griffin Campbell sat next to the fire, getting roaring drunk on wine. Probably not a good idea given their situation, but Jamie didn't really blame him. In one day the man had lost his fiancée, saved his fiancée's lover, been punched by his fiancée's lover, almost been captured by the British, and been taken in by gypsies. Not a bad day's work in all, and well deserving of a little relaxation.

Jamie glanced down at Jix again and ran his gaze lightly over her slim body, then frowned. There was still something between Jix and Griffin. He knew it. He felt it. He didn't like it. And yet, he knew she didn't love the man. She loved him. He would stake his life on it.

The gypsies had built up the fire and four women danced around it, their bright skirts whirling, castanets and tambourines chiming out the rhythm of the music. They were all dark-haired and vivacious, with long legs and heavy breasts. He didn't wonder that the men sat spellbound, watching them, including Griffin Campbell. He hoped Griffin found a nice little gypsy to warm his bed tonight. It would ease his mind that much more about Jix and Griffin's relationship.

A new dancer joined them. This woman wore a black mantilla over her head. She laughed as one of the men tried to kiss her and the lacy black veil fell to her shoulders. She shook out a voluptuous mane of long, white-blond hair, a red bandana tied around it like a headband.

Jamie straightened. Samantha Riley whirled in frenzied abandon, her skirt swirling out in a huge circle from her waist. He couldn't help admiring her. She wore a brilliant blue peasant-style blouse, off the shoulder, tucked into a skirt that contained every color in the rainbow. A dozen bracelets or more covered her arms, and at least six or seven necklaces adorned her throat. Huge triangular silver earrings dangled beneath her blond hair, which hung past her waist. She was a far cry from the staid Samantha he remembered meeting.

The music ended and before Jamie could move, Griffin stumbled to his feet. He crossed to Samantha and pulled her into his arms. She laughed up at him, then kissed him on the mouth. Giving her a lopsided grin, he headed away from the camp, pulling her behind him.

"Och, Griffin," Jamie said, more to himself, "now I have to wake up Jix." He shook her shoulder. "Jix, love, wake up."

She raised her head to look up at him groggily, then fell face first back into the blanket. "This had better be important, MacGregor," she muttered.

"Just a bit. I just found yer friend, Samantha, and she's gone into the woods with Griffin."

Jix lay motionless for half a second, then sat up quickly. "What? What did you say?" she said, sounding dazed.

"I said your friend Samantha is here. She's with the gypsies and she and Griffin just left the camp with big smiles on their faces."

"That doesn't sound like Samantha," Jix said, lifting one hand to her head and frowning. "Are you sure?"

Jamie shrugged. "As sure as I can be. I only saw her the once, ye remember. Do ye want to go and see?"

"Yes, but if she and Griffin—" Jix clapped one hand over her mouth, then jerked it away. "Griffin? She went with Griffin?"

"Aye, he's a bit drunk and—"

"Oh no! They can't—I mean, Griffin can't—" She grabbed Jamie by the sleeves. "We've got to stop them, Jamie. Which way did they go?"

He pointed and a very wide awake Jix tore off across the gypsy camp, her auburn hair flying behind her. Jamie stood staring after her, his good humor over the situation gone. So Jix didn't want Griffin to sleep with Samantha. What the hell was going on?

Jamie caught up with her just outside camp. She stood on a rise, watching Samantha and Griffin cross the meadow below, hand in hand. "Lass, wait a minute!" He gestured toward the two runaways. "I know ye're anxious to see Samantha, but do ye really want to take a chance on, well, interrupting something? They are both adults."

"Jamie, you don't understand! Something's wrong. Samantha would never do something like this! I've got to stop them. Besides, Griffin—" she broke off. "I've just got to stop them."

Jamie let her go. Why would it be so important to stop Griffin from seducing Samantha unless—maybe he was just being naive. Jix had tried twice now, or was it three times, to give him the old heave-ho. And maybe her feelings for Griffin Campbell had been at the bottom of it all along. He released his breath explosively and followed her, his heart weighing heavily in his chest.

By the time Jix caught up with the two, Griffin was throwing up in the bushes, and she doubted it was because of too much drink. A blond-haired woman sat on a stone nearby, twiddling her thumbs and gazing up at the moon. Jix approached stealthily around the side of a huge boulder, ready to slip away unnoticed if Jamie's eyes had been playing tricks on him. She peeked out.

Samantha. Tears burned Jix's eyes. It really was Sam. She had on the most horrendously bright clothing Jix had ever seen her wear and a ton of costume jewelry that she couldn't imagine her best friend getting within ten feet of, but it was Sam. Jix jumped out from behind the rock and ran across the short distance.

"Oh, Sam, Sam, I've been so worried!" she cried. "Can you ever forgive me? Are you all right?" She laughed with relief and hugged her friend tightly, kissing her hair, her face, her forehead. Sam hugged her back and for a brief, wonderful second, everything was all right, just as she had known it would be. Then she realized Sam wasn't hugging back, she was trying to get away from her.

"Who the hell are you?"

Jix took a step back. Okay, so this wasn't going to be that easy. Apologies were in order and she was happy to make them. "Now look, Sam, I know you're upset with me and you have every right to be."

The woman frowned. She didn't really act particularly angry. Jix knew when Sam was angry. She seemed . . . puzzled more than anything.

"I can explain everything," Jix assured her. At that moment Griffin came out from behind a bush, and even in the moonlight she could tell he was green around the gills. He wiped the back of his sleeve over his mouth and hiccuped.

"Griffin," she scolded, crossing to take his arm. "What are you doing? This is my friend, Samantha—she's the one we've been looking for!"

"Is she?" he said, swaying against Jix. "I dinna know. She smiled at me." He grinned at Samantha who rolled her eyes.

"Look," Sam began, "I don't know what this is all about but he still owes me twenty shillings."

Jix laughed. "Good one, Sam."

Samantha put her hands on her hips and glared. "And why do you keep calling me that strange name? My name is Finnuala."

Jix's laughter faded. "Now that's not funny, Sam. We don't have time for paybacks. We've got to get you back to the castle and—"

"Paybacks? Castle?" She shook her head. "I don't know what you're talking about and I'm not going anywhere. I live with the gypsies and I never saw you before in my life!"

Jix was leading Griffin back toward the camp and at Sam's words she stepped on a rock and fell flat on her face. Griffin sat down beside her, giggling. Samantha stalked over to him and shook her finger in his face.

"I want my money! It's not my fault you couldn't do the deed!"

Jix scraped her hair out of her eyes and looked up to find Jamie staring down at her, a kind of angry amusement in his eyes.

"Jamie, you remember Samantha don't you?"

"Aye," he said, darting a quick look at Griffin who was trying to balance a rock on his head, and then at Samantha who stood tapping her foot against the ground. "I do."

Jix propped her chin on both hands. "Well, gee, guess what? She doesn't remember us."

"Are you with these monkeys?" Sam asked, glaring at Jamie. She pointed at Griffin. "He owes me twenty shillings. It's not my fault—"

"Yes, it's not her fault that Griffin is better at throwing up than—" Jix caught herself just in time. Griffin trusted her with his secret and just because she was frustrated didn't mean she was going to betray him. She scrambled to her feet. "I mean, it's obvious that he's sick from something he ate," she explained to Sam. Jix walked over to the woman and looked at her carefully. Was it possible she wasn't Sam? Could she be Sam's great-great-great-great-grandmother or something?

"Listen, y'all," Sam said. "I want my money!"

Jix smiled. Only if her ancestor spoke in twenty-first century Texan. Yep, it was Samantha.

"If someone doesn't pay me my twenty shillings, I'm going to get Malkov and he's not going to be happy."

"Aye, lass, aye," Jamie said, his voice soothing. He crossed to Griffin and knelt down beside him. Pushing the man flat, he opened the sporran at his waist and dug around inside. He found a few coins in the leather bag and handed them to her.

"Samantha, you can't mean that you do this all the

time," Jix said, suddenly appalled at the thought of what Sam's demand for money implied.

The blond's haughty chin lowered just a bit. "Well," she said, pocketing the coins, "actually your friend was going to be my first try at it. The gypsies took me in and everyone has to earn their keep, so I thought I might as well see what all the fuss is about."

Jamie stood. "He's out," he said, jerking his thumb toward Griffin. "Tell me, Sam—"

"Finnuala."

"Finnuala, how long have ye been with the gypsies?"

Her gray eyes clouded. "The leader said they found me almost dead about three months ago. They nursed me back to health and kept me with them." A wry smile touched her lips. "They think my golden hair brings them luck." She shrugged. "And I discovered I knew a lot about healing. That's what I've done to pay my way, but no one is sick right now and Malkov is getting kind of pushy about me bringing in some money."

"You were hurt?" Jix asked in concern. "You mean, you were knocked out and then you woke up and you didn't know where you were or—"

"Or who I was: Malkov gave me the name Finnuala" Sam finished for her. Her eyes widened. "Are you people telling me you know who I am?"

Jamie nodded. "Aye. Your name is Samantha Riley. I'm Jamie MacGregor and this is a friend of yours, Jix Ferguson."

"Jinx?"

Jamie raised one brow. "Well, some might say so but—"

"Jix," Jix corrected, shooting him a narrow look. "It's a combination of my three initials. Don't you remember, Sam? It was your idea. It stands for Jessica Isobel Xavier. You gave me the nickname when we were little kids."

Sam frowned. "I did?"

"Sure. You're my best friend, and you're the most understanding, kind, forgiving person in the—" Jix glanced up at Jamie. He was frowning. "Okay, so we've had our problems, but, Sam—wait until you hear! We've all been on the most incredible—"

"Maybe we should discuss all of this back at the camp," Jamie interrupted, shaking his head slightly at Jix. So he didn't think she should tell Sam about the time traveling. Maybe not. It might be a hard concept for her friend to handle if she didn't even remember her own name.

Sam walked over to Jamie and looked up at him, her gaze searching his face as if to find some hint of recognition. "Are we engaged?"

"No, we're just friends."

"That's strange. All I can remember is that I was supposed to get married, and it seemed like the guy was Scottish."

Jix mouth fell open. Was Sam remembering Jix's recount of the dream, or was she having her own psychic experience?

Samantha sighed and leaned against Jamie, her arm linked through his as she pouted up at him. "Do you know how terrible it is not to know who you are? And worse—to know that you don't fit in anywhere? These people"—she gestured toward the gypsies' camp—"they're kind but we might as well be speaking different languages. At times we *are* speaking different languages!"

Jix and Jamie exchanged looks. "Samantha," she began, "I know this has been hard for you, and that's why you must believe me when I tell you that we're your friends. There are things you don't know—"

"Then tell me!" she said, her tawny brows pressed together over her troubled gray eyes. She glanced up at Jamie and her voice softened. "If you can, tell me anything that will help me remember, please!"

Jix considered. Sam didn't remember a thing. The old Jix would have seen this as an opportunity to play some pretty wild practical jokes on her friend—give her a lot of false information, tell her wild things that weren't true about her past. But the new Jix, the improved, mature Jix wouldn't dream of—wouldn't dare to—

"Well," she said, "you once were a Yugoslavian phone sex—"

"Jix!" Jamie was trying not to laugh, she could tell, but he gave her a stern look and she shrugged.

"Oh, all right." Jix started over. "Listen, Sam, there's a lot we have to tell you, but first you have to come with us when we leave the gypsies. It's the only way you'll ever get back home."

"Home?" Sam echoed the word wistfully.

Jix had never seen her friend look so vulnerable. This was a side of Samantha she'd never thought existed. She reached out and hugged her friend tightly, even though the woman didn't respond. "I promise, Sam, when this is all over, I'll explain everything." She pulled away slightly. "Can you trust us, just a little?"

Sam hesitated, then at last nodded. Jix hugged her again, then dropped her arms away from the woman and smiled encouragingly. "Yes, something else?"

"There's just one thing I need to know," Sam said.

"What is it?" Jix hoped desperately that she wouldn't ask something she couldn't answer. She wasn't sure when a good time would be to tell her about their trip through time!

Samantha shook her head. "Every time I see you, I remember something about . . ." she frowned and tilted her head to one side ". . . a skunk?"

Jamie burst out laughing. Jix shot him an angry look, but he ignored her and smiled down at Sam gleefully. She looked completely bewildered by his amusement. But the look of confusion quickly changed as Jamie continued to gaze at the blond beauty, his dark eyes alight with interest. Samantha shifted her hips against his as she gave him a provocative smile and lowered her thick eyelashes demurely.

Jix's heart fell as she watched Jamie return the smile, but she pushed down the pain. This was good. This was a great start for the two of them.

Samantha put her hand on Jamie's arm and looked up at him from beneath her lowered lashes. "Well, sexy, since

we already know one another, how would you like to b
my first instead of puke boy over there?"

Jix expected Jamie to suggest that Samantha join ther
back at the camp, or tell her about their trip through tim
Instead, he gave her one of those heated looks that alway
melted Jix right down to her toes.

"Och, what a tempting offer," he said, his voice silky
"I've never been with a gypsy before."

"She isn't a gypsy," Jix said before she could stop th
words. Jamie could hardly take his eyes from Sam lon
enough to glance her way.

"Hmm? Well, she looks like a gypsy, and I can dream
can't I?"

And don't talk about dreams, she wanted to scream.

He laughed. "Maybe later, lass." He looked over at Ji
and his smile faded. "Jix and I have a few things to discus
first."

"That's fine. I'll just wait over here for you, shall I?
Sam slid him another smile.

Jix watched her best friend slide away, her hips undu
lating like a pinup girl from a 1940s black-and-whit
movie. Jix turned back to Jamie, only to find he was sti
watching the woman. She cleared her throat and h
dragged his gaze away from Sam's behind and back to Ji

"So what's the problem, Jamie?" she asked.

Jamie scowled and pointed to Griffin passed out on th
ground. "That's the problem. I want to know what's goin
on between the two of ye?" he asked, a hard tone in hi
voice. "Why did ye rush out here to stop Samantha fro
making love to him, if ye dinna care for him?"

Jix was too weary to even think about finding a way
explain Griffin's predicament without betraying his conf
dence or embarrassing him.

"Gee, I could've sworn that wasn't what had your a
tention tonight. But I can't tell you, Jamie," she said. "An
you're just going to have to trust me on that."

"I see." Jamie took a step back and glanced down
Griffin. "So yer loyalty to him supercedes any ye mig

feel to me." His fingers tightened on his waist until his knuckles were almost white.

Jix looked up at him. In that frozen moment of time, she wanted to forgive his lack of faith. How could she explain to Jamie that she and Griffin had formed a close friendship in the last few days? How could she make him understand that what she felt for the big Scot was nothing—a vague glimmer of the raging fire that churned inside of her every time she spoke Jamie's name? His jealousy hurt her along with his obvious attempt to make her jealous in return, and Jix realized she still had it in the back of her mind that somehow she and Jamie would end up together. They wouldn't. Sam was back, and all they had to do now was get the sword and go home. Then the rest would take care of itself. So Jamie's belief or disbelief really didn't matter. Of course it didn't. Jix took a deep breath.

"Jamie, have you thought about what this means? We've found Samantha. All we have to do is—"

"Take Samantha with us to the castle, aye, I know. Then Griffin will get the sword to us and we'll return to our own time."

The wind picked up just then and lifted his hair almost straight up. Jix's heart began to beat a little faster. In the moonlight, with his hair rising with the wind, Jamie looked like some specter from the faerie world. His eyes bored into hers and she shivered with the strength of that look.

"And after we return to our time, Jix, then what?"

Jix bit her lower lip. If they made it back to their own time, then her first dream would be the one that must come true. Jamie and Samantha would be married. There would be no Meadbrooke Castle, no evil black-eyed, black-haired captain with a sword. That dream would be canceled out by time. Wouldn't it? But what if they couldn't get back?

"I don't know, Jamie." She rose from Griffin's side. "Let's just get Sam and get out of here."

"Aye," he said. The wind had waned and Jamie was no longer a mystical specter but simply a man, a man that she loved. A man she couldn't have.

"Talking about me?" Sam asked, suddenly at Jamie's side again.

"No," Jix said shortly. "Do you think some of the gypsy men would come and carry Griffin back to camp? Jamie's hurt his shoulder and his ankle."

"Of course. I'll send them back. Or why don't you stay here with him and"—she glanced up at Jamie,—"what did you say your name was, lover?"

"Jamie MacGregor."

The blonde slid him another heated look. "And Jamie and I will go and find some men to come and carry Griffin back."

"Jamie doesn't like me to be out here alone," Jix said, irritated with Sam's high-handed manner and her come-hither looks. Of course, Jamie was giving them right back to her.

"Och, lass, I'm sure ye'll be fine for a few minutes," Jamie said, unconcerned. "Come along, Samantha."

"Finnuala."

"Whatever, lass, whatever."

He put his arm around the woman and guided her toward the camp, leaving Jix to stare after them, completely dumbfounded. As they disappeared through the woods, Jix sank down on a rock beside Griffin, the silence of the glen interrupted only by his rumbling snores.

Jix leaned her chin against the palm of one hand. "This is great. Sam and Jamie getting along right from the start. And I do mean getting along. This is terrific. Great. Fantastic. Damn it to hell." She kicked a rock and it went smashing against a larger one to ricochet back against Griffin's side.

"Wha-Wha-What?" He sat bolt upright and looked blearily around. Jix put her foot on his chest and pushed him back to the ground. He closed his eyes again and sighed.

"My sentiments exactly," she said.

Chapter Eighteen

Jamie led Samantha back to the camp, limping across the clearing where the campfire lay, dodging dancing gypsies, and into the woods beyond. As soon as they were alone, he stopped and swung her into his arms.

"What do you think you're doing?" she squealed, slugging him in the arm.

"Ouch. I'm giving ye what ye asked for of course. Ye said ye wanted me to be yer first, didn't ye?" Jamie pinned her arms behind her. "Of course I took that to mean yer first man in yer new career as a whore, not yer first man in general, since we both know how unlikely that would be."

"Why you—"

Jamie had expected a struggle. He didn't expect her to bite him.

"Damn it to hell, woman!" he yelled, letting go with one hand to cover his chin. She twisted her arm, trying to get her other wrist out of his grasp, but Jamie held on. He pulled her to a small tree and flung her around it, then jerked the red bandana from her head and tied her hands together around the slim trunk.

She was shooting daggers at him now. "When I get loose from here I am going to cut off your—"

"Now, now, Ms. Riley, let's not be graphic," he said mildly, finishing the knot and spreading his hands apart. "When we get back home, I might report yer violence to the authorities. Remember, I'm with Scotland Yard."

"That's *Doctor* Riley to you—and when we get home I'm going to tell Scotland Yard that you were a party to—" she stopped as a broad smile spread over Jamie's face. She lifted her chin and stared at him, sullenly. "When did you catch on?"

He chuckled and touched his chin again. "When ye started comin' on to me. Believe me, darlin', I ken as well as ye do that there's nothin' at all between us and never could be."

"Just air," Sam retorted, "a whole lot of hot air from your side of the fence."

"So what's with the act?"

"Let me go and I'll tell you."

Jamie shook his head. "No, I don't think so. Tell me and then I'll let ye go."

Sam shot him a look that might have bent steel if she'd had telekinetic powers, but as it was, it just made Jamie step back a pace and grin, mockingly.

"Fine," she snapped. "The act is about making Jix Ferguson pay for what she's done to me."

"Ye mean the kidnapping."

"I mean the kidnapping, her stupid dream, sending me back in time—do you know how long I've been here? Three freaking months!" She jerked her wrists, trying to break the bandana and glared at Jamie again. "I have had to live by my wits—"

"I can tell ye were ill prepared for such an endeavor," Jamie interjected.

"—*and*"—Sam went on, furiously—"it is all her fault and I intend to make her pay!"

"By flirting with me?" Jamie folded his arms over his chest and leaned back against a tree opposite hers. "How would that make her pay? Doesn't seem too creative if ye ask me."

"Who asked you?" she shot back. "She's in love with you, you twit. Don't you know that? My gosh, it's written all over her sappy face! And since she was determined that you and I would get together—according to her dumb dream—*I've* decided, now that she's in love with you, to get even!"

Jamie shook his head. "What are ye talking about? What dream? Why would Jix want ye and I to be together if she loves me?"

Samantha stared at him, her full, pouty lips open in disbelief. Damn, but she reminded him of Cathy, his ex. Another good reason not to have much to do with her.

"You mean she still hasn't told you about her dream?" She laughed shortly and narrowed her eyes. "She's probably afraid to tell you, afraid you'll dump her here and go home without her." Sam glared at her bound hands. "I would if I knew how."

"Tell me about her dream," Jamie demanded.

Sam sighed and tossed her blond hair back from her face with a practiced movement as she shrugged. "Ever since we were kids Jix had these dreams that she claimed always came true. I never bought into it. She had such an absolutely wild imagination that I always thought it just sometimes got away from her."

"You mean she's a liar." It wasn't a big revelation to Jamie, but the thought that Jix might not be what she seemed to be bothered him.

"Oh, I don't think it was ever that she meant to lie. In spite of her faults, Jix has a good heart," she admitted begrudgingly. "I really think she just told such good stories that she actually started believing them herself."

Jamie laughed. "That sounds like Jix."

"Doesn't it?" Sam shook her head. "She's an original, there's no doubt about it."

"So ye didn't believe her dreams. What kind of dreams?"

"She told me once she dreamed her mother abandoned

269

her before it actually happened. And she's supposedly had dreams that helped her brother, Thomas, with his FBI work."

"Her brother's in the FBI?"

"She has four, you know. She was adopted by a big Irish family." Sam seemed calmer suddenly. "Jix really did have it tough when she was little."

"Aye, I figured that out. So what was the dream that made her kidnap ye and bring ye to Scotland?"

Sam lifted one tawny brow in his direction. "She dreamed that I was marrying you."

"Marrying me?" Jamie straightened away from the tree and glanced back toward the gypsy campfire. Through the trees he could see Jix on the other side, looking their way. Though he couldn't tell if she could see them, he moved to stand in front of Samantha, blocking Jix' view. "But ye didn't even know me. We'd never met until ye came to Scotland."

"Exactly." Sam leaned her head back and let her blond hair cascade down her back for a moment, then jerked her head back up. The tousled hair danced around her face and he had to admit she looked sexy. Just not sexy to him. It was strange to realize that he was now the crazy-redhead type.

"But somehow," she went on, "Jix believes she had a dream about me marrying some man in a kilt—so she kidnaped me and took me to Scotland. Oh, she also had a story in there about my fiancé planning to steal my trust fund. But when we got to Scotland the pièce de résistance was when we met you and she claimed that you were the man in her dream."

"So this is why—" He broke off abruptly. Jamie felt thunderstruck. So this had been at the bottom of her resistance, her strange behavior, all along! Jix must think that by loving him, she was somehow betraying her friend.

Sam's eyes widened. "Don't tell me—she's been holding back on you out of some misguided loyalty to me."

"Aye."

She shook her head. "That nitwit. When we get back

home I'm taking her—not sending her mind you, but taking her—to a psychiatrist!"

"Why didn't she tell me about the dream?" Jamie couldn't help feeling hurt. Did Jix think she couldn't trust him with the knowledge that she had such a wonderful gift? Or was Sam right? Was this just part of some fantasy Jix had created, and not true at all?

"Who knows?" Sam's cocky attitude faltered a bit, and she glanced away. "I haven't been exactly supportive of her 'power,' if you know what I mean. Maybe she was afraid you'd make fun of her, or think she was crazy."

Jamie nodded. More pieces falling into place. "I take it those were yer reactions."

Color rose into Sam's cheeks, but the sheepish look on her face disappeared as she turned on him. "Look, it's easy for you to judge—you haven't been friends with her for twenty years! If you knew the stuff she's put me through—"

"I'm no' judgin' ye, believe me. But I'm sure she meant well."

"Oh, sure, she always means well," Sam said, rolling her eyes. "But it really doesn't matter that she meant well when you're getting rabies shots because your best friend told you a skunk was tame!"

Jamie couldn't help but smile. "I get yer point. But Samantha, truly"—he shook his head and lifted one shoulder in a shrug—"she's Jix. Would ye really want her to be different from who she is?"

Sam looked down at her bound hands. "Mr. MacGregor, I've been kidnaped, forced to miss my own wedding, sent back in time where I've had to live with gypsies, and am now being held captive by a wild Scotsman." She glanced up at him. "And whom do I have to thank for these pleasures? My dear friend, Jix."

"She's been sick with worry over ye," Jamie said softly. "An' from the looks of how happy ye were when ye're dancin', I dinna think ye've suffered all that much."

"Well, I have discovered an interest and a talent for

271

dancing that I didn't know I had. But that's beside the point!"

"She loves ye more than anything." Jamie reminded her.

"Oh, not more than anything." Sam raised both brows and smiled knowingly. "Not more than she loves you, Mr. Righteous Defender. Now, let me go before I start screaming and bring the wrath of the gypsies down on you."

"Och, that would be terrible. I wouldna want to be danced into my grave."

Sam laughed and Jamie had to admit that maybe Samantha wasn't as bad as he had originally thought. It was obvious she still cared about Jix in spite of her anger. He grabbed the knotted bandana and cut it with a small dagger he had appropriated from the castle.

She rubbed her wrists and glanced up at him. "All right, Mr. MacGregor, what do you say we call a truce?"

"Agreed."

"But—I forbid you to tell Jix that I didn't really lose my memory." She put her hands on her hips. Jamie could tell she was going to make a great doctor. She had the I'm-a-god-obey-me-or-else part of it down pat.

"And why would I agree to that?" he asked.

Sam tilted her head back and slid him a provocative look from beneath her lashes. "Because, silly boy, I can make Jix stop playing this martyr game and admit her true feelings for you."

Although warning bells rang in his mind telling him not to get caught in between the two friends, Jamie was intrigued.

"How?"

"Look—Jix is in love with you." Her gaze raked over him. "Personally, I don't see the attraction, but it's her life. And in spite of everything I do want her to be happy."

"And if ye get to dig the knife in just a little, while ye're working toward that goal, that's no' so bad, either, eh?"

An appreciative smile slid across her glossy lips as she folded her arms over her chest, pushing her ample bosom higher. Did she do it on purpose, he wondered? In any case, she left him cold.

"I didn't say that," she said, sliding her hands into her lush blond hair and lifting the mane from her neck. "We'll simply beat her at her own game."

"And what game is that?"

She dropped her hair and widened her eyes. "Why, the green-eyed monster game of love, of course. Oh, I've been watching the three of you since you came into camp. I see the way she fawns all over Griffin in front of you—what do you think she's doing?"

Jamie shook his head. "Trying to drive me crazy?"

"Exactly! She's trying to make you jealous because she thinks then you'll dump her and go for me."

"How could she think that? No offense," he added.

"None taken." Sam tapped her chin thoughtfully with one finger then lifted one shoulder. "You have to realize that Jix sees things her own way—lives in her own world in a sense. But she has a strict code of loyalty to those she loves. And the only way we're going to get past that code, big boy—" she moved closer and slid her arms around his waist. She ran her tongue over her lips and pressed her firm breasts against him.

"—is to make her absolutely miserable."

Jamie gazed down at her warily. "I'll think about it," he said. "But in the meantime"—he pulled her hands away and clasped them together in front of her—"keep your hands to yourself."

"You have to go with us!"

Jamie sat shaving his two-day growth of beard with a sharp knife he'd borrowed from Malkov. Jix's anguished cry from Samantha's wagon made him jerk his hand and he winced as he nicked his jaw. He pressed his fingers against the wound, wondering what mischief Jix had gotten into now. After he returned from the woods last night with Sam, he'd found Jix asleep on her blanket and Griffin beside her. The sight of the two of them lying so closely together had sent jealousy coursing through his veins. He'd

273

had to walk it off before he could even sleep.

"I dinna think ye can spare anymore blood." Griffin Campbell's voice interrupted his thoughts. "Ye've lost enough in the last day or so."

Jamie ignored the man's overture at conversation. As far as he was concerned, the farther he stayed away from Griffin, the less likely he was to trounce the big Scot. He lifted his chin to scrape more of his blasted beard. What he wouldn't give for a disposable razor.

"She's a bonny lass, is she no'?" Griffin asked.

Jamie almost cut his own throat. He lowered the knife and watched as Jix stalked across the campground. She had changed her clothes and now wore a gypsy skirt and blouse. The dark green blouse was loose, low-cut, and displayed the top of her breasts for any man who cared to look. The swirling skirt of green and lavender and blue hit her just below her knees. A good length by twenty-first century standards, but provocative in this day and age. The eyes of every man in the camp turned toward her. Her long hair hung unbound, curling down her back, and the way she tossed it over her shoulder, with fire in her green eyes, fury on her face, there wasn't a man alive that wouldn't look at the woman and wonder if he could be the one to tame her.

"Watching over that woman is like being responsible for a load of nitroglycerin in a truck with no shocks."

"I dinna ken nitroglycerin or truck, but I ken yer meanin'," Griffin said with a grin. "Ye're a lucky man."

Jix knelt next to the fire, trying to pour some tea from a metal pitcher settled in the embers. She wrapped the end of her skirt around her hand and picked up the container, raising her skirt up over her knees. Three gypsies jumped up to help her.

Jamie groaned and rose to his feet.

"Do ye want me to go?" Griffin asked. "Since yer ankle is—"

"No!" Jamie growled. He limped to Jix's side, ignoring Griffin's chuckle. After a night of debauchery, Griffin looked refreshed and apparently unaffected by his hard drinking. He was trying Jamie's patience, and so was Jix! "Now what do ye think ye're doin'?" he demanded, glaring down at her.

Jix smiled at the gypsies hovering around her. One of them gave her a cup and another helped her pour the tea. The third one simply gawked at her. Jamie watched the men and saw their gaze wander again and again to her hair. That was it then, her red hair. Just as they'd believed Sam's blond hair brought them luck, maybe red hair meant something too. Uninhibited hoyden, perhaps? She thanked them profusely, then waved them away. With a sigh she stood and turned to Jamie.

"Sam says she isn't going with us to the castle," she said, taking a cautious sip of the hot tea. Her face twisted and she stuck out her tongue. "Ugh. Boiling hot paint thinner, anyone?"

"Why doesn't she want to go?"

"She says she doesn't know us and the gypsies have been good to her and why should she go with us."

Jamie nodded. "She has a point."

"Right on top of her head," Jix said. She poured the tea on the ground. "Jamie, we've got to take her with us. I guess I'll have to kidnap her again."

She sighed, her brows pressing together thoughtfully. Jamie watched her face as the Jix wheels started turning. She truly was incredible. He could almost see the lightbulb appear over her head as her latest idea took form in her brain.

"All right," she said, "you round up the rope, I'll find something to use to gag her and—"

Jamie couldn't help but laugh, even though he was still angry with the lass. "I think there might be an easier way."

Jix raised both eyebrows. "Really, MacGregor?" She put her hands on her hips and smiled doubtfully. "Well, by all means, don't let me stand in your way."

Ten minutes later the gypsies had agreed to take them to Meadbrooke Castle as soon as the full moon began to wane.

"I'm impressed," Jix said, spreading her skirt over the

blanket on the ground. Her bright skirt, layered over several petticoats, flared up around her, making her look like a lovely flower. "What magic wand did you wave, Houdini?"

"No magic, lass, I simply had Griffin invite the gypsies to come and stay at Meadbrooke for a time. They're always lookin' for a sponsor or a handout. What better way to get Samantha to do what we want without causin' her undue stress?"

Jix stared down at a twig she held in her hands, for several minutes. Jamie sat down beside her and frowned. It wasn't like her to be silent for so long. "What is it?"

"I could have found an easier way to stop Sam's wedding, I guess."

Ah, so that was what was on her mind. In spite of his ultimatum the night before, she had such a dismal look on her face that he had to comfort her. "Come here, lass." He put his arm around her shoulders and drew her against him.

Jix leaned her head on his chest and twirled the twig between her fingers. "I have a real problem with the dramatic, you know?"

"I'm sure ye did what ye thought best at the time," he said. Her green blouse slipped off one shoulder, exposing her creamy skin. Jix shrugged and it slipped further. She kept talking, oblivious.

"No, I didn't think. That's my problem. I acted. I saw my best friend headed for disaster and I thought, 'This calls for drastic action!' It never occurred to me that there might be a less drastic way to handle it."

"Maybe there wasn't."

"Maybe." Jix turned, her face so near to his he could have kissed her. "Do you think I've changed since you met me?"

Jamie chuckled softly and with hard-won control did not drop a kiss to her mouth or her bare shoulder. "If ye're asking me if ye've grown a bit since we arrived in the past, I'd have to say yes."

"I was pretty awful in the beginning, wasn't I?"

Her hair brushed against his chin and Jamie inhaled

deeply. Somehow she always smelled of lavender, even though they were both dirty, disheveled, and had been two days on the road. What had she asked him? Awful? Aye, if by awful she meant exciting, wild, uninhibited, spontaneous, and absolutely lovable. But it might not do to tell her that. After all, she was making an effort to calm some of her more outrageous character traits. And besides, he wasn't sure where he stood with her anymore.

"Aye," he agreed, "ye were." She popped him in the ribs with her elbow. He laughed. "Och, Jix," he said, his mouth against her ear, "dinna change too much."

They sat there for a long, pleasant moment, then Jix pulled away from him. He could see the reluctance in her eyes, but at the same time could sense the distance she was putting between them. More than physical, it was as though she had emotionally separated herself from him.

"When will we leave for Meadbrooke?" she asked.

"Not until tomorrow morning. The gypsies willna move until the moon begins to wane."

She nodded, rising from his side, then looked down at him, uncertainly. "Why don't you want me to talk to Sam about where we're really from?"

Oops. He'd forgotten this would be likely to come up. He rose, brushing dirt from his trews. He pulled his long hair back and refastened the leather thong he'd found that morning. For two cents he'd cut the whole mess off. He smiled as he remembered their first day in the past—how Jix had threatened to do that very thing with her long mop.

"What are you smiling about?" Jix asked, frowning slightly.

"Och, lass," he lifted one long lock of hair from her shoulder. "I was just wonderin' how ye're farin' with yer long bounteous hair these days."

She smiled and gently pulled the strand of hair from his fingers. "Just fine, thank you. What about Sam? You didn't answer my question."

Jamie sighed. Something had definitely changed between them. Was it because of his jealous outburst about Griffin? Because of his ultimatum? Because he had openly flirted with Samantha? Three strikes—was he out? It had been childish of him on all counts. If only he knew what was going on inside Jix's mind—if only she would trust him enough to tell him about the dream.

He'd promised Sam that he wouldn't tell Jix the truth about her "amnesia" until they left for Meadbrooke. Now he was keeping secrets, too—so how could he be angry with her? And yet, he sensed that Sam was right. Jix was holding back out of loyalty to her, and the only way to make the redhead admit the way she truly felt was to force her to feel what she didn't want to feel. Jealousy.

"I just think it would be better if ye wait for a bit," he finally said. "Ye dinna want to upset her."

Jix gave him a long, searching look, then nodded. "All right. Maybe once we're back at the castle. I've got to go. I promised Sam I'd help her with supper."

"Perhaps ye'd take a walk with me after?" he asked softly.

Jix hesitated. "No, Jamie," she said, "I told you, it just won't work." She turned to go.

"Ye know ye can trust me, don't ye, Jix?" he asked suddenly.

She stopped and slowly turned around, her gaze stricken. "Where did that come from?"

"From last night." He moved to her side and took her hand. "Ye couldna tell me about Griffin and it's made me wonder, what else do ye feel ye canna share with me?"

She shook her head and looked away. "Let it go, Jamie."

He lifted her chin and her lashes swept upward, letting him drown for a moment in her forest green gaze. "Och, lass, I canna let it go, for I canna let ye go. Tell me, tell me what keeps us apart."

A panicked look flashed into her eyes and Jix wrenched her face from his hand. "I don't love you, Jamie," she whispered. "That's what keeps us apart!" She was gone before he could open his mouth to declare his disbelief.

Cursing, Jamie spun around and almost ran headlong into Samantha Riley, dressed all in red. Her blouse left ittle to the imagination and she seemed to revel in her appearance.

"Well," she said, "come to any earth-shattering conclusions since last night?"

Jamie turned and watched Jix. She walked across the campsite to where Griffin Campbell stood grooming his horse. He watched the way she rested her hand on the man's arm for a moment, then smiled up at him.

"Aye," he said fiercely. "Let the games begin."

Chapter Nineteen

Jix sat beside the campfire feeling numb. Supper was ove
and the gypsies once again had taken out their musica
instruments and their wine and prepared for a night o
gentle debauchery. Jamie had ignored her through tha
meal, choosing to sit beside Sam, who had also ignore
her completely and utterly. Griffin sat beside her, than
goodness, or Jix would have felt totally alone. As sh
stared across at Jamie, she noticed the top of a bandage a
the deep neck of Jamie's shirt. His foot was wrapped a
well. Samantha had been taking care of him.

Good, that was just excellent.

God, why do you hate me?

As soon as supper ended, Jamie stood up and extende
his hand down to Sam. He led her into the woods near th
campfire. They didn't come out for almost an hour, an
when they finally did, Sam's face was flushed, her clothin
askew, and Jamie had a satisfied look on his face.

Yes, indeedy that was good.

Jix felt her heart sink as Jamie stopped halfway to th
campfire and pulled Sam into his arms. He buried his fac

against her neck and she leaned backward, laughing, caressing his head. No, Jix didn't buy it. It was possible Jamie had just made love to Sam in the woods, but Jix found that hard to believe. Not after the way he had looked into Jix's eyes last night and confessed his love for her. Jamie wasn't another Dirk the Jerk. Was he? She shook the thought away. No, he was just trying to make her jealous. Wasn't he?

Well, what did you expect, Jix? She thought in disgust as she turned away from the sight of her best friend pawing the man she loved and vice versa. She got up and stalked over to the place Jamie and Griffin had appropriated for their sleeping quarters and threw herself down on a blanket, blinking furiously to keep the tears at bay.

He's angry and he wants to hurt you, so he makes out with your best friend. She glanced across the fire at the two. Jamie had Sam pressed up against a tree and she was still laughing. Okay, if he wanted to hurt Jix, that was one thing, but he wasn't being fair to Samantha—she didn't even know who she was! And if Jamie still loved Jix and was just using Sam to try to make her jealous, the dream still might come true. A cold chill danced down her spine.

The answer was simple: Somehow she had to make Jamie hate and despise her—but how? Griffin stumbled up just then and sat down beside her, his breath potent enough to intoxicate half of Austin.

"H'lo, Jixie darlin'," he said. "I think I'll just have a wee sleep for a minute or two." He fell over on the blanket and promptly began to snore.

Jix raised both brows as she looked down at her friend. Jamie was jealous of Griffin. If he thought Jix had slept with him, he would hate her. No doubt about it. Especially after what had happened with his ex-fiancée and his exbest friend back in their own time. Her heart began to pound. It would be cruel, an awful thing to do, but it would save Jamie, because if he married Sam, he wouldn't die.

"Griffin," she said, shaking the man by the shoulder, "wake up."

He opened his eyes. "What ish it, Jixie darlin'?" he asked, his words slurring.

"Can you stand?"

"Of coursh I can shtand," he said. He pushed to a sitting position and fell over sideways into her lap.

"Great." Jix rolled him off and stood, bending down to slide her hands under his armpits. She pushed him to a sitting position and somehow managed to provoke him into standing. He leaned heavily against her and Jix groaned, propelling them both forward into a halting walk toward Samantha's wagon. She had her work cut out for her as she tried to push the heavy man up the three wooden steps leading to the interior of the wagon, and by the time they were both inside, she was exhausted. There were two narrow beds with a space between them about a foot wide. Somehow Jix got him into one of them, then stood with her hands on her hips, her lips pressed together grimly as she gazed down at him.

"Okay, Griffin. Here's where I turn you into a man, and turn Jamie against me, all at the same time."

To her surprise, Griffin opened his eyes and smiled up at her. "Ye're goin' to make a man of me, lash?"

Jix sat down beside him and bit her lower lip. Would she actually have to do the deed with Griffin to get through to Jamie? She'd planned to only make it look like she and Griffin had become lovers, but maybe Jamie would see through that—see through her. How could he not look at her and see the love in her eyes, unless she betrayed him with Griffin? If she really went to bed with the Scot, there was no way she could ever look Jamie MacGregor in the eye again without feeling shame. And Jamie would know.

She took a deep breath. "Yes, Griffin, I've decided that I want to make love to you."

His beleaguered grin broadened. "Och, do ye now?" His mouth drooped. "But wha' about Jamie? Ye shaid ye were in love with him."

Jix nodded. "I know. I was wrong." She began tugging on Griffin's shirt. "I want to make love to you, Griffin. Sit up, would you?" He pushed up with both hands and sat unsteadily, looking at her in confusion. She managed to get his shirt over his head, but one hand caught in the sleeve and she had to practically sit on top of him to get it out. By the time she got through and was ready to start on his trews, Griffin was pushing her off of him.

"Get off, lash, get off!" he cried, shoving her aside. He clapped one hand to his mouth and ran to the door of the wagon. Jix shook her head with pity as she listened to the poor man retch a few yards way. He returned, a few minutes later, his face ghastly pale, to collapse back onto the bed.

"Dinna look on me," he begged her. "I'm a disgrash."

"Nonsense," she said, feeling a little desperate. If Griffin couldn't make love to her, how would she convince Jamie to stop loving her? "I have faith in you, Griffin. Let's just get these trousers off of you and I'll bet—" she untied his trews and started tugging. When she had them to his knees he sat up again and stumbled to his feet. He almost made it out the door, but tripped on the trousers dragging behind him and landed flat on his face.

Jix sighed and rose from the bed. She crossed and knelt at his side, feeling for his pulse as she brushed the hair back from his face. He was all right, just out cold. With a shrug she started pulling his pants down his muscular legs.

"I hate to take advantage of you, Griffin, but this is a matter of life and death."

Jamie and Samantha swayed to the tune of the gypsy violins, his ankle killing him, his shoulder burning, until he finally noticed that Jix was nowhere to be seen. He led the blond abruptly from the campfire circle as he limped to his blankets, then pulled her down beside him. He frowned as he searched the camp with his gaze.

"Where is she? This charade isn't doing me any good if she doesn't see us together."

Sam yawned and shrugged. "Maybe she went back to help Griffin. Let me ask around." She rose gracefully and walked away. Jamie leaned back against the tree trunk, his arms folded over his chest, his jaw locked so tightly his teeth hurt. Where was Jix? Surely she hadn't gone away from the camp by herself? He shook his head in frustration. By now he should know that there was no "surely" with Jix Ferguson.

Sam returned in a matter of minutes, a worried look on her face.

Jamie lowered his arms and sat up a little straighter. "What's wrong?"

Sam hesitated, then gave him a pitying look. "Jamie, I owe you an apology. I really thought Jix loved you, but maybe I was wrong."

There was a sudden roaring in his ears as he gazed into Sam's eyes. He knew the answer before she opened her mouth again.

"She's with Griffin—in my wagon," Sam told him.

"Which?" he asked hoarsely.

"The blue."

Sprained ankle forgotten, he was across the camp in three strides, at Sam's wagon in five. Sam caught up with him just before he took the first step onto the wooden platform.

"Wait! Let me go in first," she said. "There's no sense in you subjecting yourself to this."

"Get out of my way, Samantha." His hand closed around her arm. "Or I willna be responsible for my actions."

She shrugged and moved aside. "Okay, but I won't let you kill her, in spite of what she's done to both of us."

The door wasn't locked, but Jamie took great pleasure in kicking it open. There was the sound of a woman's scream as he ducked under the doorway and stood stoop-shouldered in the gypsy wagon.

Jix sat in a narrow bed, naked to the waist, her beautiful breasts bare for his burning glance—and the touch of the man she lay beside. Griffin Campbell, also naked if his broad, bare back was any indication, lay sprawled against her, his arm thrown across her lap. At the noise he raised up on one elbow, blinking sleepily at the intruder.

"What's the screamin' about?" he asked.

Jix slowly pulled the blue blanket up to cover her nakedness, her green eyes boring into Jamie's. "I'm sorry, MacGregor," she said softly, "I tried to tell you. To warn you. It was fun—that was all. I don't do commitment."

Jamie clenched his fists at his side, fighting against the pain slicing through his heart, the horror bursting inside his mind, the violence erupting in his soul.

"Damn ye," he whispered. "Damn yer conniving little soul to hell."

Meanwhile, back at the castle . . . the thought brought no smile to Jix's face as she and Samantha rode in the gypsy wagon toward Meadbrooke Castle. She sighed and shifted uncomfortably on the hard seat. On Firestorm, Griffin rode beside them in silence, his face troubled.

"I had such a wonderful night after Jamie saw you with Griffin," Samantha said, stretching her arms over her head and smiling languidly at Jix. "My, what endurance that man has. And sensitive—why, I have tingles in places I didn't know I had."

Jix felt her face burning and clutched the reins more tightly. "Yes, he's amazing," she said shortly. "But not as amazing as Griffin. And you can tell Jamie I said so."

"All right, maybe I will." Samantha straightened in her seat. Jix shot her a glance and her heart ached at the dreamy look in her best friend's eyes.

Well, are you happy now, God?

Jix fought back tears. She'd done the right thing. Jamie and Samantha would be together and Jamie wouldn't die. She should be happy. Ecstatic even. So what that she'd lost the only man she'd ever loved? So what that he actually thought her capable of such cruelty, such betrayal? Jamie would live and that was what counted. But it hurt—and what hurt the most was how easily he had believed the little scenario she had staged.

Oh, sure, she had wrestled with the idea of actually bedding Griffin, but she truly didn't think she could've gone through with it. Thankfully, Griffin passing out had taken the decision out of her hands. But Jamie should've thought better of her. She realized, belatedly, that there was a part of her that had hoped he wouldn't believe it, wouldn't buy it. She'd hoped he would burst into the wagon and laugh, telling her to put on her clothes and stop being such a silly fool. But he hadn't. He'd believed every bit of it.

Of course, she'd done a good job of making him believe, so it wasn't really fair to blame him. Did he have to jump between the sheets with Sam just minutes afterward? Yes, she supposed it was only fair. But did she have to hear a blow-by-blow account of their mad, passionate fling?

Bad choice of words, she thought, as Sam launched yet again into a detailed report of how good she had made Jamie feel in return.

"Griffin—" Jix said abruptly, cutting Sam off in mid-description. He turned toward her, his eyes bleary from his hangover, his dark brows colliding.

"Aye, lass?"

"We had a wonderful time last night, too, didn't we?" She smiled at him brightly, feeling like her head might explode from having to keep up this happy facade.

He nodded, but there was a sadness in his eyes. What was all that about? She'd thought he'd be thrilled to think that he had finally been able to be with a woman. "Aye, lass, we had a dazzlin' night. I thought yer screams of delight would overshadow the gypsy music."

Jix forced a laugh, thankful he was willing to fall in with her improvisation. "Aye, and I thought the same when you were voicing your enthusiasm as well."

Griffin glanced over at Sam as his horse rocked along beneath him at a steady pace. "And I dare Jamie Mac-Gregor to make any woman feel better," he said.

"Is that so?" Jamie was suddenly beside the wagon, at Samantha's side, his face as dark as a blue northern sky, Jix thought, unable to keep from staring at him. His gaze touched hers briefly, then he leaned over and kissed Samantha. Jix turned away, afraid he would see the stricken look she couldn't hide.

"Hello, love," he said softly to Sam.

"Hello, Tiger," she returned, her voice like silk. "Why don't you ride with me today?"

"Nay, I came to let ye ride with me."

Sam squealed as Jamie leaned down and gathered her into his arms, then tucked her in front of him on his saddle. He tossed Jix a triumphant look from his midnight blue eyes as he dashed away with Samantha pressed against him.

Jix watched them go, wistfully. Apparently Jamie hated her as much as she had hoped that he would. She should be delighted. Yep. Dee—lighted.

A single tear traced a path down her dusty face and Jix blinked as a gentle hand swabbed it away. Startled, she turned to find Griffin in the wagon with her.

"I tied my horse behind. I thought ye might use some company."

"I'm fine," she said, handing him the reins. "But I am kind of tired."

"Tired of lyin'?"

Jix stared down at her hands and didn't answer for a moment. How could she explain to Griffin the way she felt inside? Like her heart had been cut out. Like her soul had been destroyed. Jamie thought the worst of her, and it hurt more than any pain she'd ever known.

"Why do ye no' tell him of yer dreams?" Griffin asked, the steady clip-clop of the horses threatening to drown out his soft words.

"You don't understand, Griffin. In my time people don't believe things like this so readily. I mean, some people don't. Jamie would think I was crazy—or trying to scam him somehow."

"Scam?"

"Trick him." She shook her head. "Besides, what if by telling him it messes it all up? I mean, if he knows about the dream, would that keep him from falling in love with Samantha? Or if he knows about the—the—beheading dream, would that make him decide to take things into his own hands?"

"An' what would be so bad about that? If ye warn him, will ye no' be givin' him a better chance at livin'?"

"I don't know!" she cried, covering her face with her

287

hands. "Don't you see—I just don't know!"

Griffin patted her on the back and Jix allowed a few tears to squeeze past her lashes, then gulped back the rest. She lifted her head and dashed away the moisture from her face. "Besides, the second dream isn't going to come true, now—he's with Samantha. We'll get back to the castle, you'll give us the sword, and we'll go back to our own time."

"Och, lass, I hope it's that easy. But I think ye are a bit premature about Jamie and Samantha."

"Why?" Jix couldn't help the bitterness creeping into her voice. "He obviously slept with her last night—"

"After he thought I bedded ye," he said reproachfully. For a moment there was only the sound of the horse's hooves. "Why did ye make him believe such a lie?"

Jix laughed uneasily. "It wasn't a lie, Griffin. We made love last night—you just don't remember. Now you don't have to be afraid anymore. Even after I'm gone, you can find a nice girl, marry her, be happy, with no qualms. You're a terrific lover!"

Griffin glanced over at her, a wry smile on his face, and Jix felt her face turning red. "Och, lass," he said, "I was drunk. I wasna dead. I dinna make love to ye. I would know. I would feel it, ye ken? There is no' that between us."

She took a deep breath and let it out slowly, then threw up both hands with a laugh. "Okay, you got me. I confess!"

"While ye're about confessin'," he said, "why do ye no' confess to Jamie the truth? That ye are afraid to love because ye've lost everyone ye ever cared about?"

"Except my brothers," she whispered. "That's why I stay away from them as much as possible. Maybe if I'm not around, nothing will happen to them."

"Och, lassie, do ye think ye cause the bad things, then?" He shook his head. "Ye must ken that—"

"Griffin, please—I don't want to talk about this anymore!" She slipped her arm through his and leaned against his shoulder. "Let's just get to Meadbrooke so we can go home."

"Aye, lass," he said. There was a moment of silence, then he sighed. "I dinna like bein' used, lass."

Jix had the grace to duck her head and blush. "I'm sorry, Griffin. I was just trying to—"

"I ken what ye were tryin' to do. When will ye learn that the truth is always better than a lie?"

"I don't know." She looked ahead and saw Jamie holding Samantha in front of him. Her dress was hiked up over her knees and Jamie's hand rested on her thigh. "Griffin," she said, desperate to turn her attention away from them, "you told me once that Worthington is superstitious—tell me more about that."

"Och, 'tis well known around here that he is a great believer in the old ways, which is unusual for an Englishman."

"What kind of superstitions?"

"What I've heard is that he's fascinated with the occult, but frightened of it as well. He believes that some people have the power to see into the future," he nodded toward Jix with a half smile. "He believes in the fairy folk, and in omens, both good and bad. He willna look upon a man that he has killed, fearing the man will take his soul with him, and as I told ye, he cuts off the heads of his enemies to prevent their returnin' to haunt him." He frowned thoughtfully. "Och, and I've also heard that he is terrified of spiders. Strange, is it no', for a man who has killed so many to be afraid of such a thing."

Jix shivered and pulled the dark green shawl Sam had given her more firmly around her shoulders. "There ought to be some way to use this information against him." They rode along in silence for a few minutes, then she glanced over at her companion.

"Griffin, I didn't mean to hurt you."

He shrugged. "Och, I know ye dinna, lass. And it was no so much that it hurt me, it's just that, well, seein' ye with Jamie is hard because—" he broke off.

Jix sighed. "Because you love me. I'm sorry, Griffin."

His dark brows lifted, his eyes widened and he ran one

hand through his light hair, then threw his head back and laughed loud and long.

She folded her arms over her chest and sniffed indignantly. "Well, you don't have to be so rude about it. It was a logical conclusion."

"Och, lass, I'm no laughin' at the thought of lovin' ye." His lips curved up. "Life with ye would have never been borin', that I ken!"

"Then why—"

"I'm laughin' because ye are so concerned about everyone else's feelin's that ye no have time for yer own." His voice softened and he tousled Jix's hair, just like one of her brothers. "The problem with seein' ye and Jamie together is that it makes me long for the same kind of love. And makes me all the more determined to have it, no matter what."

Relief flooded over her. "But that's wonderful, Griffin—and don't you dare settle for less. I really believe that you'll find the right woman, if you just keep looking."

The humor left his eyes and he sat in silence for a moment. "Aye," he finally said, "I only hope she doesna mind a tremblin' schoolboy for a lover."

Jix shook her head. "Don't be so hard on yourself. I truly believe when you find the right woman, everything will work out."

"I hope so, lassie." He sighed.

"I know so, laddie," she quipped. He gave her a broad smile.

"Thank ye. Now, dinna fash yerself about Jamie and Samantha. Rest a while. It will all work out the way the good God intended."

Jix closed her eyes and took a deep breath, determined not to weaken now in their final hour. Their final hour. Okay, so maybe having a dramatic nature wasn't all it was cracked up to be. She tried to find some kind of caustic remark to throw at God, some accusation or challenge. For the first time since she was four years old, the words wouldn't come.

* * *

"Jix didn't sleep with him," Sam said casually as she bounced in front of Jamie on horseback.

Jamie's arm tightened around her. "What?"

"Ow, not so hard," she admonished, slapping his arm lightly. "I said, she didn't sleep with what's-his-name, Griffin baby."

Jamie felt cold, right down to the center of his being. Seeing Jix in bed with Griffin had been a blow he didn't think he'd ever get over. Forget finding Cathy in bed with his best friend. That was nothing—a mere ripple in his emotional well-being compared to how he had felt last night. Last night he'd wondered why she didn't just thrust his sword through his heart and be done with it.

"How do ye know?" he asked, afraid to hear the answer. Afraid it was just another one of Samantha Riley's caustic remarks. "Griffin said—"

"Griffin said, Griffin said—" she gave him a disdainful look. "Since when do you believe what another man tells you about his sex life? Besides, I know Jix. I can tell when she's lying and believe me, that load of dung she was shoveling today in the wagon stunk to high heaven."

Jamie couldn't help but smile. "Ye certainly have a way with words."

"Listen, Jamie, I was right about Jix. She loves you."

He laughed without humor. "Of course she does, that's why she went to bed with Griffin Campbell."

Sam rolled her eyes. "Oy vay, you are dense. She didn't!"

"I saw her—she was lying with him, stark naked!"

"That doesn't mean they did the deed," she insisted, shifting slightly in front of him. "Ow, when do they invent softer saddles?"

"Not for another hundred years or so." They rode along in silence for awhile before Jamie could speak his thoughts aloud. "What if you're right—why would Jix be so cruel?"

"Isn't it obvious? She's still trying to push us together. I'm guessing you made some big declaration of love the other night, am I right?"

"Aye."

"So, she got worried about this dumb dream of hers."

Jamie shook his head. "It doesn't make sense. So what if that dream didn't come true? What if ye and I dinna get married? Would the world come to an end? Why would she work so hard to sabotage what we had together?"

Sam shrugged. "I know it's hard to figure, but Jix is very, very loyal to me."

"No," Jamie said, "ye dinna understand. We had something—" he broke off, unable to go on for fear his voice would break.

"Yeah, yeah, I know. The earth moved, the stars fell, yada yada." Sam reached up and turned his face toward hers. Startled, Jamie looked directly into her gray eyes. "Look, MacGregor, do you love her?"

"Aye," he said.

"Then fight for her," Sam told him. "And try believing the best about her instead of the worst."

"Maybe ye should follow some of that advice," Jamie said, wondering if he dared do as Sam suggested.

"Aye," she agreed, thoughtfully, "maybe I should."

Sam leaned back against his chest and fell silent. Jamie glanced back at the bright blue wagon behind them and saw Jix sitting beside Griffin, leaning against his shoulder.

Try believing the best about her.

He hated to even entertain the thought, but maybe Samantha Riley was right. The question was, could he do it? Did he have the guts to find out the truth?

Chapter Twenty

"So the English have taken over the castle," Jamie said, his voice low as he stared out the open door of the gypsy wagon at the pouring rain. They had arrived at Mead-brooke Castle and set up camp about a half-mile from the gates. The gypsy leader Malkov had gone to request permission to stay for a few days, and returned with the news that *Captain Worthington* had given his approval.

Malkov, Griffin, Jamie, Jix and Samantha sat silently in the wagon as the storm outside raged. Worry lined their faces.

"Did ye see my father?" Griffin asked the swarthy man, breaking the silence.

"Your father seemed vell," Malkov replied in his unusual accent. Jamie frowned, trying to place it. Romanian? Some derivation, no doubt. Even though these people had probably been born in Scotland, their parents and the closed world of the gypsies had kept them isolated from change.

"Did he seem to be under duress?"

Jix scooted closer to Griffin and slipped her arm through

his. He clasped her hand tightly, gratefully, and Jamie had to look away. He turned to put his arm around Samantha. She looked up in surprise, then he saw understanding quicken into her eyes as she fell into her role and snuggled back.

"I could not say, young laird," Malkov answered. "He appeared . . . distressed, I vould say."

Griffin stood and almost banged his head on the low ceiling of the wagon. He bent over slightly. "I must leave at once. My father needs me."

"Aye," Jamie agreed, "but dinna run off half-cocked. We must have a plan."

The blond Scot looked at him suspiciously. "An' why would ye want to help my father?" he asked.

Jamie met his accusation coolly. "I want to help myself, Griffin. Ye no doubt remember that yer father has something belongin' to me. I dinna wish for it to fall into English hands."

Griffin's mouth flattened into a thin line. "Aye. I dinna need yer help, MacGregor." He walked to the door of the wagon and stooping down beneath the archway, headed into the rain. Jix hurried after him. Jamie waited thirty seconds, then with a sigh, stood and followed.

"If you think I'm going out in that rain—" Sam began.

"Stay where ye are," he ordered. "I wouldna have ye damage yer dainty appearance."

"Good."

Jamie glared into the downpour and saw Jix and Griffin beside the man's horse, arguing.

"This is crazy!" Jix was shouting as she grabbed Griffin's shirt front. "I won't let you go."

Jamie walked up beside her. "I hate to admit it, Campbell, but she's right. This will do no good. Wait and let us arrive at a plan together that will no' cost ye yer foolish head."

"I canna take the time."

Jamie stepped in front of Jix and laid one hand on Griffin's saddle horn, blocking him from the horse, practically shoving Jix backward.

"Hey!" she shouted. "Watch where you're stepping—you almost knocked me into the mud!"

"Get out of my way, MacGregor!" Griffin said, his fists clenched.

"Ye helped save my life," Jamie cried, "and I willna stand by and watch ye throw yers away—in spite of Jix!"

"What do I have to do with this?" Jix said, as she circled around the two men. She stepped between them and pushed them apart, one hand on each chest. The gypsies had gathered, Jamie saw, noting that even Samantha was in the crowd, getting drenched.

"Get out of the way, lass," Jamie said, wiping rivulets of rain from his face.

"Now, come on guys, let's not get into a macho shoving match—please?" Jix implored them. "We've got to figure out a plan."

"Leave them alone," Sam said, stepping up and pulling Jix back by one arm. "They've been itching to go at each other for days. Let them, it will be good for them."

"Oh, yeah, black eyes and broken bones are always helpful," Jix said.

Money started changing hands between the gypsies, and Jix shot them a dark glare.

"Stay out o' this, lass," Jamie said again.

"Aye," Griffin agreed. "It's time I taught yer man a few manners."

"He's not my man!" Jix shouted.

"That's right, he's mine!" Sam declared.

"Oh, he is not!" Jix said, pushing her back slightly. "You barely know him."

Sam whirled on her. "He is too!" She pushed her friend, hard, and Jix fell backward into the mud.

Jamie and Griffin looked down at the sight of the woman sprawled in the muddy sludge, her mouth open, her gypsy garb soaking wet, her hair hanging in stringy strands about her face, her backside coated with mud, her blouse clinging to her breasts. They looked at each other, the corner of their mouths lifting.

"Are ye goin' to let her talk to ye like that, Jix?" Griffin demanded, his voice irate.

Jix struggled to her feet. "No, I am not!" She stalked over to Samantha and shook her finger in her face. "You've been asking for this ever since I met you!" She put both hands on Sam's shoulders and shoved her down.

Furious, Sam tried to get up, but her foot slipped and she went flying facedown in the muck. Jix threw her head back and laughed, but lost her own footing and slid on her rump next to Samantha.

"Are ye goin' to take that lyin' down, Finnuala?" Jamie called to Sam, trying not to laugh out loud.

Samantha rose up on her knees and grabbed Jix by the hair. "I've been wanting to do this since you were six years old!"

"OW! Let go of my hair!" Jix grabbed a handful of Sam's long, now-dirty-blond hair and jerked.

"OW! Let go!"

"You let go!" Jix shouted.

The two women rolled in the mud, wallowing like pigs he'd once watched at his uncle's estate. Jamie couldn't help himself any longer, laughing so hard he had to bend over and clutch his stomach. Griffin roared alongside him.

Sam and Jix stopped rolling in the mud and landed with Jix on top. She glared up at the two men. "What's so blasted funny?" she yelled.

Jamie pointed at her. "If ye could see yerselves, ye wouldna ask," he gasped out, then raised his voice to a falsetto. "Ooh, ye let go!" He raised his hand limply.

"Och, no"—Griffin said in an equally high voice—"ye let go!"

"No, ye!" Jamie poked Griffin with one finger.

"No, ye!" Griffin poked him back.

Sam and Jix had stumbled to their feet and both women stood bedraggled and muddy. Jamie saw, too late, the fire in their eyes.

Jix glanced at Sam who nodded. Then they both pushed at the same time and the men went flying backward, down into the muck. Jix jumped on top of Jamie with a wad of mud in her hand and rubbed it vigorously across his face, while Sam did the same to Griffin.

"Ye'll be sorry for this, lass!" Jamie cried as he flipped Jix over and fell on top of her. Grabbing a handful of mud he scrubbed it into her hair as she screamed at the top of her lungs.

"All right! All right!" Griffin cried, capturing Sam's hands and pinning them to her side. "Do ye give up!"

"Never!" Samantha cried.

"Yes!" Jix shrieked. "We give up!"

Griffin let Sam go and she slid to her feet. "Quitter!" she yelled at Jix.

Jamie stared down into Jix's dirty, lovable face. Her breath was coming quickly and so was his, either from exertion or the fact that with their clothes soaked they could feel every nuance of each other's body.

Jix gazed up at him for a long moment, then bucked him with her hips. "Get off of me, you big side of Scottish beef!"

Jamie rolled off of her. "Beef?"

"Yes! What's the big idea—are you trying to squash me into the ground? You hate me so much that you want to kill me?"

Jamie pushed up off the ground and managed to gain his footing. "I dinna hate ye, lass," he said. He glanced at Griffin. "I hate him."

"Me? What have I done to ye?" Griffin demanded, his blond hair streaming around his face.

"What have ye done? Ye bedded her last night!"

"Nay, I dinna bed the lass—she just said that!"

"Griffin!" Jix cried.

"If ye canna be honest on yer own then I find I must help ye!" Griffin said and turned to Jamie, spreading his hands apart. "Nothing happened."

Jamie shook his head, confused. He stared at the man, afraid to believe him. "Then why—"

"Because of her dreams, MacGregor—the dreams she's afraid to tell ye about!"

Jamie spun on Jix. "Ye told him about the dreams but ye couldna tell me?"

Jix's mouth dropped open. "How did you know about the dreams?"

"Samantha told me!"

"Samantha? But Samantha doesn't remember—" Jix turned on the blond woman, her fists clenched at her side. "So you've been waiting to do this since I was six years old? You don't remember who you are but you told Jamie my dreams?"

Samantha held up both hands. "Dream—I told him your dream about us getting married." She raised her muddy brows. "What? Have their been more?"

"You didn't lose your memory!" Jix shrieked, and with that she lunged for her friend. The two women went down again, rolling across the wet ground amid the cheers of the gypsies. By the time Jamie and Griffin pulled them apart, Jix and Sam were so coated with mud they were hardly recognizable as human beings.

"Let me go!" Jix shouted, her arms flailing as Jamie picked her up around the waist. He lifted her off her feet but she kept shouting and kicking. "Do you know how worried I was? How many nights I cried because I didn't know where you were or what had happened to you? And then when we finally find you—you pull this kind of scam?" She reached up and grabbed Jamie by the hair. "And you—you knew she remembered and you didn't tell me! You're just as bad!"

"Ow, lass, stop it! I was desperate to figure out why ye didn't want to be with me and she had the answers! I had to do things her way!"

Griffin had Sam in the same hold and she leaned forward from the waist, shaking one fist at Jix who continued to wrestle against Jamie. "How does it feel, Jix? How does it feel to be lied to? To have your life messed with?"

"What are you talking about?" Jix demanded, abandoning her attempts to pull out Jamie's hair but still kicking. "I saved you from a fate worse than death!"

"And I was trying to save you from losing Jamie forever—but how did it feel in the process? It hurt like hell, didn't it?"

Jix stopped struggling and Jamie felt the breath leave her body. She turned in his arms and looked up into his eyes. Confusion shifted to understanding, then joy. "You mean—you and Sam were just pretending? You didn't really—you didn't—"

"No more than ye and Griffin," Jamie said.

"Oh, Jamie, we didn't—I just tried to make it look like we did." Jix sagged against him and he gathered her closer.

"But why? I dinna understand—why would ye do all of this because ye dreamed I would marry Samantha? What difference can it possibly make whether I do or not?" The rain grew heavier as Jamie spoke, sending the betting gypsies running for their wagons.

"Uh, do you think we could step out of the monsoon, kids?" Sam asked from behind them. "It's not going to matter what she dreamed if we all drown."

"Come on, lass," Griffin said, taking Sam by the hand and pulling her toward the wagon. The two ran to the bright blue cart, barely visible in the rain.

But Jamie didn't move. He stood in the rain with Jix in his arms, gazing into her eyes, letting the downpour wash the mud from them both, letting it wash away the fear and confusion and lies from both of them.

"I love ye, Jix, and that's the truth," he said. "Now, tell me yer truth."

"Oh, Jamie," she said, a catch in her voice, "I love you so much I hurt inside. I love you so much that I can't sleep at night for thinking about you. I love you so much that I almost risked your life instead of letting you go."

"How, lass?"

"I had another dream after we came back in time and now I'm afraid that the second dream somehow cancels out the first because they can't both come true—so I have to make sure the first one does come true! Do you understand?"

Jamie smoothed her rain-soaked hair back from her face, trying to follow her rambling method of reasoning. "But if the first dream canna come true, then that would mean that Samantha and I were no' fated to be wed, and wouldna that mean ye and I could be together?"

Jix lifted her hand and touched the edge of his jaw with her fingertips. Jamie watched tears run down her face to mingle with the rain.

"No," she said, her voice scarcely louder than a whisper, "that would mean you're going to die."

Jix didn't think she'd ever get warm again. Standing in the rain with Jamie had been wonderfully romantic. Why was it every joy had a price tag? As she, Jamie, Sam, and Griffin sat huddled on the two narrow beds in the blue wagon, she sneezed and sniffled her way through the entire account of her dream about the castle and the evil, black-haired captain, and Jamie's head on a platter. She felt sure stopping to blow her nose every two minutes had done nothing to help her convince Jamie of the validity of her dream, but to her surprise when she finished, he nodded, his gaze on the wooden floor of the cart.

"All right then, lass, we'll just have to find a way to thwart this dream."

Jix blinked and lowered the kerchief from her nose. "You mean you believe me?"

Jamie glanced up at her and the warmth in his dark blue eyes chased every chill from her body and filled her with a dry heat. "Aye, lass, I believe ye. Listen, we've both done some crazy things, but I ken now that we did them because we loved each other and were afraid of losing that love. Do ye love me?" She nodded. "Then I believe ye."

He believed her. He wasn't laughing at her. He loved her. Jix released her pent-up breath in one explosive rush and threw herself into Jamie's arms. He fell over backward into the narrow bed laughing, cradling her to his chest.

"Och, lass, give us a kiss."

Her mouth found his and Jix couldn't help the tears that flooded down her face as she held onto him for dear life.

"Would you like us to leave?" Samantha asked dryly.

Jix froze. Samantha! In all of this she had forgotten

about Samantha. She sat up, straddling Jamie's lap, then realized how awkward her position looked and quickly slid off of him to stand beside the bed.

"Oh, Sam, I'm so sorry. I never meant for this to happen."

"Yeah, well, unfortunately you have a lot of accidents, don't you, Jix? And I have a few things to say about this whole Jamie-Samantha-Jix triangle." She cleared her throat theatrically. "First of all, sit down." Jix sat down beside Jamie. "Second of all, I forgive you."

Jix blinked. "What did you say?" She stuck her finger in her ear and twisted it, then shook her head. "It sounded like you said you forgave me."

"I did."

Jix's mouth dropped open. "But—but—you said you'd never forgive me. You said you'd make me pay for the rest of my life. You said—"

"I know what I said, but since I was able to exact at least a little revenge out there in the mud, I've decided to let it go." The arrogance in Sam's gray eyes wavered a bit. "I know that what you did, you did out of love. And as crazy as you make me, I couldn't make it without your friendship."

Jix slowly stood, feeling afraid to hope it could be real. Gingerly she reached out and enfolded her friend in a gentle hug, fearful she would jerk away. "I promise, Sam," she said softly against her blond hair, "things are going to be different when we get back. When you and Jamie are married I'll—"

Sam pushed her away abruptly and held up one hand like a traffic cop. "Whoa. Stop right there. Sit back down." Jix sat. "I am not going to marry Jamie MacGregor."

"But my dream—"

"Is that clear, Jix? Not if we get back to our own time. Not if we're stuck here forever. I will never marry Jamie MacGregor."

Jix sighed. "Sam, you feel that way now, but once you get to know Jamie—"

301

"Excuse me," Jamie interrupted, sitting up, "but would ye stop acting like I'm not even here?"

"I don't even exist to these lasses," Griffin put in, "how do ye think I feel?"

"It won't matter how long I know him, or how well I get to know him," Sam said, ignoring both men.

"But Sam—"

She cut Jix off. "Here's the scoop, kids"—she reached over and patted the side of Jamie's face as though he were a child—"you, Mr. James MacGregor, do nothing for me. Zip. Zero."

"I dinna do anything for ye? What does that mean?"

Sam shrugged. "You don't ring my chimes, rock my world, light my rocket, pump—"

"We get the idea!" Jix said, aghast. Sam was never like this—outlandish and cocky. Well, sometimes she was cocky. "So there's not much sex appeal?" Jix asked. "You don't think you could ever, er, you know?"

Samantha hooted. "Much sex appeal? Honey, there isn't enough chemistry between the two of us to power a lightning bug. No offense, laddie, but you just don't turn me on."

Jamie looked worried. "I have no sex appeal?"

"To me," Sam said. "But with my darling friend here, it's obviously a different story. So, kids, here's the rest of the story—you have my blessing. Love each other. Go at it all night, every night, for all I care. Find a way to get us out of this blasted place and back to our own time and I'll throw the two of you the biggest wedding Austin, Texas, has ever seen. Just leave me out of this triangle you keep trying to design."

"What's gotten into you?" Jix asked, amazed at Sam's attitude. "You never act so—so—"

"Spontaneous? Free?" Sam tossed her hair back from her shoulder and gave Jix a smile that truly lit up her face. "Maybe being a gypsy for a little while was good for me. Or maybe I'm just trying to give you a dose of your own rotten medicine."

"I've reformed," Jix promised, crossing her heart with

one hand. "No more Yugoslavian accents. No more lies. No more interfering in other people's lives. If you want to go home and marry Mark, well, I guess losing your trust fund isn't the worst thing that could happen to you."

"I'm not marrying Mark."

Jix's heart leapt up inside of her and she pulled her legs up on the narrow bed and clasped her hands together over her knees. "Really, Sam?"

"Really." Sam glanced away, then back again. "I guess it was a pride thing. I didn't want to admit that I could've chosen such a loser, but after I had time to think about it— three freaking months, thank you—I realized that you and my dad wouldn't have done something so drastic if there hadn't been a real reason."

Jix blinked back hot tears and leaned back against the wall of the wagon, feeling as though half the world had just rolled off her shoulders. "Oh, Sam, you just don't know what that means to me. So maybe you understand a little, why I did what I did?"

Sam gave her a cautious look. "Maybe."

"And maybe you can admit now that I really did save you from a fate worse than death?" Jix couldn't help it. Sam's arrogance just begged to be taken down a notch.

But instead of getting mad, her friend's smile just got wider. "Sure, Jix. You saved me from Mark. And you only had to send me to seventeenth century Scotland to do it. I think that's a record, even for you."

Jix straightened. "How do I know you just aren't being noble and giving Jamie up when you really want him for yourself? Especially now that you don't plan to marry Mark?"

Samantha glanced over at Jamie, who had lain back down on the bed. She stood. There was only a foot of space between the two beds and all she had to do was lean over. He put his hands behind his head and smiled up at her as she made an obvious appraisal of his assets. Jix's eyes widened as Sam's gaze skimmed over his taut body, pausing meaningfully at his trews. He went along with her

303

gambit, lifting his fist and making his biceps bulge for her perusal.

"Very funny," Jix said. "The two of you don't realize how serious this is. If one dream doesn't come true then the other one has to!" She tried not to sound panicky, but her voice still squeaked over the last words.

"Oh, Jix, you of all people should know that Jamie does nothing for me," Sam said. "I'm not attracted to the burly he-man types."

"Thank ye very much," Jamie said.

"An' what am I? Chopped haggis?" Griffin asked.

Sam ignored them both. "I like the pantheresque men, you know, wiry, sleek"—she lifted one brow—"intellectual?"

"But—" Jix protested.

"Let me put it this way," Sam interrupted. "If Jamie and I were the last two people on the planet, I would become celibate."

"Thanks," Jamie muttered. Jix turned to him, still not completely convinced.

"What about you, Jamie? Do you feel the same way?"

"Well, lass, ye have to realize, I'm a man and—"

"Just answer the question," Jix said, narrowing her eyes.

He grinned and propped one foot on the wall of the wagon. "I'm just playing with ye. I have a better analogy—if ye lock me and yer friend in a room for a night, when ye came back the next morning ye wouldna find us in one another's arms. In fact, ye wouldna find us at all—we'd have torn each other to shreds."

Jix frowned. "But there are lots of instances where people who hate each other in the beginning actually have strong feelings for each other and—"

"Not in this instance," Sam declared. "Jix, believe me, I'm not being noble. He's yours, all yours. He just doesn't float my boat."

Jamie cast her a sour look from the bed. "And I have to say that being around yer friend has never, uh, how can I put this? Gotten a rise out of me?"

Jix smiled. She felt the gesture stretch across her face,

eal, genuine, unabashed. "Oh, Jamie," she said, sinking down to lie beside him. Her gaze locked with his and suddenly a wave of desire swept over her, down to her fingertips, down to her toes, filling her with a fire so sweet and so hot she felt she might spontaneously combust right on the spot. He was hers. Jamie was hers.

Sam glanced over at Griffin. "I think this is our cue."

"Our what?"

"Our cue." She held out her hand. "Come on, I'll tell you all about it."

"But it's still rainin'," Griffin protested, gesturing to the door.

"I'll make you an umbrella," she said, pulling him up and moving to duck under the doorway.

"But I dinna want to be an umbrella," Griffin grumbled, following her out the door. "What's an umbrella, lass?"

Jix giggled, then laughed out loud as Jamie pulled her down on top of him. Their mouths met and Jix closed her eyes, letting his tongue dance with hers, letting his hands roam where they wanted as she slid hers over his chest. His clothes were still wet and when he pulled his shirt off, his bandage came with it. Jix ran her fingers across the puckered wound, glad to see it seemed to be healing well. Getting his soaking wet trews off almost ended their passion before it got started, but Jix finally managed to work the wet material down to his knees.

Jix didn't bother shedding her clothes, instead she covered his body with her own, her full, damp skirt billowing out like a bright flower over his nakedness as she slid over him, taking control. There was no need for preliminaries, or words. Jix made love to Jamie, uninhibited, giving as freely as she received, possessing and being possessed, rocking that bright blue wagon as it had never been rocked before.

305

Chapter Twenty-one

Making love in a gypsy wagon was rather like making love in a sleeping bag, but Jix wasn't complaining. Sam and Griffin didn't come back and she and Jamie spent the rest of the day alone, listening to the gentle rhythm of the rain on the roof of the cozy cart, making love, then listening some more to the rain and to each other.

"Who'd have ever thought this would happen?" Jix said softly, running her fingers through Jamie's soft dark hair.

"Not me," he admitted. He captured her fingers and brought them to his lips. "I thought we were over. I thought I had lost ye."

The joy of the moment faded a bit as Jix pulled Jamie closer. "Oh, Jamie, I'm still afraid I'm going to lose you. The dream—"

"We'll find a way to thwart the dream," Jamie promised, sliding his hands down her bare back and sending a shiver over her skin. "If we return to our own time, how can Captain Worthington ever cut off my head?"

"Don't even say it," she whispered, cupping his face between her hands and smoothing her thumbs over his lower lip. "I can't lose you."

"Ye won't, lass. We just have to find a way to get hold of my sword."

"I found a way to get hold of your sword several times today," she teased.

Jamie kissed the tip of her nose. "Och, ye make my heart laugh. How did I ever live without ye?"

"Are you sure you can live with my—" she hesitated, biting her lower lip. How could she put it without sounding as though she considered her life that of an escaped lunatic?

"With yer different way of looking at things?"

She nodded, grateful for the kind spin he'd put on the description. "I mean, I'm trying to change—"

"Dinna change," he said softly, tracing one eyebrow with his kisses. "I love ye just the way ye are." He kissed her mouth, deeply, longingly, and Jix felt the burn begin yet again.

But she pulled away from his seeking lips, and he looked down at her quizzically. "No, Jamie," she said, shaking her head, "I want to change. At least, in some ways. I promise that I'll never lie to you again."

Jamie slid his hand down the side of her bare leg and shifted his weight against her soft skin. "Ye dinna even have to tell me that, love. I knew it already. Change what ye will, but dinna change the things I love about ye—yer sense of humor, yer loyalty, yer passion, yer love for me."

"No, I won't, I—" Jix's eyes widened. "Oh, MacGregor, I think I found that sword again."

"Och, no, lass, it's my sword that's found ye."

Then there were no words and Jix pushed away her fears as Jamie took her to the stars again. Later, they lay together totally replete, sated with love, and Jix realized that soon, very soon, they would be leaving the seventeenth century. She refused to believe otherwise. A pang struck her, and with astonishment, Jix realized she would miss Meadbrooke and Griffin and even Red Hugh.

"What is it?" Jamie asked, rolling over on his side and propping his chin on his hand.

"I was just thinking that we'll never see this place, or

these people, ever again, once we return to our own time."

"Would ye rather stay?"

Jix smiled. "And what if I said yes?"

"I'd stay."

She reached up and pushed one long lock of hair behind his ear. "You would, wouldn't you?" She slid her arms around his neck and pressed her body against him.

"Aye." He held her tightly. "Whatever ye want, Jix, that's what I want." He lifted her face to his and kissed her mouth gently before gazing down at her. "Ye never have to be afraid again, ye ken?" He searched her eyes. "I'll never stop lovin' ye, I'll never disappear, I'll never abandon ye."

"But do you promise to never die?" she whispered, her throat suddenly tight.

Jamie smiled and shook his head. "I canna promise that, lass. I'm no' immortal. But I can promise that while I'm here, I will love ye like no man has ever loved ye before."

"You already have," she said, bringing his lips down to hers again. "Oh, sweet Jamie, you already have."

He kissed her again, then rolled to his back, pulling her with him to lie atop him, her long red hair spilling over his chest.

"Let's get some rest, love. I think we'll have a long day of it on the morrow."

Jix gave a sigh of contentment. Now if only they could figure out a way to retrieve the sword without Captain Worthington catching them, everything would be perfect. If they could go back to their own time. And if Sam and Jamie really meant it when they both said they felt nothing for one another.

Jix opened her eyes. His chest was warm and furry beneath her face. "Jamie."

"Aye, lass?"

"When you were kissing Samantha—"

" 'Twas like kissing a piranha. I took my life in my hands every time I touched her. I fully expected to draw my arm back a bloody stump." Jix giggled and he hugged her more tightly. "Dinna fash yerself, *acushla,* just trust me."

"All right, Jamie," she said softly, closing her eyes. "I will. I do."

"May yer dreams be sweet, love."

Jix's eyes flew open. If only they could be sweet. If only she could dream that they were home again, and that she and Jamie were dressed in wedding clothes, gazing with stars in their eyes at one another. And if only that dream was destined to come true. If only.

Jix walked aimlessly across verdant green meadows, the smell of heather and roses heavy in the air. She felt lost, confused. Why was she alone? How had she wandered so far from the castle and why? The blue of the Scottish sky seemed unusually bright today, marred only by a haze of brown clouds near the ground. Brown clouds?

Jix blinked, one hand flying to her throat as she saw dozens of horses galloping past her. She gathered her skirts and tore across the countryside after them, afraid she would be too late to warn those in the castle. The sky grew darker as she ran until she feared the darkness itself chased her, waiting for a chance to swallow her whole.

When she arrived at Meadbrooke Castle she rushed inside. A tall man with black hair and piercing black eyes stood behind a table. A bloodied sword lay next to a covered silver platter. He lifted the lid and Jamie's disembodied head sat bleeding there. Then he opened his eyes. Jix started to scream, but the scene faded, shifted, like a hazy watercolor painting and all at once, she was in a large room filled with people, back in their own time. She heard laughter and she turned.

Samantha smiled up at the tall, handsome man beside her, a glowing, radiant look on her face. The man had dark brown hair almost reaching his shoulders and the bluest eyes Jix had ever seen. His nose hooked at the bridge and kept him from being too perfect, too pretty. His lips were firm and chiseled, like his jaw. Jamie—with his handsome head still firmly on his shoulders. Jix's heart contracted and she took a step forward. He looked down into Samantha's eyes and Jix stopped. She'd never seen him look so happy.

Samantha was beautiful in a creamy white gown. A crown of white and yellow daisies encircled her head and she held a small bouquet of daisies and roses in her hand. Jamie wore a plaid kilt of red and green, a crisp white shirt, and a black dress jacket. A white rose adorned his lapel. It was a wedding. She was at a wedding—Samantha's wedding.

Jix came awake with a start, gasping for breath. Both dreams! She sat up on the side of the narrow bed in Sam's wagon. Jamie still slept, one arm thrown back over his head, his breathing even. Asleep, he looked much younger. He'd never really said how old he was, but she gauged him to be in his mid-thirties. Funny, the age difference between them hadn't ever been an issue. She guessed time travel, prophetic dreams, and running for your life took precedence over such a mundane thing. He was so handsome, even with the hook at the bridge of his nose. She wondered how he'd broken it. She lifted her hand to her own small bump, remembering how she'd felt when they first met. Kismet.

She checked his healing shoulder. He seemed fine in spite of all the physical activity he'd been through in the last few days. *Not to mention last night,* she thought smugly.

Jix gave him a featherlight kiss on his forehead, then rose and crossed to the back of the wagon. The rain had stopped and she opened the door, ducking down and stepping out into a brand new day. Dew sparkled on the grass and trees and she walked down the steps of the wagon, feeling refreshed in spite of her dreams. She could smell breakfast cooking on the central campfire of the gypsy camp and followed her nose. There were only a few people around, but someone had left a stool near the fire and she sat down, watching the sky lighten with the dawn.

So which is it to be, God, Jix asked silently. *Will Jamie end up married to my best friend, or dead? It's got to be one of the two. It can't be both.*

Suddenly she heard her Aunt Phronsie's voice in her head. *God works in mysterious ways.* Indeed He did. If only He would leave a few clues along the way.

She leaned her head into her hands. Both dreams. She hadn't even experienced the wedding dream since their trip back in time, and now she'd had both prophecies in one night. She lowered her hands, staring blearily at nothing, tired of trying to figure out what the cosmos or God or the universe was trying to tell her.

On the other side of the fire, two of the gypsies were laughing together, the man performing magic tricks for the woman, whom he obviously wanted to impress. He took a coin from her cleavage, made it disappear into her ear, then made her reach down his shirt front to find it again. For his last trick he gave her a box. She opened it and inside was his hand, protruding through a hole cut in the bottom. He held a ring. She kissed him joyfully and the two disappeared in the direction of one of the wagons.

Jix smiled at the little by play, her gaze returning to the box the man had discarded on the ground after his magic trick. Magic! Jix jumped to her feet and snapped her fingers, her mind racing.

Was it possible she had been looking at this all wrong? Griffin had said that perhaps God wanted her to keep the dream from coming true and that was why she had this gift—to warn those in danger. But what if all that had to take place was for the dream to come true? No one said it had to come true in any certain way, did they? She certainly hadn't gotten any regulations manual or secret decoder ring in the mail explaining the rules!

She crossed and picked up the box, a plan forming in her mind. Worthington was superstitious. She would twist a supernatural rope around the rat bastard's neck and let him hang himself! It was perfect! It was brilliant! It was—

"Well," she said aloud, "it's a definite possibility."

"Jamie—I have an idea!"

Jamie, Samantha, and Griffin sat on smooth stones around the campfire. All three looked up from their soggy oatmeal and groaned in unison. Jix stuck her tongue ou at them.

"Och, one thing at a time, lass," Jamie pleaded, tem pering his words with a smile. She'd been practically hop ping up and down since he'd joined her, wanting to tel him something. He'd put her off while he shaved, washed his face, and downed three cups of hot tea. Then Malkor had announced breakfast and he'd put her off yet again Now she fairly twitched, standing on one foot and ther the other, refusing to eat until she'd given him her news And here it was—another idea.

She wore yet another gypsy outfit today, this one red and black, and with her auburn hair swept up into a French twist, her neck bare and sexy, she looked good enough to eat instead of the mediocre breakfast in his bowl. Jamie pulled his thoughts back to her words as she gazed down at him, a hurt look in her eyes.

"I'm sorry, lass, I dinna mean that the way it came out."

"Oh, maybe you meant to groan a little louder," she said, a spark of anger glimmering in her gaze, "or maybe you meant to let the whole gypsy camp know that you think my ideas are unworthy of your attention!"

Jamie shook his head. "I dinna mean any such thing. want to hear yer idea, but first we've got to decide how to get inside the castle without the English seein' us. Wor thington got a good look at my face that night."

"He believes ye to be dead, and let's keep it that way," Griffin said, spooning another bite of watery porridge be tween his lips. He wiped the back of one hand across his mouth. "I sent one of the gypsy men in last night under the guise of needin' water for the horses. He got to hear some castle gossip and it seems that Worthington came because he doesna believe that it was a MacGregor who reived his cattle. He thinks my father is behind it."

"I told Red Hugh this wouldna work," Jamie said, using the last of his bread to scrape his bowl clean. He popped the morsel in his mouth and chewed thoughtfully. "I told him he would bring the wrath of the English down on his people, but he wouldna listen to me."

"I know how he feels," Jix said, walking back and forth in front of him, her hands behind her back like a statesman delivering an oration. "Never mind that I have the answer to everything. The *men* think that since I'm just a mere *woman,* I couldn't possibly come up with anything plausible in the way of a plan! But don't forget I got Samantha to Scotland without her ever knowing she was going!"

"Gee, and I was just starting to get over being mad about that," Sam said. "Come here so I can kick you."

Jamie tossed his bowl aside and stood. "I'm sorry, lass. Ye're right. Tell me yer idea."

She planted her hands on her hips and smiled up at him. "We're going to make my dream come true."

"We are? Which dream, lass?" Jamie asked. "I dinna think yer friend will marry me, since she says I dinna pump her—"

"Jamie!"

"No, no, thank you," Sam said brightly. "Pretending to be enamoured of your boyfriend was quite enough for me, thanks all the same."

"Not that dream, the other dream!" Jix said, hardly able to contain her enthusiasm. This had to work!

"The other dream," Griffin said, looking up from his bowl. "But the other dream is of Jamie's death."

"Exactly!" Jix clasped her hands together as Jamie stared at her and Griffin's mouth dropped open.

Sam laughed. "Here we go again"—she began to drum invisible drumsticks over invisible drums—"Bada bing—"

"We're going to kill Jamie for Captain Worthington," Jix said.

"Bada boom!" Sam struck the invisible cymbal.

"And here I was thinking ye liked me," Jamie said, shaking his head.

Jix threw her arms around his neck and drew his face down to hers for a quick kiss. He was tempted to pick her up in his arms and carry her back to the gypsy wagon, but she was obviously too distracted by her latest wild idea.

"Of course I like you. Now listen, here's what we do.

Jamie, you're the master of disguise, right?"

He shrugged. "I suppose."

"Can you make the three of us look like gypsies?"

"Ye already look like a gypsy, except for yer hair," Jamie said. "What are—och, I get it. We'll dress like th gypsies and slip into the castle with them. Why didn't think of that?"

"Maybe ye had yer mind on other things," Griffin suggested with a playful leer.

"All right, so we're gypsies," Jamie agreed. "The what?"

"Tonight," Jix said, circling the campfire, "after suppe have Malkov call on me to tell a story, then leave it t me. After the captain goes to bed, we'll put the rest of m plan into action."

"Fine, but I want to hear every last detail of this plan—no surprises," Jamie said, as she slid her arms around hi waist and smiled up at him. "And I'm not wearing a earring."

The gypsies were welcomed inside Meadbrooke Castle jus before sunset. They had barely set up camp inside the oute bailey when one of the servants from the castle came wit word that Captain Worthington still expected them to en tertain after supper. Griffin had insisted on lagging behin the gypsy caravan and riding in alone, acting as though h had just returned from collecting rent from his father' tenants.

Jix had begged him not to do this foolhardy thing, fear ful that the young warrior would pose a threat to Worthing ton and the man would kill him on sight or put him i chains. Griffin had simply smiled and said that if he wa in danger, he was sure she would have dreamed it first An icy chill had danced down her spine. She hadn' dreamed of her adopted parents' deaths. There were n guarantees and she had told him as much.

Jamie had argued with the man also, trying to convinc him that if he got captured by the British, he'd be of littl

elp to the time-travelers. The stubborn Scot had gone any-
ay.

But apparently Griffin's gambit had paid off. He'd sent
ord via one of the gypsies that he'd seen his father and
een greeted civilly by Worthington. As long as Griffin
idn't oppose the man's presence in the castle, he felt sure
e Englishman would leave him alone. There was one
iece of bad news—the sword was nowhere to be found.
riffin had searched everywhere, to no avail.

All the more reason now, Jix felt, to make a success of
er plan. If they couldn't return to their own time, she had
 make sure that Captain Worthington never wielded a
word again.

Griffin's message went on to say that Captain Worthing-
on had insisted the supper be held as a celebration of Red
Iugh's renewal of the alliance between Meadbrooke and
ngland, and that Red Hugh had refused to fight the En-
lish, knowing he and his men were dreadfully outnum-
ered. His people were not happy with his decision.

Jix and the rest of the gypsies waited in a small room
ust off the great hall, near the kitchen. Everything was
eady. Jamie had been against her plan at first, worried
bout her safety as usual, but gradually she had convinced
im, and now he stood beside her, ready to play his part.
he turned and let her gaze sweep over him.

He made a wonderful gypsy. A black kerchief was tied
round his head and with the gold hoop in his left ear, he
ooked as much like a pirate as a gypsy. He wore his long
ark hair loose over his shoulders, and his five o'clock
hadow just added to his rakish appearance. One of the
ypsy women had provided makeup in the form of kohl,
nd he had widened his brows and painted shadows under
is eyes and over his eyelids. He didn't want to take a
hance on Worthington recognizing him if by accident
heir paths crossed. His red silk shirt had huge sleeves and
vide cuffs and was open to the waist. Black, skintight
rousers, his own black boots, and a blue sash at his waist
ompleted his costume.

Jix's pulse quickened. Too bad there wasn't time to

sneak away for a little impromptu gypsy fantasy. She r*
her tongue across her lips and Jamie grinned as if he kne*
her thoughts.

"Do ye like what ye see, lass?" he whispered.

"Aye. And what about you?"

Sam had given Jix a new outfit, and this one had a sn*
low-cut white bodice, big puffed sleeves, bangles for h*
arms and several necklaces, and a wide golden sash at t*
waist of her bright blue skirt. Dangly gold earrings hu*
almost to her shoulders and a black mantilla like Sam*
covered her auburn hair.

Jamie looked her over appreciatively. "Aye, ye'll do*
he said.

Jix pouted. "Is that all?"

Jamie chuckled. "I dinna say *what* ye would do," *
murmured. "Would ye care to tell me?"

"Later," she whispered. "Right now we have an En*
lishman to scare the living daylights out of." She peek*
around the corner to watch the proceedings unfold.

At the table on the dais sat three men—Griffin, his fa*
dark with anger; Red Hugh, who looked defeated and o*
and a man with flashing black eyes and unruly black ha*
Jix swallowed hard. It was the man from her dream.

Captain Worthington sat between the two Scots, arr*
gantly gazing out over the hall. Once his black eyes m*
hers and she shivered. Worthington was sinisterly han*
some, with a cleft in his chin and a straight, autocrat*
nose. His black hair was wavy, cut to the bottom of h*
ears, and he reminded her somewhat of an old movie st*
Basil something-or-other. Except evil. Really evil.

Outside the keep, the rain had begun again and Jix se*
a prayer of thanks skyward. What she was about to *
would play out more successfully against a backdrop *
lightning and thunder. Butterflies fluttered in the pit of h*
stomach and she was reminded of her actress days. Ju*
before performing, she'd always had a slight attack *
stage fright. That's all this was now. Once she got *
stage, she'd be fine. Jix swallowed hard. She could do thi*
She could save Jamie's life.

The people seated at the trestle tables below the dais were unusually quiet this night, casting resentful glances at both Worthington and Red Hugh. Jix felt a brief pang of sympathy for the laird, whose plan had backfired so terribly. Perhaps he wouldn't make the best chieftain, but she had to admire that he was still trying to save his people from unnecessary bloodshed, even if it meant losing face with those same people. If her plan worked, even Red Hugh would come out on top.

The gypsies had been fed well in the kitchen, but Jix hadn't been able to eat a bite. While they had been offered chicken and rabbit, the cook had pulled out all the stops tonight for the laird and his guests, presenting dishes Jix had never seen before in this austere place. Beef, pheasant, chicken, ham, as well as a variety of side dishes and a plum pudding for dessert. All in Worthington's honor, of course.

" 'Tis an adequate meal," she heard Worthington telling Red Hugh. The hall was so quiet it was easy to hear their exchange, even from where she stood. "For a Scottish cook, that is. In England, of course, we have nothing but the best."

"Will ye be returnin' there soon to partake of yer better food?" Griffin asked. "Please dinna let us keep ye."

The captain chuckled. "There are some things more important than feeding the flesh." His black eyes gleamed with malice. "Like putting some arrogant Scotsman in his place, or exposing him for the coward he is."

Griffin clenched his hands on top of the table and Jix clenched her own fists in reaction, hoping he wouldn't blow the whole night by losing his temper. She watched as he slowly relaxed his hands and she released her breath in relief.

"It's almost time, lass," Jamie whispered, his breath warm against her ear. "Are ye sure ye aren't afraid?"

She shook her head. One last lie for the road. No—she had promised. "Yes," she said, "I'm afraid."

"We can still call this off," he said softly. "Griffin and

317

I can find Red Hugh alone and make him tell us where t[]
sword is."

She shook her head. "No, not with Worthington he[]
It's too risky."

"All right. I'll be watching ye while ye dance. I can[]
draw attention to myself. If Worthington recognizes me,[]
will give the whole thing away."

The musicians hurried out at a command they had bo[]
missed and suddenly Jix was not just afraid, she was te[]
rified. But not for herself, for the man she loved. She thre[]
her arms around him.

"Kiss me, Jamie," she said, pulling his face down []
hers.

Jix held his face between her hands as his lips c[]
ressed her, burning his love for her indelibly across h[]
mouth, her face, her throat as they clung to one anoth[]
His arms held her as if there was no tomorrow, h[]
mouth possessing hers as if it might be the last time. B[]
cause they both knew it just might be.

Chapter Twenty-two

The music began with the crash of a tambourine and Jamie smiled his encouragement as Jix ran from his embrace into the great hall. The women had practiced the dance a few times that afternoon and Jix went immediately into the opening move. They spun around in circles, their circular skirts rising to their hips as some of the men stood behind them clapping and stomping their feet, punctuating the tambourine with shouts of encouragement.

Then the music slowed and the women danced independently. Jix turned, finding Jamie's gaze behind a dozen other men, holding it with her own as she moved with the rhythm of the music, sliding her hands over her body, over her breasts, her stomach, her legs, then up again, sliding to her throat, her face, up into her hair, lifting it from her neck, then letting it fall. She danced for Jamie and only for Jamie. The tempo increased and the women all spun around, their arms outspread before they collapsed to the floor. Jix tossed her head back, letting her hair cascade over her back. Jamie's eyes burned into hers as she slowly rose to her knees, then her feet. She and half of the women spun off the floor to wait at the sides while the other women twirled into a different rhythm.

Samantha danced like one born to the rhythm of the violin and guitar, and Jix couldn't help but smile as she watched her best friend. How amazing, to see Sam so free, so spontaneous. Would it be something lasting, Jix wondered? Or would she revert to her old self once they returned to their own time? It was one thing to act differently in an unusual situation like this, it was another to do it under familiar circumstances. Jix bit her lip as a new thought struck her. What if she couldn't make her own changes stick? What if she reverted to her old insecure, lying ways? Jix shook her head, refusing to even entertain the thought. She would never let Jamie down.

The dance ended and applause and shouts rang out across the hall. The gypsies were bowing and catching coins thrown to them. Malkov walked into the center of the room. Jix took a deep breath.

The swarthy man spread his hands apart and the noise subsided. He bowed toward the three men. "Gentlemen, I have brought the lovely Yolanda to entertain you this night. She has spun her tales for kings and princes across the European continent and is honored this night to tell her stories for you."

Jix was ready. She crossed the room slowly, seductively, stopping beside Malkov. He bowed toward her and slipped away in the other direction. She had debated on what kind of accent to use, since the gypsies were not Scots and had their own unique dialect. She had tried to practice it a bit and could only do her best, even though she was afraid she sounded like a bad imitation of Chekov from *Star Trek.*

"Young laird and Laird Campbell," she began, "and honored guest." The words almost stuck in her throat. "I have heard zat Captain Worthington is fond of ghost stories."

Worthington shifted in his seat. "Nay, you have heard wrong. Ghost stories are for children. "Tell of something else."

"Ah, Keptin," Jix said, lifting her chin and smiling, "are you afraid of a ghostie story?"

He laughed as though her question was ridiculous, but his eyes shifted nervously. "Of course not, you presumptuous wench. Tell your tale if you must."

Jix crossed slowly to the small, upraised area of stone where the musicians sometimes performed, and stepped up on it. She stood for a moment, her hands at her sides, her gaze sweeping over those at the trestle tables, then up to the dais and Captain Worthington. Jix remained unflinching before his burning black eyes, she waited a beat, and then began.

"In ze ancient days of Scotland, zere once vas a brave young lad who loved a lass vith all his heart and soul. His name vas Ian Campbell and he vas a distant cousin of the laird of Meadbrooke Castle. One night he and ze laird came home to ze castle and found zat an Englishman had dishonored zé laddie's love, and held ze entire castle captive. Ze lad and ze Englishman battled with swords, and though ze Scot fought valiantly, ze Sassenach tricked him into turning avay, zen stabbed him in ze back."

Worthington shifted in his chair and scowled at her. The people at the trestle tables murmured, shooting dark glances toward the captain. Jix hurried on. She and Griffin had agreed it best be a short tale.

"Ze Scot lay dying in ze lass's arms," she said, sweeping her own arms out to the side, encompassing the room in a pitiful gesture, "but before he died, he made her a promise—zat he vould ne'er leave ze castle, not even after death. He promised to valk ze halls of Meadbrooke and protect her and any other lass living zhere from danger. He said zat any who sought to cause her harm vould die a slow and painful death."

Jix stepped down from the upraised stone and walked slowly across the room to stand in front of the dais. She glanced at Griffin. She had to hurry, for she feared Worthington might not let her complete the story. His face had already turned beet red and his fists lay clenched on the table top, so tightly that his knuckles were white. If Griffin hadn't been able to speak privately with Red Hugh, the laird himself might stop her story. But a glance at him set her mind at ease. He looked happy, as if the "gypsy" girl's story was striking a blow that he could not.

Jix hurried on. "Ze Sassenach heard his vords, and fearing ze Scot vould do as he promised, he took his sword and cut off his head, sinking zis vould prevent him from ever returning to ze mortal vorld." There were audible gasps from the audience. Worthington continued to glare at her, his dark eyes narrowed, lethal. Red Hugh offered the man more wine and he took it, draining the goblet in a single drink.

"Zat night ze Sassenach vent to ze young lass's chamber and zhere sought to defile her again. Ven he reached out to touch her, all at once behind him appeared ze ghost of Ian Campbell. He held his own bloody head in his hands." Jix extended her hands. "Ze Sassenach froze in horror as ze specter threw his head straight at him! Ze Englishman caught Ian's head, and paralyzed vith fear, stood like one dead until finally he roused enough to fling ze dreaded object avay from him!"

Jix lowered her voice, leaning forward slightly as if to convey some terrible information. "But it vas too late. Because ze Sassenach had held ze head for longer than a moment, ze spirits of the castle had no choice but to enter his soul. Ze Englishman trembled as he first felt his skin go hot, zen cold." She moved her hands to her face, widening her eyes in horror. "His face slowly began to darken, ze skin zhere growing green and shrunken, his eyes popping further and further from his head until at last zey snapped from ze sockets altogezer and rolled upon ze floor!"

The great hall lay hushed. Worthington sat staring at her, no longer glaring, no longer cocky. He refilled his goblet with wine and gulped it down as Jix moved in for the kill.

"Ze Sassenach ran screaming from ze hall, stone blind, but before he could reach ze castle gate, his skin began to split and rip until his very insides ver spilling from his body. He collapsed to ze ground and writhed in agony for

322

hours until at last he died, every inch of his body stripped of flesh!" She lifted her chin and looked Worthington directly in the eyes. "And so now zere are two ghosts zat wander ze halls of Meadbrooke Castle"—she concluded, winding up for the grand finale—"ze ghost of Ian Campbell who walks ze dark corridors with his head beneath his arm, protecting any who vould dare accost a lass," she paused, gazing around at her captive audience. "And ze ghost of ze Sassenach, who blindly vanders through ze castle, praying for forgiveness for his deeds."

An ominous silence fell over the hall as Jix sank into a low curtsy. Red Hugh stood, shaking his shoulders as if to ward off any wee ghosties that might have wandered in to hear the story. He lifted his goblet and for a moment, Jix thought he seemed to have regained some of his dignity. "A grand tale, Yolanda. We thank ye for it. Now, musicians, let us have something to lighten the mood.

The musicians moved into the elevated space and Jix stepped down. To her consternation Jamie met her as she crossed the great hall.

"I dinna like the way he's lookin' at ye," he said as he escorted her toward the crowd of gypsies.

"As long as he isn't looking at you, I don't care. Jamie, you shouldn't have—"

"Wait!"

The music screeched to a stop as Worthington stood. He slammed down his goblet and swayed slightly, revealing that he was well into his cups as he started down the steps from the platform. Jamie put his hands on Jix's shoulders and drew her back against him.

"Jamie, you mustn't let him get close to you, do you hear me?" she whispered fiercely. "I mean it! Back away. I'm in the middle of a crowded room. What could happen?"

Jamie's fingers tightened for a moment, then he released her and slipped back behind some of the other gypsies. He was close enough to help her if she needed him, and Jix relaxed and turned to face the black-eyed man. He towered over her, and Jix had to force her eyes to his, refusing to be intimidated.

"Did you like ze tale, Keptin?" she asked.

"Indeed," he said, his voice harsh. "I especially liked the part about cutting off the bastard's head." He reached out and grabbed the end of one long lock of her hair that had slipped out from under her mantilla, pulling her closer to him. "Although there are some heads that it would be a shame to remove."

Jix drew in a sharp breath, determined not to let the man shake her. "And zere are some zat should have rolled long ago." She followed the terse statement with a bright smile.

"Unusual hair color for a gypsy."

"My mother vas Irish," she improvised. "Please, sir, I must attend to my child, out in my vagon."

His eyes bored down into hers like two hard black marbles as he wrapped her long hair around his hand until it became painful. "Come to my room tonight," he said, his voice low, "and I will pay you more if you struggle."

The man wore a white shirt and dark blue trousers and coat for his uniform, with a belt at his waist containing a dagger. In one quick movement Jix reached down and pulled the blade from his belt, lifting it to his throat. He raised his chin and froze at her side.

"Do you know I am so damn tired of men thinking I'm afraid of them," she said, dropping the accent. She moved the blade downward, slicing through the strand of hair he still held, and with another swift move, slid the blade back into its scabbard at his waist so hard that the man jumped. Then she smiled and walked away, leaving Worthington standing there with a stunned look on his face, a lock of red hair in his hand.

Jamie quickly ushered her into the side room where they had waited before, then to a small side door. Once outside, she fell into his arms, trembling with reaction.

"Bastard!" Jamie cursed the man roundly. He tilted her face to his. "What did he say to you?"

"To come to his room later. He said he'd pay more if I struggled."

Jamie's face turned bright red and Jix wished she hadn't told him. He turned as if to go back inside and Jix stopped him, grabbing him by his shirt. "Jamie—no! He's a rat bastard and we're going to get him."

He nodded, releasing his breath explosively. He lifted the shorn lock from her shoulder. "Och, well, ye didn't like it long anyway, did ye?"

She shrugged. "I sort of like the way it feels on my back," she slid him a smile, "when I'm naked."

"I like the way ye feel when ye're naked."

"Weren't we supposed to meet Griffin?" she asked as he slowly backed her into the shadows of the castle wall. "And we have to get the makeup ready for—"

"Aye," he said, lowering his mouth to hers, "but later, much later."

Midnight. The witching hour.

Operation Worthington was about to begin. After supper ended it took the better part of two hours, but somehow Griffin managed to clear the bottom floor of the entire castle, save for those involved in the next phase of their plan. He'd convinced Worthington to camp his men in the inner bailey instead of inside the castle. That at least would slow the soldiers down if they did end up coming to the captain's aid.

Jamie and Jix stood at the top of the stairs gazing down into the deserted hall. All of the trestle tables had been pushed back against the walls except for one that now sat in the middle. A black tablecloth covered it, the edges brushing the floor.

"I wish we didn't have to do this part," Jix said. "I wish we could just find the sword and get out of here!"

"Aye, but even if we could return to our own time, right now, wouldn't the dream continue to haunt ye?"

She frowned. "I don't know." Jix shook her head. "I need an operator's manual for this stuff."

Jamie grinned. "Well, until ye find one, I think we'd best go through with yer plan. Besides," he put his arm around her shoulders and hugged her tightly to him, "I'll enjoy watching that little weasel run away. If he doesna

325

wet himself in the process, I'll let Red Hugh keep my sword and we'll stay here."

"Don't say that, even joking!" Jix said, feeling panicky. "I want to go home. I'm sick of no running water, no decent food, no central heat, no Dr. Pepper, and the darned stinking rushes on the floor—I don't want to stay here another minute!"

"So, Jix Ferguson, queen of comedy, doesna want to joke anymore."

She made a face at him and tossed her auburn hair back from her shoulders. "I don't care if I ever make another joke again in my entire life. Or tell another lie!"

Jamie grinned at her. "What? No lies to anyone? I thought I was the only one signed up for yer new honesty policy."

"No more lies," Jix stated flatly, then frowned. "Unless of course Sam asks me if she looks good in brown. She looks just awful in brown, but if I tell her she looks awful in brown, then I have to listen to her wail and bemoan the fact that I have to criticize her every move and—"

"I get the idea, lass. Ye can lie to Samantha if ye must."

"Only little white lies," she said, demonstrating with her forefinger and thumb just how small the transgressions would be.

"Just never lie to me."

"Never," she said fiercely. Jix lifted her face for his kiss. It shook her all the way down to her toes, and when he tilted her head to kiss the top of her hair, then moved away, Jix almost burst into tears. What if it didn't work? What if Worthington caught on? What if he really cut off Jamie's head? Weren't they taking a terrible risk? Would her 'great idea' end up a catastrophe—as usual? What was she thinking?

"Jamie, I—"

Griffin came to the bottom of the stairs. "It's almost time," he said.

"Maybe we need to rethink this, guys," Jix said, a nervous energy pulsing through her veins. Tonight they would save Jamie's life—or end it.

"It's a good plan, lass." Jamie turned her to face him, his hands gentle on her shoulders. "Nothing will go wrong."

"But what if it does?" she whispered.

"It willna," Griffin had moved soundlessly up the stairs and stood next to Jamie. "At the first sign of trouble, I'll terminate the bastard."

Jix laughed. "I see you've been talking to Samantha about movies again. All right, then, let's do it."

"Are ye ready for yer makeup, lad?" Griffin said, clapping Jamie on the back.

"Aye."

"And I'm ready for my close-up, Mr. DeMille," she quipped, feeling far from the lighthearted adventuress she portrayed. She reached up and pulled Jamie down for one more kiss, then he headed down the stairs with Griffin.

Jix resolved to focus on her part of this escapade. Nothing messed up a scam like inattention to detail. She walked over to the wall and leaned against it, her breath coming quickly as she mentally went over the plan for the umpteenth time. Everything had to be perfect. Everyone had to be in the right place and do the right thing if this was going to work. She paced back and forth, waiting for Griffin to give the word to begin.

Of course the only glitch in her little plan had to do with human nature. She couldn't control what Worthington's reaction would be to their little hoax. If he did the wrong thing, would that mean the dream could still come true? Jix resolved to not think about it. All she could do was try. Beyond that, it really was in God's hands. She blinked rapidly for a minute, then smiled and glanced up.

"So I had to go through all of this, just to figure that out? You couldn't have just left a note? Oh, yeah, I guess you did. But you realize, of course, I do have a back-up plan. Just in case. No offense."

"Jix!" A hushed whisper echoed across the hall. Sam stood at the bottom of the stairs, her face pale, her long, now powder-white hair iridescent in the candlelight. "Are you ready?"

Jix nodded, gathering her courage. "Yes! Are you?"

"Yes, but I still think—"

"Don't think—just do this for me!"

"All right, but you owe me big time—I mean more than you already owe me for—"

"Sam, just shut up and do it!"

Sam hurried away and from her limited vantage point Jix surveyed the flickering lights of the great hall. Every candle in Meadbrooke had been brought and placed in two rows, lining a pathway to the stairs. Jix could just see the beginning of this flaming trail they had created.

Griffin had enlisted the aid of several men and women he trusted and Jix thought she and Jamie had done a great job on the makeup for their extras. They only had limited ingredients like flour, cornmeal, and mud with which to work—although for his own disguise, Jamie planned to use more exotic items. Jix had been afraid to watch him apply his makeup for fear it would jinx the whole thing.

Instead, she waited out of sight in the upstairs hallway. She knew all that remained was for Jamie to finish his preparations and get in place, then they could begin.

After what seemed like forever Jix heard Griffin's signal—a quick, short whistle. Now came the hard part. She took a deep breath, refusing to think about the danger of what she was doing. Everything hinged on this. Everything.

Slowly Jix walked down the open corridor to Worthington's chamber door. Red Hugh had given him one of the best rooms, and luckily, one of the closest to the stairs. Jix stood there clenching and unclenching her fists, summoning the courage to knock.

"Now!" Griffin called. "Before the candles go out!"

Jix lifted her fist and brought it down heavily on the door. Once, twice, three times. Nothing happened. She lifted her fist and brought it down. Once, twice—the door opened. Jix almost tripped over her own feet backing away.

"Who the hell is—" Worthington sputtered, swaying in the doorway. He wore only his trousers and was obviously

328

drunk. "Oh, it's you. I didn't think you were comin' you little slut."

"Captain Worthington," she said in a mysterious voice, "the spirits have instructed me to speak with you. You must come downstairs, and your future will be revealed to you."

"What's wrong with your voice?" he asked, slumping against the doorframe.

Jix sighed, remembering the Chekov accent. "Please come with me now, if you vish to know your future." She turned and started walking away from him. He wasn't moving. Damn. He wasn't going to buy it.

Then he started following her and Jix blew out her breath in quick relief. She led him down the stairs and through the hallway of lights.

Jix circled behind the table covered in black and sat down on the stool positioned there. Another, smaller black cloth covered a large bump in the center of the table.

"Sit down," she said, in what she hoped sounded like an ominous voice. Worthington sat down in the chair that had been placed opposite hers. Jix produced a velvet sack and shook it in front of Worthington, then spilled the contents on the black tablecloth. She had borrowed some of the gypsy's fortune telling runes—small stones with symbols carved into each. She spread them out in a straight line across the dark surface.

"What'd' you see?" Worthington demanded, his voice slurred. "An' I don't pay for bad news."

"I only tell you vat is there," Jix said solemnly, "I can only tell you vat the rune stones reveal."

Not bad. Maybe the next time the carnival came to town in Austin, she would sign up to be the resident psychic. Aunt Phronsie would be so proud. Jix peered down at the first rune and prepared to freak out the Englishman.

"Oy vay!" she cried.

"What—what is it?" Worthington asked, jumping to his feet.

"No, no, you are right." Jix sat back on her stool,

crossing her arms over her chest. "I should not gif you bad news."

He sank back into the chair. "Tell me," he said, his voice a whisper.

"Wery vell." She pointed to the first rune. It had a marking that looked like an arrow on it. "Zis is the sign of departure." She pointed to the next one, frowning ominously. "Do you see zis stone zat it is pointing away from?" The rune had a squiggly line on it. She had no idea what it meant.

"Zat is Scotland." She nodded her head knowingly. "It is obvious. You must leave Scotland."

"Leave Scotland? But—"

"Vait!" She held up one hand. "Do not interrupt." She pointed to the next in the line she had laid out. The symbol on it looked like a lightning bolt. "Do you see how zis lies next to Scotland?" He nodded, his dark head bobbing up and down frantically. She narrowed her eyes and spread her hands in a dramatic gesture. "If you stay in Scotland, death vill be your reward. And not a noble death."

She picked up the next rune and drew in a deep breath as if to steady herself, then lifted her gaze to his, amazed to see the terror reflected in his eyes. She tossed the stone in front of him. An X blazed across its surface.

"You are a man familiar vith death. You have brought it to many people. Zis rune tells me zat, and zese"—She indicated the next two—"tell me zat your death vill be slow and painful unless you leave Scotland."

Worthington licked his thick lips. "But I can't leave Scotland."

She nodded. "I see. Of course, pain means different zings to different peoples." She picked up the next stone and frowned at it. "Do you have a problem vith . . ." she looked up, her eyes hooded with mystery, as she hesitated. Well, she hoped they looked hooded with mystery.

"Yes, yes, with what?" he asked anxiously.

"Vith spiders?"

The man physically shivered in front of her. "You see sp-spiders?"

She lowered her voice. "Yes. Many, many spiders."

Worthington stared back at her, looking as if he couldn't move to save his life.

"There is one last message." She glanced at the final rune she had set a little apart from the others. Jix stood up, her eyes wide with horror. Carved into the stone was a perfectly innocent symbol that looked sort of like the letter 'H', but Jix acted like she'd just been exposed to malaria. Or was it the plague during this time period? Yes, the plague, she decided as she widened her eyes even more and raised one hand to clutch her throat.

"What is it?" Worthington cried, rising from his chair also. "What is it?"

Her voice trembled. *Damn, I'm good.* "Ze spirits have bidden me to show you vat is beneath zis cloth," she said, lowering her gaze to the black lump on the table beside her.

"Wh-what's under the cloth?" Worthington asked.

Jix raised her stricken eyes to his and tried for a hollow sound. "Your destiny," she whispered, wishing she had just one microphone with echo capabilities.

"I-I don't want to see it."

"You must!" She lifted one arm toward him, pointing her index finger toward him, widening her eyes until they felt like they would fall out of her head. "If you do not look, ze stones say zat you will die tonight!"

"All right, all right!" Worthington cried, "What do I do?"

"Come, stand vere I am standing."

Worthington hesitated, then moved around behind the table. Jix reached under the black tablecloth and pulled out a long sword. Blood dripped from the end of it and Worthington backed away as she held the weapon out to him. She took a moment to silently thank the chicken that had given up her life for that bit of theatre. The animal was going to be dinner tomorrow anyway, so Jix didn't feel too guilty. Well, okay, still pretty guilty.

"What is that sword for?" His normally deep voice sounded almost squeaky.

"Zis represents all of ze deaths you have caused," Ji said, laying the sword across the cloth on the table. "Com here." She positioned Worthington, then moved away fror the table and into the shadows. She took her place in fror of the fireplace, standing just where she had always stoo in her dream. Jix began to tremble. Now, as Aunt Phronsi used to say, this is where the rubber meets the road. "Nov you must remove ze small black cloth."

Worthington's hand trembled too as he reached out an pulled the cloth away. A large serving platter with the kin of round, silver top Jix had only seen in magazines wa revealed. It looked large enough to contain a pheasant c even a whole turkey.

"What the bloody hell?" Worthington's terror fade "What kind of jest is this?"

"Do not resist ze spirits of Meadbrooke," Jix whispere in a raspy voice. "Pick up ze cover," she said.

Worthington hesitated.

"Pick up ze cover or die. . . ." Jix moaned.

Worthington picked up the cover.

Even though Jix knew what to expect, the sight of Ja mie's disembodied head in the center of the platter sent shock through her, right down to her toes. Blood drippe from a gash on his forehead and horrible black entrai appeared to gush from the top of his head. The color c his face was grayish green. His eyes were closed. Just lik her dream.

Worthington gasped at the sight of the head. "I'll hav *Campbell's* head for this outrage! I'll—I'll—"

Then Jamie opened his eyes.

Chapter Twenty-three

Jix stared at Jamie's disembodied head, too horrified to look away. He rolled his eyes so far back that she felt ill watching him and shifted her gaze to Worthington instead. The captain stood staring at the moving manifestation, his knees practically knocking together. Jix glanced down at the wet spot forming on his trousers and smiled. Jamie had been vindicated.

"You!" Worthington whispered, staring at Jamie's face. "But I saw you—you went over the cliff. You're—"

"Dead?" Jamie's voice was a rasping horror. "Aye. Ye killed me. One of yer men found me, and followin' yer orders, cut off my head. As ye can see, that dinna keep me from comin' back to get my revenge."

"B-b-but it wasn't my hand that killed you," the Englishman stammered.

" 'Twas yer orders," Jamie hissed. "Do ye no' order yer troops to behead the dead?"

Worthington opened and closed his mouth several times but no sound came out.

"Do ye no' order yer troops to behead the dead?" Jamie said, louder, more ominously.

The captain shook from head to foot, but he was still
soldier. He lowered his right hand, and still trembling
drew his sword from his sheath. Just what Jix had feare
he might do. The only glitch in an otherwise brilliant plan
But she was ready. She took a deep breath and let loose
bloodcurdling scream that should have roused every ghos
in Scotland.

Worthington almost fell down at the sound of the hor
rible shriek, and Jamie almost came through the table. Ji
realized belatedly she probably should've let him in on he
backup plan, but there was no time for regrets now. Th
big double doors of the castle smashed open (courtesy c
two burly servants) and Sam seemed to float across th
rushes, her face white (with flour), her hair white (wit
flour). She wore a filmy cream gown that billowed aroun
her feet and streamed behind her like the mist from som
ethereal being. In front of her, she held a cross that sh
and Jix had fashioned from two pieces of wood. Sh
walked toward Worthington.

"God shall judge you for your sins," she intoned, in th
voice of the dead. "Take your swords and beat them int
plowshares." Her voice got a little louder. "Take you
swords and beat them into plowshares!"

Stumbling away from her, Worthington dropped hi
sword and turned to run. A small army of ghouls and ghos
ties—more castle servants—had quietly moved into posi
tion while he was distracted by Jamie's head, and now the
stood blocking his way, waving their arms and groanin
his name.

"Ye killed me in battle," one man sighed, his face gray
ish green.

"Yer men murdered me and my babe," said a white
faced woman. She clutched a baby-shaped bundle to he
chest and began keening.

"Murderer," another hissed.

"Murderer," the taunt was taken up by the rest. "Mu
derer, murderer, murderer . . ." their voices rose as Wor
thington stood frozen, his black eyes stricken.

". . . murderer, murderer, MURDERER!" They reache

a crescendo, then as if from a signal, the ghouls and ghosties disappeared into the shadows.

Samantha was the only ghost who remained, and she performed like a pro, Jix observed from the dark corner in which she hid. Sam stood in the center of the candles and lifted the cross high, pointing at Worthington with her other hand. "Leave," she whispered, "and never return. Else suffer the fate of those you have slain."

Worthington didn't move. Then a hoarse voice echoed through the hall.

"Leaaavvveeeee . . ."

The eerie moan coming from Jamie's severed throat would have felled the bravest warrior, and coupled with his macabre head, it was no contest.

Worthington's eyes bulged from his head, the whites visible around his black irises. He stumbled backward but couldn't seem to wrench his gaze from Jamie's head as he retreated. Jamie suddenly smiled at him, showing all of his teeth in a terrible grimace, and the captain's legs gave way beneath him. Sobbing like a little girl, Worthington crawled across the nasty rushes on the floor until he managed to scramble to his feet. He ran forward, almost fell, then righted himself before plunging headlong out of the room in his frantic, terrified flight from the hall.

As soon as he was out of sight, the "ghouls" reappeared from their hiding places and shut the double doors behind him, then began quickly cleaning up. If Worthington returned, there would be no evidence of the scam. If he dared to come back, he would think he had experienced a purely supernatural happening. Somehow, Jix didn't think it likely that they would ever see Worthington's evil face again.

The reaction came over her all at once and with it, Jix almost collapsed to the floor. She sat down on the hearthstone, realization setting in. It was over. Her dream had come true. If nothing else happened—if they never went home again, if Sam married Jamie, she could bear it, because Jamie would be alive.

"Lass? Uh, lass, could ye come over here?"

335

Jix drew in a deep breath, and blinking back tears of relief, strolled over to the platter on the table, striving for a jaunty tone of voice.

"I think you were put in the wrong category," she told Jamie mildly as she paused beside the table, hand on her hip.

"What do ye mean?" He frowned up at her, his ghastly greenish gray face making her skin crawl.

"You were listed under 'beefcake' on the menu, but I think you're definitely a ham."

Jamie chuckled. In spite of her bravado, Jix was unable to keep a slight tremor from her voice as she leaned over and kissed his forehead. "It's over, Jamie, it's really over."

"Aye, lass," he said softly. "Thanks to ye. Now, I don't want to disturb yer moment of triumph, but could ye please get me out of here?"

She frowned and slid one finger through his hair. "Ugh. Did you really gut a chicken for the brains oozing out of your head?"

"No, a fish. Get me out."

Jix pretended to consider. "Well, I don't know. I kind of like having you a captive audience for a change. I might have to—"

"Jix, get me out of this crazy thing!"

Jix laughed and came to her feet, slowly lifting the silver platter from his neck and over his head, careful not to let the sharp edges touch his skin.

"I hate that we had to ruin this beautiful silver tray," she said, holding it up and looking through the very large hole in the bottom. Jamie sat smiling at her, his head protruding from the matching hole cut in the top of the table.

"Just be glad we could put a hole in the damn thing. It wasna easy." He disappeared, then emerged a few minutes later from beneath the table and picked up the discarded black cloth from the floor. He scrubbed it across his face and the top of his head and in a minute, Jix could stand to look at him again.

"Where do you think Worthington's going?" she asked, nodding toward the doors.

Jamie's mouth twisted in amusement. "Antarctica? Probably just as far from here as he can go," he said taking her hand. He bowed over her fingers, then brought them to his lips. A tingle ran over Jix's hand and up her arm, as he kissed her palm softly. He straightened, his dark blue eyes filled with new respect. "My compliments, milady," he said. "I promise, I'll never groan at one of yer ideas again. Although what was that little improvisation with Samantha?"

Sam stopped picking up candles and grinned up at him, her face still caked with flour. "Jix was afraid Worthington might panic and try to kill you all over again, so she had me stashed as a sort of spiritual distraction."

Jamie laughed. "I never thought of ye as the guardian angel type, but thanks." He gave Jix a stern look. "Although I thought we agreed, no surprises."

Jix shrugged. "I only promised not to lie, MacGregor. I'll always be full of surprises."

He pulled her into his arms and kissed the top of her head. "Aye, lass, I'll wager that's true. And I wouldna have it any other way."

"I wouldn't have let anything happen," Griffin said, coming back from following Worthington out of the castle and catching the end of their conversation. "I had my word at the ready."

Jix saluted him. "I was a Girl Scout, I can't help it. Always be prepared." She put her arms around Jamie's waist and leaned her head against his chest.

"It's over, Jamie. My dream came true, and you're still alive."

"Aye, thanks to ye, Jix. Only thanks to ye." He gazed down into her eyes and Jix felt she might melt into a puddle right then and there.

Griffin cleared his throat. "I think I'll follow Worthington for a bit and see what he does." He turned to Sam. "Samantha, would ye like to go with me?"

"Follow that guy? What would I—" she broke off. Jix couldn't take her eyes from Jamie, but she heard Sam laugh with understanding. "Sure, sure, I'll go with you,

Griffin. Did Jix or Jamie ever tell you anything about ou world?"

"There hasna been time."

"Well, let me clue you in. . . ."

Jix laughed against Jamie's shirt as the two left. "She' going to set Scotland back a thousand years."

Jamie tilted her face up to his. "Ah, lass, as much as hate to be the one to rain on this lovely parade, we've go to remember—there's still one little glitch."

"There's always a glitch. What is it now?"

Jamie kissed the tip of her nose. "We still don't hav my sword."

"No!"

Red Hugh's face lived up to his nickname. It turned bee red as he stood, hands on his broad hips, facing Jamie an Jix and their fellow co-conspirators. They had all agree there was no reason to tell the old Scot about their journe through time. Griffin feared his father would burn them the stake for witches at worst, imprison them at best. Ja mie, accompanied by the other three, had approached hir in his chambers and quite respectfully asked for the retur of his sword. Red Hugh had still refused.

"I willna return Jamie MacGregor's sword until Maigre marries Griffin. That was the agreement."

"Now that's gratitude for you," Jix grumbled.

It was the morning after Captain Worthington had ru screaming from the great hall, a victim of just revenge Griffin had seen him grab a horse in the outer bailey mount it without saddle or bridle and ride hell for leathe across the Scottish countryside. Worthington's men ha left early that morning to look for him, and the story tha made it back to Meadbrooke claimed that Worthington ha left immediately for France to join a monastery, after rec ommending to his superiors that all efforts to subdue th Campbells be abandoned.

Jamie had smiled grimly when he heard the report. All' well that ends well. *Or does it?*

Jix began trying to cajole Red Hugh into giving ove

the blade, reminding him of what their trick had done for him, but Jamie had had enough. He pushed past her and grabbed the older man by the front of his shirt, lifting him into the air.

"Jamie, don't hurt him," Jix said, "he can't help that he's an honorless jerk!" Apparently she had abandoned her Scottish brogue all together. He didn't blame her. He was sick and tired of the whole charade.

"The agreement," Jamie said, his face an inch from Red Hugh's, making his voice as dark and threatening as possible, "was that if I reived the English cattle, ye would return my sword."

Red Hugh glared down at him, looking rather comical as he dangled from the bigger Scot's hands. To his credit, he maintained some degree of decorum. "But ye dinna bring back any cattle! That was part of the agreement as well! So ye dinna fulfil the entire bargain."

Jamie shook him. "Why, ye lying bastard—that was no part of the bargain, ye said it dinna matter if we brought them back or no!" He shoved the man against the wall, three feet from the floor.

"Jamie," Griffin stepped up and laid one hand on his shoulder, "my father is no' trustworthy, ye ken? And he put honor aside long ago for survival's sake."

Jamie let go of the laird, letting him slide in a heap to the floor. He wasn't going to hurt Red Hugh. It would be like stepping on a brown wooly caterpillar. With teeth. "Aye, ye're right. What am I wastin' my time for?"

"That is no' true," Red Hugh said, standing and straightening his clothing. He jerked his whiskered chin up, his beady eyes fixed first on Jamie, then on Griffin. "Verra well. The two of ye have joined together against me and so I have no reason to spare yer feelin's, Griffin."

The blond Scot raised both brows. "My feelin's? What are ye talkin' about?"

"I know about yer problem!"

Griffin's face went white. He glanced at Jix, his eyes stricken.

"Don't look at me, I didn't tell him," she said.

"What problem?" Jamie and Sam asked in unison.

"He knows of what I speak," Red Hugh said, his dark red brows bristling above his eyes as he frowned at his son. "And I will tell the whole castle—the whole clan— unless Maigrey fulfills her promise."

Griffin's face turned scarlet. "Ye would do that to me, to yer own son?"

"Och, are ye no' taking sides against me with these MacGregors? But I am no' being vengeful in my request."

"Request?" Jamie laughed shortly. "Sounds like a threat to me."

"Because I ken his problem, I must be certain that my son is worthy to be my heir and will continue the family line. He must marry so he can have a son." He put on a mournful look. "Last night made me realize, made me think—I am no' immortal. When Worthington stormed the castle, I could have been killed."

"I don't think you were in any immediate danger," Jix said dryly, "since you didn't resist him. And how can you even doubt that your son is more than worthy enough to be your heir, Red Hugh?"

Jamie shot her a glance. He knew she and Griffin were just friends, but he still couldn't help the slight pang of jealousy he felt as she defended the man.

"But is he *man* enough?" Griffin and Jix exchanged glances. "I received a message this afternoon from the council of Clan Campbell," Red Hugh said. "News travels fast in the Highlands. They are impressed with what we did to Worthington."

"Oh, now it's what *we've* done to Worthington," Jix muttered. "Have you got a mouse in your pocket?"

Red Hugh frowned at her. "No, I've no mice. What's wrong with yer voice, lass?"

"Never mind—what did the chieftain have to say?"

"Actually, he dinna say a word. He's dead. Tripped over a goat and fell against a rock. Split his head open."

Griffin moved forward. "Then there is no chieftain of the clan? This is yer chance, Da."

"Nay, this is yer chance."

"What do ye mean?" Griffin's excitement for his father drained from his face.

Red Hugh gazed up at the muscular man and for an instant Jamie saw the real love the old Scot had for his son. Begrudgingly, Jamie realized Red Hugh had done what he thought would keep his people safe from men like Worthington, but he was still a selfish man, and his insistence that Jix and Griffin marry meant there was something in it for him.

"I mean that the clan has heard of yer part in the goings on last night and they want to offer ye the chieftainship."

"Me!" Griffin's eyes widened. "But I dinna want it. I'm no chieftain."

"Aye, they think ye are."

"But that is yer dream, Da, no' mine."

Red Hugh clapped his son on the shoulder and shook him with one strong hand. "Aye, but they will never allow it. And do ye not ken that this honor being paid to ye is mine as well? But I fear they will withdraw the offer if they get wind of yer problem."

"What is Griffin's problem?" Jamie demanded, curious in spite of himself.

"Does it have anything to do with excess body odor?" Sam asked. She'd donned her gypsy costume again and now sat on the window sill behind Red Hugh, her skirt hiked up and her legs crossed, one foot swinging. "Because I have to say, in his defense, that I've noticed all you Highlanders have to deal with that particular little problem."

"Look," Jix said, "we can put all this discussion to rest very easily." She turned to Griffin. "Griffin, I'll marry you—on one condition," she looked back at Red Hugh, her eyes narrowing.

Jamie folded his arms over his chest. He loved watching Jix when she had her ire up like this. She had such spirit, such spunk. He couldn't wait to get her back home and marry her. Marry her? He grinned. Yes, marry her. He took a deep breath and released it, feeling like a great weight had been lifted from his shoulders. He would marry Jix

Ferguson and they would live happily ever after. Was it possible? Was it too much to ask? But what was she saying? Marry Griffin? He dropped his arms to his side.

"Now wait a damn minute—" he began.

"What condition?" Red Hugh asked.

"That Jamie's sword is at the wedding," Jix said. "It has to be there, in your hands, and you have to be ready to give it to Jamie as soon as Griffin and I recite our vows."

Jamie started to protest again, but she shot him a quelling look. He frowned. Maybe she was right. This could be their only chance to get the sword back, damn the stubborn Scot!

After Worthington's departure, the four had searched the castle from top to bottom, even the secret passageways Griffin revealed to them. Jamie was beginning to doubt the sword was even in the keep. If they wanted to go home, it looked as though they were going to have to play it Red Hugh's way. But only to a point. He shot Jix back a warning that he knew she'd understand. She nodded without hesitation.

Jix might go through with the marriage ceremony, but he'd be damned if she'd go through the wedding night. As soon as the ceremony was over, Jamie would take his sword and the three of them would go home. Griffin would understand. He relaxed his shoulders. Sure. It was simple. What could go wrong? He almost groaned aloud. What had gone right in this crazy adventure?

"Ye agree?" Red Hugh was openly surprised at Jix and Jamie's lack of protest. His beefy face broke into a glorious smile. "Well, all right then, 'tis settled! I'll make the arrangements and tonight, all will be as it should be." He turned toward the door, but Jamie stopped him.

"If the sword is there, my laird," he said. "I promise ye, if the claymore isn't in yer hands, Maigrey willna go through with the weddin'."

"Aye, I ken the agreement." He glanced at Jix and frowned. "But try to do something with yer voice, lass, before the ceremony. Half the clan is on their way here to attend. I'd no' like them thinkin' ye're a Sassenach."

Jix sighed. "Fine. I'll gae them a taste of my Scots."

The laird's smile reappeared. "Grand, grand." He hurried out the door and the four stood staring after him.

"Jix—" Jamie began.

"Jix—" Griffin started to say.

"When's lunch?" Sam put in brightly.

"Wait!" Jix held up both hands. "Jamie, I'm marrying Griffin. Griffin, as soon as I marry you I'm leaving—we're all leaving, if the sword will take us back through time."

"And what if it doesn't?" Jamie demanded, irritated by the way she had taken over the planning. Some day she'd have to learn that her ideas were not the only ideas. "Then we'll be married to him."

She bit her lower lip. "That won't happen, but if it does . . ." she hesitated.

"Then the two of you can run away together," Sam interjected, "and I'll marry Griffin."

"What?" Jamie and Jix said at the same time.

"What?" Griffin echoed.

Sam shrugged. "Why not? You're a nice guy. You're buff and not bad to look at."

"Buff?" Griffin frowned. "What is buff?"

"And uh, I think I can help you with your problem."

Griffin looked like she'd punched him in the stomach. He turned on Jix. "Ye promised ye wouldn't—"

"I didn't—"

"She didn't—"

"All right!" Jamie moved between them and grabbed Jix. "Enough. I personally dinna care what Griffin's problem is, particularly if it pertains to body odor." He stroked one hand down the side of Jix's face and saw the fire quicken into her forest green eyes. "But we have a few hours until you get married, Miss Ferguson. Let's make the most of it."

Jix stood waiting at the top of the stairs on her wedding day. Two of the maids had spent the better part of an hour arranging her long hair in a beautiful curling mass down her back. How they had managed it, she'd never know.

She smoothed one long sleeve of the heavy cream-colore
brocade wedding gown that had been Griffin's mother'
She felt absolutely beautiful. Too bad it was all a farce.

Jix felt a sharp twinge of guilt. She hated that Griff
would be left without a wife, and without a way to prov
at least to his father, that he could be the chieftain of th
clan. But Griffin had assured her that everything wou
work out the way "the good God intended." She smiled
the thought. She would miss Griffin, and in fact, consid
ered him practically one of her brothers. Yet she'd be
happy to return to her real brothers.

Jix blinked. It was probably the first time in her li
she'd ever thought of them in that way. The Ferguson
were her real family. Maybe not her blood family, but wh
did that matter? They loved her from the bottom of the
hearts and souls, and she loved them. Jix bit her lower li
wishing her parents were alive so that she could tell ther
and yet—she glanced upward. Somehow, she felt sure the
knew.

Two strong arms wrapped around her middle witho
warning and pulled her away from the stairs. Jix squeale
then looked back over her shoulder into Jamie's rugge
face.

"Hello, lass," he said softly, "ye are a vision."

Jix put her arm around his waist as he guided her arour
the corner to a shadowed alcove, out of sight of any c
rious onlookers. They had spent the afternoon locked
their chamber, making love, then talking, then making lo
again. She still tingled all over from his touch.

"Oh, Jamie," she said, feeling torn inside, "this seem
so unfair to Griffin, and even to Red Hugh."

Jamie tilted her head up and planted a kiss on her mout
"Dinna fash yerself. They are both grown men. I've n
doubt they'll survive even yer loss."

She punched him lightly in the stomach. "That's n
what I meant and you know it!"

He linked his arms around her, lacing his hands togeth
at the small of her back. Jamie had on his own clothes
freshly laundered—and the sight of his bright plaid wa

344

somehow reassuring to Jix. A symbol of returning home. He had worked three small braids into his long, dark hair and Jix reached up to tug on one, teasingly. He kissed the hand that held it, then kissed her mouth again. But when he started to deepen the kiss, she pulled away.

"Jamie, I'm about to marry another man and I'm standing here making out with you," she tugged the braid again, lowering her gaze to the tiny bead at the end. "I feel . . . immoral."

He laughed softly and Jix looked up, irritated by his casual attitude. But as he gazed down at her, his eyes so deeply blue, his dark lashes sweeping down as he took in the décolletage of her gown, then up again as he gave her another heart-stoppingly sexy look, Jix knew she was doing the right thing. They had to do whatever necessary to get that sword so they could go home.

"So ye think that was making out? I can see I have a few things to teach ye after we're married."

"I think you taught me quite enough this after—Married?" Jix looked away from his smiling eyes, feeling suddenly shy. Neither of them had mentioned marriage before, except in connection with her wedding to Griffin. She smoothed the tartan crossing his chest with the flat of her hands, then glanced up and grinned. "Och, laddie, in that case I may have a few new ideas for you as well."

"It's time," Sam called, hurrying up the stairs.

Jamie gave Jix another quick kiss. "Remember what to do," he said. "Soon we'll be home again." He gave her a tender smile. "And when ye're taking those vows, just keep yer fingers crossed behind yer back." He turned and headed in the opposite direction.

Jix watched him go and sighed. How she wished it was going to be Jamie waiting at the altar for her. When they returned to their own time—if they returned to their own time—did he really want to marry her?

Samantha hung over the stair railing, speaking to someone below. Jix stood watching her, waiting for her signal, when suddenly her infamous dream of Jamie and Sam's wedding flashed through her mind yet again. Jix closed her eyes.

One day at a time. Heck, one century at a time. Just focus on getting out of here, then deal with what comes next.

She opened her eyes to find Samantha smiling directly at her. Although the concept of a bridesmaid was a foreign one in this time period, Jix had insisted Sam be at her side. Her best friend wore a pale blue gown, cut low and laced up the front, and a white, gathered blouse with a scattering of tiny blue flowers, beneath it. Her eyes were a beautiful gray blue, and for once, she looked extremely happy.

"What are you so excited about?" Jix asked with a laugh. "You'd think I was really getting married—and to someone you approved of!"

"I'm excited because we're going home," Sam gave her a tight hug, then spun her around in a circle. "No more lukewarm baths once a week! No more au natural! And chocolate—oh how I've missed chocolate." She stopped spinning her friend and gazed at her, a kind of awe in her eyes that surprised Jix. "But I wouldn't trade this, you know? The whole experience?"

"Have you been in the wine?" she accused. "You know you told me never to let you drink before you fly again."

"Gosh, that seems years ago now, doesn't it," Sam said, linking her arm in Jix's and pulling her toward the stairs. She laughed. "Or centuries."

"A lifetime ago." Jix took a deep breath. In a matter of minutes their fate would be decided. Either they would return to their own time, or this would likely be their home for the rest of their lives. Jix almost missed a step and Sam tightened her grip on her elbow.

"Careful. It wouldn't do for the bride to go tumbling down the stairs, headfirst."

Jix smiled ruefully. "I don't think anyone would be surprised if I did."

Sam patted her arm. "I think you're wrong about that."

Jix shot her a look. "What do you mean?"

"I mean, you've changed, Jix. Matured." They made it

o the bottom step without mishap and Sam turned to her, reaching up to tuck a stray curl back in place. "I'm proud of you, Jixie-Pixie."

Jix blinked back quick tears. "Thanks," she whispered. "And thanks to you."

Jix shook her head. "Thanks for what? Ruining your wedding? Getting you lost in time?"

Sam smiled and leaned nearer. "For the ride," she whispered.

Tears spilled down Jix's cheeks. "Oh, Sam," she sniffed and wiped the back of one hand across her face. "I promise, in the future—" she broke off laughing. "I mean, in our own time, I won't let you down anymore."

"You never have," Sam said softly, squeezing her hand. "Don't change too much, kiddo. There was a lot of good stuff in the old Jix." She hugged her, then turned and walked into the great hall.

Jix brushed the last bit of moisture from her face and began walking toward Griffin. Her throat tightened as she moved slowly down the informal aisle created by the people standing on either side.

They had decided on a simple ceremony, but Red Hugh had insisted on a bit of pomp and circumstance, since some members of the clan council had arrived that afternoon. A grand supper had been served, then the bridal party had retired to prepare, and the great hall had been cleared of its usual trestle tables.

Now, Griffin waited in front of an arch decorated with heather and greenery, and next to him stood a man dressed in black. A clergyman she supposed, or a priest. A silken pillow lay on the floor in front of them. To kneel upon? To pray to God? To sanctify this sham of a marriage?

Jix stopped beside Griffin and smiled hesitantly up at him. Red Hugh stood next to the clergyman, and Jamie stood on the other side of Griffin, between the man and his father. Sam stood at Jix's right hand.

Jix drew in a quick breath as she saw that Red Hugh held the MacGregor sword. The point rested on the floor and the laird leaned on the hilt like a walking stick.

Red Hugh beamed at her and Jix smiled back, thankf[ul]
for Griffin's arm to cling to as the ceremony began i[n]
Latin. She didn't speak the lingo but she caught the gi[st]
of it—she was about to take a holy vow before God. O[f]
course, she had taken holy vows before, with Dirk the Jer[k]
and meant them. But she felt sure God had released he[r]
from those because of extenuating circumstances, o[r]
maybe that was what she wanted to believe. But if she ha[d]
learned anything at all during this wild trip, it was tha[t]
God loved her and had an infinitely wonderful plan for he[r]
life, if she would only listen. So could she stand here an[d]
lie to His face? Hadn't she sworn to only tell the trut[h]
from now on?

"Wait," Jix said, interrupting the clergyman. He looke[d]
up from his prayer book, startled. Griffin glanced down a[t]
her, blinking in surprise. Red Hugh glowered. Jami[e]
looked at her and shook his head slightly. Sam widene[d]
her eyes and laughed out loud.

"I—I—" Jix began.

"Wait!" A voice behind them shouted.

Everyone turned. Fergus, Red Hugh's right-hand ma[n]
strode boldly across the great hall, a dark-haired man an[d]
a woman hurrying behind him. Jix gasped. The man wa[s]
the spitting image of Jamie MacGregor, and the woma[n]
just a more feminine version.

"Stop the ceremony!" Fergus cried.

"Uh-oh," Jix said.

Fergus shoved his way through the assembled crow[d]
pulling the man and woman with him until they reache[d]
the arch. The big, black-haired Scot shook a finger in Jix'[s]
face.

"This is no' Maigrey MacGregor!" Fergus said, the[n]
swept his arm back to point to the dark-haired woma[n]
behind him. "This is Maigrey MacGregor and her brothe[r]
James. These people"—he nodded at Jix and Jamie—"ar[e]
imposters!"

"Oops," Jix said. "Best-laid plans."

"Well, that explains the resemblance," Sam muttered be[-]
side her.

"Not Maigrey?" Red Hugh was saying, his gaze stricken. He turned to the two new MacGregors. The woman had the high cheekbones of a Highland lass, her hair a burnished chestnut brown, her eyes proud and blue. "Ye are Maigrey?" he asked, and his mouth curved up.

"Aye, my laird," she said, dropping him a low curtsy.

"And I am James." The new James and the old James stared at one another. "I dinna know who this man is," the new James said after a moment, "but I canna deny he must be a MacGregor, or some relation. Still, he wasna sent from the clan MacGregor."

Red Hugh was livid. He started to lift the sword, but he was too late—with one broad sweep of his leg, Jamie knocked the point of the MacGregor claymore upward. The momentum wrenched the hilt from the laird's hand. The sword flew toward Jamie and he caught it by the hilt, then backed away swinging the blade around in a circle, keeping Fergus and the Scotsmen suddenly pouring into the great hall at bay.

"Jix! Sam!" Jamie called. Jix blinked and hurried to his side, Sam right behind her. "This time, Samantha, hang on!" he cautioned. "Jix, your hand on the stone, Sam's on the hilt." He stared down at the glowing green stone. "Me in the middle," he said softly. " *'S Rioghal Mo Dhream.*"

The crowd in the hall stared at them, their faces stunned by the drama unfolding in front of them. There was a tense, pregnant pause, then Jix could almost hear the anticlimatic movie score fizzling downward around them. She cleared her throat.

"Jamie, nothing's happening."

" *'S Rioghal Mo Dhream!*" Jamie cried again.

"Another fine mess you've gotten me into," Sam said dryly.

" "Wait a minute!" Jix shouted, dropping her hand from the sword. "Last time I was on the left! We're on the wrong sides! Sam, trade places!"

They switched sides and Jix reached for the stone again as Sam touched the crosspiece on the hilt.

"That's more like it," Jix whispered as a shock tingled

through her fingers and up her arm. She glanced up an
saw Griffin smiling at her. "Good-bye, Griffin," she sai
a slight sadness in her heart, "thanks for everything. An
just remember—practice makes perfect." Her gaze sof
ened. "You'll find the right girl. Don't let anyone pus
you into anything less."

"Good-bye, lass," he called, "have a bonny life."

"I canna let go," Jamie cried, his voice joyous.

"And neither can I!" Sam echoed. "Do you think—"

This was the part Jix had dreaded. But she had one la
message for Scotland before they departed.

"Red Hugh!" she shouted over the roar beginning in he
ears. "Change the stinking rushes on your floor!"

It was as though the world had suddenly turned to glas
As though the reality of Jix and Jamie and Samantha ha
been flattened into a picture upon a sheet of glass, trappe
inside, and sent spinning through eternity. Jix spun throug
the blackness, voiceless, frozen, then the glass shattere
Free but blind, she cried out, the darkness swallowing he
voice as the void wrapped around her. Falling, she reache
out into the darkness and found . . .

Everything.

Epilogue

God's in his heaven—all's right with the world!

As Jix and Jamie danced together for the first time as man and wife, she couldn't help remembering the poem she'd learned as a child. She smiled up at her husband. Everything was certainly all right with her world.

Knowing they wouldn't be able to leave Scotland any time soon, what with Jamie resigning his job at the Yard and taking over the running of his uncle's estate, they had planned their wedding quickly and quietly. A few telephone invitations and a week later, surrounded by the people they loved, Jix and Jamie had stood before God and man and promised to love, honor, and cherish one another for all time.

For all time. How fitting, Jix thought, looking up into Jamie's smiling face. He looked wonderful in his Scottish kilt and tartan. He had considered wearing his sword for the ceremony, but they decided not to tempt fate. Instead, his family claymore had been sealed in a case with a glass front and now hung over the fireplace in Angus Campbell's study.

"Still planning to write a romance novel?" Jamie asked, nuzzling the side of her neck as they danced.

"Of course," Jix told him. "The next five years are dedicated to becoming a published author—and becoming the perfect wife." She frowned thoughtfully. "I wonder if a time-travel romance would sell?"

"Lass," Jamie chuckled, "ye never cease to amaze me."

He whirled her across the smooth, polished floor and Jix stopped thinking, instead admiring the million tiny stars that twinkled above them, courtesy of Samantha Riley's high-powered, high-dollar wedding planner. Sam had outdone even her usual outlandishly generous self, creating a veritable fairyland of lights and flowers for the reception at Meadbrooke Manor. Their wedding ceremony had been held inside an ancient Scottish chapel that morning, but even there Sam's touch had been seen in the fragile bouquets of baby's breath and heather at the altar, and the candles on the sills of the stained glass windows.

Of course there had to be a few glitches, Jix thought wryly, or it wouldn't have been her wedding. At the last minute Sam's personal seamstress had been called away on a family emergency and her assistant had shipped the wrong bridesmaids' dresses to Scotland. She and Sam had opened the packages just that morning and discovered two beautiful dresses—in white.

Jix didn't care. She had her own incredible cream-colored, vintage wedding gown—a present from a Scottish laird, she delighted in telling everyone—and the fact that both her bridesmaids were wearing white didn't bother her at all. Her oldest brother Travis had brought her adopted mother's wedding veil—no, her *mother's* wedding veil—and made the day complete.

Jamie twirled her past Sam and Chelsea, who seemed to be arguing over something. Jix waved at them and Sam waved a long lemon-colored scarf back at her. She had insisted on adding the touch of color to the neckline of the bridesmaids' dresses, matching the daisies in their hair and in their bouquets. Jix loved her own beautiful bridal bouquet, made up of white roses, daisies, daylilies, and heather.

They danced past Jamie's uncle and his old partner, Tavish, deep in conversation, and Jix smiled. Jamie had asked his Uncle Angus to be his best man, and Tavish, his groomsman. The three Scotsmen had looked handsome and dashing in their Scottish regalia as they stood at the altar.

And yet, there was still one thing marring her joy. Jix sighed, just a little, as she and Jamie danced. Just last night she'd dreamed about Jamie and Sam's wedding again. Sam had spent the night with her, since Jamie was forbidden to see the bride, and Jix had awakened, breathing hard, convinced all over again that Jamie and Sam were destined to be together. Sam had implored her not to worry about the dream, and Jix had tried really hard, but sleep had been long in coming.

Even during the ceremony, at the back of her mind, there it was, that sense that everything was not yet complete. Not final.

"Is something wrong, lass?" Jamie asked.

For a moment, just a brief moment, she considered telling him, then shook her head. They had been through time and space and life and death together. Surely even her dreams couldn't separate them now.

The dance ended and the bride and groom took their applause in stride as they walked off the floor and a rock and roll song began. Sam rushed up, dragging their friend, Chelsea, behind her.

"Jix, I can't get Chelsea to dance—tell her it's your wedding and she has to dance!"

Jix glanced at mousy little Chelsea. Her hair hung limply under the flowers at her crown and she gave Jix a pleading look from behind her horn-rim glasses.

"Sam, don't bully her," Jix commanded. "She doesn't have to dance if she doesn't want to. Just because you think you're the new Pavlova—"

"Oh my gosh—look!" Sam cried. "They're serving the groom's cake! You know the thing I missed the most on our little 'side trip'?"

Jix rolled her eyes in Chelsea's direction, reminding Sam to play it cool. They had decided not to tell anyone about their adventure in time. Chelsea and Colonel Riley believed Jix had taken Sam to a place in the Highlands where there were no phones. Well, it was true, Jix rationalized.

"I can't imagine," Jamie said. "Uh, hot water?"

"Chocolate." Sam headed for the groom's table.

"Gee, no kidding." Jix laughed, watching her friend hurry across the room. "Ever since we got back she's a complete chocoholic. She's lost every bit of self-discipline she ever had."

Jamie chuckled. "Maybe that's a good thing.'

"There's no hot water or chocolate here in Scotland?" Chelsea asked, pushing her glasses up on her nose. "I didn't know that."

"Well—" Jix was saved from having to explain when Sam came hurrying back again, carrying a huge piece of chocolate cake on a glass plate. She ate it with relish as the other three watched, then licked her fingers.

"You know, you've changed, Sam," Jix said in wonder.

"I have?" Sam caught a piece of frosting just as it fell from her plate and stuck it in her mouth, a beatific smile on her face. "How?"

"You're a lot more fun," Jix grinned. "A lot weirder, but more fun."

"Hey, if there's one thing I learned from the gypsies, it's how to enjoy life."

Chelsea frowned. "Gypsies?"

Jix elbowed Samantha in the ribs. "Yes! We saw gypsies at a fair on our trip."

"Really? Oh, I'd love to see gypsies—did you get to ride in one of their wagons?"

Jamie smiled down at Jix's shy friend. "Aye, lass, Jix and I had quite a lovely ride in one."

Jix jabbed her other elbow in Jamie's side. "And here I've been trying to turn over a new leaf," she muttered.

"Now that's a shame," a deep voice behind her said. "Who's going to carry out my next assignment?"

Jix spun around to find Colonel Patrick Riley at her side, her four brothers behind him—Travis, Thomas, Sean and Sebastian. Her heart swelled at the sight of them and with tears in her eyes she opened her arms. She would never take her family for granted again. Each one hugged her tightly, whispered his congratulations, then turned to shake Jamie's hand. Jix smiled so hard she thought her face would split.

The colonel pulled her aside from the rest. All at once Jix realized she hadn't spoken to him alone about Mark since right before the wedding, and even then he only had time to tell her that Sam's *ex*-fiancé was in jail. Samantha had told her father personally that she never wanted to see the slimeball again. As far as Jix was concerned, that was just as big a cause to celebrate as her wedding. She beamed up at the colonel and saluted.

"Mission accomplished, sir," she reported.

His gray eyes clouded with tears and he pulled her into his arms for another gentle hug. "Thank you, Jixie," he whispered against her ear, "more than words can say." He straightened and took her hands in his. "Well, Sam doesn't seem any the worse for wear. In fact, I think she's found a whole new lease on life!" His salt-and-pepper gray brows knit together quizzically. "What did you do?"

Jix shook her head. "Gave her a look at a real man?" she guessed, glancing over where Jamie stood talking to her brothers. "Or five real men?" She smiled up at him. "Of course, she always had you for the best example."

"Well, whatever happened, I've never seen her look so happy."

"I think that might be because of the chocolate cake," Jix said, then frowned.

Her brothers had wandered off to hit on unsuspecting women, leaving Jamie and Sam standing alone. Sam had discarded her lemon-colored scarf, but the elaborate white dress still complimented her pale blond looks, as almost anything she wore always did. She had just finished another piece of chocolate cake and set her plate aside with a big smile, standing in easy camaraderie with Jamie, her arm linked in his.

Jamie wore black knee-high boots, a black velvet dress jacket over his MacGregor tartan kilt, his tartan scarf across his jacket and white shirt, and his plaid hanging from his back, anchored by a beautiful silver brooch at his shoulder. Although Jix had left her hair long for the wedding, Jamie had cut his the day after their return, and it was the same shaggy length as when they first met. Samantha gazed up at him, looking happier than Jix had ever seen her. Dressed in white, a circlet of daisies in her hair, holding her bridesmaid's bouquet, Sam smiled up into Jamie's face. Samantha looked rather like a happy bride herself. Jix frowned again.

Circlet of daisies. Bouquet. Happy Bride. Sam and Jamie.

Her dream!

"Sam! Sam—did you do this on purpose?" Jix cried, rushing across to her. Jamie put his arm around his new wife, concern in his dark blue eyes.

"Lass, what's wrong?"

"Did I do what on purpose?" Sam asked, her perfectly made-up eyes widening innocently.

Jix gestured toward the white bridesmaid's dress. "This—you—Jamie—your dress—the bouquet—" she took her friend by the arms and shook her. "This is my dream—*this is my dream!*"

Sam glanced up at Jamie, then back at Jix. "Do you know what she's talking about?"

"I confess that I often dinna know what she's talking about," Jamie admitted. "But I guess I'll learn."

"Sam! Did you—"

"You'll never quite know for sure, will you, Jix?" Sam

said, a slow smile easing across her lips. She dropped a wink. "Now we're even."

She sashayed toward the chocolate cake as Jix turned to Jamie, relief and happiness flooding through her soul. She pulled him across the center of the room and down the hall, into the wide alcove where she had met him on that rainy day so long ago.

"Jamie," she said breathlessly, flinging her arms around his neck, "it's over. My dream came true—not the way I thought it would, but the best way possible—and I didn't lose you!" She laughed out loud and leaned back, her eyes on the ceiling. "Thanks, God—great sense of humor!"

Jamie cupped her face between his hands, his dark hair falling over his forehead. "Och, lass," he gently touched his lips to hers, "do ye know that ye are my dream come true?"

"I am?" Jix asked, his nearness sending shivers of anticipation through her veins.

"Aye, and I plan to spend the rest of my life trying to fill yer heart with happiness. I will love ye forever."

"I love you, Jamie MacGregor," she whispered, "and I'll spend the rest of my life making all your dreams come true. As a matter of fact I have—"

Jamie stopped her words with a kiss and a smile. "Och, no, lass, please dinna say it—"

"—a great idea!"

He covered her mouth again with his and kissed her until Jix felt weak in the knees.

"Still want to talk about ideas?" he asked, his voice silky, his arms holding her close.

"I have another one," Jix said softly, pulling him toward the stairs. "But it involves a lot less people."

"Are ye going to tell my fortune?" Jamie asked, following her up the wide staircase.

She turned on the step above him and smiled. "Aye, laddie—I see a glorious future ahead of you, but it involves whipped cream and a crazy redhead. Interested?"

"Aye, lass." Jamie picked her up in his arms and carried

her the rest of the way up the stairs. At the top he paused and wiggled his eyebrows suggestively. "An' just when will this 'makin' my dreams come true' part begin?"

"Right now, MacGregor," Jix said, her voice a caress. "And straight through forever."

TESS MALLORY
HIGHLAND DREAM

When Jix Ferguson's dream reveals that her best friend is makir
a terrible mistake and marrying the wrong guy, she tricl
Samantha into flying to Scotland. There the two women met th
man Jix is convinced her friend should marry--Jam
MacGregor. He is handsome, smart, perfect . . . the only proble
is, Jix falls for him, too. Then a slight scuffle involving the Sco
ancestral sword sends all three back to the start of th
seventeenth century--where MacGregors are outlaws ar
hunted. All Jix has to do is marry Griffin Campbell, steal Jami
sword back from their captor, and find a way to return herself ar
her friends to their own time. Oh yeah, and she has to fall in lov
It isn't going to be easy, but in this matter of the heart, Jix knov
she'll laugh last.

___52444-9 $6.99 US/$8.99 CAI

Dorchester Publishing Co., Inc.
P.O. Box 6640
Wayne, PA 19087-8640

Please add $2.50 for shipping and handling for the first book ar
$.75 for each book thereafter. NY, NYC, and PA resident
please add appropriate sales tax. No cash, stamps, or C.O.D.s. /
orders shipped within 6 weeks via postal service book rate.
Canadian orders require $2.50 extra postage and must be paid
U.S. dollars through a U.S. banking facility.

Name_____
Address_____
City_____ State_____ Zip_____
I have enclosed $_____ in payment for the checked book(
Payment **must** accompany all orders.❏ Please send a freecatalo
CHECK OUT OUR WEBSITE! www.dorchesterpub.com

BUSHWHACKED BRIDE
EUGENIA RILEY

"JUMPING JEHOSHAPHAT! YOU'VE SHANGHAIED THE NEW SCHOOLMARM!"

Ma Reklaw bellows at her sons and wields her broom with a fierceness that has all five outlaw brothers running for cover; it doesn't take a Ph.D. to realize that in the Reklaw household, Ma is the law. Professor Jessica Garret watches dumbstruck as the members of the feared Reklaw Gang turn tail—one up a tree, another under the hay wagon, and one in a barrel. Having been unceremoniously kidnapped by the rowdy brothers, the green-eyed beauty takes great pleasure in their discomfort until Ma Reklaw finds a new way to sweep clean her sons' disreputable behavior—by offering Jessica's hand in marriage to the best behaved. Jessie has heard of shotgun weddings, but a broomstick betrothal is ridiculous! As the dashing but dangerous desperadoes start the wooing there is no telling what will happen with one bride for five brothers.

___52320-5 $6.99 US/$8.99 CAN

Eugenia Riley
Bushwhacked Groom

When Cole Reklaw offers a prime parcel of ranchland to the first of his five children to marry and produce a grandchild, his daughter Molly vows to win. She heads for Reklaw Gorge—where her pa had once "bushwhacked" his future bride off a stagecoach—only to watch that very vehicle comes crashing into the gorge, bringing with it Molly's own "hero" from across time, Lucky Lamont.

All Lucky ever wanted was to get even with his girlfriend for betraying him. Instead he finds himself in the clutches of a hellcat who declares she will marry him, or else. Then Molly Reklaw goads Lucky into a reckless kiss that soon results in a shotgun wedding! With the bride set on gaining the prize and the groom burning for revenge, can love find a way for *both* of them to win?

AN ORIGINAL SIN
NINA BANGS

Fortune MacDonald listens to women's fantasies on a daily basis as she takes their orders for customized men. In a time when the male species is extinct, she is a valued man-maker. So when she awakes to find herself sharing a bed with the most lifelike, virile man she has ever laid eyes or hands on, she lets her gaze inventory his assets. From his long dark hair, to his knife-edged cheekbones, to his broad shoulders, to his jutting—well, all in the name of research, right?—it doesn't take an expert any time at all to realize that he is the genuine article, a bona fide man. And when Leith Campbell takes her in his arms, she knows real passion for the first time . . . but has she found true love?

___52324-8 $5.99 US/$7.99 CAN

Dorchester Publishing Co., Inc.
P.O. Box 6640
Wayne, PA 19087-8640

Please add $1.75 for shipping and handling for the first book and $.50 for each book thereafter. NY, NYC, and PA residents, please add appropriate sales tax. No cash, stamps, or C.O.D.s. All orders shipped within 6 weeks via postal service book rate. Canadian orders require $2.00 extra postage and must be paid in U.S. dollars through a U.S. banking facility.

Name_____
Address_____
City_____State_____Zip_____
I have enclosed $_____ in payment for the checked book(s).
Payment <u>must</u> accompany all orders. ☐ Please send a free catalog.
CHECK OUT OUR WEBSITE! www.dorchesterpub.com

Nina Bangs
Master of Ecstasy

Her trip back in time to 1785 Scotland is supposed to be a vacation, so why does Blythe feel that her stay at the MacKenzie castle will be anything but? The gloomy old pile of stones has her imagination working overtime.

The first hunk she meets turns out to be Mr. Dark-Evil-and-Deadly himself, an honest-to-goodness vampire. His voice is a tempting slide of sin, and his body raises her temperature, but when Darach whispers, "To waste a neck such as yours would be a terrible thing," she decides his pillow talk leaves a lot to be desired.

Dangerous? You bet. To die for? Definitely. Soul mate? Just wait and see.

DEE DAVIS
WILD
❧ HIGHLAND ❧
ROSE

Marjory Macpherson feels rebirth at hand. Ewen—the enemy son she'd been forced to marry—is dead, killed by a rockslide. Marjory rejoices. She can shed her thorns . . . at least, until her husband's father returns.

When Marjory goes to retrieve Ewen's body, she finds instead a living, breathing man, covered in blood, talking strangely but very much alive.

Though he wears her husband's face and kilt, Marjory recognizes salvation. Whether this is a kinder Ewen or another who, as he claims, has been transplanted from the future, the man she finds is a strange new beginning, the root of something beautiful to come.

SANDRA HILL
A TALE OF
TWO VIKINGS

Toste and Vagn Ivarsson are identical Viking twins. They came squalling into this world together, rode their first horses at the age of seven, their first maids during their thirteenth summer, and rode off on longships as untried fourteen-year-old warriors. And now they are about to face Valhalla together. Or maybe something even more tragic: being separated. For even the most virile Viking must eventually leave his best buddy behind and do battle with that most fearsome of all opponents—the love of his life.
